D1041815

The COLOR *of* LIGHT

KAREN WHITE

FICTION FOR THE WAY WE LIVE

NAL Accent
Published by New American Library, a division of
Penguin Group (USA) Inc., 375 Hudson Street,
New York, New York 10014, USA
Penguin Group (Canada), 10 Alcorn Avenue, Toronto,
Ontario M4V 3B2, Canada (a division of Pearson Penguin Canada Inc.)
Penguin Books Ltd., 80 Strand, London WC2R 0RL, England
Penguin Ireland, 25 St. Stephen's Green, Dublin 2,
Ireland (a division of Penguin Books Ltd.)
Penguin Group (Australia), 250 Camberwell Road, Camberwell, Victoria 3124,
Australia (a division of Pearson Australia Group Pty. Ltd.)
Penguin Books India Pvt. Ltd., 11 Community Centre, Panchsheel Park,
New Delhi - 110 017, India
Penguin Group (NZ), cnr Airborne and Rosedale Roads, Albany,
Auckland 1310, New Zealand (a division of Pearson New Zealand Ltd.)
Penguin Books (South Africa) (Pty.) Ltd., 24 Sturdee Avenue,
Rosebank, Johannesburg 2196, South Africa

Penguin Books Ltd., Registered Offices:
80 Strand, London WC2R 0RL, England

First published by NAL Accent, an imprint of New American Library,
a division of Penguin Group (USA) Inc.

First Printing, June 2005
10 9 8 7 6 5 4 3 2 1

FICTION FOR THE WAY WE LIVE
REGISTERED TRADEMARK—MARCA REGISTRADA

LIBRARY OF CONGRESS CATALOGING-IN-PUBLICATION DATA:
White, Karen (Karen S.)
The color of light/Karen White.
p. cm.
ISBN 0-451-21511-7 (trade pbk. original)
1. Pawleys Island (SC)—Fiction. 2. Mothers and daughters—Fiction. 3. Seaside
resorts—Fiction. 4. Missing persons—Fiction. 5. Pregnant women—Fiction. 6. Single
mothers—Fiction. I. Title.
PS3623.H5776C65   2005   2005003505
813'.6—dc22

Set in Adobe Garamond
Designed by Ginger Legato

Printed in the United States of America

*This book is dedicated to my precious Meghan,
who gave me the title, and to my God,
from whom all good things come.*

ACKNOWLEDGMENTS

This book was a few years in the making, with lots of stops and starts. I would like to thank the many people who supported me during the stops and made me keep going: my fellow writers in GRW, especially Debby Giusti; Sandra Popham, my "number one fan"; and the most wonderfully supportive critique group imaginable: Wendy Wax, Susan Crandall and Jenni Grizzle. A heartfelt thanks to all of you for being the soft buffer against the hard knocks.

Thanks also to the patience, love and support of my long-suffering family: Tim, Meghan and Connor. Thank you for not complaining (too much) about the packaged meals and piles of laundry and for making me laugh when I'm banging my head against the wall.

To the gracious people of Pawleys Island, South Carolina, thank you for sharing your inspiring island with a native wannabe, and to Chief of Police Guy Osborne, for insight on Pawleys Island law enforcement. I apologize in advance for any creative license on my part to make fact work with fiction.

Thanks, too, to Wally Lind, Senior Crime Scene Analyst. Your knowledge and willingness to help went way and above the call of duty and I am truly grateful.

Last, but not least, thank you to my agent, Karen Solem, for not giving up; to my editor, Cindy Hwang, for believing in this book; and to St. Jude, who really does listen.

But such a tide as moving seems asleep
    Too full for sound and foam
When that which drew from out the boundless deep
    Turns again home.

—"Crossing the Bar"
Alfred, Lord Tennyson

CHAPTER I

JILLIAN PARRISH STOOD BAREFOOT IN HER BACKYARD, HER TOES curled into the cool grass, and wrapped her hands around the neck of her telescope. Peering through the narrow opening and pushing back her fear of dark spaces, she focused on the pinpoints of light that made up the constellation of Centaurus. She stepped back slowly, gazing out at the night sky, pretending the grass beneath her feet was gritty sand and that she could actually hear the ancient rhythm of the ocean rocking the stars to sleep. She thought of the immortal centaur as he begged the gods to end his suffering, and how Zeus had mercifully let him die and then given him a place among the stars.

She sat down on the grass, wishing she had such an option. She spun the rings on her finger and shrugged. Her ex-husband wouldn't care and her parents would simply not allow it. It would cause them the inconvenience of having to recall her name for the police report and see her each time she rose high above them in the heavens, her celestial face a constant reminder of their failure to create a child worthy of their notice.

She looked at the tiny diamond engagement ring nestled next to her grandmother's gold band. Yes, there were other points of refuge besides being relegated to dangling in the sky for eternity. But as she had learned, they each carried a price. With one swift motion, she wrenched the diamond ring off her finger and threw it high into the night sky, the white stone blinking once in the light from the back porch bulb and then dropping back to earth like a falling star.

Hoisting herself up, Jillian sighed, silently thanking her grandmother for teaching her about fairy tales and mythology to soften the sharp edges of the life into which she had been born. Not that they had done anything to prepare her for ambitious young waitresses at Hooters or a husband who had finally given up trying to get as much love as he gave in a marriage.

Closing up the tripod and lifting the telescope, Jillian stumbled through the overgrown grass to the house to finish packing. She paused on the back steps, staring out into the Georgia night sky one last time. A shooting star blazed away its brief life across the heavens, and just as suddenly Jillian Parrish Ryan saw her life with the clarity of a woman full-grown. At thirty-two years old she could finally stop believing in fairy tales and happily-ever-afters and begin to recognize what really lived in the dark space under her bed.

"Jilly-bean?"

Keeping a hand on the expanding girth of her pregnant belly, Jillian turned to her seven-year-old daughter, the late March sun kissing her light blond hair and spinning it into gold. She slammed the back door of the Volvo wagon before answering. "What, sweetie?"

"Will the Easter Bunny be able to find our new house?"

She had forgotten all about bunnies, chocolate eggs and pastel hats. In the blur of the three months since the divorce she had found it difficult to remember to wash her hair or get out of bed, much less remember that Santa Claus and the Easter Bunny still roamed the landscape of her life. She lifted her hands and rubbed at her temples in the feeble hope that it might dissipate the headache that seemed to loom just below the surface. "Damn," she said under her breath.

"You shouldn't swear." Grace tilted her face expectantly toward her mother. Jillian looked at her as if really seeing her for the first time in months and noticed that the blond bangs were too long. Her gaze dipped lower and she saw the sparkly red Dorothy shoes on the little feet, shoes she vaguely remembered throwing in the garbage. At least they weren't white. Never white shoes before Easter. Jillian stopped herself in time. Her mother's teachings always seemed to pick the worst times to come back and haunt her.

Jillian moved the hair off her daughter's pale forehead. "Sorry—you're right. I shouldn't swear. And the Easter Bunny will find you, Gracie. Promise."

Grace climbed into the backseat of the car. "Where's Spot?"

As if on cue, a black-and-gray-striped feline streaked past Jillian and into the car, settling his plump bottom onto Grace's lap. He gazed at Jillian with cool green eyes, and a look of understanding settled between them. *I'll tolerate you in these close quarters and you'll tolerate me. It's just the three of us and we've got to learn how to get along.* Jillian watched as Grace hugged the cat that thought it was a dog, and sent him a look of acknowledgment before shutting the door.

With one last look at the brick colonial that had been the cornerstone of her life for almost ten years, she spied Rick's rocking chair, the one piece of furniture he wanted and that had not been sold, moved or put into storage. It shifted in the wind as if waving good-bye, the final assault on Jillian's nerves. Climbing up the steps, she took the piece of gum out of her mouth and stuck it to the wicker seat where it would melt in the unseasonably hot March sun. Then, without another glance, she climbed behind the steering wheel, the child inside her kicking furiously in protest, and put the car in gear to begin the longest journey of her life.

The distance between Atlanta and Pawleys Island, South Carolina, was not particularly long or difficult, yet her hands clutched the steering wheel in a white-knuckled grasp the entire way. She'd never been on her own before, never traveled any distance at all sitting in the driver's seat. She'd always been a granddaughter or daughter and then a wife, all of which excused her from the necessity of sitting behind the steering wheel and determining which direction she should go. Inching forward in the right lane, she hugged the shoulder and ignored the glances from other drivers as they veered around her, leaving her in their hasty dust.

Gracie sang to herself as she colored in her coloring books, and then slept. Spot nestled next to her, his watchful eyes finally closing. Jillian risked another glance in the rearview mirror and saw Grace's little mouth turned upward in a smile. Grandma Parrish said Jillian used to smile in her sleep, too. It's what happens, she'd explained, when little children talk to the angels. Jillian smirked as she faced the road again. If only the angels would give her a few minutes of their time, she could give them an earful.

Her daughter sighed and turned her head, and Jillian caught sight of the single dimple on her left cheek as she grinned a lazy sleeper's grin. Jillian's throat tightened, and she realized anew why she had named her Grace. Since her birth, her daughter had been the one patch of thick, green grass on the stony mountain of her years in this world. They didn't have anything in common, and they didn't even resemble each other, but somewhere, deep down, she felt that there was something that anchored the two of them together. She just wasn't sure what it was.

Jillian looked away, feeling the gnawing guilt hit her again. The guilt of knowing that she had never wanted to bring a child into this world in the first place. She almost laughed when the baby inside her kicked her ribs, reminding her of his presence. *Two children.* How had this happened? She did laugh softly this time, finding it so much easier than the alternative.

Traffic thinned as she turned off onto Highway 501 South, and she found the courage to reach over to the radio and turn up the music from a country station. A heavy veil of purple-tinged clouds cupped the sky like a father's hand under his newborn's head, and her spirit shifted in the sludge around her soul. Although she had called Atlanta home for more than thirty years, the briny air of the salt marshes of South Carolina's low country always welcomed her back as an absent and much-loved daughter.

Perhaps it was the memories of South Carolina summers that made the humid air and waving palmettos seem more like home than the city she was raised in. Jillian had been allowed to visit her grandmother at her beach house on Pawleys Island every year, and those summers still lived in Jillian's memory as bright spots on the bleak horizon of her childhood. The long days spent with Grandma Parrish had been days filled with clam digging and shell collecting and then, as she grew older, her first crush and her first kiss. But those summers had been her refuge, and she knew that she and her daughter could use a dose of that now. Even with her grandmother long gone, the abiding affinity Jillian felt for her grandmother's island was as fresh in her heart as the smell of summer grass.

Jillian squinted in the dimness, following the signs for US Highway 17 toward Georgetown. She drove even slower, noticing the new putt-putt golf courses, beach furniture stores, and garish tourist shops with front doors disguised as the mouth of a shark. She turned away, looking straight ahead, passing Murrells Inlet and Litchfield Beach. She checked the map again on the seat beside her without really seeing it. Almost there.

Dusk descended lower, the purple clouds now giving way to hulking dark shadows as she pulled off the highway onto the small two-lane North Causeway Road. It had been more than sixteen years since she had last been to Pawleys, but the way was as familiar to her as the back of her own hand. The night sounds of the marsh hovered close, filling her with an odd mixture of apprehension and excitement. She turned down the radio, now playing oldies Carolina beach music, to listen more closely to the bellowing bullfrogs.

Grace stirred in the backseat and then bolted upright, wide awake. "Jilly-bean—stop the car. Lauren says we need to stop the car now."

Jillian's hands slipped on the steering wheel. *Why that name, Gracie? Of all the names you use for your imaginary friends, why that one?* She forced her voice to remain soft. "We're almost there, honey. I think you were just having a bad dream." She glanced to the side of the road where the right shoulder seemed to disappear into the marsh, the lights from the old Pelican Inn glowing in the distance. No other car lights gleamed ahead or behind. "Everything's fine."

Something quick and dark and low to the ground ran out in front of the car. She pressed hard on the brakes, the ABS pumping rhythmically. Glowing yellow eyes stared back at her as she waited for the sickening thump of solid steel hitting the soft body of an animal. Instinctively, she jerked the steering wheel to the left, sending the car careening across the road and into a metal guardrail, the air bag jabbing her sharply in the face.

Blinking her eyes as she sat in the suddenly still car, she tried to focus on the dashboard, where the lights glowed with dim persistence, while something warm and sticky dripped from her forehead and into her lap.

Grace unbuckled her seat belt with a soft snap, then climbed on top of the armrest to stroke her mother's cheek. "It's all right, Jilly-bean. Everything's going to be all right."

Jillian reached toward her daughter, skimming her hands over the small, delicate bones, relieved to see that the child was uninjured. The little girl squinted up at her mother. "You're driving like a woman."

Something dripped over Jillian's eyes and she touched her forehead, feeling the wet stickiness of blood. She leaned back against her seat and gave a heavy sigh of resignation. "Thanks, Gracie. I appreciate you letting me know."

She closed her eyes for a moment, listening to the sudden silence. The baby moved inside her then, reassuring her of his presence, and she let out a mouthful of breath she hadn't been aware she was holding.

Grace's hand continued to stroke her mother's cheek. "It will be all right, Jilly-bean," she insisted. "Lauren said a policeman was right behind us."

She jerked abruptly around to look at her daughter's face. Grace stared back sweetly, with no concern etched on her face. Again, she thought, *Why that name?*

Since Grace had been able to talk, Jillian and Rick had been aware of Grace's extraordinary perception and imagination. They'd listen to her on the baby monitor, speaking to imaginary friends as she drifted off to sleep. Her pediatrician assured them that it was normal and that she would grow out of it. But she had not, and Jillian had learned to ignore it. Until now.

Jillian's composure fractured. "Stop it, Gracie. Do you hear me? I said to stop it. It's not helping anything."

The words were barely out of her mouth when the flashing lights of a vehicle behind them sliced through the darkness, illuminating all with its strobe-light effect. Spot leapt over the seat back, landing with practiced precision on Grace's lap.

Jillian heard the crunching of gravel as footsteps approached the beached car. A flashlight shone inside, blinding her, and she held up her hand to block the glare. The sounds of the crickets rushed in as the officer pulled open her door and leaned in, the scent of Old Spice mixing oddly with that of burnt rubber and salt.

"Are y'all all right in here?"

The last word came out with two syllables, like "he-yah." She had been surrounded by so many Northern transplants in Atlanta that the sound of a genuine Southern accent caught her by surprise.

Jillian looked up at him, and he lowered his flashlight a fraction so that it no longer blinded her. "I think so. I just got a little scratch on my head from the air bag, but we're all fine." She twisted a little in her seat. "Right, Gracie?"

Grace answered by lifting the cat up to her nose and rubbing her face in his soft fur. "I told you there would be a policeman." Her words were devoid of recrimination or bravado.

"I think it was a raccoon. It ran out in front of me and I tried to avoid it."

The officer shook his head. "And if that ain't the damnedest thing. I was on my way home, and somehow I had the urge to head up the causeway again to check on things." He shook his head. "If this don't just beat all." He reached into a back pocket and brought out a neatly folded handkerchief and handed it to Jillian. "Here, now. You hold this to that cut on your forehead and I'll go call an ambulance. And next time, don't worry about the raccoon." He winked, then let his gaze stray to her belly.

She shook her head, feeling numb with weariness and wanting nothing more than to reach their destination. "I know it was stupid of me—I guess my reflexes took over. But I promise you, we're fine and there's really no need to call an ambulance. And we're almost to where we're going. If you can just help me move the car off the road and drive us a mile or so, I'll call a tow truck in the morning."

He stood for a moment, looking down at her, his broad face creased in concentration. "Where are you staying?"

"On Ellerbee Road. Off Myrtle Avenue."

His brow furrowed. "You must be talking about the old Parrish house. Are you the new owner?"

Frowning up at him, she said, "Yes. I am."

Jillian grabbed her purse, then pushed at the door to open it farther. The officer stepped back, holding it for her. Gracie yanked her door open at the same time, and the three of them stumbled onto the solid pavement of the road.

Jillian reached for her daughter's hand, and felt her own fingers tremble. The accident had shaken her more than she cared to admit. Gracie gave her hand a tight squeeze and snuggled up to her side.

The policeman hitched his pants to cover a large paunch and looked at her with a frown. "I'll need to write up an incident report for your insurance company. Why don't you two come and sit in my backseat while I do that, and you can think about letting me take you to the hospital. I think you should see somebody about that cut on your head, and check out that baby."

Her hand went to her belly and felt the roil of her baby under the tightly pulled skin. She shook her head wearily. "We're fine—really. We just need to get some sleep. It will be good to wake up in a familiar place in the morning instead of some hospital."

He looked at her closely, his eyes widening in recognition. "You're the Parrish girl, aren't you? Julie, Jill—no, wait—it's Jillian, isn't it? It's different enough that I'd remember it. I thought you looked familiar. I think I caught you on lovers' lane a couple of times, huh?" He smiled at her, as if waiting for her to say something. She felt the heat rush to her face and wondered if this interminable nightmare of a night would ever end. When she said nothing, he continued.

"You probably don't remember me, 'cause it's been a while, but I'm Chief of Police Joe Weber. I was involved in the nasty business of the Mills case when their daughter disappeared."

The blood seemed to freeze in her veins, stealing her breath. Grace appeared to feel it and squeezed her mother's hand tighter.

Chief Weber didn't seem to notice, and continued. "Of course, you probably don't recognize me—I've changed a bit since then." He gave a sheepish grin. "I've got a little less hair and a lot more stomach." Scratching his chin, he said, "You'd think I'd remember that girl's name, too. . . ."

"Lauren," she forced out. "Her name was Lauren."

He looked at her sharply. "Yeah—that's it." He shook his head somberly. "I remember now—you two were good friends, weren't you? We never did find her, poor child. And those two houses have stood empty all these years, boarded up and a real eyesore. Until that architect from Charleston bought 'em both dirt cheap and decided to fix 'em up. Just started the Mills house, but he's only gotten as far as repairing the roof. Nobody here can believe you bought your house so cheap. Most of those old ones are going for three times more."

She tried to keep her movements calm, her voice steady. Guiding her daughter, she walked toward the police car, a white Jeep SUV with the word POLICE emblazoned on the side. She paused, remembering the gentle people who had once lived in the Mills house, and the family they had become to her in the short time they had spent together. She faced the chief. "It was certainly lucky finding that my grandmother's old house was available." She didn't mention the feeling of destiny fulfilled that had possessed her when her low-ball offer had been accepted, nor the feeling of unease that the owner had dropped the price considerably to an affordable amount. But the healing call of the swaying sea oats had beckoned her, and the tall house behind the dunes had been the one sanctuary of her childhood, and the only part of it that she would ever care to revisit.

Grace slid into the backseat of the chief's vehicle, Spot cradled in her arms, and Jillian followed. After handing Chief Weber her driver's license and registration, she settled back and listened to the static of the radio, the disjointed voices mixing with the insect song of the night. She closed her eyes, hoping the policeman would notice and stop digging up old memories that were best left buried alongside adolescent humiliations and deep loss.

A pen scratched across paper and Jillian felt herself drifting off to sleep. His words jerked her awake.

"Will your husband be joining you?"

Gracie's head sagged limply against her mother's arm, and Jillian felt some relief that the child wouldn't have to hear this conversation yet again. "I'm divorced." She spared the officer the sordid details of how easily her husband's head had been turned by a twenty-one-year-old woman whose greatest asset appeared to be her bra size. She was sure that the whole ordeal would have been a lot easier on her ego if the woman had only been a rocket scientist or a neurosurgeon.

The pen stopped as Chief Weber half turned his head, his profile covered in shadow. "I'm real sorry to hear that." His face seemed to shift downward in an expression of sorrow and it made her want to cry. She closed her eyes for a moment and swallowed.

"Seems like you'll be having your hands full, then, with two little ones."

She nodded, afraid to trust her voice.

"Lots of friendly neighbors here, Miz Parrish, that will be glad to help—including my wife. We've had eight of our own, and my Martha just loves babies. Don't you worry about a thing."

"Thank you," she managed, before dropping her head and letting the tears fall onto the soft hair of her daughter. Grace stirred in her sleep, then nuzzled into Jillian's side with a contented sigh. She thought of Grandma Parrish telling her that babies in heaven choose their parents, using a wisdom that seemed to elude them once they are born. She grinned at her watery reflection in the window, wondering how such a choice could have gone so awry in two generations of the same family.

Chief Weber put the luggage they would need into his Jeep before moving and locking up the Volvo. "Hope you don't mind if I keep the key—don't expect you'll be needing it tonight, though." He gave her a small grin. "I'll call for a tow in the morning and have Richie Kobylt look at it in his shop and fix the air bags. If everything's fine, I'll have him bring it to your house."

"I don't know how to thank you for all your help."

He started his engine, then waved his hand in dismissal. "It's nothing. I'm just glad I was here." The car moved off with the crunch and pop of loose gravel, as Spot moved from Grace's side and settled by Jillian's. He didn't settle down to sleep, but remained on his haunches, an alert sentinel as they moved under the canopy of streetlights and toward the lure of salt-drenched waves.

Even in the pitch darkness, Jillian recognized the two houses nestled behind the dunes in a tangle of sea oats, cedars and myrtles. Handmade arches and columns adorned the wide porches that surrounded the lower floors, while their elevated, strong-timbered foundations clung fiercely to the ground upon which they were built. The shadows of the houses sat together with identical eaves and roof pitches, matching dormers and a single turret on opposing sides, like two sisters frozen in time in a perpetual shoulder shrug.

They were each more than one hundred fifty years old, built by two brothers for their families to escape the summer yellow fever epidemics inland. Each brick and length of timber had been floated by boat down the Waccamaw River, then lovingly assembled on the island. Despite more than a century's worth of hurricanes and beach erosion, the houses stood intact, facing the wind with sheer defiance. Perhaps it was their jutting profiles, indicating a confident bravado she had never felt, that pulled her close to this place. The arched pillars of the front porch had always reminded her of her grandmother's arms, and standing beneath them she could almost remember being loved and cherished.

Her weariness didn't allow Jillian any time to study her new yet familiar surroundings. She opened the front door with the key the Realtor had sent and allowed Chief Weber to carry their bags into two upstairs rooms. She called up after him, "Do you mind switching on all the lights? I don't like a dark house."

He answered by flicking on the upstairs hall light, and then the rest of the rooms followed like a dance sequence, slowly making the house grow brighter and brighter.

The house had been completely furnished by the architect who had restored it, and as she glanced around, she was struck with the uncanny feeling that the furniture had been placed in the same locations as she remembered. She walked from room to room, switching on lights, smelling the newness of everything, but recognizing the furniture and layout as if nothing had changed in the past decade and a half.

She was relieved to see fresh linens covering the beds, and a huge welcome basket of kitchen items with a card from Lessie Beaumont, the real estate agent, monopolized the kitchen island. Lessie had insisted on preparing the bedrooms with linens, a welcome treat Jillian hadn't argued with, but this was a much-appreciated bonus. She'd call Lessie in the morning to thank her. Assuming she didn't sleep through the next day and a half. Exhaustion pulled at her, making her struggle to stay on her feet and keep her eyes open.

Officer Weber joined her in the kitchen. "I guess my Lessie's got you all set up here."

Jillian's eyes widened in understanding. "That's right—she used to be a Weber. Lessie mentioned that in our first phone conversation when I called her real estate office. I was surprised she remembered me, since I was only here during the summers and she's at least four years younger than me."

"Yeah, well, Lessie's sort of Pawleys honorary historian—she knows everything about everybody who spent more than five minutes on the island—things people might not even know about themselves." He winked, gave Jillian his numbers at work and at home, then left with a warm and sympathetic smile and a promise to have Martha stop by in the morning. She made herself busy getting Grace ready for bed, ignoring the throbbing of a headache that had been brewing since after the accident.

Grace stood groggily in the middle of her room, her stuffed bunny, Bun-Bun, held suspended by an ear, and Spot pacing restlessly at her ankles. Jillian led her to the bathroom, and while Grace sat on the toilet her mother pulled off her dress and slipped her nightgown over her head.

Jillian let her skip brushing her teeth, helped her to the white iron bed covered with a frilly white lace coverlet, then pulled back the covers to allow Grace to crawl in. Spot dutifully plopped down on the pillow next to her as she snuggled Bun-Bun in the crook of her arm. Jillian eyed the feline with grudging acceptance. "Spot still thinks he's a dog. I think we should change his name to Tinkles or something more catlike."

Gracie smiled a groggy smile and snuggled deeper into her covers.

The distant thrum of the ocean crept through the open windows, spilling the salt air onto the pillows and into the corners of the room. She breathed deeply the smell of her youth, and let her hand fall gently on her daughter's forehead. She was still awake, looking at her mother intently, as if awaiting the questions she knew she had to ask.

"Who is Lauren, Gracie?" Her voice came out as a whisper, barely louder than the breeze blowing the ruffled curtains.

Spot lifted his head and narrowed his eyes.

"She's my new friend. She wants to help us."

Jillian swallowed. "I see." She measured her words carefully. "I want you to understand something. These people in your head are only in your imagination, all right? They aren't real, and anything that happens is just a coincidence and would have happened, anyway—like the policeman showing up tonight. And when you pretend it's otherwise, you scare me."

Grace's lower lip quivered. "I don't want to scare you, Jilly-bean. But they're *real*."

Jillian stood, her sciatic nerve throbbing from the weight of her pregnancy. She rubbed her hands over her tired face. Maybe it was a coincidence. Or maybe her daughter needed help. She remembered her grandmother's final year as she descended further and further into senility, and how she would call the police every night, insisting she could see naked people having sex on the beach. Jillian stared in trepidation at her little girl.

"You're not seeing naked people or anything, right?"

The girl stared up at her mother in blank confusion.

Feeling foolish, Jillian smiled. "Good. Now, I think we're both overtired. We'll both feel a lot better in the morning after we get a good night's sleep."

Gracie didn't move. "Lauren told me you wouldn't believe me."

With frustration borne of weariness and grief, Jillian leaned her hands on the bed and looked into Grace's light brown eyes, their only similarity. "We're starting over here, Gracie. Please don't start with your imaginary friends again. Let that be over so we can begin to put our lives back together. I don't want to hear any more about Lauren. Do I make myself clear? It's not helping anything."

The little girl's throat bobbed as she swallowed. Then, slowly, she nodded. "All right, Jilly-bean."

Jillian kissed Grace's forehead. As she turned off the light and left the room, she was aware of two sets of eyes watching her intently. She hesitated, then left the door open a crack, letting the light from the hallway filter into the darkened bedroom.

She limped from the room, rubbing her back. Her suitcase lay unopened on the four-poster bed in the largest bedroom, and she collapsed next to it. As if on their own, her fingers unlatched the lock and spread open the case. Heedlessly tossing aside support hose, maternity underwear and a couple of blouses, she reached into the back corner and pulled out a small wooden box about the size of her open hand.

It had been carved from a solid piece of pine and polished until it shone. She pulled the lid off and stared inside. A tiny wooden star, its edges uneven and unpracticed, nestled in a corner along with a withered note, its seams torn from years of folding and unfolding. She didn't know why she had clung to this relic of a time in her life she never wanted to revisit. Maybe it was because it represented a door in her past that had never been closed. Or maybe because it was all she had left of the two people she had once loved with all the fervor of a young girl's heart, and then lost forever.

She cradled the box in her hands for a long time, not touching the note. She had not returned to the island to revisit her past, but to recover from her present and perhaps find a future. Still, she could almost see the strong hand of the boy who had carved the beautiful box and written the note, the pencil clutched tightly in his long-fingered grip. She let her fingers trace the two carved initials on the top—two *L*s intertwined with each other in wood, as solidly as the two names they represented remained in her memory.

She placed the cover back on her past, then shoved the box into the back of the nightstand drawer to gather dust. She slipped into her nightgown and crawled into bed, and waited for sleep that seemed to evade her despite how tired she was, her bedside lamp burning brightly. The empty hours before dawn populated themselves with memories of this house and her grandmother, and of the boy she'd first danced with and with whom she'd shared her first kiss. She lay awake until the dawn sky pinkened the white walls around her and the seagulls began to cry.

CHAPTER 2

SIX-YEAR-OLD JILLIAN DUG INTO THE SAND WHERE SHE HAD SEEN AN air hole from a clam, her small fingers gripping the soggy grains and pushing them aside until she found her prize. She held it up for her grandmother to see before dropping it into her bucket with the others.

Grandma Parrish stood next to her, wearing a wide-brimmed straw hat and her pants rolled up to her baggy knees. She winked at her granddaughter, then turned her attention back to the sand and its hidden treasures.

Jillian moved ahead of her grandmother, eager to fill her bucket and already tasting her dinner. Something ahead in the sand caught her attention, and she moved toward it. A small mound of sand stood scraped away from a large crescent-shaped hole, the small claw marks of the digger still evidenced in the moist sand. Peering inside, she spotted chunks of white eggshell and yolk smeared against the edges of the vandalized nest.

She fell to her knees with a soft sob, her bucket tipping over and spreading clamshells like an offering. Her grandmother came and knelt beside her.

"It's a little early yet for loggerheads to be laying their eggs."

Jillian simply nodded, staring with unspeakable sadness at the wrecked nest of unborn baby turtles.

Grandma spread her hand, soothing down the mound as a mother would ease a child's ache. "Looks like a raccoon. See these claw marks?"

Jillian sniffed, hating raccoons with every fiber of her being. "Why'd he have to ruin all of them? Couldn't he just take a few and leave the rest to get born?"

Pushing up her broad brim, Grandma Parrish smiled. "Nature's not always so tactful, is she?" She stared out at the ocean, squinting. "At least their mommy doesn't know about it. She thinks they're all safe in the perfect little nest she made for them." She looked at Jillian for a long moment before turning back to the nest.

"Why can't their mommy stay and make sure they're all right until they're born?"

She shrugged. "It's just what they're wired to do. They dig a hole, lay their eggs and then spend a great deal of time and energy burying and disguising the nest so their enemies can't hurt them."

Jillian wrinkled her forehead, examining the wreckage. "She didn't do a very good job, did she?" She stared at the ruined eggs, wondering how a mother could ever let that happen.

Grandma Parrish pushed out of her granddaughter's eyes the hair that had escaped dark brown braids. "Jillian, sometimes mothers can only do their best. It's all God ever asks of us. And all he can expect with what we're given."

Something in the deepest part of the nest caught Jillian's attention and she leaned forward, scraping sand away from a scrap of white. Gingerly, the old woman moved Jillian's hand away and finished unearthing a small Ping-Pong ball–shaped egg. They both smiled at her prize.

With what sounded like relief, her grandmother said, "See? Sometimes we survive, anyway." Very carefully, she put the egg back where they had found it, then covered the hole with the sand. Grandma emptied her pail of clams into Jillian's, then walked up toward the dunes to grab dry sand and scatter it over the nest, along with dried sea oats.

She winked at Jillian. "And sometimes we rely on the kindness of others to put us back in our nests." With a final pat, she reached for her granddaughter and pulled her up. Jillian felt the reassuring rub of her grandmother's gold wedding band against her fingers before letting go and bending to gather the clams and replace them in her bucket.

A tall shadow fell on them, and they both looked up.

It was Mason Weber, oldest boy of the chief of police. He was all of nine years old, but already taller than her grandma Parrish. "Y'all aren't messing with a turtle nest or anything, right? We're supposed to be leaving nature alone."

Grandma Parrish pushed the brim of her hat back and stared down her regal nose at the young boy. "Now, Mason, you know we're just here digging for clams. Nothing wrong with that, is there?"

He took off his baseball hat and wiped the sweat from his forehead with his forearm. "No, ma'am." He peered down at Jillian. "Your parents just pulled in at the house. I reckon they're waiting to take you back to Atlanta."

She clung to her grandmother's hand but didn't blink an eye. "I don't have any parents. I'm an orphan."

Mason slid his hat back on his head, giving Jillian a peculiar glance that made her think he'd just bitten into a lemon.

Grandma Parrish squeezed her hand. "Thanks, Mason. We were just leaving, anyway." With her grandmother tugging on her hand, Jillian looked at her bare feet and the sand clinging to her knees and hands. She knew her father would make her bear the humiliation of stripping naked in the backyard to use the shower there before she'd be allowed inside their car.

As they approached the dunes, Jillian looked back and watched as a wave spilled up over the shore and erased the footprints they had made, filling in the dips and hollows made by their heels and toes as if they had never existed at all.

Jillian's leg twitched, and she flicked her eyes open. She stared at the unfamiliar ceiling, her heart beating erratically. She could still smell her grandmother's perfume of baby powder and soap, and feel her absence with the poignancy of deep and abiding loss. She wiped her face of the tears she could only shed in her dreams, and sat up.

She jerked with a start, realizing somebody was banging on the front door. Out of habit, the thumb of her right hand slid to her ring finger and found the small dent in her grandmother's gold wedding band. With bleary eyes, she stumbled from the bed, throwing her sweater over her nightgown, her bathrobe still buried somewhere in a suitcase. She tripped on a small area rug, catching herself from falling by grasping the door handle.

Her sciatic nerve always ached worse in the morning, and she cursed under her breath, remembering her stupidity in leaving her heating pad in the Volvo.

"Don't say 'shit,' Jilly-bean."

Grace stood in the doorway to her room, the sun passing through the pink curtains and flooding her and the room behind her in a soft rose. Her beloved Bun-Bun dangled by a long, floppy ear.

"Sorry. I didn't know you were up."

"I know. I was being real quiet so I wouldn't wake you. Do you want me to get the door?"

"Yes, thanks. It will take me a while to get down these steps."

With exuberant enthusiasm that can only be found in the very young, Grace bounded down the stairs, slid back the dead bolt and threw the door wide.

A woman stood on the doorstep, a large canvas tote dangling from an arm and a white covered casserole dish clutched in her hands. She was of medium height, with medium-length hair in a medium shade of brown streaked with gray. There was nothing remarkable about the woman except for the brightly colored oven mitts shaped like crabs that she wore on her hands, and the warmth of her smile. She moved her gaze from Grace to Jillian, where she stood halfway down the stairs, then seemed to notice all the glaring lights that were still on from the previous night.

She held up the dish. "I don't know if you remember me, but I'm Martha Weber. My husband, Joe, brought you here last night and thought y'all might could use a home-cooked breakfast this morning." She indicated a medium-sized box at her feet. "And Lessie suggested I bring her old college dishes until your shipment arrives."

Jillian smiled and took a step toward her grandmother's old friend. "Of course I remember you. I suppose I should have made the connection when I saw your husband last night." She took a step toward Martha, grasping the railing tightly for support.

With a no-nonsense voice, Martha said, "You stay there while I go put all this stuff in the kitchen, and I'll be right back to help you down."

Jillian heard her bustling in the kitchen before Martha quickly reappeared to help her down the stairs. Too tired to protest, she allowed Martha to take over, settling Jillian and Grace in chairs at the kitchen table, then placing steaming plates of hot ham and grits in front of them.

When she set a cup of coffee down next to Jillian's plate, Martha joined them at the table, a mug held between her hands.

Jillian stretched out her leg, trying to find a comfortable position, and looked across the table at her guest. "I really can't thank you enough for all this. You're too kind."

Martha waved a hand in dismissal. "I'm just glad to help. Annabelle—your grandmother—and I were good friends, you know. It's the very least I can do for her granddaughter and great-granddaughter." She grinned down at Grace, who smiled back without guile.

Jillian relaxed a bit, glad to see a familiar face who wasn't aware of the humiliation of her recent past. Martha was more gray and more round than she remembered her, but she was so familiar that it was as if a piece of her grandmother had walked into her kitchen with Martha Weber.

Spot entered the room cautiously, pausing to look up at the visitor. Purring softly, he snaked between Martha's ankles, then retreated to a corner to silently watch them with wide green eyes.

Grace looked up at her mother. "He's hungry, Jilly-bean. What should I feed him?"

"There's a couple cans of cat food in my tote upstairs in my room, if you want to go get them."

The little girl slid back from the table, and the two women listened as her feet pounded up the wooden stairs.

Martha leaned forward. "She doesn't call you Mama." She stated it as a fact, without reproach.

Jillian looked down at the steam rising from her mug. "No. I . . . I didn't want her to call me that. I know it's odd, but she came up with Jilly-bean almost as soon as she could talk. . . ."

Martha reached over and placed her hand over Jillian's. "You don't need to explain anything to me. I knew how it was between you and your parents, honey. You don't need to explain a thing." She pointed upward. "And your little girl. I don't think she minds. She's an old soul, that one."

Jillian stared at her companion for a moment. "Do you really think so? A gypsy at the state fair once told me the same thing. I wasn't sure what she meant then, but I'm pretty sure I know now. Sometimes with Gracie, I'm not sure who's the adult and who's the child."

Martha smiled down into her mug. "I think we're given the children we need to make our lives whole." She winked. "I've had eight, so I know what I'm talking about."

Looking away, Jillian avoided Martha's gaze. "I think some children get misdirected and end up in the wrong place altogether."

Martha patted her hand in the most sympathetic gesture anyone had offered Jillian in the past three months. She had the sudden and unmistakable urge to cry and to confess every awful hurt she'd suffered in the past three months. Before she could stop herself, she blurted, "I didn't even tell my parents about the divorce—I didn't want to hear them say something like 'It took Rick a long time to come to his senses.' Which is probably true, since I know he hadn't been happy for a long time, but I mean, if all he wanted was bigger breasts, he could have just hung around for a couple of months. . . ."

She stopped, mortified at what was running out of her mouth. Maybe mental instability did run in her family. Maybe she'd be the one to see naked people in her backyard. "I'm sorry, Martha. I think these pregnancy hormones . . ."

Once again, Martha reached across the table and squeezed Jillian's hand. "Honey, I've been a mother for thirty-eight years. There's nothing I haven't seen or been made to understand. And there sure as heck's not anything left that can surprise me."

To Jillian's relief, Grace clattered back down the steps with the cat food and Spot's bowl, then rummaged around the kitchen until she found a can opener in the basket from Lessie Beaumont. Settling herself cross-legged in the corner, she put her elbows on her knees and watched Spot eat. Jillian knew that posture well. It was meant to make her disappear so that the others in the room couldn't see her listening to every word. Jillian had always wondered if Grace had learned that from her.

Martha stood to begin clearing plates. "Well, I'm glad you've found your way back here. It will be like having a little piece of Annabelle back." China dishes pinged together as she loaded the dishwasher.

"Please, Martha. Stop. I can do that. . . ."

"Nonsense. You're limping, child, so let me help you. I like doing for other people—which is probably why I had eight children. Most of them have moved away, so let me play mama again." She paused for a moment, holding a dish in midair, her shoulders slumped forward slightly. "Let me help you. I reckon you and your little girl will need it, so you might as well say yes."

Jillian couldn't argue with the bent figure at the sink. She smiled to herself as a flash of memory shot through her mind. Her grandmother standing by this same sink, handing her a glass of iced tea, forbidden by her mother. She could still feel the way the glass chilled her young fingers.

"Thank you," she said, and didn't say anything else.

Martha found a sponge and began wiping the counter. "I suppose you'll recognize lots of people—it's a small island, and us locals don't move away much. Except for the Millses, but I suppose you know that. After"—she paused—"after poor Lauren disappeared, they moved away, and pretty much lost touch with everybody here."

Jillian stood stiffly, then made her way to the coffeepot to refill their mugs. "So you don't know what happened to them?"

Martha closed the dishwasher with a final thud. "I do remember hearing that they had lost a lot of money in bad investments a couple of years ago and had to sell pretty much everything—including their house next door. It had been lying here empty for so many years, I couldn't believe anybody would buy it, but it sold right away. That was the last I heard about them." She took a dish towel from the basket on the counter and began to wipe drops of water off the chrome faucet. "I heard they hung on to the house as long as they could, hoping their girl would eventually come back. I guess they finally gave up hope."

Jillian clutched her mug tighter, staring down at the muddy coffee. *Lauren.* She had carefully sifted through her memories, taking out the large chunks of unwelcome ones and keeping the ones as fine and easy as powdered sand. The summers before her sixteenth year were the ones that sifted down into the stronghold of her memory. Everything else was left in the sieve.

Martha reached for a small bowl in the box she'd brought and filled it with milk before setting it in front of Spot and Grace. She patted Grace on her head, startling her as if she was surprised to find that they remembered she was there.

"And that boy—what was his name? The one they questioned about Lauren's disappearance. He's never been back, either. Which I guess is just as well."

Jillian's hand shook slightly as she placed her mug back on the kitchen table. "His name was Linc." It was a name she had not said out loud in sixteen years, and it shocked her to do so now. But there was something about being on Pawleys Island again, traversing a world she knew yet didn't know, that made his name leap to her lips.

Martha sat down slowly. "Yes. I believe you're right." Her pale eyes were warm and inquisitive, but she wouldn't say anything else. "I don't suppose you've come all this way to dredge up the past, though."

She shook her head. "No, I didn't. I came here to start over."

"It's a peaceful place, and I do swear that the salt air is a great healer." Martha rose, taking their two empty mugs with her and putting them in the dishwasher.

Jillian pushed her chair back. "Thank you for coming, Martha. You've been a great help."

"Glad to do it. Don't get up—I'll let myself out. Joe had your car towed into town to check it out. He'll have it brought back here if there aren't any problems. He told me to ask you if there was anything in the back that you needed in the meantime."

Jillian's sciatic nerve began to throb as if in answer to her question. "Yes, actually. I left my heating pad, but I could probably live without it for another day. . . ."

"No, you shouldn't. I'll have him bring it by when he comes home for lunch." Martha put her hand on Jillian's arm. "You know we're not that far away—we're right down Myrtle Avenue. Just a phone call away if you need anything. Here's my number." She scribbled it on a pad of paper by the phone. "Now—is that it? Any toys for Grace, or cat food?"

Jillian stood, leaning heavily on the table. "If . . . if it's not any trouble, could he get my telescope, too? My grandmother gave it to me and it's pretty special."

The older woman laid a hand on Jillian's arm and gathered up her crab oven mitts with her other. "Honey, you don't need to explain. My Joe will be happy to do it."

She bustled to the door, and Grace and Jillian followed.

"Oh, before I forget, seeing how Sunday's Easter, we were hoping you and Grace would be able to join us for dinner. A few of our children and grandchildren will be there, and I always make a huge ham."

Grace tugged on her hand, and Jillian looked down into pleading eyes.

"We'd love to—but only if you allow me to bring something."

Grace piped up. "My mommy loves to cook. She curses like a sailor when she burns herself, but she's really good."

Jillian bumped her with her hip, belatedly telling her to be quiet.

"I ran a small catering business from my home in Atlanta. It's been a while since I spent any time in a kitchen, and I think I'm due."

Martha looked at her skeptically. "Only if you really want to. Otherwise, we'll have enough for everybody."

Jillian could almost smell the sweet aroma of baking bread in her Atlanta kitchen, and the need to create, to make something wonderful and desirable with her own hands pulled at her. "I'd really like to."

"Then I look forward to it. Say, about two o'clock? I'll send Joe to come pick you up. We're only on the other end of Myrtle Avenue, but it's a bit of a hike for a pregnant lady and a little girl. You're a bit isolated up here on this end, you know." She winked at Grace. "Just make sure you both know where my phone number is so you can call me if you need anything."

"Thanks again," Jillian said, waving, then watched Martha leave. She felt reluctant to close the door, wanting Martha's presence to linger in the old, empty house and the salty breeze to blow through the rooms. Gracie ran back inside, but Jillian stayed in the doorway and gazed out across the dunes.

Loud buzz saws erupted with sound at the twin house next door, and she stepped out onto her porch, hiding herself in the shadows of the arches. She was embarrassed to still be in her pajamas at eleven o'clock in the morning. Since childhood, she had been an early riser, unwilling to face the consequences of languishing in bed. Old habits died hard, and the guilt would follow her until she was showered and dressed and doing something productive.

A black Mercedes sedan pulled into the driveway next door and a man stepped out, several rolls of what looked like blueprints tucked under his arm. He wore jeans and a long-sleeved shirt with a button-down collar. Despite the casual appearance, there was nothing casual in this man's stance.

He slammed the car door, not with deliberation but with a honed strength that seemed to unleash itself without provocation. He was tall, with long legs and broad shoulders, and seemed to emanate a power that had nothing to do with his physical attributes.

The sun bathed him in its glowing light for a brief moment, reflecting off his dark brown hair, then threw all into shadow as a cloud obscured the sky. He tilted his head back and looked at the house, and

Jillian almost smiled. His jutting chin and determined profile nearly matched that of the house. She sobered quickly, recalling how her grandmother had once said the same of her.

A misty breeze blew up from the ocean, bringing with it the smell of rain. Angry black clouds skimmed toward them, whipping at the waves. A strange, tingling sensation rippled up her spine, and the baby inside slammed against her ribs, nearly taking her breath away. She bent over, grasping at a column, then glanced across the sandy grass.

The man was staring at her, his eyes hidden behind dark sunglasses. She quickly ducked behind the column, her breath coming in quick gasps. There had been something strangely familiar about him, and it wasn't a pleasant familiarity. She recalled the sign in the front of the property—RISING & MORROW, CHARLESTON. The firm's name was foreign to her, and she was sure she didn't know anybody in Charleston.

Too late, she realized she was attempting to hide her pregnant body behind a relatively slim column. From the man's vantage point, she must closely resemble a snake swallowing a toaster.

Straightening her shoulders, she ventured another look. The man was now leaning against his car but still staring in her direction, his eyes hidden behind the sunglasses but his expression making it clear he was watching her.

Pretending she hadn't noticed him, she moved to the front door. Fat drops of rain began hitting the tin roof of the porch as she hurried inside, closing the door firmly before the deluge began.

CHAPTER 3

JILLIAN KISSED GRACIE'S FOREHEAD AS SHE TUCKED HER IN BED, HER Bun-Bun tucked securely under her arm and the ever faithful Spot on the pillow beside her. In the three days they'd been in the house, Grace had not said anything more about her new imaginary friend, Lauren. Jillian could sometimes hear her whispering quietly in her room, in the midst of a heated conversation, but when she knocked, all would be silent.

Jillian moved over to the window to close the curtains, using the opportunity to stare out at the house next door. Not that she wanted to see that man again, of course. But there had been something about him, something that made him stick in her mind like bubblegum on the bottom of a shoe.

"Are you seeing naked people, Jilly-bean?"

Peering closely at the dark windows next door, she muttered, "I wish."

"What?"

The curtains forgotten, Jillian walked back to the bed. "Of course not, Gracie. I'm just looking at all that construction rubble next door and hoping they'll clean it all up when they're through."

After a quick good night kiss and tucking the quilt under Grace's chin, she left the room and went downstairs. The golden glow of a tired sun in the early evening sky lent the rooms its weary light. This had always been her favorite part of the day. The new stars would appear, lighting her way through the night, as if making promises that the following day would be better.

She busied herself in the kitchen, clearing away the dinner dishes while waiting for Gracie to drift off into a deep sleep. She longed for nothing more than to curl up in her own bed and sink into oblivion, but she had promised her daughter that the Easter Bunny would find them.

As she draped the dish towel over the faucet, a time-honored sig-nal that her kitchen chores were done, she listened carefully for any noise from up above. Nothing disturbed the almost eerie stillness of the house, and she heard Martha's voice in her head, commenting on how isolated these two houses were. She walked to the window and slid down the sash, locking it with a solid snap.

Kneeling down in front of the counter under the sink, she reached behind the garbage can and pulled out the two bags of stuffed plastic Easter eggs. She stared at the brightly colored eggs, trying to sense the sheer bliss of a child on Easter morning, but could not. No one had ever hidden eggs for her, and her classmates' chatter about their own Easter mornings had been as if in a foreign language.

Straightening, she began hiding eggs in obvious spots around the first floor. She almost stopped then, thinking that there was more than enough candy to satisfy a single child. But she had another bag full of stuffed eggs that she had spent the last four nights assembling after Grace had gone to bed. Rick had always been in charge of these things, and she had obviously overestimated the number of eggs it would take.

Assured that everything remained quiet upstairs, she flipped on all the lights, then quietly let herself out the back door. Clumping around the porch, feeling large and ungainly and glad no one could see her, she hid the eggs under the arches, behind old flowerpots and under the rocking chairs that had arrived the week before. When she was down to the last egg, she sat in a chair and cracked open the smooth pink shell, allowing herself this one treat. Sweets had always been considered con-traband in her parents' household, and she still could only enjoy them on rare occasions when nobody else was near to see her sin.

As she sat and chewed on the miniature candy bar, she allowed her gaze to stray to the house next door. The twilight sky bathed the man-gled house in soft shades of pink and orange, making it beautiful again. Part of the roof was missing, with wooden beams meeting at a point in the middle like the sun-bleached ribs of a beached whale. Lauren's bed-room window looked out at Jillian with a vacant, staring eye, and the sadness that she had managed so far to keep at bay washed over her.

Not even realizing what she was doing, she stepped off her porch and began walking next door. Stray boards and nails lay scattered in the sandy grass, and she gingerly walked around them. As she stood in front of the porch, a strong gust of wind blew at her back like unseen hands pushing her forward.

She walked up the cracked steps, almost smelling the corn bread cooking in the oven and feeling the welcoming hugs and smiles of Lauren and her parents. Tears stung her eyes at the memory, and she quickly tucked it back where it belonged.

The door was open and blew in and out at the whim of the wind. She placed her flattened hand on it and pushed it before stepping into the foyer. Blinking in the dimness, she waited for the familiarity to settle over her again.

Fluffy pink insulation covered the spaces between the wood studs of the walls and ceiling, reminding her of cotton pulled from a stuffed animal. The soul had been removed, leaving only the skeleton and a host of memories, which seemed to cling to the bare floors and open joists. The entire place had been gutted, with little to resemble the house that it had been, though she could still see the floral chintzes and bright yellow walls when she closed her eyes. She hesitated, listening to the stillness, until the breeze pushed at her back, encouraging her to move deeper inside this shadow of a house.

The floor plan was opposite of hers, with the kitchen on the left instead of the right and the stairs curving up toward the beach side of the house. Holding tightly to the makeshift banister, she began to climb the stairs slowly, not quite sure why or what was propelling her to do so.

As she stood on the top step, she paused to listen. The thrum of the ocean stroked the quiet house like a mother soothing a child to sleep. She closed her eyes for a moment, rocking with the gentle rhythm of it. The quiet house seemed to close in on her, and she abruptly opened her eyes, propelled again to move forward.

The door to Lauren's room was missing and she stepped through the doorway, feeling almost as if her old friend was in there, waiting for Jillian to hear a long-kept secret. This room seemed to have fared better than the others, as the walls and flooring were intact, though the rosebud wallpaper and pink shag carpeting had been removed. She walked toward the corner of the room where a deep window seat nestled inside the bay window, and sat down.

She started to tuck her knees under her chin as Lauren and she had always done, then laughed at her attempts to bring her legs past her extended girth. The sun dipped a fraction lower, sending a bright ray into the room like a gentle benediction. She raised her right hand into the light, letting the sun reflect off her grandmother's wedding ring, and wondered whose presence she felt more at that moment.

Her hand dropped and brushed against a hinge, reminding her of the opening in the window seat. A rush of excitement coursed through her, and she quickly climbed off the seat. She lifted the lid, the rusty hinges groaning, the sound exaggerated by the dead silence of the house. Squatting down as much as her belly would allow, she reached inside to the corner, her fingers searching for the hidden compartment she knew to be there.

After several minutes of fumbling, she was rewarded when her fingertips found the small release button. Eagerly, she pressed it as Lauren had shown her how to do, and felt acute disappointment when nothing happened.

She was leaning over into the opening when she heard the distinct sound of a car door being shut. Quickly rising and closing the seat, she pressed her face against the glass and looked down. She couldn't see anything and was left wondering if the visitor had come to this house or her own.

She thought of Gracie asleep alone in the house next door, and she felt the first tinges of panic. She moved toward the doorway as fast as she could, sliding off her shoes to make less noise. As she leaned against the threshold of the room, she heard the distinct sound of the front door closing and the latch being thrown. Her heart beat loudly in her chest and she swallowed, the sound seeming to echo throughout the hushed house.

A footfall came from below, and it was apparent that whoever was in the house was climbing the stairs. Holding her breath, she watched a long shadow slide up the stairwell, stretching around the bend until the visitor stopped on the landing and looked directly at her.

The face was familiar and not familiar. Gone was the soft earnestness of youth; the invincible, indestructible aura held only by the very young and those who had not yet acquired the disillusionment of adulthood. In its place were the hard planes of a man who had severed his roots with a final, deft blow. He had left behind the good with the bad in a desperate attempt to escape the world into which he'd been born and become the person that the same world said he could never be.

But the determined stare had not changed in sixteen years. The dark gray eyes still regarded the world with barely concealed animosity, hiding the scars and a gentleness in his heart that very few were allowed close enough to see.

"Linc," she managed before one of her shoes fell from her hand, sliding down the stairs toward him. She sat down heavily on the top step and waited. Of course it was him. She had probably known it since she'd spotted him outside the house, staring back at her as if he knew her.

With a quick and precise motion, his hand struck out and grabbed her shoe between those long, sensitive fingers, and held it up just out of her reach. He stared at her and raised an eyebrow.

"What are you doing here?" Her voice echoed in the empty house.

"I was about to ask you the same question." His voice had not changed. It still carried the soft accent of a native, calling to mind summer storms, sudden and unexpected but full of sultry heat.

She laughed nervously. "You mean this isn't my house? Sorry, I must have gotten confused and taken a wrong turn on the dunes."

His lip twitched before his face settled back into stony perusal. "I see." He kicked a nail down the stairs, the sound loud in the thick silence. "You're pregnant."

She let her gaze drop to her belly that now completely obscured her legs when she sat. "Hey, I think you may be right." She gave him a lopsided grin. "I must be blocking your way. If you step out of the house, I should be able to slide by and give you room to move."

As if he hadn't heard her, he said, "Married?"

She looked at him, unblinking. "Divorced." When he didn't say anything else, she said, "Look, I'm sorry if I'm trespassing. I've bought my grandmother's old house—next door. I wanted to see what all the renovations were about over here." She swallowed nervously. "I'll leave."

Still, he didn't move, nor did he give her the shoe. "I saw you the other day. You were watching me."

She blushed, remembering the man staring at her as she hid on her porch. "I didn't recognize you. Otherwise, I would have come over sooner."

He looked at her with obvious disbelief.

"I saw the blueprints under your arm and assumed you were one of the architects. . . ." Her voice trailed away as his expression darkened. She swallowed again and continued. "I didn't recognize any of the names on the sign, so of course I didn't suspect. . . ." Again, her voice failed her, and they stared at each other in the darkened stairwell for a long moment. "Which one are you? Morrow or Rising?"

He leaned back against the stairwell wall, crossing his arms over his chest in a defensive gesture. "Rising. Since my mother didn't know who my father was, I figured I could pick any last name I wanted. Found Rising in a cemetery in Charleston. Thought it was appropriate for a guy running away and starting over."

The baby kicked, and her hand instinctively went to her swollen abdomen. His gaze flickered briefly at her hand, then went back to her face, his eyes unreadable.

His voice had an edge to it when he spoke. "You shouldn't be here. There's lots of garbage lying around and it's not safe—especially for a pregnant woman. It's real easy to trip and fall."

She grabbed hold of the banister and struggled to stand and put on her shoe. His presence unsettled her, caught as she was between memories of the boy she had known and this man he had grown to be. She tried to speak to the boy she remembered. "It's been a long time, hasn't it? I've thought about you a lot."

"I bet you have."

"I would have written if I'd known where you'd gone. You didn't have to run, you know. There were some who believed you innocent."

An uncomfortable silence settled between them as he regarded her. "And you would know about running, wouldn't you, Jillian? You ran back to Atlanta the minute the chief picked me up in his cruiser."

Her breath stuck in her throat as she gripped the railing with both hands. "Give me my shoe, please, and I'll go." She didn't care that he heard her voice shake. She needed to leave, to get back to Grace, to ignore past hurts and start the healing her soul so desperately needed. Linc's presence had pressed on old bruises, bruises she wanted to fade forever.

He held up her shoe, and she grabbed it. Carefully, she made her way down the stairs. When she paused on the landing, she looked up at him. His face was closed to her, an ability he had honed to perfection in the years since she had last seen him, but she noticed his hands were pressed tightly against the wall. It was almost as if he were forcing them there to stop them from helping her down the stairs.

She made to move past him when she heard him swear under his breath.

"Damn," he said, as he swept his hands under her and lifted her up to carry her the rest of the way down the stairs and across the piled lumber on the front steps.

She felt his heat first, and the strength of the muscles that supported her. And then she caught his scent, of new wood and salt, and she knew then, with all certainty, that this was the Linc she had once known.

When he set her down on the other side of the debris, he gazed at her with gray eyes that seemed to darken to slate as they reflected the inside light.

"I don't need your help," she said, pushing away from him.

"You never did, Jillian. But I always ended up being there for you, anyway."

She caught his double meaning and turned away, her pulse beating erratically. With as much dignity as she could muster and with what she hoped was more grace than a stuffed flounder, she poked her way through the sandy grass, not wanting to stop until she was on her own property.

Pausing for a moment to catch her breath and slow her heartbeat, she chanced a look behind her. He stood outlined in the doorway, silently watching her. She could almost believe he was making sure she made it home safely.

With renewed strength, she cautiously moved between the houses, relief flooding her as she made it to her back porch. She leaned against one of the columns and stared out over the ocean that she couldn't see but knew was out there, crashing against the shore in an age-old rhythm of approach and retreat. It had always reminded her of human nature's acts of hurt and forgiveness, and she wondered again why so many drowned in the surf, unable to reach the hard-packed sands of redemption.

With her last reserve of energy, she entered the house and snapped the door shut behind her.

Linc stared at the closed door, feeling ashamed at the way he'd spoken to her. He wasn't sure what made him angrier: that he had spoken so harshly to her or that he felt ashamed for doing so. Despite what he thought of her role in his past, he still couldn't reconcile it with the look of hurt on her face as she had left.

He climbed the rest of the way up the stairs and entered Lauren's room, wondering if Jillian had been in there and if she had found anything that he had not. He sat down on the window seat and looked across to the house next door.

The light went on in the corner bedroom, and he saw Jillian walk across the room to the bed, where the little girl lay. He watched Jillian place a hand on the child's forehead but not bend down to kiss her. Her dark hair, still worn straight and shoulder-length, fell forward as she bowed her head for a moment, as if in prayer.

Damn, she was beautiful. And her pregnancy only added to it. It gave her a vulnerability that had caught him by surprise. It made it difficult for him to hate her, as he had been telling himself to do for the last sixteen years.

When he had first seen the child and Jillian's obvious pregnancy, it had startled him. Just as fervently as he had sworn he would one day become an architect, she had just as adamantly sworn she'd never become a mother. He wondered what part of her soul she had bargained to get herself to change her mind.

He watched as Jillian smoothed the covers under the child's chin and then moved toward the window to close the curtains. In the seconds before she spotted him, he saw her face as she would never let the world see it. Instead of the composure of the eternal optimist, he saw the face of a woman who wore her griefs and disappointments right below the surface of her skin, keeping them hidden even from herself. It unsettled him to see it, and he wished that he hadn't.

With one hand clutched on the pink frills of the curtain, she looked toward the other house, and they stared at each other for a long moment. It wasn't a look of forgiveness or reconciliation, but merely acknowledgment, and it left Linc with a feeling of unfinished business.

Another white palm showed in the window as Jillian reached up for the second panel and closed the curtains, blocking his view. A few minutes later, the lamp went out in the room and the dunes were once again left to the feeble light of the moon and stars.

CHAPTER 4

JILLIAN FELT THE WARMTH OF THE SUN ON HER FACE, AND FOR A moment she thought she was a young girl again, safe in her grandmother's house, and Lauren in the house next door. And then she opened her eyes and the baby kicked, and she knew she'd never be that girl again.

Sitting up, she swung her legs over the edge of the bed, judging the slant of the sun. With alarm, she glanced at her bedside clock and saw it was nearly nine in the morning. She made her way to the door and threw it open, and saw Gracie's door standing wide open across the hallway.

"Gracie!" she shouted, but heard only the distant crash of the ocean's waves in answer. She searched Gracie's room and then the rest of the house, her voice escalating with panic.

Still wearing just her nightgown, she stumbled out of the house and onto the back porch, then over the rise of the dunes and onto the narrow boardwalk, until she could see the long stretch of beach. She stopped suddenly, hearing her own pulse beat in her ears as she spied the small figure of her daughter. Still in her nightgown, Grace nestled in the sand with her full Easter basket next to her. On her other side, sitting with his knees up, heedless of the sandy wind that was being tossed back and forth between the ocean and the dunes, was Linc.

Jillian rushed forward off the boardwalk and tripped over a low-lying scrubby sandwort, and found herself on her knees in the soft, warm dune. "Crap," she muttered under her breath as she struggled to stand again, the shifting sand making it more difficult to find her balance.

"Gracie!" she shouted again as she neared, perturbed at the two calm faces that turned in her direction. Spot lifted his head from Gracie's lap, sending Jillian a disdainful look. She stood before them, trying to catch her breath, her white nightgown billowing out around her.

Gracie held up her Easter basket. "Look, Jilly-bean—the Easter

Bunny found us!" Placing the basket back into the sand, she squinted up at her mother. "And you shouldn't curse."

Jillian looked down at her daughter, wondering how she had heard, and just as quickly decided she didn't want to know.

The little girl smiled. "This is Linc."

Jillian pressed her hand against her heart, willing it to slow down. "I know. But what I don't know is what you're doing out here in your nightgown."

She pressed her hand over her mouth and giggled. "You're wearing yours, too!" Gracie looked at Linc. "My daddy said that only trailer trash run around outside in their pajamas."

Defeated, Jillian sank down on the dune next to Gracie. "And he would know."

Linc sent her a questioning glance but didn't say anything.

"Gracie, you know better than to leave the house without telling me—especially so near the water. And you definitely know better than to talk with strangers."

"I didn't want to wake you up, Jilly-bean. And I saw some Easter eggs on the porch, so I figured it was okay if I got them. And Linc's not a stranger. I saw him out the window, looking up at the house, and Lauren told me to go talk to him."

Grace put her hand over her mouth as soon as she'd uttered the forbidden name. Linc stood abruptly and stared hard at the little girl before sending an accusing glance at Jillian.

Jillian picked up her daughter's Easter basket and handed it to Grace. "I want you to go in now and get dressed. Wear one of your Sunday dresses, because we're going to church and then we're going to Mrs. Weber's for supper."

Gracie ducked her head. "I'm sorry, Jilly-bean. I know I wasn't supposed to say that name."

Jillian tugged on Grace's fingers. "That's okay. Just remember that she's only in your imagination, all right?"

Grace hesitated for a moment, as if she wanted to say otherwise. Instead, she turned to Linc and offered him a small smile. "Good-bye, Linc."

The tight lines around his mouth seemed to soften. "Good-bye, kid. Thanks for keeping me company." Then Grace turned and left, clutching her Easter basket and running up the dunes toward the house, Spot following faithfully behind her.

Jillian floundered in the sand for a minute, trying to find purchase so she could stand. Tanned, long fingers stretched out in front of her and she startled, realizing Linc was offering to help her up. Taking both hands, she allowed Linc to hoist her, admiring his lack of a grimace from the effort.

Before she let go, she noticed the short, darkened scar on his right hand in the space between his thumb and index finger. She touched it gently and looked up at him. "I remember when you got this. You were making that box for Lauren and your knife slipped. You bled for hours, but you kept working. Like you knew time was running out."

He pulled his hand away, as if it had been too close to a fire, and she saw a flash of pain in his eyes before he shuttered them again and perused her coolly. "What did you tell Gracie about Lauren?"

She stared out toward the horizon, at the blurred line where the sky and sea met. "Nothing. I've never mentioned that name to her before." Her eyes settled on his. "Or yours. She just has imaginary friends, and she picked the name Lauren for her latest one."

"Why are you limping?"

Smoothing the white cotton nightgown down over the mound of her belly, she said, "My sciatic nerve. The baby's pressing on it and it makes it painful to walk. Or sit. Or stand." His expression remained bland, and she had the tugging desire to get a reaction from him. "My ex-husband suggested I get a cane, but I wasn't in the mood to listen to him. He made the suggestion right after the one about him keeping my grandmother's bedroom furniture after the divorce, because his new girlfriend thought it was cute."

He didn't even blink. "When's the baby due?" His words were reluctant, each one doled out like a precious commodity. Each one vainly hiding a slow-burning resentment indicating he didn't want to be there. Still, he stayed and faced her.

She shrugged. "One more month until I can see my feet again. But it feels like I've been pregnant forever."

His gray eyes settled on her, an empty beach full of unasked questions between them. "Forever's a long time."

Maybe forever's not long enough to let go. "Maybe." His expression closed itself to her and he remained silent as a gusty wind buffeted her from behind, as if propelling her toward him. "Why did you come back, Linc?"

Facing the two old houses, their turrets frozen in time in their perpetual shrug, Linc shoved his hands deep into his pockets. "Home is where the ghosts are."

The wind billowed out her nightgown again, blowing in her mouth hair that tasted of salt and sand. "That sounds cold. And lonely."

He continued to stare at the houses as if she hadn't said anything. Turning to leave, she felt a strong grip on her arm. "You'll hurt yourself."

With reluctance, she allowed Linc to guide her through the thick sand toward the boardwalk. His hand was warm against her skin, and it occurred to her for the first time that she wasn't wearing anything under her gown. She felt the blood rush to her face.

"Are you all right?" Linc's voice was solicitous but impatient.

Flustered, she said, "I'm fine. Just get me to the boardwalk and I'll be fine."

Slowly, they made their way to the firm footing of the boardwalk, where Linc quickly dropped her arm.

"Thank you. And thanks for taking care of Gracie."

"She's a neat little girl." He looked away for a moment. "I have to admit, I was surprised to find out you were a mother. I expected a lot of things from you, but never that."

Quickly, she turned toward the house, unwilling and unable to voice her reasons to anyone, much less this man. "Thanks again," she said, walking as quickly as she could to her back door.

Inside, she shut the door and leaned against it, knowing that Linc still stood on the boardwalk, the ocean-borne wind tousling his hair, staring after her with cool gray eyes.

At nearly two o'clock, Linc stood on Jillian's front porch and rapped loudly on the door. He hated the idea of being a subject in Mrs. Weber's machinations, but realized that in the end it simply made it easier to get the information he needed from Jillian. And the sooner, the better. Her vulnerability tugged at him, making him care more than he wanted to.

He smelled something wonderful coming from the open front windows, and then heard small, quick footsteps before the door was thrown open by Gracie. "Hello, Linc," she said somberly, her pastel green dress neatly starched and devoid of wrinkles. A small smile lit her face as she lowered her voice. "I knew you'd come. Jilly-bean's in the kitchen." She stepped back for Linc to enter, and then led him quietly to the back of the house.

Jillian was leaning over the oven, two huge oven mitts on her hands, pulling out a baking pan. As she turned toward the kitchen island, she startled at seeing him, almost dropping the pan. Lowering her eyes, she put the pan down and slid off the mitts. Her cheeks were flushed from the heat of the oven, and it was then he realized that she wore only a slip under her apron. It was an oddly appealing sight, and it made him want to kick off his shoes and sit at her kitchen table. The thought bothered him, and he quickly buttoned his jacket.

"Hello, Linc. Sorry about the outfit, but I wasn't expecting visitors."

"Sorry. I guess I should have mentioned earlier that Mrs. Weber wanted me to drive you and Grace to her house. I'm invited, too, and seeing as how your car isn't back yet . . ."

His words trailed off as Jillian's eyes widened.

"What's wrong?"

She shook her head and began stabbing a knife around the edges of another pan that had been set atop the stove to cool. "Nothing. Just that . . . nothing. But thanks. I'll just get these onto a plate and throw my dress back on, and I'll be ready to go."

He waited for her to say more, and watched her as she set about preparing a plate, her movements full of purpose and graceful, despite her pregnancy. Somehow, her condition seemed to make her more beautiful, filling out her cheeks and giving her a glow that encompassed more than just her skin. So different from how he remembered her: a reed-thin girl who tiptoed around life as if afraid to draw attention to herself. The sharp bones of her face and body had jutted out like those of a starved child, but he had known even then that she was only starved of all those things that were freely given to other children.

He shoved his hands in his pockets and began to look around the kitchen, noting the personal touches Jillian had added in the short time she'd been there. Lace curtains framed the large kitchen window, and bright copper molds, all used but polished to a high sheen, hung on the walls. A child's artwork, probably Gracie's, was placed in light wood frames and displayed in prominent spots on all the walls, along with a huge star chart of the night sky.

He felt her presence at his side and turned to see her thrusting a piece of pound cake on a china plate and a coffee mug at him. "This will keep you busy while I get changed."

She left before he had a chance to thank her, and he sat down at the table, wondering how he had found himself to be there. Gracie joined him, sitting across the table and regarding him with serious eyes.

Resting her chin on her hands, she said, "I knew you'd be here."

Linc paused with his fork halfway to his mouth. "You did, did you? And how would you have known that?"

"Try the cake. Jilly-bean used to bake things for other people and get paid. She's really good."

Obliging her, he took a bite, immediately wishing he'd been given a bigger piece. It was still slightly warm from the oven, the cake moist and sweet, the drizzled sugar and fruit bits on top the proverbial icing on perfection.

"It's good, isn't it?"

Linc nodded, then finished chewing before taking a sip of coffee. "You didn't answer me. How did you know I'd be here?"

She leaned forward on her elbows and whispered, "Lauren told me. She said you would know her."

His next bite stuck in his throat and he quickly took another sip of coffee. Before he could ask another question, Jillian reappeared.

"The clouds have come out and the wind's a bit chilly, Gracie. Go get your sweater."

As the little girl ran upstairs, Linc stood and put his plate and mug in the sink. Slowly, he turned to face Jillian. "Gracie said she knew I'd be here. How does she know these things?"

Jillian's mouth tightened and a wary look passed through her eyes. "She just . . . knows. She says her imaginary friends tell her things."

Linc shook his head. "I can't believe that. Maybe she heard you on the phone to Mrs. Weber or something. . . ."

Jillian interrupted him and took a deep breath. "Tell me, Linc, are you by any chance wearing one dark brown sock and one black sock?"

Silenced for a moment, he regarded her warily. "Of course not. And what's that got to do with anything?"

"Humor me, then."

"Okay, fine. Look." He pulled up his pants legs, and the light from the large kitchen window illuminated the gleaming wood floor and his feet. And the two socks, each a different color.

Gracie bounded down the stairs, her sweater in her hand, and Linc dropped his hands from his pants and met Jillian's gaze. Her face had paled as a look of resignation settled there.

"Come on, Gracie." She stuck out her hand and the child clasped it as they left the house for the waiting car. Linc followed, wanting to ask a hundred questions, but kept silent. He wasn't going to get involved with Jillian or her daughter. He had things he needed to know, questions he needed to ask about what had happened sixteen years ago. But that was all. Because in the end, nothing else mattered.

CHAPTER 5

SPRING IN THE LOW COUNTRY WAS AN ETHEREAL THING TO JILLIAN. Although most of her time spent on Pawleys had been during the summers, she had also spent two Easter vacations with her grandmother, times when the air was cooler and the summer crowds had yet to descend on the island.

As she stepped out of her house, she could smell the spring air, a green scent ripe with hope and new beginnings. It made her think of her grandmother and all the things she'd taught Jillian about Pawleys. She noted the blooming dogwoods and azaleas, and knew they signaled the time the ospreys would be building their nests and the red-beaked oystercatchers would be arriving to claim their spots in the life cycle of the island.

She glanced over at Grace as they piled into Linc's car. Soon she'd take her out to the marsh to see the osprey nests and the beautiful egrets. The marsh was full of things to capture the imagination of a child: fiddler crabs, periwinkle snails, snapping shrimp and all the animals that lived in the tall grass world of the marsh. *And ghosts.*

As she walked toward the car, she pictured her, Linc and Lauren in the thick marsh mud, capturing fiddler crabs in clear jars. She hesitated for a moment before opening the car door. She'd take Grace soon. She couldn't avoid it forever.

Jillian surreptitiously studied Linc as he drove the short distance down Myrtle Avenue to the Webers'. The promise of his youthful good looks had been fully realized, even though he appeared not to be aware of it. She watched the long fingers grasp the steering wheel, remembering those same fingers brushing back Lauren's hair as they'd watched the sun set over the marsh. She saw the newly acquired tight, unforgiving lines around his mouth, and the hard set of his eyes, and couldn't imagine this man and his fingers doing anything gently.

Linc broke the silence. "They don't know who I am, by the way, and I'd appreciate it if you wouldn't enlighten them. They know me as William Rising, architect from Charleston who's renovating the old Mills house, and I'd like to keep it that way."

"Don't you think they already recognize you?"

He shrugged but kept his voice low. "I guess the long-haired son of a Myrtle Beach prostitute doesn't grow up to drive a nice car, wear suits, and restore expensive houses. It would never occur to them to look deeper."

She shifted uncomfortably in her seat and glanced back at Gracie, who was pretending to study the salt marsh creek on the other side of the road but was listening to every word. She lowered her voice. "Why the secrecy? The Webers seem to be understanding people. Besides, you were never charged with anything."

He slowed the car and stared hard at her. "But that doesn't make me an innocent man, does it, Jillian?"

She stared back at him, unblinking. "No, it doesn't. But there were those who believed your innocence, regardless of what other people said."

With a jerk of the steering wheel, he parked on the side of the road in front of a crisply painted white cedar house. A wide porch criss-crossed by hammocks surrounded the house on three sides, the main floor raised by brick pillars. Four dormers capped the front of the house under a tin roof, with white lace curtains waving at them through the open windows. Martha Weber opened the front screen door and left the porch to greet them, wiping her hands on a bright yellow apron. Jillian smiled when she read the words on the apron: MARTHA STEWART IN TRAINING.

Before Linc could open his door, Jillian grabbed his arm. "Your secret is safe with me—although I think you should tell them. But it won't come from me."

His gaze flickered, as if torn between trusting her or not. When he pulled away from her and opened the door, she wasn't sure what he'd decided.

Martha approached and opened Gracie's car door. "Come on in, y'all. Hope you're hungry, because we've got a mess of food." She clucked her tongue when she saw the plate of pound cake in Jillian's hand. "Aw, now, you didn't have to do that. I hope you didn't go to too much trouble."

Jillian tried to juggle the plate and her purse and make it out of the car without dropping anything. She was relieved when Linc reached in to hoist her out. She noticed how quickly he let go of her hand as soon as she was on steady ground, and how closely he stayed by her elbow as they walked toward the house.

"It was no trouble at all. I love to cook, and I especially love to cook for other people."

"Well, you're a real dear. And so are you, William, for bringing Jillian and Grace. I know it's a short distance, but I didn't think Jillian should be walking it in her condition."

"It was my pleasure, Martha."

Jillian cast him a sidelong glance, surprised not to see a sarcastic smirk. His hand grasped her elbow as she reached the porch steps, guiding her as she made her way to the door.

A young woman in a bright red floral jumpsuit, with heels and lipstick to match, appeared at the screen door with a girl about Grace's age. She smiled brightly at Jillian as she held open the door.

"I bet you don't recognize me—I look a little different now than the last time you saw me. I'm Lessie Beaumont—your Realtor. My husband, Ken, is around here somewhere." She checked behind her to see if her elusive husband or anybody else might be in hearing distance, and lowered her voice. "I'm so glad I was able to help you get your grandmother's house—and at such a steal!"

Jillian remembered Lessie as a little girl about four years younger than her, and who walked around the island wearing a rhinestone tiara and her mother's high heels. Jillian held out her hand with a smile. "Well, I can't say I'm not glad to see you ditched the crown, and you are a bit taller, but I think I'd still recognize you. And I can't thank you enough for everything you did to get the house ready for us. I felt as if I were home the minute I stepped foot through the door."

Lessie smiled warmly. "It was the least I could do. You were always so nice to me when I was a little girl—never laughing at my crown the way that other kids did—and when you told me you were expecting and bringing your little girl here all by yourself, well, I figured you could use a little taking care of."

Jillian remembered her grandmother reburying turtle eggs, and something she had once said about relying on the kindness of others to put us back in our nests. She hid the sting of tears in her eyes with a bright smile. "Well, you did that and more, and I owe you a wonderful dinner."

Lessie laughed. "And I'll hold you to that." She pulled the skinny blond girl to her side. "And this here is my Mary Ellen. I think Mama said that she and your Grace were about the same age."

The two girls eyed each other warily before Mary Ellen spoke. "My brother found a busted alligator egg. Wanna come see it?"

Grace widened her eyes at her mother, and when Jillian nodded, she followed Mary Ellen and disappeared into the back of the house. Lessie winked. "She'll be fine. Mary Ellen's brothers always look out for her and her little friends."

Jillian felt herself being led with Linc into the crowded house, where the shouts of children blended in with the adults' chatter, and the enticing aromas of baking ham and stewing oysters drifted in the air. A hand touched her shoulder, and she found herself face-to-face with Mason Weber. He was a few years older, his skin weathered from constant exposure to the sun, making his shock of blond hair bright against his forehead. She smiled broadly, remembering how she had once had a huge crush on him.

"Mason Weber. You're a sight for sore eyes." Leaning forward, she kissed him on his cheek and watched as his dark cheeks turned redder.

"Hey, Jillian. It's good to see you. I was wondering if you'd ever come back."

Tilting her head, she noted his uniform for the first time. "Yeah, I thought it was time. So, are you working with your dad?"

"Sure am. He's still chief—although he swears every year that he's going to retire—but I'm an officer. Never could find it in myself to leave the island. Pretty boring, huh?"

He smiled shyly, then looked over at Linc and offered his hand. "You must be the famed architect I've been hearing so much about from Lessie and my mama. I'm Mason Weber."

With a hint of wariness, Linc took his hand and shook it. "Nice to meet you." Not waiting for the inevitable pleasantries, he excused himself and left the small group.

Jillian stared after him until she realized Mason was watching her closely. "I think he's shy," she said, wondering at the same time why she was coming to his defense.

Mason just nodded. "Maybe I can come by some time and we can catch up on old times."

"I'd like that," she said, meaning it.

"I'll call you." He turned away, not quite hiding another blush, and allowed the swarm of people to crowd around Jillian.

After introductions were made, she gravitated toward the kitchen, where most of the women seemed to be, and turned to see Linc standing in the family room with the men, watching television. He stood slightly to one side, a cold beer pressed into his hand, a part of the group but separate, too. She noticed he stood on the opposite side of the room from Chief Weber, and wondered if it was intentional. As an impartial observer, she could agree that he looked good—real good—leaning against the wall with a leg crossed casually over the other, his button-down shirt rolled up over tanned forearms, his expression one of mild aloofness as he studied the room.

As if sensing somebody was watching him, he turned his face and caught her staring. Before his eyes could meet hers, she ducked into the kitchen, the swinging door vibrating behind her.

Nobody asked her about Rick, and she reminded herself to thank Martha and Joe later for prepping everybody. She found herself in her element in the kitchen, and was soon pressed into service by a grateful Martha. She welcomed the busyness, thankful that she could take her mind off of Linc for a little while. *Home is where the ghosts are.* His words haunted her more than any filmy specter could. And so did his eyes. Despite his outwardly show of success, they told her that he was as lost and alone as she was.

Pushing aside a pan to make room for another, she burned her finger. "Crap."

Martha looked over and went to the freezer for a piece of ice, and handed it to her without saying anything. Jillian stood by the sink, watching the ice drip, and thought of Linc again. *Crap.* She wanted to dismiss him as much as he evidently wanted to dismiss her, but couldn't. Lauren's presence seemed to hover over them, between them, near them. Eventually, she'd have to confront Linc. Until then, she'd try to ignore him as much as possible. She'd returned to Pawleys to heal and to start over. Resurrecting old ghosts had never been part of the plan.

"I hear you bought your grandmother's old place for a song. You know, the Nesbit-Norburn house went for more than two million. Sure, it's a bit bigger, but still. You really lucked out."

Jillian turned to face Donna Michaels, a teacher at Low Country Day School who lived in another old Pawleys house. "I had no idea. Lessie says my offer was accepted right away without negotiations. I was . . . eager to leave Atlanta, and didn't give it much thought."

Donna's next comment was drowned out by Martha's announcement that the ham was ready to be carved. In the bustle of getting the serving plates onto the dining room table, Jillian forgot all about the conversation.

She found herself in the living room with Lessie, Donna and several more women, all settled like roosting hens on chairs placed about the room and their plates perched on knees. Grace and Mary Ellen, already inseparable, found spots on the floor. Linc came in, too, but leaned against the doorframe to eat, as if making it clear he was just a bystander.

Lessie set her iced tea glass on the floor by her chair and turned to Jillian. "I don't know if Mama mentioned this to you or not, but I'm taking a correspondence class in historical preservation. One of my assignments is to do research on some of these old houses here on Pawleys, and I was wondering if you'd let me come over some time to study your house."

"Sure. I don't know anything about it, but you're welcome to come in and look around."

Donna Michaels spoke up. "I know there's a hidden room at Tamarisk—that's the old Lachicotte place—that was used to hide from Indians and pirates. Maybe you've got something like that at your house." She looked up at Linc and batted her eyelashes. "We've got a bona fide architect right here. I bet he'd know."

Linc casually placed his plate on a side table, and Jillian wondered if she was the only one who sensed his cool disdain. "I have the blueprints to Jillian's house, as well as the one next door, and I've seen nothing on either one of them that would indicate hidden rooms or anything like that." He took a swig of his beer as if signaling that his part in the conversation was over.

Lessie turned her brilliant smile on Linc. "Well, then, maybe you're the man I should be talking with. Can I call you some time this week for a more in-depth discussion?"

Casually wiping his hand on a napkin and placing it on top of his plate, he gave her a perfunctory smile. It looked at first as if he'd refuse. Then he reached into his wallet and pulled out a business card to hand to her. "Sure. Page me and leave a message at the number on top. I'll get back to you when I can."

Lessie settled back in her seat, looking like a pleased and well-satisfied tomato. "Thanks, William. I'll do that."

"You know, Lessie, the one person I've found who seems to know a lot about everything on Pawleys is Janie Mulligan." Donna primly tucked her bleached blond hair behind her ears.

There was an odd silence as everyone stared at Donna.

A small stir of memory brushed through Jillian. "Who's Janie?"

"She's that crazy woman who lives in the pink cottage facing the marsh on Morrison Avenue. She carries a rag doll around and calls it Baby. I can't see why you'd think she knows so much, Donna. She's barely coherent." Lessie shook her head and stabbed a piece of ham.

Jillian remembered Janie, a woman whose beauty seemed to be as frail as her mind. She would be about in her late forties or early fifties now, and Jillian couldn't imagine how age could have benefited her in any way. Her grandmother had taken Jillian to bring her food or just to visit on many occasions, and the one thing she remembered about Janie was the doll.

"Is it the same rag doll? She used to wear it in one of those infant carriers over her chest. I think she had a crib in her bedroom where it would sleep."

Lessie nodded. "Same one. And she still uses the carrier, too. Mama and I still visit every week to help with paying her bills and such, and she still cradles that doll. It's really sad, but she seems happy."

Martha, who had crept in to sneak a bite to eat before her hostessing duties claimed her again, spoke in a firm voice. "Janie Mulligan has her strange ways, but I sometimes think she's the sharpest woman I know. And she's definitely the person to talk to about our old houses and their history. She's like a walking encyclopedia. People just need to learn how to be patient with her, that's all."

Lessie placed her empty plate at her feet. "Maybe you're right,

Mama. Maybe I will talk with her about it next time I'm there." She beamed up at Linc again. "But I still think a walk-through and chat with William will just about make my paper write itself."

Linc just smiled and took a long swallow of his beer without comment, as the room quieted and people turned back to their food.

Mary Ellen took a sip of her lemonade, slurping a bit as she got to the end. "Miz Parrish, are you going to have a little boy or a little girl?"

"I'm not sure. I guess we'll find out in about a month, though."

Gracie announced to the room, "I know where babies come from."

Sweet corn bread stuck in Jillian's throat as she tried to signal with her eyes to her daughter to stop. But Gracie, for the first time in her life, seemed to have found the courage to speak before a crowd.

"The mommy and daddy have to get naked in bed together, and then the daddy gives the mommy a sunflower seed and it becomes a baby inside her."

The adults sat in stunned silence as Mary Ellen enthusiastically piped in, "And the mommy and daddy have to be in love for it to work."

Grace glanced over at her mother, and her little face flushed. Lowering her head, she said, "That's not true, Mary Ellen. My daddy didn't love Jilly-bean, but she's going to have a baby, anyway."

Jillian noted how everyone pretended to eat, focusing on their plates instead of on her reddening face, and felt her stomach turn.

Linc crossed the room in two long strides and squatted in front of the two young girls. "I spotted a chocolate cake on the kitchen counter, but I don't know if it's good or not. I'd appreciate it if you two would taste it first and let me know if I should have some."

The girls jumped up and ran out of the room toward the kitchen. Linc faced Jillian and took her plate from her knees, setting it aside on a table. Stretching out a hand toward her, he said, "Come on, you look ill. I'll either take you outside or lead you to the bathroom—your choice."

Gratefully, she took his hand and allowed him to lead her to the powder room. She'd barely managed to close the door before her lunch came back up and left her wondering how much more humiliation she could take. She suddenly and desperately wanted anonymity, her grandmother and peace. Instead, all she had to show for her troubles was a bitter divorce, a troubled daughter, a belly big enough that she couldn't see her feet and a man waiting outside the bathroom door who seemed to want to have nothing to do with her and probably didn't even like her all that much.

She rinsed her mouth and face with cold water. With a heavy sigh, she unlocked the door and left the bathroom, and found Linc waiting for her, leaning against the hallway wall with his legs crossed at the ankles.

"Thanks for coming to my rescue. As much as you'd like to pretend you're not, you're a pretty nice guy."

He straightened and stuck his hands in his pockets. "I just didn't want you throwing up in my car."

Stifling a grin, she walked past him with as much dignity as a lumbering elephant could muster.

Linc took a last swig from his beer bottle and stared at the bobbing light from a flashlight next door. He'd been sitting on the second-floor porch, watching as the ocean shifted from blue to gray and the sun drowned in the waves far on the horizon, casting the island in the buttery light of sunset.

And now the first stars were appearing in the purple-hued sky as darkness descended, and his new neighbor was struggling with a flashlight and what appeared to be a telescope. He watched as Jillian wobbled down the boardwalk and paused at the edge, staring out into the thick sand of the dunes. She took two hesitant steps before she stumbled, dropping the flashlight.

"Damn." The word drifted over the dune toward him.

Gritting his teeth, Linc stood and headed toward the stairs. *She's going to kill herself if I don't help her.* By the time he'd reached her, she was still in the same spot, staring out at the sand as if negotiating her passage.

"What are you doing?"

She didn't look back, as if she'd been expecting him. "I'm trying to get my telescope to the beach so I can watch the sky. I've missed a few nights, and I can't miss another one."

His chest tightened, remembering other nights, balmy nights spent
on the edge of the water, toes clenched in the wet sand, his young heart
not unbruised but still full of hope and dreams. He wanted to turn
away, leave her. But when he saw her rounded silhouette against the sky
and the defeated slant of her shoulders, he knew he couldn't. He cleared
his throat. "Still looking for a new star?"

She turned to him then, her light brown eyes luminous against the
purple sky. "Still. There's a guy in Portugal who found two in a single
year. All I want is one."

He wanted so much not to feel the need to help her, to talk with
her, to make her pain go away. But he couldn't seem to stop. Without
asking, he took the telescope and flashlight from her, for the first time
noticing the binoculars around her neck. "I was wondering what the
star chart was doing on your kitchen wall."

Slowly, she began moving over the dune toward the beach. "I've
memorized it. So, when the new star appears, I'll recognize it immediately." She stopped and stared into the darkening sky. "Do you remember watching the stars with me, Linc? We'd lie on our backs in the
sand and stare up at the sky. We'd find constellations and calculate their
distances from the earth. Then Lauren would stop us and make us wish
on shooting stars."

The moon, once translucent against the fading sky, now seemed to
take on strength from the growing blackness, showing its power to pull
the ocean's tides across the giant earth.

She stopped and her voice was soft. "Did you, Linc? Did you ever
make a wish?"

He looked at her, his gaze focusing on her mounded belly, unable
to lie to her face. "No. I never believed in wishes."

She watched him in silence for a long moment. "I'm sorry." She
moved on, and he followed behind her.

When she'd found a suitable spot, she stopped and reached for her
telescope. He turned off the flashlight and dropped it in the sand to
help her.

She whirled, her voice almost panicked. "Where's the light?"

"We don't need it yet. We've got a good ten minutes before total
darkness."

"Turn it on. Please. I like it to be on when it gets dark."

He bent and retrieved the flashlight before flipping it on again.

"Thank you." Her relief was a palpable thing.

"I'm sorry. I'd forgotten."

She gave him a feeble laugh. "Most children outgrow their fear of the dark. I never have."

He remained silent as she continued to set up her telescope, aiming the flashlight in her direction. *Why am I still here?*

He watched as she first scanned the sky with her binoculars and then positioned herself behind the viewfinder of the telescope and peered up at the shining pinpricks of light above. She pulled away, a huge grin on her face. "Nothing's changed—all stars present and accounted for. I've still got a chance."

He couldn't help but return her smile. For a woman who at the moment closely resembled a blowfish, he couldn't remember ever seeing a more beautiful one. Damn, but she was addictive. *But she's one of them.*

"Do you want to look? You taught me everything I know about the night sky, remember?"

His smile faded, and he listened to the beat of the surf against the sand for a moment. "I don't look at the stars anymore. Haven't for years."

Her voice was barely audible above the crash of the waves. "I'm sorry to hear that. I sometimes think that what's going on up there makes so much more sense than what's going on down here."

Suddenly, Jillian bent over, her hands clenched over her belly and an odd moan erupting from her lips. Alarmed, Linc rushed to her side. "What's wrong?" He looked back to see how far they were from the dune, wondering if he could carry her through the thick sand and beyond without killing them both.

She glanced up at him, her breathing seeming to come a bit easier. "I think . . . I think I might be pregnant."

He stepped back, shock, surprise and then laughter rushing through him simultaneously. She laid a hand on his arm. "It's just the baby kicking me in a sensitive spot, that's all. I'm fine." She straightened and touched his cheek, sending warning bells throughout his system. "It's good to hear your laugh, Linc. You're not as tough as you like to pretend, you know."

He moved, making her drop her hand, his laughter gone. "You don't know me at all."

She regarded him through the darkness, and he shifted under her scrutiny. Then she returned to her telescope and peered through the viewfinder again. "Since you're planning on staying until I'm done to make sure I don't beach myself like a stranded whale, would you mind sitting over there? And just shine the flashlight on the ground in front of me so I can see where I'm stepping."

Grunting, and not sure where he'd left his backbone, he lowered himself in the sand, the flashlight cutting a pie slice of light out of an entire island of darkness. When she was finished, he helped her pack up her things and walk back to the house.

"Thanks, Linc. I think from now on I'll just watch the sky from my porch. It'll be a lot easier."

He just nodded, and then, before he turned, he asked the question that had been niggling at the back of his brain. "Why does Grace call you Jilly-bean and not Mom?"

"It . . . it sounded better to me. She doesn't know any different."

He understood. He had known her parents and her relationship with them, and understood. But he didn't say anything. Small gossamer strands made a formidable web if enough were tossed together. He wanted nothing that would tie him to her.

"Good night," he said, and turned away to walk toward his house.

"You never asked about your socks and how I knew."

He faced her again, the distance between them comforting. "I didn't have to."

A silent creature flew overhead, its eyes focused on prey in the sea oats below, its steady wings stirring slowly in the night above them as if the air had become too thick. Linc thought she would say more. Instead, all she said was, "Good night, Linc."

By the time he said good night, she had already closed her front door, leaving him alone on the dark dunes, his way illuminated by the moon, and all his ghosts following closely behind as he made his way back to his car across the sand.

CHAPTER 6

JILLIAN SAT ON THE EDGE OF THE BOARDWALK, WATCHING THE retreat and approach of the waves and Gracie dancing on her toes as she raced to avoid the salty foam, her arms thrown wide as if to embrace the wind. The tide was low, leaving in its wake the ocean's debris and a child's treasure. She twisted the gold ring on her finger as she watched. *Ebb tide, flood tide.* Her grandmother had always said that each life would have a bit of both, each to even out the other. But even at ebb tide, when the dried, packed sand seemed to gasp for water and the ocean seemed so far away, there would be things left behind to comfort you until the ocean returned with the flood tide.

A part of her wanted to join her child and dance in the sand, to race with the wind and tease the sea. Instead, she stayed where she was, studying her child and wondering where Grace had learned to laugh and to sing and to dance.

Grace stopped and squatted down to pick something out of the sand, then squealed as she held up her prize. "Jilly-bean—look! It's a sand dollar. And it's not even broken!"

Sensing her excitement, Jillian met her halfway on the beach and cradled the treasure in her hand, feeling the sun's warmth transferred to her skin. "It's beautiful, Gracie." With her fingernail, she traced the pattern on the front. "Look here. This is supposed to be the Easter lily, and this, in the middle, is the star of Bethlehem."

Grace's eyes widened. "Ohhhh. That's so neat."

Jillian smiled and flipped the sand dollar over. "They say if you break it open, five doves of peace will fly out."

"Really?" Then Grace's face closed in alarm. "We don't have to break it if we don't want to, right?"

Her voice soft, Jillian reached to smooth back the fine blond strands off Grace's face. "Never, Gracie. Never."

"Look what I brought back, Mama. Me and Grandma found them on the beach, and we made jewelry." Feeling suddenly shy, she tucked the bag of shells and sand dollars behind her. "I made you a necklace."

Her mother looked up from the glass menagerie she'd been dusting. Gently, she replaced a pink-colored swan and turned to Jillian. Her eyebrows were raised and she wasn't smiling. "May I see that?"

Jillian took a hesitant step backward, bringing the bag out in front. "I . . . I made you a necklace. With a sand dollar. Grandma showed me how." Very carefully, knowing how delicate it was, she lifted the necklace out of the bag, beaming at the beautiful white roundness of the perfect sand dollar. She'd spent hours combing the beach for just the right one.

Too late, she heard the spattering of sand spilling on her mother's freshly swept hardwood floor.

She looked up and saw her mother's face. She wasn't looking at the necklace, but at the mess on the floor.

Jillian's right knee started trembling first, and then her other leg and arms, and she hated it for the way it made her voice shake. That always seemed to make her mother even madder. "I'm sorry, Mama. I didn't mean to. I'll clean it up myself. I'll . . ."

She wasn't allowed to finish her sentence. Her mother jerked the bag out of Jillian's hand, making her drop the necklace. She heard the snap of the sand dollar breaking as it hit the floor, but she didn't look down.

Her mother pointed at the sand that lay scattered on the floor like tiny tears. "Look what you did! Look what you did! And you won't clean it up—you never do. You just make a bigger mess. You think I'm your servant, waiting on you hand and foot just to clean up your messes. I'm sick of it. Do you hear me? Sick of it!"

Her mother's voice was higher now, almost a scream but much, much scarier. She wished her daddy were home. Her mama was never this bad when he was home.

"I'm sorry, Mama. I'm sorry."

"I'll show you sorry." With a tight grip that made Jillian yelp, she grabbed her by the arm and dragged her into the hallway.

"No, Mama. No. Don't. Please don't." She was crying now, knowing the tears always made it worse, but she couldn't stop. But she couldn't go in there again. She couldn't. She knew she'd die if she had to go in there again.

With her free hand, her mother opened the door to the crawl space. "We'll see how sorry you are now."

Jillian screamed and threw out her hands to grab ahold of something, anything, but her hands slipped over the painted wood of the doorframe as her mother forced her into the crawl space and locked the door. Fear choked her as the dark swallowed her like a monster's mouth, and she thought she could see faces in the swirling blackness. It was like a wind that she couldn't see or hear, but she felt it up close to her skin, touching her up there on the back of her neck and the curve of her spine.

When she couldn't scream anymore, she closed her eyes. She fell asleep pressed against the door, the skin on her hands worn and raw, and dreamt of light and of the sun dancing on the ocean's waves.

A small hand touched her cheek, bringing Jillian back to the present. "Why are you sad, Jilly-bean?"

Jillian took Grace's hand and held it, trying to find her voice as she forced a smile. "I'm not, Gracie. I think I'm just tired." She stood, brushing sand off her knees. "Come on, I'll show you where to find more sand dollars, and then we'll make sand dollar necklaces. Maybe we can make one to give to your new teacher."

Grace stared at her mother with steady eyes, and Jillian once again had the feeling of role reversal. She brushed Grace's hair off her forehead. "You're an old soul, Gracie. And maybe one day I'll tell you what that means."

Tugging on her daughter's hand, Jillian led Grace back to the beach, where the sand met the water and treasures waited to be discovered.

The sound of buzz saws and hammering punctuated the warm morning with their odd music. To Linc, there was no better symphony, and no better smell than the scent of freshly cut wood. It made his fingers itch to watch the workmen on the roof joists, wishing that he could be using his hands to do the actual building. The love of creating something out of nothing, to see something of beauty emerge from his own hands, had been the undertow of his life; the pulling force that led him to pursue his dreams and study architecture.

It was the one thing in his life he'd always been sure of—the one thing he'd allowed himself to believe in. And now it had made it possible for him to reach his other dream—his dream of owning this house, of making it his. But as he stood back and looked up at its old and graceful lines, he frowned. He was so close to the realization of his dreams, yet he still felt far, far away from them.

Rolling up his sleeves, he grabbed his tools and boom box and entered the house. He had custom designed the new kitchen, allowing himself the luxury of handcrafting the cabinets in his workshop and having them shipped to Pawleys. He'd finish them himself, too, staining the cherry wood to a dark, rich finish—just like the original cabinets had been sixteen years ago.

As he set up his boom box and flicked it to a local station playing Carolina beach music, he surveyed the wreck of a kitchen, much like he supposed an artist surveyed an empty canvas. He was lucky his business partner was understanding of his need to spend so much time down here on the island. Maybe all builders were artists, and it hadn't been too much of a stretch for George to allow Linc all the time he needed to oversee this project.

The Chairmen of the Board came on the radio singing "Carolina Girls," causing an involuntary smile to cross his lips. It made him think of dancing barefoot in the sand, with the scent of salt and sea and sweat and coconut oil heavy in the air. And it made him think of a girl with hair the color of the sunset and skin a honey brown from baking in the sun. He could almost see her, standing in the kitchen. If he reached out his hand, he sensed he could touch her.

"Hello, Linc."

Startled, he jumped as he turned around and spotted Grace standing in the doorway to the kitchen, a threadbare bunny held in her arms and a necklace strung with shells and a large sand dollar hanging from her other hand. There was something about her face; although the features were soft and small and round like a child's, her light brown eyes and the set of her mouth were almost those of a full-grown woman. It was arresting and unsettling at the same time.

"Hello, Grace." He smiled and squatted in front of her. "Who's this?" He pointed to the stuffed bunny.

"It's Bun-Bun. Jilly-bean gave her to me when I was born."

He looked at the scratched eye buttons and the matted fur. "I can tell she's been loved a lot."

She gazed at him with those bright brown eyes. "It's not so easy to tell with real people, is it?"

Disconcerted, he stood, touching her head lightly. "No, it's not. And it's too bad, really."

Giggling, she turned around to survey the kitchen. "I guess we'd look pretty silly with all our hair rubbed off and our noses missing."

She began humming to the song on the radio. "I like this song." She continued humming as she looked around at his tools and the cabinets that now sat crowded together in the middle of the kitchen floor. "Lauren liked to dance to this song. And she told me that Jilly-bean has the thing you're looking for."

His breath lurched. "What thing?"

Grace shrugged and bent to blow a pile of sawdust off the counter.

Completely unsettled now, Linc moved to stand in front of Grace. "I'd love to visit with you some more, but I've got a lot of work to do, and besides, this is a dangerous place for a little girl. There's open electric wires, sharp tools, and nails all over the place." He looked down at her pink-polished toenails peeking out of bright yellow flip-flops. "I'd hate to see you get hurt."

With a bland expression, Grace said, "You don't like it when I talk about Lauren, do you? She said you wouldn't."

He pretended he hadn't heard her, and bent to pick her up. "I'm going to carry you back to your house, okay? We don't need you stepping on any nails."

She allowed him to lift her, and when she was at eye level to him, she said, "I made this for you." She held up the necklace, the mis-matched shapes of the shells reminding him of something Wilma Flint-stone would have worn.

Touched and somehow pleased, he said, "It's beautiful. Thank you," and ducked his head so she could slip it on. "Come on. Let's go find your mother." He carried her out of the house and across the sand to the house next door.

Jillian stood in the backyard, hanging laundry in the sun. She was reaching up to clip something large and white to the line when they rounded the corner of the house. He saw her necklace first, the sand dollar a bright white against the dark blue of her sundress. He stopped in front of her, gently putting Gracie on the ground.

"Nice jewelry," she said, holding up her matching necklace.

He smiled, and he saw her face warm to him. "It sure is. And here I thought I'd been given an original."

Jillian looked down at her daughter. "And where have you been? I thought you were reading upstairs in your room."

"I was. And then I saw Linc and I wanted to say hi."

She opened her mouth as if to scold her, but Linc touched her on the arm. "I already explained to her how a construction site isn't a good place for a little girl. I'll be happy to show her around another time when the workers aren't there, though."

Mollified, Jillian nodded. Her gaze settled on his hand where he'd been patting Grace's head as he spoke. She smiled and squinted up at him. "Thanks for bringing her back." She turned away to put the other clothespin up on the line, and he dropped his hand.

He didn't notice when she faced him again, as his attention had fo-cused on the clothes flapping in the breeze behind her. His eyes were widened slightly, trying to register what he was seeing.

She turned to see what he was looking at and saw her maternity un-derwear, fluttering like a huge white sail at full mast.

Facing him again, she said, "Oh, that. You might think that those are pairs of underwear, but they're really sails. I'm thinking of starting a sail shop."

For a moment, her face reminded him of the girl he remembered with the quick smile, the salty remarks and eyes that always held something back. It gave him a little sense of coming home, and it settled uncomfortably in him. He wasn't coming home. He was starting over.

Grace giggled as Jillian bent to take several bath towels and the largest bra he'd ever seen out of the basket and began to hang them on the line next to the underwear. Realizing what she held in her hand, she quickly dropped the bra and continued hanging up laundry.

The breeze teased her dark brown hair off her forehead as she concentrated on her work. "I've made lemon bars if you'd like one."

He almost said yes. "No, thanks. I've got to get back to work."

She gazed steadily at him. "You can't avoid me forever, you know." She dropped her hands and picked up the empty laundry basket. "Come on in the kitchen and I'll get you some iced tea and a couple of lemon bars. If you're nice, I'll even give you a few extras to take with you."

Without waiting for his answer, she started walking across the backyard toward the kitchen door, the basket balanced on one hip, and moving relatively fast despite her pregnancy. Seeing no other choice, he followed her, Grace close at his heels.

She called after her daughter. "Your daddy called. He left a message on the machine. You'll have to call him back in the morning, because it's already in the middle of the night in Singapore."

Grace skipped in a circle before stopping in front of her mother. "You shouldn't let him talk to the machine, Jilly-bean, if you're there."

Jillian flushed and didn't meet Linc's eyes as she hitched the basket higher on her hip and continued walking. "Rick is on a temporary overseas assignment in Singapore for his law firm. He calls every other day to speak with Grace. I don't necessarily feel the need to chat with him when he calls."

Linc didn't feel the need to question why, and silently followed her toward the house.

When they got inside the kitchen, Jillian made a plate for Grace and sent her into the den to watch TV. Then she placed two plates and two glasses of iced tea on the table and motioned to Linc to sit. She looked ridiculously appealing, sitting at the kitchen table behind her lemon bars, a dusting of powdered sugar on her chin and her waistline stretched beyond the width of the chair.

They looked up at the same time at the sugar bowl still on the counter. She moved as if to get up and get it, but Linc stood. "I'll get it. You just sit." He turned one of the chairs to face her. "Here. You should probably keep your feet up."

She grimaced. "I might be shaped like an egg right now, but I can promise you I won't break." Despite her protest, she did as she was told.

He put the sugar bowl and a clean teaspoon in front of her. Leaning over, he wiped the sugar off her chin with a napkin, then took a bite of the best lemon bar he'd ever tasted in his life.

"Thanks," she said. She leaned forward on her elbows. "I heard your music while I was outside. It reminded me of Lauren teaching us the shag on the beach. Do you remember?"

The lemon bar melted on his tongue as he washed it down with iced tea. "Yeah. I was a pretty good dancer. You were lousy."

She threw back her head and laughed. "Really, Linc. You should try to be more honest."

An involuntary grin crossed his face. "It was like you had three feet. I thought you were going to hurt yourself."

Still smiling, she said, "Careful. You might hurt my feelings." She took a bite out of a lemon bar, severing it in the middle, and chewed thoughtfully before swallowing. "But Lauren was wonderful. She could really move. It was almost as if the music were part of her."

Uncomfortable, he took another bite and turned away, spotting the star chart and noticing how she'd highlighted certain stars. *After all these years, still looking for a new star, something with a one-in-a-million chance of happening. But she actually believed she could.* He looked back at her, at her filled-out cheeks and her solemn eyes, and wondered where she found her resources of such boundless faith. He admired it in her, but would be damned if he'd ever admit it. He had no allies, and she had proven herself firmly entrenched behind enemy lines sixteen years ago.

Her voice was soft. "You know, we can tiptoe around it or we can start by talking about Lauren now. Either way, we need to talk."

He stood abruptly, brushing powdered sugar from his fingers. "Okay, fine. Since you've softened me up with sugar, I guess that makes me ready. I loved Lauren, she disappeared and everyone, including your father, Lauren's parents and the chief of police, thought I'd killed her and tried pretty hard to prove it, despite the fact that they had no body and no evidence. They let me go, and I left. That's pretty much all of it."

With deliberation, she stood and carried the dirty plates to the sink. "Not quite, Linc. You'd never have come back here if that was the end of the story." She rinsed off the plates and then turned off the faucet. Not turning around, she said, "You told me the other night that home is where the ghosts are. Maybe you're right. And maybe we're both here because they've asked us to come back. Maybe there's unfinished business."

Slowly, she turned to face him, and her eyes were troubled.

He walked toward her and stood close enough to smell the fragrance of ocean breezes in her hair as he placed his empty iced tea glass in the sink. Quietly, he said, "Maybe you're right."

He stayed next to her for a long moment, somehow unwilling to move away. Then, with a hard mental shove, he forced himself to leave her side and strode across the kitchen toward the door. "I've got to get back to work. Thanks for the lemon bars."

He had barely made it across the sand when Gracie came tearing after him, a plate with lemon bars wrapped in plastic wrap balanced precariously in her hands. "Jilly-bean wanted you to have these."

Unable to help himself, he returned her smile. "Thanks. They're pretty good."

She swayed in front of him with her hands behind her back. "The necklace looks good on you."

He looked down to where the sand dollar necklace lay against his shirt. "Yeah, it sure does."

"Are you going to wear it all day?"

"Of course. It's my favorite necklace. Wouldn't even dream of taking it off."

"If it gets in your way, you can tuck it inside your shirt."

"I'll do that."

She waved, then turned to go before stopping suddenly. "You should ask Jilly-bean to show you that thing."

"What thing?"

"The thing Lauren talked about. Remember? I told you before."

Without waiting for a response, she waved again and took off over the sand toward her house.

He stood watching her, the plate of lemon bars in his hand shaking slightly. Why was the fertile imagination of a little girl so disturbing? And almost so convincing? Trying to clear his thoughts, he made his way back into his house.

After placing the plate next to his boom box, he flicked it on and settled back into the rhythm of working with his hands, listening to beach music and trying not to remember too much the feel of a warm, slender body in his arms as he danced in the sand. Or the solemn brown eyes of a ghost from his past who was very much alive and who seemed to know how to weaken his defenses with sugary confections from her kitchen. If only she weren't so wounded. If only she weren't so fragile. If only he didn't care.

He flipped off the radio, preferring the silence for now, and bent over his work, allowing his hands to mold and create and temporarily exorcise a past that was best left buried.

CHAPTER 7

IN THE GRAY LIGHT OF DAWN, JILLIAN SAT UP IN BED, NOT SURE WHAT it was that had awakened her. Her gaze drifted around the room, finally coming to rest on the bedside table. She leaned forward and pulled open the drawer. Her fingers groped until they grabbed hold of what they were searching for. Leaning against her headboard, Jillian stared down at the smooth, wooden box, the beautifully scripted *L*s sitting on top.

Slowly, she opened the box and pulled out the well-creased paper, not opening it, but smoothing it between her fingers. The voices from her past seemed to speak louder to her now, as if the box were a transmitter to the deepest reaches of her memories.

The door creaked slightly and she looked up, startled. Spot, in feline nonchalance, strolled into her bedroom before stopping for a moment and then jumping up onto the foot of the bed. Settling down into a black ball of cat fur, he meowed, as if to make sure Jillian realized she was in the presence of greatness, and stared at her and the box.

A cool breeze brushed her neck, and she looked up to see if the air-conditioning vent was pointed at her. That was before she remembered that there weren't any air-conditioning vents anywhere in the house. She looked back at Spot, who seemed to be staring intently at something in the middle of the room, his head moving almost imperceptibly as if following the movement of a person slowly walking across the rug toward the door. The door creaked slightly again as it shifted on its hinges, and then Spot snapped his head back to stare at Jillian. Her eyes widened as she scooted up against the headboard. His hair stood completely on end.

Gracie.

She dropped the box next to her before jumping out of bed and moving across her room, intent on reaching Grace's bedroom as quickly as possible. She passed through the hallway with all the lights still on, their bright glowing bulbs defying the gloom of the morning.

Placing her hand on Grace's partially open door, she paused, her heart thumping wildly in her chest. Grace was talking, her childlike voice low but animated, as if in intimate conversation with a close friend.

Jillian pushed the door open farther, and the talking stopped. She peered around the door to scan the room for another person. Finding it empty, she turned to Grace on the bed, her calm voice surprising herself. "Who were you talking to, sweetie?"

Spot came up behind Jillian and stopped, not even approaching when Grace patted her bed in welcome.

Biting her lower lip, Jillian glanced down at the cat, noticing again how he seemed to be watching something at the empty side of Grace's bed. Firmer now, she asked, "Who were you talking to?"

Grace glanced briefly toward the side of her bed before sliding farther down into her covers. Quietly, and not very convincingly, she said, "Nobody."

Jillian again glanced down at Spot, who had tilted his head back as if watching something much taller than he approach. Without a sound, he turned tail and ran out the door. It was then that Jillian noticed how cold it seemed in the room, making her think of the nonexistent air-conditioning vents again. She noticed with some detachment that every hair on her arm stood on end. At the same time, she realized that Grace was speaking.

"Don't be afraid. I'm not."

The coldness seemed to evaporate with the suddenness of a switch being thrown. She looked behind her, trying to make sense of what had just happened, but all she saw was the rose wallpaper and the lone burning lamp on the bookshelf.

Slowly, she approached Grace and sat down on the edge of the bed. She didn't want to ask, didn't want to know. But somehow, she heard the words coming out of her mouth. "What's going on, Gracie? Who were you talking to?"

Somber, frightened eyes peeped up at her from over the edge of the covers. "You told me you didn't want to hear her name again." Spot appeared as if conjured and leapt up onto the foot of the bed before nuzzling up against Grace's side.

Jillian felt her chest tighten. Not with fear, but simply with not knowing. "Lauren?" she asked, staring intently into her daughter's eyes.

Gracie simply nodded.

"She's not real, you know. You do understand that, right?"

Grace stared at her for a long moment before slowly giving a brief nod of her head.

Jillian stood, leaning on the footboard. "Okay, then. Let's forget all about this." She clutched her hands together and looked about the room, her gaze coming to rest on the window whose drapes had been thrown wide, allowing the pink rays of the early sun to wave its good morning.

The little girl sat up in the bed. "I opened the curtains to see the sun rise."

Jillian looked out at the dunes, taking in the gentle surf and the swaying sea oats moving gracefully in the breeze as if stretching after a night's sleep. Her blood seemed to swish slower in her veins, and for a brief moment all was right in her world again.

With an optimism she hadn't felt in a very long time, she turned to face her daughter. "It's low tide right now. If you can get dressed in a hurry, I'll take you to the creek and maybe we can spot an egret."

A smile lit Grace's face. "Can I wear what I wore yesterday? It'll be quicker."

Jillian's gaze followed Grace's to the pile of clothes on the floor. She couldn't suppress a grin. "Sure. Just don't forget to brush your teeth."

Impulsively, she kissed Grace on the forehead before heading toward the door.

"Jilly-bean?"

A note in the child's voice filled her with apprehension as she turned around. "Yes?"

"The light bulb in the living room lamp is burned out. You might want to take a new one down with you to replace it so you won't be scared tonight."

The tension slid away from her. "Thanks. I will."

After quickly dressing, Jillian grabbed a light bulb from the upstairs linen closet and headed downstairs. It wasn't until she'd reached the tenth step that she remembered the living room lamp had been turned on after Grace had gone to sleep. So how could she have known it had burned out?

Jillian descended the rest of the stairs, promising herself that she would ask Grace about it later. Later, in the bright light of day, when it was so much easier to hear the answer to questions she didn't want to ask.

Jillian and Grace wore matching wide-brimmed straw hats that Jillian had bought when they'd stopped for gas right after crossing over the border from Georgia into South Carolina. Despite it only being March, the sun beat down on them as they let themselves out of the front of the house, and sweat began to trickle between Jillian's breasts. They were fuller now, preparing to nourish the child that grew inside her, and felt heavy beneath the cotton of her blouse.

Pausing in the heat, Jillian pressed her hand to her swollen belly, feeling the baby kick. Martha had given her the name of an obstetrician in Charleston, and Jillian had every intention of going. Soon. It was so easy to let nature take its course: her swelling body and growing child, the engorged breasts and increased blood pumping through her veins. She felt like the marsh at high tide, teeming with life-giving substance, yet completely uninvolved in the entire process.

As they crossed the road that ran the length of the island, sandwiched between the ocean and the creek, Jillian found herself holding her breath. It was as if she were afraid that her beloved marsh would have disappeared along with her grandmother, pulled from her grasp finger by finger until it was no more.

The pier jutted out into the creek, and they walked slowly down the length of it, letting their senses slowly accommodate the scents and sights of the marsh. Gracie helped Jillian spread a beach towel at the end of the pier, and they sat down side by side and stared out over the creek at low tide. The roots of recently exposed plants gleamed wetly at them as they swung their legs in unison, as if both hearing and keeping the beat of the marsh's liquid music.

Using the brim of her hat to shade her eyes, Jillian stared out across marshy land, seeing an old friend after a long absence, and felt her heart tighten in her chest. She had always had an affinity for this place, almost as if salt marsh water ran through her veins. She squinted at the intertwining rivers and creeks of the island stretched out before her.

They wove a treelike pattern: tentative fingers of water reaching forever outward, searching for the source that filled their banks with teeming life, craving with outstretching arms the one thing that increased their territory and made their depths dance with being.

Jillian took a deep breath, smelling the salt and the cordgrass heated by the sun, and let her gaze rest on an osprey nest settled in the high branch of an exposed bald cypress. *I'm home,* she thought, feeling her grandmother's touch in the warmth of the sun on her back. It was as if her heart, cold and rigid, had been suddenly plucked from the wet marsh mud and rinsed clean in the salt water, jolting it into beating again.

With quiet alabaster poise, a great white egret moved from behind tall grass, standing in the shallows of the marsh creek. It craned its long, crooked neck over the surface, searching for food, oblivious to its own gloriousness.

Grace slid her hand into Jillian's, her skin warm and smooth.

Startled, Jillian looked at the small hand clasped in hers, then down into the pale brown eyes of her daughter and at the smattering of freckles on her upturned nose, as if she were seeing this child for the first time. She cleared her throat. "It's beautiful, isn't it?"

Grace kicked out her feet, and Jillian noticed the old sparkly red shoes again. The same ones that were a size too small and had already been thrown away once. She opened her mouth to say something about them, but the softness of her daughter's profile as she stared at the snowy egret made her close her mouth without saying anything. Jillian turned back to look at the beautiful white bird, her own legs swinging in rhythm with Grace's.

Grace whispered, "Is this your favoritist place in the whole wide world?"

Jillian felt a small smile start at each corner of her mouth. Without taking her eyes off the egret, she said, "Yes, I believe it is."

Grace squeezed her hand a little tighter. "Mine, too."

They sat for a long time without speaking, holding hands and watching the beauty of the marsh unfold. The osprey set sail out of its nest, its wings in the telltale V and its underside a brilliant white. Madly flapping its wings, it soared across the water, then crashed feet first into the creek, lifting its struggling prey in its talons. It settled on a branch of a bald cypress tree and began to eat, allowing the creek to return to its low buzz of insects and the occasional slap of water.

"She and her mate return each March to that nest. They mate for life, you know."

Jillian and Grace turned at the sound of Linc's voice. He wore sunglasses so she couldn't see his eyes, but she felt his gaze on her. "What an admirable quality," she murmured while trying to find the best way to get herself into a standing position.

Linc reached her in two long strides and put his hands in hers to pull her up. Brushing off the seat of her maternity pants, she said, "Thanks. Hope I didn't throw your back out."

Black sunglasses stared back at her. "No problem. I once helped haul a beached pilot whale back out to sea. You're nothing compared to that."

She scrutinized him for a moment, feeling slightly stunned, but her mouth twitching, anyway.

He frowned. "I'm sorry. I didn't mean to say that."

Jillian waved a hand at him. "Yes you did, and don't apologize. That was pretty funny." She stared closely into his face, trying to see past the dark glasses. "You always had a great sense of humor, and I hate to see it hidden under all that grumpiness."

"Hi, Linc! We saw an egret," Grace piped up, sparing him a response.

Jillian grimaced. "That's Mr. Rising to you, Gracie."

Linc lifted Grace and set her on her feet. "I don't mind."

Gracie looked up, her expression serious. "I know not to call him Linc in front of other people because he doesn't want them to know his real name. I promise I won't forget."

Startled, Linc looked at Jillian, who shrugged. "She hears everything. I've long since stopped trying to censor things from her."

Gracie beamed up at him, and Linc sent her a reluctant grin before returning his attention to Jillian. "Lessie Beaumont's here with Janie Mulligan. I was about to give them a tour of my house, and Lessie wanted to know if she could get inside yours while she's here."

Jillian nodded. "Sure," she said, as she bent to gather up the towel.

"I was replacing the wooden sill in the front bedroom, and I saw you and Gracie cross the road."

Jillian squinted at him. "You don't have to explain yourself, Linc. I didn't think you were spying on us."

He looked at her again, as if he didn't know what to say. Jillian watched as Grace stuck a hand into Linc's. "Come on. Let's go find Lessie before somebody sees me and alerts Sea World."

Jillian slid him a sidelong glance and was sure this time that a full-fledged smile was brewing on his lips. With her own smile she faced the twin houses, each frozen against the horizon as if in a silent shrug, and wondered anew how such structures of timber and mortar could survive for so long with the constant onslaught of ocean winds and time.

A small hand crept into hers, and she looked down at the child beside her. Jillian suddenly thought of the ancient dunes that had sheltered the houses for nearly two centuries, taking the brunt of storms and the ocean's encroachment upon the shore, protecting the old houses in their solid, sentinel arms. She squeezed her daughter's hand as the child in her womb kicked again, and for a brief moment Jillian thought she understood something that had been denied her for a lifetime and remained elusive still. But when she looked down into Gracie's eyes, she felt the first glimmer of hope.

Jillian watched as Linc slowed his pace, waiting for them to catch up. She continued moving forward, toward the old houses, finding an odd comfort in the tall shadows they cast.

Linc waited as Jillian and Grace approached, wondering, from the expressions on their faces, if he had just witnessed something startling. He looked away, not wanting to be more involved than he already was.

"Have you spoken to your husband yet?" His words were hard and clipped, as if constructing a deliberate barrier between the past few moments of companionship and the distance he wanted to keep between them.

Jillian blinked before lowering her head, the brim of her hat hiding her face. "He called again this morning, as a matter of fact. Couldn't get to the phone in time, so he left a message on the machine. Mentioned something about him and his new wife going to Bali for the week. I sure appreciated him letting me know."

He started to say something, unable to let Jillian bypass the topic, but felt his hand grabbed by Grace.

"Linc's a funny name," she said, swinging her arm.

Linc's eyes narrowed as he glanced down at her, wondering yet again how she had an adult's ability to know when to change the subject. Although she apparently hadn't yet mastered the ability to know which subject would be appropriate to change it to.

"Gracie, why don't you run ahead and feed Spot? We're going to be going out this afternoon, and I'd hate for him to starve."

Grace shot back a knowing glance at her mother before letting go of Linc's hand and skipping away.

"It *is* an odd name." Her eyes held a challenge, as if welcoming the chance to retaliate against his mention of her ex-husband.

He felt his face flush, the embarrassment over the origins of his name flooding through him as if it were the first time he'd heard it. "Right. And Jilly-bean isn't."

She stiffened beside him, and he suddenly felt like a small boat navigating a riptide. He heard her take a deep breath before she surprised him by answering his unasked question. "I . . . I didn't really care what she called me when she first learned to talk. As long as it wasn't Mama."

The hurt and pain emanated from her like rippling waves, making him cringe. He hadn't meant to do that to her. His long-held anger was easily dislodged, its escape effortlessly nudged.

He held her arm, making her stop and face him. "I never knew my father. The only thing my mother remembers about him was that I was conceived in the back of his Lincoln. That's where my name comes from."

She didn't recoil or make excuses. She just regarded him gently with soft brown eyes. "Why are you telling me this now? You would never tell Lauren and me when we asked."

He tried not to flinch at the mention of Lauren's name. "To make us even." He hoped she couldn't read that for the lie it was. There was something about her that brought out the confessor in him. Maybe it was her maternal shape, or maybe it was that deep understanding between them that hadn't dissipated in nearly two decades. Whatever it was, it didn't sit comfortably on his shoulders, but he was powerless to consider her without sympathy.

He tucked her hand into the crook of his elbow. "Hold on to me. It'll make it easier to walk."

Evading her probing look, he led her off the pier and across the street toward Lessie and Janie, now standing by Lessie's parked Buick. Jillian leaned on him slightly, and he promised himself that this would be the last time he'd help her. But before the thought had even been completed, she pulled away, walking away from him, and calling out a greeting to the women who awaited them. She straightened her shoulders and moved slowly, picking her steps carefully.

Linc stopped, watching her. *I don't need you either, Jillian.* Slowly, he followed, denying the unsettled feeling that suddenly seemed to clutch at him and propel him after her.

CHAPTER 8

LESSIE CAME FORWARD WITH HER ARMS OUTSTRETCHED. "WHAT ARE you doing wandering out to the creek in your delicate condition? We need to make sure she takes care of herself, don't we, Mr. Rising?"

Linc coughed. "Call me William."

Lessie beamed. "I'll do that, thank you." Tucking Jillian's hand into the crook of her elbow, she looked around with a frown. "Now where did Janie run off to? I'm not sure if she remembers you, but she insisted on coming here with me."

As they turned to face Jillian's house, they spotted Janie and Grace sitting on the front-porch steps, playing cats in the cradle with an orange circle of yarn. As Lessie and Jillian approached, Janie and Grace glanced up with remarkably similar expressions. Even their eyes, one pair a deep brown and the other a lighter shade, held the same light.

"Hi, Jilly-bean. This is Janie. She's teaching me some new moves." Pulling the yarn free from the older woman's fingers, Grace stood with her hands held out and the bright orange yarn pulled tight between them, the garish stripes pulled into a pattern. "Look—it's a witch's broom!"

Jillian smiled at Grace. "That's pretty cool. You'll have to show me how later." Then she looked down at the woman who still sat on the step, her thin arms wrapped around her drawn-up knees, her small feet enclosed in white patent-leather sandals. "You must be Janie. It's been a long time, but I remember you. I used to come visit with my grandmother."

Pale blond hair, worn long but held back with a headband, whipped across the surprisingly smooth skin of the older woman's cheeks. Jillian guessed Janie to be in her late forties or early fifties, but for the slight lines around her mouth and eyes, she more closely resembled an adolescent girl than a woman whose youth was far behind her.

Janie tilted her head, a small smile touching her lips. "I remember you. I let you hold Baby."

For the first time, Jillian noticed the small bundle lying next to Janie on the step. At first glance it resembled a pile of blankets, but upon closer inspection, she could see it was a papoose-type carrier with an old rag doll peering out the top.

Jillian carefully knelt and laid her hand on the doll, brushing away yellow string hair that had drooped onto the faded cloth forehead. "Yes, I remember Baby." She smiled into Janie's eyes, somehow saddened by what she saw there; brown pools of deep loss and old grief. She picked up the bundle and handed it to Janie before standing. "I'm glad you came."

Turning toward the others, Jillian said, "I've made some pecan tarts. Why don't y'all come sit on the porch while I go get them and a pitcher of iced tea?"

Linc opened his mouth as if to refuse, but Lessie overrode him. "We'd love to. Can I help?"

"Yes, thanks. It's hard to carry things when I can't see my feet."

Lessie followed Jillian into the kitchen while the others found seats on the porch. Before the screen door shut behind her, Jillian caught the flashing image of Grace and Janie sitting next to each other on the porch swing, with Grace holding Baby and singing softly.

Lessie sniffed hard as she entered the kitchen. "Something smells divine in here."

"It's probably the tarts—or it could be the shortbread torte I did earlier." Jillian reached into the refrigerator and pulled out a full container of iced tea.

Lessie lifted a tart off the cooling rack on the stove and held it poised in front of her mouth. "I think I'm going to cry if I don't try this right now."

"Go ahead. There's plenty more."

Needing no further encouragement, Lessie took a huge bite, almost half of the tart going into her mouth. She chewed for a few moments, then closed her eyes. "Oh. My. God. I think I just died and went to heaven. What did you put in this?" She sighed again, chewing thoughtfully. "And the crust—it just about melts in my mouth."

Jillian began filling glasses with tea. "I added a little bit of bourbon, which I think enhances the flavor. And the secret to the crust, well, I could tell you—but then I'd have to kill you."

Lessie choked and took a glass from the tray Jillian had begun filling. As soon as she could speak again she said, "And it would probably be worth it. I have never tasted anything so heavenly. Really. You truly have a gift."

Jillian felt her face flush with pleasure as she arranged napkins on a tray. "I sometimes wonder, well, this is going to sound silly, but I think everybody is born with one special thing—some gift or talent." She fiddled with the napkins, studying them and her fingers while she searched for the right words. Looking up, she said, "Most of us know early on what it is, while others never really figure it out. And the rest of us"—she shrugged—"well, the rest of us just kind of muddle around, trying different things until we find that one thing, or at least a close substitution, that makes our hearts sing." Smiling, she handed the tray to Lessie. "Sometimes I think I've found it with my cooking."

Lessie licked her fingers. "Trust me, Jillian. You've found it."

Flushing again, Jillian began arranging tarts on the tray. "I used to be a caterer back in Atlanta. I was sort of toying with the idea of maybe doing the same thing here on Pawleys."

Lessie's eyes opened wide. "That would be wonderful! My hips would hate you forever, but I would happily sacrifice my figure to help you start up your business." She stuffed the rest of the tart into her mouth, chewing slowly with her eyes closed. "Trust me. You would never hurt for customers."

"From your lips to God's ears." Feeling inordinately pleased, Jillian picked up the tray with the tarts and motioned Lessie to follow her with the iced tea onto the porch.

Linc watched Grace and Janie join hands and move through the dunes toward the boardwalk. Janie wore the papoose over her stomach, the thin blankets wrapped around the doll and their ends flapping in the wind. They stooped in the sand, the sea oats bowing around them and kissing their bare legs, and Janie reached to pick something up, holding it for Grace to see. Their foreheads nearly touched as the two bent to examine Janie's find.

Despite the age difference between the child and the woman, there was definitely an affinity there. Linc had never really thought about Janie Mulligan, just acknowledging her on the periphery of life on the island as an unfortunate existence—a handicapped mind in a world that spun too fast for her to latch on.

Now, though, as he watched Janie with Grace, his perception shifted. She was speaking slowly to Gracie, and the little girl was nodding her head as if in comprehension. Then Janie said something that made Gracie throw back her head and laugh out loud, the sound carrying up to him on the porch, reminding him of forgotten words from a favorite song. He noted the smile on Janie's face matched his own, and he realized that it was the first time he'd heard Grace laugh like a child. Her laugh was high and bright, so much like what her mother's used to be that Linc was flooded with memories of the young Jillian he had once known—the girl with the laugh that made others smile and the eyes that hid so much from the world.

He looked at Janie again, and she wore a look of satisfaction. It was as if she'd ordered something therapeutic for the child and was reveling in her success. Linc squinted into the sunlight at Janie, feeling his perceptions shift and turn, and wondered if it was everyone else's outlook on the world that was out of focus instead of the other way around.

Jillian cupped her hands around her mouth. "If you two want a pecan tart, you'd better come up quickly before they're all gone." She set about putting tarts on plates as Janie and Grace ran toward the porch, kicking sand and sending it flying into the breeze.

She handed a plate to Janie. "I knew that would get Grace's attention."

Janie took the plate and smiled. When she spoke, her voice was light and airy and almost childlike in its directness. "Do you have a baby in there?" She pointed at Jillian's stomach with her fork.

Jillian's hands found the mound of her abdomen and smiled. "I think so. I don't remember swallowing a beach ball."

Janie took a bite of her tart and chewed it thoughtfully, her eyes focused on Jillian, who was trying to settle herself in the porch swing. She held her tea in one hand and her plate in the other, and every time she tried to back into the swing it moved with her, preventing her from finding purchase on the seat.

"I have a baby, too."

Jillian paused in her attempts to sit and let her gaze settle on the yellow head of the doll that hung out of the papoose. "I've held Baby before. She's very sweet."

A deep frown hung over Janie's face. "They didn't want me to keep her, so they tried to take her away. But she's mine. She'll always be mine."

Jillian tried another vain attempt at seating herself in the swing. "She has a mother who loves her and will always protect her. She's very lucky, you know."

Grace looked up from the porch steps where she'd been sitting. "Like me, Jilly-bean. Right?"

A look of surprise filtered over Jillian's face. She regarded her daughter and seemed to chew over the thought, as if it were the first time it had ever occurred to either of them. "Yeah, sweetie. Like you."

Pulling words from around her full mouth, Gracie added, "And just like my baby brother or sister who's growing in your tummy, right?"

Jillian turned to stare at the swing in mute frustration, her whole body registering defeat. Ignoring the little voices in his head, Linc strode over to her and took the plate and glass from her hands. After placing them on the porch railing, he held the swing steady. "Go ahead and sit, and I'll bring your food to you."

With an ungainly move that consisted of hiking her maternity dress above her knees, Jillian managed to seat herself on the swing. When Linc brought her the plate and glass, she looked up at him with grateful eyes.

Gracie stamped her foot with impatience and repeated her question. "Right, Jilly-bean?"

A sigh crept out of Jillian without her noticing, but it seemed to diminish her before his eyes, reducing her to something small and fragile. He walked away from her and sat back down in his chair, putting in a mouthful of tart that seemed to stick in his throat.

With her eyes on her untouched plate, she said, "Yes, Gracie. Like the baby, too."

Lessie drained her glass of iced tea and interrupted the silence, as if unaware of the tension between the other adults, as she addressed Linc. "Donna Michaels says that you're moving in next door on a permanent basis. I guess this means I'll be needing to bring you a Welcome Wagon basket of goodies."

Linc placed his empty plate and glass on the ground by his chair. "Don't worry about the basket. I'm only going to be a temporary resident until the house is completely refurbished and sold. With me doing so much of the work, it made sense to be closer. I'll still have my town house in Charleston, but this will work for the time being."

His gaze stole over to the neighboring house, at the raw wood and empty windows, and he felt its aloneness as if he, too, were standing naked and alone on the edge of the dune, waiting for the next strong wind.

"Well, it will be good to have you in our community. I don't think we've ever had an architect living among us before. Unless you count the summer people. I'm sure there must have been one or two over the years." Lessie smiled, then rose to start gathering plates. "I'm really surprised, though, William, that you didn't move into this house instead of selling it to Jillian. I would think that would have been easier than living in a house that's being renovated around your ears."

He felt Jillian's gaze on him and he turned to meet her eyes.

"I wasn't aware you owned this house, William. I don't remember seeing your name on the papers. And I'm pretty sure you never mentioned it."

He shifted uncomfortably in his chair. "Yes, well, my firm owned it, actually. And I never thought it was important enough to mention." Avoiding her eyes, he stood and handed his dirty plate to Lessie.

"I guess we'd better get started with our tour, Jillian, before we overstay our welcome." Lessie stacked the dirty plates on a tray and headed inside, followed by Grace and Janie.

Linc moved to follow, but Jillian called him back. For a moment, their gazes locked and he waited for what she would say to him.

"I need help. I can't get off the swing."

Relief flooded through him, and he felt angry with himself for even feeling relief. He had nothing to hide, no guilty feelings. He moved toward her and took her arm and helped her off the swing.

He held the door open for her and she walked past him but stopped, leveling her cool brown eyes at him. "Don't think this conversation is over, Linc. I may be fat and have as much grace as a hippo, but I'm not stupid." She moved past him and into the house.

He watched her walk away as he shut the door behind him, and wondered why he had to force down a smile.

They walked through Jillian's house first, with Linc leading the way and Lessie close on his heels with a notepad, busily scribbling. Linc made a great show of opening up all doors—most newly painted or stained—except for the downstairs coat closet. He turned the knob and yanked on it, but it didn't open. "I think the house has shifted, because this door is firmly wedged inside the frame and I can't budge it. We'll figure something out." He slapped his palm against the surface, then moved on.

Because her back was hurting, Jillian stayed downstairs when the entourage climbed to the second level, and Janie and Grace stayed with her. Jillian wasn't sure what to make of Janie. When she watched her talking with Grace, it was as if Janie were just another seven-year-old. It was there in the way she held herself, with the loose-limbed poise of a child who is blissfully ignorant of the world's perception of her. But when she caught Janie's gaze on her, there was a depth in her eyes that reminded Jillian of her daughter and of something Martha Weber had said about Gracie, about her being an old soul.

Jillian sat down on the bottom step and watched Janie and Grace sitting cross-legged on the parlor floor, facing each other and playing with Spot. They both looked up as if on cue, and Jillian stared. The faces were different, as was their coloring, but the light in their eyes, light that seemed to shine beyond their years and through a person's heart, was the same.

Lessie's voice drifted down from upstairs, along with knocking against plaster. "I was so hoping to find a secret passage or at least a secret room. It would make my assignment so much more interesting."

"Sorry to disappoint." Linc's voice sounded bored and strained with impatience. "Like I mentioned before, there's nothing on any of the blueprints that show anything like that. Besides, both of the houses were completely remodeled in the 'twenties, and if there had been something before then, it would have been discovered."

Lessie let out a heavy sigh. "Well, maybe we'll find something at your house."

Jillian pulled herself to a stand when she heard their footsteps approaching the stairs.

Lessie spoke again. "Then again, what if the people who did the remodeling were bootleggers or something? I mean, that was Prohibition, right? Maybe they found something and just kept it quiet for a reason."

They came into view at the top of the stairs, and Jillian saw Linc roll his eyes. "I guess anything's possible, but I know every inch of these two houses, and I haven't found a thing."

As they passed by her, Jillian said, "I know there are hidden nooks and crannies at the other house. William can show them to you. Not big enough to hide a person, I don't think, but certainly interesting enough to include in your paper. I believe they were original to the house."

Lessie's brows raised with interest. "Thank you. I'll definitely check it out. But it's odd, isn't it, that these two identical houses wouldn't have the same hiding places?"

Linc gently pressed on Lessie's back as if to propel her more quickly to the door, but she didn't seem to notice. "Maybe they were added later by one of the owners. That would explain it."

Lessie paused in the doorway and looked back at Jillian. "Are you coming with us?"

She shook her head. "No, I'll stay here with Grace and Janie. Take your time. I know William's just dying to show you every square inch of his house."

"That's right. Just dying to." Linc narrowed his eyes at Jillian before closing the door in her face.

Jillian waited until Gracie was asleep and all the lights were turned on in the house before leaving it just before sunset to go find Linc. She could hear his radio and the music of the Tams dancing with the sand across the dunes. Gingerly, she picked her way toward the house next door, a flashlight in one hand and a peace offering of the remaining pecan tarts in the other.

She stood for a long time watching him before he noticed her. He had a sawhorse on level ground, and he seemed to be turning small sections of lumber into a saw blade. He had removed his shirt and wore only jeans and work boots, revealing more male skin than she'd seen in a very long time. She couldn't help but notice that he was no longer the skinny, gangly boy she remembered. Oh, Lord, not at all.

He looked up at that moment and she felt hot blood flood her cheeks. *Damn these pregnancy hormones.* "I brought you a tart . . . um . . . some tarts. I figured my waistline didn't need them, and you seemed to enjoy the three you had this afternoon."

After flipping off the saw and the radio, he moved to the porch steps and put on his shirt. She watched as long, tanned fingers moved over the buttons, the movement flicking off some of the wood chips that had stuck to the sweat of his hands and forearms. They were artist's hands, hands meant to create things of beauty from solid blocks of nothing special. Just, she supposed, like he had done with his own life. His hands dropped to his sides, and she remembered the carved box with the intertwining *L*s, and met his eyes again.

"Thanks." He took the plate from her hands and put it on the porch.

She faced him, trying again to find the boy she'd once known, the boy she could talk to about anything, but couldn't. Somewhere on his journey into manhood, he'd found the need to hide behind William Rising—a man she wouldn't have recognized except for his hands.

"I'd like to know why you took a loss on this house to sell it to me when you could have made a decent profit by selling it to somebody else."

He looked out behind her to where the sun had begun its long descent. "I was just trying to help you out. I knew how much you loved your grandmother's house, and when Lessie told me you were looking at it, I made a quick decision."

Her eyes narrowed as she considered him. "That's a bunch of crap and you know it."

Half of his mouth turned up, but there was no humor reflected in his eyes. "Come on, Jillian. Tell me what you really think."

She placed her hands on her hips, as she remembered her grandmother doing when Jillian was a child and had done something wrong. It seemed to give her strength. "Okay. I will. I've been thinking about this all day—ever since Lessie dropped her little bombshell about you selling me the house for under market value." She dug her toe into the sand with a hard thrust. "I think you wanted me nearby for something.

Did you think you'd check my mail every day to see if Lauren was writing to me? Or visiting me? Do you think I've kept her existence a secret all these years just to punish you for a crime we both know you didn't commit? What is it, Linc? What made you do something underhanded when all you really ever needed to do was just to ask me?"

His jaw worked as he clenched his teeth, and she knew she had pushed him too far. It didn't matter, though. Nothing mattered except for her and Grace and the new baby, and their ability to find whatever peace they could in their new home. Dealing with Linc was just a detour—something that needed to be taken care of before the peace could come.

Linc took a step toward her, but she didn't back away. His voice was quiet when he finally spoke. "I don't know. Maybe it has something to do with the way I remember your father accusing me of murdering Lauren and making sure I was hauled into jail. And then the way that you disappeared right after that, and I never saw you again. Maybe I was thinking that after all these years I might finally get some answers if I could have you nearby long enough to figure out what I needed to know."

Her fingers lightly touched his arm before falling away. "All you had to do was ask, Linc."

"You never wrote. You never tried to contact me. Why would I think that you would want to answer any of my questions?"

"My parents sent me back to Atlanta, and I didn't know how to reach. You had left the island and nobody knew where you'd gone. I did try, Linc. I did."

He finally stepped away, as if making sure she was more than touching distance from him. "Well, obviously not hard enough. And he was your father, Jillian. That makes you guilty by association."

A tight ball formed in her throat. "I never doubted your innocence, Linc. Please don't put me in the same corner as my daddy. There's a lot of things I can forgive, but that's not one of them."

"It was pretty easy for me to do, Jillian. Your father said that you never wanted to see me again. That you blamed me for Lauren's disappearance." He stuck his fists into his pockets and stared up at the sky for a brief moment. "He tried to give me the star I had made for you—said you didn't want it anymore. I didn't take it back."

Jillian felt stunned for a moment, as if all the breath in her body had been beaten out of her. "I never gave that to him. It meant too much to me—you know that. He must have taken it from my drawer and put it back without my ever knowing about it." She swallowed, fighting tears. "But you didn't even try to contact me to make sure!"

"He was pretty convincing, and when you never showed up to tell me different, it made it easier for me to believe that you thought the worst of me, along with everybody else."

They faced each other in the fading light, listening to their own hard breathing and the crash of the waves below on the beach. Finally, Jillian said, "Good night, Linc." Grasping her flashlight, she carefully began her slow, lumbering journey back into the circle of light around her house.

She heard the note of belligerence in his voice and wondered if he did, too. "Why did your husband leave you?"

She didn't expect his words to hurt as much as they did. She took a deep breath and faced him again. "What makes you think it wasn't the other way around?"

There was a long pause, and for a minute she thought that he wasn't going to answer her. Then he spoke. "Because you would never give up. In all those years I knew you, if there was a speck of hope to hold on to, you'd find a death grip and wouldn't let go. I don't imagine you've changed all that much."

She looked away, noting with dread that darkness was falling, and curious that he would remember that about her. "No. I don't guess I have." A wave of exhaustion hit her, as if she'd just run for miles, and she found it difficult to hold back her shoulders. She managed to suck in a breath before speaking again. "Good night, Linc." Clutching her flashlight, she again began to make her clumsy way across the dunes.

"Grace said you have something I'm looking for."

She stopped again and turned around. "What do you mean?"

"I'm not sure. She said Lauren told her that you have whatever it is I'm supposed to be looking for."

She managed to keep the trembling out of her voice. "My daughter has a vivid imagination. She talks to imaginary people like they were real."

"But why Lauren? Why would this one be called Lauren?"

"I don't know. Before we came here, she'd never heard me say the name." She watched as he took something out of his shirt pocket and slid it over his head. It was the sand dollar necklace Grace had made for him.

He turned as if to walk away, then faced her again. After several deep breaths he said, "I feel her here. I feel her presence whenever I'm in this house. And I can't help but wonder if that means she's really dead."

A lump formed in her throat. "Don't say it, Linc. I have lived all these years with the hope that she's alive—somewhere. And that one day she'll come back. I can't stand to consider anything else."

Total darkness had fallen now, and she turned to face the vast blackness that separated the two houses. She turned on the feeble glow of the flashlight. A light touch brushed her elbow. "I'll walk you across."

Grateful, she nodded. When they had stopped in front of her house, Linc asked, "Are you going to look for your new star tonight?"

"I'm only going as far as the boardwalk, and I'm not bringing my telescope. I can see what I need to see with my naked eye. So you don't need to worry about me."

He looked at her for a long moment without speaking. "I wasn't worrying. I just don't want any dead bodies on the beach. It's bad for resale value."

She gave him a shaky smile. "Thanks for your concern. But I'll be fine."

"I know. You've always been like a cat, haven't you? Always landing on your feet."

Before she could ask him what he meant, he had started walking home. It was then that she recognized the old Linc; it was in the way he walked, with his shoulders thrown back and his hands clenched in fists of bright energy. It was the walk of a boy who always pictured himself alone in the world, someone who always had to fight his own battles. And to some extent, he always had.

He flicked on his radio, and she heard the music again, dredging up memories of long-past summer nights. With a sigh, she looked up at the ribbon of stars above, marveling how such objects of light and beauty could be tethered to nothing, but still find the strength to shine with brilliance night after night, showing lost souls the way through the darkness.

She hummed to herself as she made her way up the steps and into the house, the music following her until she closed the door behind her.

CHAPTER 9

JILLIAN DIDN'T FEEL FIFTEEN AS SHE WIPED THE TEARS OFF HER FACE with the back of her hand and lay back in the sand, staring up at the darkening sky and at the stars that had begun to blink. Her birthday had slipped by completely unremarked, but she had thought she'd at least feel older.

She could feel the rhythm of the surf under her head, and beyond that the heavy tread of someone running. Turning, she spotted Linc running toward her, long, tanned legs spinning in her direction under short cutoff jeans. As usual, his hair was too long and too wild, but Jillian thought it suited the spirit of the boy underneath it.

He skidded to a stop in front of her, spraying her with sand, and she threw her arm over her eyes so he couldn't tell she'd been crying.

His voice sounded out of breath. "Where's Lauren?"

She kept her arm over her eyes. "I haven't seen her. She said she'd meet me here before sunset." She bit her lower lip to stop it from trembling. "She knows I don't like the dark."

"Why are you crying?"

She moved her arm away and stared at him, wondering not for the first time how he always knew everything about her. "It's not been much of a birthday."

"Sorry." He sat down next to her, then reached into his pocket and pulled out a small object before poking her in the arm with it. "This is for you."

"For me—really?"

He gave her a halfhearted shove on her shoulder. "It's *your* birthday, right? Happy birthday."

She sat up with her palm out, and he laid a beautiful wooden star in her hand. "I carved it myself."

Jillian examined the five-pointed object, marveling at the rounded edges and smooth curves. It was as if he had pulled a shining star from the sky and transformed it into a material she could hold next to her heart. "It's beautiful," she said, and then began to cry.

Awkwardly, he put his arm around her. "Don't cry, Jillian. I don't want you to cry anymore."

Sniffling, she said, "I'm not crying."

"Right. So stop moisturizing your eyes."

She kept her eyes focused on the star. "My mother said she's not celebrating my birthdays anymore because they make her feel old. Grandma was baking me a cake, but it won't be ready by the time we leave."

She felt Linc stiffen beside her. "You're leaving? You've only been here a week. Aren't you supposed to stay all summer?"

Jillian nodded. "They've been fighting about me ever since we came. I don't know what it's all about—but I think my grandmother wants to tell me something that my parents don't think I'm ready to hear. And now my mother is saying that my grandmother isn't fit to take care of me, and she's going to put me in summer camp in Atlanta for the rest of the summer." She was silent for a moment, and then added, "I overheard my mother accusing him of having an affair with one of our neighbors in Atlanta. I think that's why she wants me there—to help her keep an eye on him."

She heard Linc gritting his teeth, and turned to see his hard profile in the fading light. "I'm sorry."

He scooted away and lay back in the sand, and Jillian did the same, the top of her head pressed against his. He touched her hand when he spoke. "What were you looking at?"

"The Big Dipper."

"You mean Ursa Major."

"Same thing."

"Not really. Haven't I taught you anything? The Big Dipper is an asterism, not a constellation, and is actually part of Ursa Major."

Jillian raised her hand, holding up the wooden star, placing it along the flank of the great bear in the sky. "According to some Indian legends, the bowl of the Big Dipper is a giant bear, and the stars of the handle are three warriors chasing it. It lies low in the autumn evening sky, so it was said that the hunters had injured the bear and its blood caused the trees to color their leaves red."

He turned his head toward the sound of water over sand for a moment. "You have been paying attention."

Jillian blinked back more tears. "I want to be up there, with them. I want to die and fly up, and hang my star in the sky."

Linc reached up and placed his hand over hers, sealing the wooden star in their closed fists. "Don't you ever say that, Jillian. Don't. Here's your star—right here on earth." He squeezed their hands tighter, digging the wooden points into her skin, the pain making imprints on her memory. "You can make it shine, and don't ever let anybody tell you different."

She lowered her arm and his fell away. Impulsively, she turned and kissed the top of his head. "We're a lot alike, aren't we? I guess some people are made to create their own light. God knows our parents aren't going to do it for us."

Jillian heard a shout in the distance and sat up, staring over Linc toward two silhouettes approaching them across the dunes. "I think that's Lauren. But who is that with her?"

Linc stood, wiping sand off his shorts. He waited until the figures were closer, then said, "I think it's your dad." He reached down and helped her up, and she stood next to him, not touching. He stood slightly in front of her, as if to protect her, and it made her want to cry again.

Lauren, who had been walking with Jillian's father, ran ahead as they approached the two on the beach.

Linc took a step toward her and bent to kiss her lips, but she turned her head and he kissed her cheek instead.

"Happy birthday," she said, throwing her arms around Jillian. She swayed slightly, and Jillian smelled the beer.

Lauren leaned in a little closer and whispered, "Your dad caught me buying beer, so I gave him one and everything's cool." She kept her arm around Jillian, her skin still warm from the sun and the faint smell of suntan oil mixing with that of the beer. She wore only a halter top and shorts, her feet bare.

"You're drunk." Linc took a step toward Lauren, then stopped.

Lauren held a wavering finger in front of her lips. "Shhh. It's a secret." She winked at them and raised her eyebrows in a silent signal to let them know that she was as sober as they were. Then she giggled and stumbled over to where Jillian's father stood in the sand, his arms crossed over his chest and his eyes coolly appraising the three teenagers. His gaze stayed on Linc for a long moment, but he didn't say anything. He didn't have to. He'd made it clear many times what he thought about his daughter's association with a boy whose mother hung around the street corners in Myrtle Beach when money got tight. Jillian knew her punishment would be harsh.

Lauren watched Mr. Parrish glaring at Linc, then seemed to throw herself against Jillian's father. Mr. Parrish stuck his arms out to catch her, and she fell into him, his breath knocked out with a quiet swoosh. He didn't let go.

She looked over her shoulder at the other two teenagers and winked again. "I thought your dad and I could have a reasonable conversation over a little drink." She hiccupped and held her hand over her mouth for a moment. "He's agreed that you can stay another week—but he and your mama are gonna be staying, too. That was our bargain. I hope that's okay with you." She hiccupped again, then giggled, this time swaying toward Linc until he opened his arms and caught her. Lauren blinked up at him. "Hello, gorgeous."

When she reached up to kiss him, he turned his head. "You smell like beer."

She pulled back and narrowed her eyes for a moment before sinking into a sitting position in the sand, her back resting against Linc's legs.

Jillian looked at her father. "Is that true, Daddy? Are we really staying another week?"

He lit up a cigarette as his dark-eyed gaze settled on her, but she felt as if he weren't really seeing her. She was used to this, having considered herself the invisible child for quite some time. "Yeah, I figured we might as well. We've already driven all this way. Your mother and I have just decided that we don't want to have to drive all the way here and back at the end of the summer to retrieve you, so we'll just take you back with us when we leave."

She felt the tears lodge in her throat but swallowed them back, knowing that his decision had been made and her crying would only make him more disgusted with her.

"Thanks," she said weakly, and was surprised to feel Lauren's hand slipping into her own and squeezing.

"Let's go." Her father dropped the cigarette into the sand, then motioned with his head for her to follow.

Jillian pulled Lauren up to a standing position. Quietly, she said, "Thanks, Lauren. I don't know what you said to him, but thanks."

Linc stepped forward and put his arm around Lauren. "Happy birthday," he said again to Jillian. Lauren dropped her head on his shoulder and closed her eyes.

Jillian's father turned his gaze toward Lauren. "Be good," he said, using the same words he always said to Jillian before leaving.

He moved toward the dunes, and Jillian started to follow before stopping suddenly and turning around to face Lauren and Linc again. They stood together in the deepening twilight, their arms linked around each other, and Jillian smiled and waved, and wondered how she could ever survive without them.

She turned around again and began to follow her father, avoiding his footsteps in the sand, and squeezing the small wooden star in her hand as if her pressure could somehow give it light.

Jillian looked up from the wooden star in her hand and caught Gracie watching her closely.

"What's that?"

Slipping it into her pocket, Jillian said, "It's just something somebody gave me a long time ago." She stood, slapping her legs to signal that she was through with the conversation. "Aren't you supposed to be practicing your letters? School starts back tomorrow, and you don't want your new teacher to think they don't teach writing in Atlanta."

Grace stared back solemnly. "It's from Linc, isn't it?"

Spot jumped up on the couch and cuddled up to Gracie's side and gave Jillian an accusatory glare.

Jillian couldn't ignore both of them. "Yes, Gracie. Linc gave it to me a long time ago. Now, get back to your practicing. Do you need any help?"

A light rapping sounded on the front door, and all three heads turned.

Tucking her hair behind her ears, Jillian headed toward the door. "I wonder who that could be."

Gracie called out behind her, "He's allergic to chocolate, so give him the shortbread instead."

Jillian paused for a moment, trying to absorb what Gracie had said, then opened the front door. The sight of the uniform gave her a start before she recognized the face and smiled.

"Mason. Good to see you." She pulled the door open wider. "I'm hoping this is a social call." She looked past him at the police Jeep in her driveway, relieved to note there were no flashing lights. She glanced up at the sky, noticing gathering clouds, and frowned. The weather forecast that morning hadn't mentioned any rain.

He slid his hat off his head, his fingers rolling the brim, and gave her a boyish grin. "Yes, ma'am, uh, Jillian. It's strictly social. I thought I'd stop by and say hey, and see if you needed anything. I also heard that you've been creating miracles in your kitchen, and I figured it was my duty as an officer of the law to come investigate."

Jillian gave one more look at the clouds, then stepped back and allowed Mason to come inside. When he stood next to her, she had to crane her neck back to look into his eyes. His was a comfortable face: a familiar face that brought back pleasant memories—like that of a flan. A comfort food that didn't stay long on the tongue but was pleasant going down. The corners of his eyes crinkled as he smiled down at her.

She smiled back at him. "What a coincidence. I just finished icing a chocolate torte, and I was hoping for a taster."

He frowned for a moment. "Well, darn. I'm allergic to chocolate. Maybe I could just bother you for a cup of coffee, then."

Her eyebrows knitted and she opened her mouth to call to Gracie, then stopped. Instead she said, "I have some freshly made shortbread, too. Come on back to the kitchen and we'll talk."

After settling down at the kitchen table with two mugs of coffee and a plate of shortbread between them, Mason turned toward her with appraising eyes. "You're still just as pretty as ever, Jillian. You haven't changed a bit."

She raised her eyebrows, and he colored.

"Well, except for that baby in there, I mean." He took a sip of coffee, looking eager to change the subject. "How are your parents? I don't think they've been back here since, well, since . . ." He colored again, as if belatedly realizing he was treading in dangerous territory for the second time in as many minutes.

She played with the shortbread crumbs on her plate, swirling them in a circle. "I don't know. I don't see them anymore."

He nodded his head as if he understood. And she realized he probably did. Not as much as Lauren and Linc had, but Mason had been around enough to know how things were in her life.

"There's no denying that you had it tough growing up. But I always got the feeling it was more problems with your mother than your dad. I always thought it strange how you sort of thought of them in the same way."

Jillian stared at him. "He always deferred to her, regardless of what he really might have thought. And he never stuck up for me—he'd just sneak behind her back and apologize to me afterward. But I always saw it as them against me."

Mason reached over and stilled her hand where her finger was stirring crumbs. "I'm sorry. I didn't come here to upset you. Some men are just weak, and there's no excuse for what he allowed in his house. But I thought you did a great job of growing up despite them."

Needing to change the conversation, Jillian slid the plate of shortbread closer to him, and he took another. "And you must have found the fountain of youth, because you look just like the kid who gave me my first kiss."

He colored again and ducked his head. "I can't believe you remember that. I was so green. You must have thought you were kissing cardboard, for all my expertise."

She touched his arm, and his eyes met hers. "That's not how I remember it at all. I treasure that memory, actually."

Sliding back in his chair, he stretched his legs in front of him and cradled his mug. "Then I'd say you really need to get out more."

Throwing back her head, she laughed. "No doubt about that, Mason. It's just a little more difficult now than it once was."

Serious now, he nodded. "I'm sure I can only imagine."

She looked past his shoulder and out the large picture window, noticing how dark the clouds had become. "Have you heard anything in the forecast about a storm? Last time I checked, it was supposed to be blue sky and sun. But I don't like the looks of those clouds."

Mason followed her gaze. "Oh, those will blow over. I was just listening to the weather report on the way here. They said gathering clouds would be expected to blow south by evening. It's a shame, really. We could really use the rain." He smiled reassuringly at her knitted eyebrows. "You know how unpredictable the weather is here, Jilly. But it's not supposed to rain, so go ahead and hang out your laundry."

She smiled back, remembering old storms in this house, storms of electrifying intensity that had made her crawl under the covers in her grandmother's bed. The power on the island was a fickle thing and needed no encouragement to flicker off. Definitely not a situation she wanted to encounter alone. "Yeah, you're right. I just hate storms—I tend to worry when it starts to sprinkle."

"Hey, if it makes you feel any better." He pulled out a card from his shirt pocket. "Here's my card with all my numbers on it. Call me if you need anything, all right?" He looked directly in her eyes, serious again. "I mean it. Anything at all, any time of the day or night. Call me."

She nodded, reassured.

He stood, came around to her side of the table, then helped her up from her chair. She kept her arm linked in his as she led him to the door. "Thanks so much for stopping by. I'll make sure to always have a nonchocolate item on hand for you in the future, just to make sure you come by again. I could always use company—and tasters."

"You got it. And you make sure you call me if there's anything you need, you hear?"

She nodded and waved as he pulled away in his cruiser, dust from the sandy driveway billowing toward her. She noticed the darkening of the sky again and the fat, cumulus clouds that clung to the horizon like huge dust balls. Shutting the door, she went inside to make sure all the windows were closed and that she knew exactly where her flashlight and batteries were, just in case.

The flash of light in the pitch-black sky startled Linc as he bent over his work. He looked up from his task of touching up the final coat of finish on the cradle, ignoring the questions as to what he was doing in the first place. He remembered his tour of Jillian's house the previous week and how there hadn't been a single thing set up for the baby. It had bothered him. Bothered him enough to make a cradle so that the baby would at least have a place to sleep when it arrived.

The lights flickered briefly, and he looked down at his watch, silently cursing. It was after one o'clock in the morning. He had to be up by six a.m., but instead of getting sleep, he was here making a damned cradle.

Thunder rattled the sky at the same time the rain and wind hit the house with a force Linc felt all the way down to his bones. He stood, facing the walls, knowing their strength. They would hold against whatever onslaught Mother Nature threw at them. Maybe that's why he had chosen his profession. Maybe he had wanted to build things that couldn't be destroyed easily by the whims of weather or man. He was living proof that it could be done.

He set down his tools and decided he'd clean up tomorrow. It was late and he was tired and the sawdust wasn't going anywhere. Pushing in his stool, he picked up his beer can and took a last warm swallow and grimaced. The lights flickered again, staying off this time for almost a minute before turning back on.

As he made his way to the kitchen, he flicked off lights, not wanting to forget them if the power should go out completely. He didn't want to be awakened any earlier than he had to with bright lights suddenly turning on throughout the house.

Once in the kitchen, he threw away his beer can, then made his coffee for the next morning and set the timer for six a.m. He calculated his sleep time and groaned again. Before he left to head upstairs, he grabbed a flashlight from a drawer and checked the light. Satisfied, he flipped off the kitchen light and headed up to bed.

He hadn't made it to his room when the electricity flickered again, this time staying off. The central air-conditioning went silent, the only sounds in the empty house that of the wind and rain pushing at its walls. Linc set the flashlight down on his bedside table and moved about the room, stripping off his clothes while his shadow crept along the wall like a trapped ghost.

Before he unbuckled his pants, he moved to the window to pull a draped blanket over the glass and noticed that the house next door was shrouded in darkness. Lightning flashed again, illuminating the house against the scarred sky, and he thought for a brief moment that he'd seen a small face in the upstairs window, peering out at him.

The window rattled as the thunder answered the lightning's call, and he glanced out again at the darkened house. He remembered her, then, out on the beach, when she'd grown frantic because he'd turned off her flashlight. *Most children outgrow their fear of the dark. I never did.* Something slammed against the side of the house, scraping along new lumber. She was there now, in that house. He reached for the phone to call, but knew before he held it to his ear that it would be dead. He gripped it for a long moment and stared at the rivers of water weeping down the windowpanes. *I never did.*

Rain pelted the roof as he stumbled around the room, looking for his clothes. He found his shirt and slid it back on, but left his socks and shoes. He grabbed the flashlight, then raced down the stairs, ignoring the splinters that stabbed into his bare feet, barely remembering to shut his front door before he ran across the dunes toward the house next door.

He dropped the flashlight once and it went off, leaving him completely in the dark. The ocean seemed to roar in his ears as he waited for the next flash of lightning to show him where it was. He retrieved it, his feet sinking into the wet sand as he continued across the two properties, not even noticing how soaking wet he was until he reached the shelter of her porch.

Panting heavily, Linc banged on the door. "Jillian! Grace! It's me, Linc!" He heard nothing but the storm and the wind and the sea and he banged again, bruising the side of his hand. The next roll of thunder shook his teeth as the wind pushed him against a fallen rocking chair. Another chair swayed drunkenly in the gusts that barreled in from the ocean, spraying everything with sand and water.

Linc swore silently under his breath, wondering why he was here instead of in the warm sanctuary of his bed, then turned the doorknob. It was unlocked and slipped easily in his hand. He pushed the door inward, then shut it with force against the wind that demanded entry.

Despite the raging storm outside, the house held a tomblike still-ness, almost as if the air was textured to mute the sounds of the storm. "Damn," he swore again, feeling foolish. Any minute Jillian would appear at the top of the stairs and ask him why he was in her house in the middle of the night.

He turned to leave, and touched the doorknob again. A soft sound came from upstairs, something between a moan and a sob. "Jillian?" he called again. "It's Linc. Are you all right?"

There was no response, but he was already moving up the stairs, holding his flashlight in front of him. He paused at the threshold of Grace's room and looked in, shining the light on the bed. The child slept with her arms around her stuffed bunny, oblivious to the world raging around her. Glowing green eyes from her cat gazed steadily at him from the foot of the bed.

With long strides, he closed the distance between the rooms and entered Jillian's bedroom. The flashlight illuminated her empty bed in a bright circle of light, then skipped off the bed and around the room. She was in there. He felt her.

He moved forward and stumbled over something that rolled across the wooden floor. He bent down and picked up the object, realizing it was a battery. The smashed flashlight lay several feet in front of him, and beyond that he found Jillian.

She was curled in a corner, her bare feet lonely beacons of paleness under her dark gown. Her head was pressed down on her upraised knees, her hands holding down her head. Her teeth were chattering, holding back the sobs that seemed to leak out between her lips.

"Jillian?" He showed the flashlight beam against the wall near her so as not to blind her when she looked up.

"Jillian?" he said again as he moved closer to her.

Her head jerked back, and he saw that her eyes were clenched shut, closed against a blackened world that hid things that even he didn't want to see.

"Don't . . . leave me . . . in here."

Oh, God. Her voice sounded like that of a child. He reached for her hand and she grasped it, her fingers cold and clammy. Her eyes flew open and focused on his face.

He kept the flashlight on, but put it on the floor before he got down and placed his arms around her. She shook in his arms but didn't try to pull away. "I'm not going to leave you, Jillian. I'm staying."

She curled into him and he felt her softness, her body full and ripe with motherhood. It startled him; he hadn't expected that, despite the way she looked. He bent his head closer so she could feel him, so he could make her chattering stop. He caught her scent then—an odd mixture of rain and ocean, an intoxicating perfume that couldn't quite hide the scent of her fear.

The wind lashed at the house, the rain tap-dancing across the roof and windows, the sky alternately dark and light as the lightning flew through the sky. She pressed her forehead into his shirt. "I . . . don't like . . . the dark."

He held her tighter, and he noticed with absurd detachment that he was rubbing her back, the soft cotton of her nightgown bunching under his fingers. "I know, I know. It'll be over soon." He stared down at her, wrapped in his arms as if she belonged there, and felt with dread the fingers of need curl inside him. Part of him wanted to push her away, to leave and run through the rain to his cold, empty shell of a house. But he knew he wouldn't. He'd always been such a coward where she was concerned.

Her breathing slowed as she clung to him, and he moved her head so that it rested against his chest. He shifted restlessly under her, his wet clothes sticking to them both, a tight roiling of her belly feeling natural under his arm. *What has she pulled me into now?* He realized he had spoken aloud when she raised her head.

A bright flash illuminated the room, creating a halo of light around her. Her voice was quiet but calm. "I'm not trying to make your life miserable, Linc. Not on purpose, anyway. Besides, you seem to be doing a good enough job on your own."

She was still trembling, so he bit back his first response. "I knew you were afraid of the dark." He groped in the blackness for words that would somehow excuse his rudeness and also hide whatever reasons had propelled him across the dunes in such a storm. "When the lights went out, I knew I couldn't leave you and Gracie here. I can't even say that you spoiled a perfectly wonderful evening. I was just getting into bed."

Her hand gently cupped his cheek. "Thank you." She had to lean close to his ear to be heard against the storm's newest efforts. "Did you check on Gracie?"

"Yes. She was sound asleep."

"Good." He felt her nod against his chest, her shivering slowly subsiding.

He must have dozed off, because he was jerked awake when she leaned toward his ear again. "Are you really going to stay?"

Linc nodded, his eyes scratchy with dried sand.

"Good." She paused, and he felt her muscles tighten. "Because I think I'm about to have a baby."

CHAPTER 10

LINC FELT JILLIAN'S MUSCLES TIGHTEN AGAIN BENEATH HIS FINGERS, and he closed his eyes. Maybe this was just some horrible dream he was having trouble waking from. Hadn't she just said that she wasn't trying to ruin his life?

She gasped, and he tightened his hold on her. She was flesh and blood and mother-to-be under his hands, and conflicting emotions coursed through in equal measure: anger at being there in the first place, and gratitude that she didn't have to go through this alone.

He waited for the spasm to pass. "Do you have a cell phone?"

She shook her head, clumps of hair sticking to her forehead. He realized she was wet from his shirt.

"I'm going to have to go back to my house and see if my cell phone's working and try to call for help." He looked nervously down to her abdomen. "Can you hold off that long?"

With a crooked smile, she said, "It's not soft-serve ice cream, Linc. It generally takes a little longer than that." A wave of pain seemed to grip her and she gritted her teeth, her hands clutching at her nightgown. When it had passed she said, "Although these contractions seem to be coming pretty close together."

He tried to keep the panic out of his voice. "Like, how close?"

"Well, longer than soft-serve, but much less than a turkey."

He shifted her off his lap so that he could maneuver to lift her in his arms. "How can you joke about this? You're about to have a baby and all you've got is me."

"I'm not trying to be funny, Linc. I was just trying to put it in a man's terms."

Bending over, he lifted her up with a soft grunt. She placed her arms around his neck and brought her face close to his, her voice strained. "Besides, you're here. Everything's going to be fine now."

Gingerly, he carried her to the bed and laid her on it. As he pulled the sheets up, he noticed his hands were shaking. "I'll hurry." He picked up the flashlight and left it on the nightstand, the night parting in a triangle of light around her. "I'll leave this here."

She gripped his hand tightly, her legs drawing up under the covers. Slowly, her grip relaxed and she looked up at him. "Sorry to ruin your evening."

A grin twisted his lips. "I'll go tell the exotic dancers they need to go home." A blast of wind knocked into the house, as if reminding them of its presence. A splattering against the windows rattled and quieted in a pulsing rhythm, moving with the giant waves of ocean-borne wind. He squeezed her hand and let it drop down on the mattress. "I'll be right back."

As he turned to go, something fell to the floor, hitting it with a dull thud. He looked around to see where it had come from, but saw no place from where it could have fallen. In the glow from the flashlight, he made out a dark spot on the floor and bent to pick it up. He felt the smoothness of the wood and knew what it was before he held it inside the beam of light: a small wooden star, hand-carved and warm to the touch, as if it had just been held in someone's hand.

A sharp grunt exploded from Jillian: half scream, half whimper.

He took a step toward her, but she held up her hand. She didn't lift her head from the pillow, as if she were conserving her strength. "Don't. Just . . . hurry."

Without thought, he slipped the star into his pocket and ran from the room. The rain was now being blown in horizontal sheets, cutting into Linc's face and bare arms as he made his way in the dark across the dunes. He stumbled on sea oats and sandspurs, and sucked sand in his mouth when he fell. Each flash of light in the sky seemed to linger for several seconds, lighting his way to the house next door.

An eerie sense of calm filled him as he stumbled his way into the kitchen, searching for another flashlight. He would move as fast as he could, trying not to think of Jillian and the baby and of what might be happening right now while he stood shivering and pooling water on his kitchen floor.

He remembered one of the workmen leaving his toolbox on top of the stove, and he groped his way over to it. Digging his hands inside, he carefully felt the familiar curves and edges of a carpenter's tools, nearly shouting with relief as his hands felt the round, cool metal of a flashlight. Flipping it on, he dashed the light around the room, searching for the cell phone he remembered putting down somewhere.

He heard the scream of the wind outside and imagined he also heard a woman's scream, and his movements became more frantic. He slid his hands along the countertops, knocking things on the floor, then stepping on them with his bare feet.

With a conscious effort to calm down, he grabbed a plastic garbage bag, then made his way to the stairs and ran up to his room. Using deliberate movements, he threw dry clothing into the bag as he searched every available space for his cell phone. The beam from the flashlight found it lying on the floor next to the closet. He snatched it up and punched the ON button, watching the screen search for a calling area. He didn't realize he'd been holding his breath until the phone beeped, and he knew that it would work. Dialing 911, he ran down the stairs, barking information into the phone.

Satisfied that they were aware it was a real emergency, he kept the phone on but snapped it onto the waistband of his pants, under his soaking shirt, and headed to the door. He placed his hand on the doorknob, then turned back to run into the kitchen and pick up the cradle. Throwing the plastic bag inside and bending low over the baby's bed, Linc dashed outside in the rain, trying as best as he could to protect the cradle from the teeming rain that seemed to have no end.

Jillian heard the slam of the door downstairs and pulled the baby closer to her chest, feeling the stickiness of blood and afterbirth and the feel of the cord that was still attached to the baby. With more energy than she thought she still possessed, she reached down for the blanket and pulled it up to cover them both, but not out of modesty. She just didn't want Linc to faint before the ambulance came.

The baby made a mewling sound and began to root for a breast. Close to exhaustion and near to passing out, she smiled at the child's determination and helped him find what he was looking for, using a corner of the blanket to wipe his face clean. She hurt and she was tired, but the sound of Linc's returning told her that everything was going to be all right.

He stopped in the doorway, his skin and hair glistening with rain, and stared silently at her. He was carrying something in his arms, but he put it down before walking over to the bed and looking down where she nursed her new son.

His voice cracked. "I thought you said it would be longer than soft-serve but shorter than a turkey."

She shrugged, a weary smile crossing her face briefly. "I lied."

He wiped a hand over his face, shaking water down on her, but he didn't appear to notice. "An ambulance is on the way." He glanced down nervously. "Are you all right? Is there, well . . . can I . . . I mean . . . are you done?"

If she hadn't been so tired, she would have laughed. "Mostly— nothing that can't wait for a doctor."

"Good." He sounded relieved. "Is it a boy or girl?"

The baby stopped his nursing, finding his fist to be a satisfactory substitute. She touched his cheek briefly with her knuckle. "A boy."

He spoke softly. "Figures. Us guys don't like to dawdle when something needs to get done." His smile faded as he regarded her in the dim light from the dying flashlight. Rain continued to pelt at the windows, but the sky lay dark and silent. "I'm sorry. I tried to get back as quick as I could. I'm sorry."

Her fingers strayed to his knee, where she patted him gently. "You showed up, Linc. That's probably more than anybody has ever done for me."

He shrugged, looking uncomfortable. "Are you warm enough? I could get that afghan off the blanket stand." She could tell he wanted to help, that he wanted to somehow make it up to her for not being there when the baby came.

At her nod, he carefully settled the afghan over her and the baby, gently tucking the top sheet around her. He sat on the edge of the bed and stuck his hand out toward the baby before pulling it back.

Her eyes were getting heavy. "It's okay, you can touch him." Her lips turned upward in a tired grin. "I already cleaned him up."

Linc's long fingers gently cupped the down-covered head, a play of shadow on light, before brushing the soft cheek. "Does he have a name?"

She nodded, her eyes closed, the need for sleep pulling at her. "He didn't. Not until just now."

When she didn't continue, he asked, "Do you need me to call your ex-husband?"

Her eyes popped open. "No. He should hear it from me. I'll call in the morning."

Linc watched her as her hands touched the baby, feeling the small, perfect fingers and the smoothness of his skin. The umbilical cord was still attached, and she didn't want to move him. The child of her body now lay cradled in her arms, looking up at her as if he were actively pursuing becoming the child of her heart. He was tiny and perfect, and she could almost believe that their bond was real and lasting and that she could be the mother he deserved. Almost.

"Two kids, Jillian. I didn't think . . ." He looked up at her with guilt haunting his dark eyes. "Never mind. It's none of my business."

She looked down at her son, trying not to see her own failure reflected in his eyes. She licked her dry lips. "Rick wanted children. It seemed like a small price to pay—first, to thank him for saving me, and the second time, to get him to stay." The exhaustion fell on her like a palpable thing, and not just the exhaustion of childbearing, but the eternal defeat of being pushed aside and rendered invisible. She sighed. "Seems he got tired of giving more than he got in our marriage."

She felt the nausea hit her, and she looked to see if she could recognize revulsion in his eyes. But all she saw was understanding. "We don't have to repeat our parents' mistakes, Jillian." He even looked as if he almost believed it himself.

He was silent for a moment. "Was he a good husband?"

She looked away, then nodded her head once, not having the energy to do more. "He loved me—in the beginning, anyway. And I, well . . ." She closed her eyes, seeing the hurt on Rick's face every time he told her he loved her and she couldn't answer back. She opened her eyes and looked back at Linc. "My grandmother once told me that every point of refuge has its price. And she was right. I was and still am angry and humiliated, but I don't blame him for leaving. I only wished I had had the courage to do it myself years ago." Tears of pain and exhaustion stung behind her eyelids. "But yes, he was a good husband."

The faraway sound of sirens wailed in the distance. Linc looked relieved to move away from the intimacy of their words, as if he'd tasted some forbidden fruit and knew that punishment wasn't far behind. "I'm going to go let them in." He stood and moved toward the door, and a small smile crossed his lips. "Don't have another baby while I'm gone, okay?"

She was too tired to respond, and he must have thought she'd fallen asleep because he turned to leave. With a last burst of energy, she called out, "Linc?"

He paused in the doorway, a frown creasing his brow. "Yes?"

"Aren't you going to ask what I named him?"

"Yeah, sorry. What's his name?"

"I'm naming him after you."

He looked horrified. "Linc?"

She shook her head. "I'm calling him Ford. Ford Parrish Ryan."

It looked like he wanted to laugh out loud. He had always hated his name and how it had come about, but she could tell he was pleased. "Thank you. I think."

Jillian cradled the baby on her chest and turned her face toward the window. Bright streaks of pink and purple claimed the sky, the rain finally ending. Her voice held surprise. "It's not dark anymore."

"No, it's not." He leaned down and slid something heavy over against the wall. When he straightened, he looked almost embarrassed, as if he were trying to hide whatever it was that he had brought in. Then he turned and headed for the stairs, leaving her alone with her son, who slept peacefully in her arms.

The flashlight on the night table sputtered and died, as if it had been patiently waiting for dawn. Despite the sound of people downstairs, she let her eyelids drop until her eyes closed and she slept.

Linc sat across from Gracie at Jillian's kitchen table. She stabbed her fork into a frozen waffle and frowned. "It's still cold."

"I'll stick it back in the toaster." He stood and took her plate, staring at the offending objects dripping with maple syrup. Ripping off a paper towel from the dispenser, he proceeded to wipe off the syrup before sticking it back into the toaster oven. Gracie regarded him with raised eyebrows but didn't say anything.

Linc joined her at the table again and took a sip of his coffee, grimacing at the bitterness. Jillian had one of those fancy European coffeemakers, and he hadn't quite figured out how to use it in the two days she'd been on bed rest and he'd been keeping an eye on Gracie.

"How come you don't have kids?"

He paused with his mug held halfway to his mouth before he thought better of it and put it back down on the table. "Because I'm not married."

She rolled her eyes. "Like that makes any difference nowadays."

"You're not supposed to know about that stuff, you know."

She leaned back in her chair, and the expression in her eyes almost made him forget that he was talking to a child. "I know." She swung her legs back and forth under her chair. "Are my waffles ready yet?"

He stood and pulled the waffles out of the toaster, touching them in the center to make sure they were cooked this time. He placed them in front of her along with the bottle of syrup, and patted her on the head before he realized what he was doing. He heard the sound of the hammer pounding next door at his house and he wondered, not for the first time, what the hell he was doing babysitting when he had work to do.

Gracie looked up at him with one of her impish grins. "We can go over there after I'm finished with breakfast, if you want. I'll color or something so you can get to work."

He looked at her with narrow eyes. *She's an old soul.* He didn't know where the thought had come from. But he remembered Martha Weber, when she'd arrived the previous day to see Jillian and the baby, saying that to him. He wasn't sure what she had meant, but he was beginning to suspect that he'd learn very quickly.

Linc studied Gracie for a long moment, looked at the round face that hadn't lost its baby fat and the way her feet were too short to touch the floor when she sat in the kitchen chair. She was a child, although one who referred to her own mother by her first name. He thought of Jillian at that age, on the beach with her grandmother, and knew he couldn't go back to work. Not yet.

"Let's go look for shells. We'll have a contest to see who can find the most."

She had jumped off her chair and was running out of the kitchen before he finished his sentence. Her voice carried down the stairs to him. "You'll have to get your own bucket. I only have one."

With a smile and a shake of his head, he followed her up the stairs to check in on Jillian and tell her where they were going. He tapped on the slightly ajar door and pushed it open when he heard Martha's voice telling him to come in.

The room was filled with flowers, three bouquets alone from Mason Weber in an attempt to alleviate some of his guilt at not being able to predict a bizarre shift in the weather. Jillian was propped up on starched white pillows, her hair neatly brushed and settled over her shoulders. Her eyes were closed, her head tilted toward the light from the windows, and he almost wouldn't have recognized her without the large mound of her pregnant belly. Even her face seemed thinner, her hair more glossy, reminding him more than ever of the young girl he had once known. *She's beautiful,* he thought. Had he always known that? Or had he simply acknowledged it when he first saw her again after all those years—when there was no Lauren to compare her to?

He looked away to where Martha sat in a rocking chair next to the bed, quietly knitting beside the cradle he had made. Inside, surrounded by brightly colored blankets, lay Ford Parrish Ryan, looking much smaller than his name but quite content to lie back and stare at the swaying of the rocking chair. Linc wasn't sure why, but he squatted in front of the cradle and touched his finger to the tiny palm, and was rewarded with a tight squeeze.

Taking his finger back, he stroked the baby's cheek. "There's a little guy joke I can teach you about pulling fingers, but it'll have to wait for when there aren't any ladies present."

"He's already got the belching down pat. All I'll need to do is get him a recliner and a remote control, and he'll be all set."

Linc looked up to where Jillian was peering over the side of the bed, her hair streaming around her head like a halo. He stood up, feeling self-conscious under Jillian and Martha's perusal. "I didn't mean to wake you. I just wanted to know if it would be all right if I took Grace down to the beach to hunt for shells."

She smiled at him. "Yeah, that would be nice. Thanks."

"Well, there's not a lot of work going on next door right now, so I had a bit of free time. . . ."

His voice died, and she looked at him with a half-smile. "I didn't get a chance to thank you for the cradle. It's beautiful. You didn't have to do it, but I'm glad you did."

Martha's knitting needles stilled as she looked up at him, an amused expression on her face. Linc shrugged under her gaze. "It wasn't any trouble. I had some extra wood and I figured I'd make something useful."

The baby burbled, as if giving his opinion on the truth of Linc's words. He was saved from speaking by Grace, who raced into the room, carrying two sand buckets. She handed the pink Barbie one to Linc and smiled innocently up at him. "You can have this one. I forgot I had it."

She moved over to the cradle and squatted in front of it, then leaned over and kissed the baby on his forehead. "Can Ford come with us?"

Jillian settled back against the pillows. "Not yet. I wish I could go, too, but for some reason Mrs. Weber thinks I need to stay in bed for another day, even though the doctor said I was fine."

Mrs. Weber stopped rocking. "With each of my eight children, I stayed in bed for a whole week and was pampered. It's not right that they expect mothers to be up and about so soon after giving birth."

Linc took Grace's hand. "We'll let you two argue it out. Grace and I have shells to find."

As they headed toward the door, he heard Martha say to Jillian, "I still can't believe how that little girl slept through the storm and her mother giving birth."

Grace stopped and turned slowly around. "I did wake up. But she told me that Mr. Rising was coming and that everything would be all right. So I went back to sleep."

Jillian was sitting up straight in her bed now, her eyes focused on Grace. "Who told you, Gracie?"

Grace looked at her mother, then up at Linc, then back again. Quietly, she said, "Lauren did."

Martha Weber dropped a knitting needle, but she didn't stoop to pick it up.

Linc tugged gently on Grace's arm, leading her out of the room. He called back to Mrs. Weber, "She's got one heck of an imagination, doesn't she? Her imaginary friends seem so real to her. We'll be back later."

They rushed down the stairs as fast as Grace's short legs could go. Linc paused on the boardwalk and looked down at the little girl. "Your mother gets upset when you talk about Lauren, doesn't she?"

Gracie looked down at her pink-tipped feet strapped into white sandals. "I'm not supposed to say her name."

Linc knelt in front of her. "But she's real to you, isn't she?"

Grace nodded. "She *is* real. And she tells me things."

A prickling sensation touched the back of his neck, and he rubbed it quickly to make it go away. "Like what?"

She turned her head toward the beach. "Let's go get shells." She pulled her hand away and raced down the boardwalk and onto the sandy beach. He followed slowly behind, his attention focused more on the child than on any of the shell specimens spilled on the beach.

The beach was strewn with the storm debris; shells, rocks, and twigs scattered across the sand and dunes like dandelion spores blown from an unseen mouth. Linc bent to pick up a broken sand dollar, and when he straightened, he recognized a familiar figure approaching them on the beach. She wore sandals similar to Grace's, her hair pulled back in an unruly braid. The pouch with her baby doll was strapped across her chest, but bounced in rhythm with her walking.

Linc held up a hand. "Hello, Miss Janie."

"Hi," she said, sounding like a young girl. Gracie ran to stand next to her, and Janie patted her on her head before smoothing hair away from her forehead. "I've come to see the baby. I've brought a present." She held up a handmade yellow knit bonnet, old and faded but clean.

Grace placed her hand on the pale yellow-and-white ties. "Is this your baby's?"

"Yes, it was. But she doesn't need it anymore. She understands."

Grace's hand slid down to where a monogram had been stitched in pink—J. M. "Did you make this all by yourself?"

Janie sent a conspiratorial wink toward Linc. "When Baby was in my tummy, I knitted this bonnet to keep her warm after she was born."

Linc looked up in the direction of the house, wondering if it was wise to let Janie see Jillian. And then he remembered the no-nonsense Mrs. Weber, and knew that she was in safe hands.

"She might be sleeping, but knock on the door and Mrs. Weber will answer it."

Janie placed a light hand on his arm. "They're not going to take the baby away, are they? They did that to me, you know. They took my baby away."

Her eyes were looking at him but not seeing him, and he felt an unfamiliar rush of pity. "Miss Janie, look—here's your baby. Nobody's taken her."

She stared vacantly down at the rag doll. "No, I guess not."

"Do you want me to walk you up to the house?"

She looked at him, her eyes clear again. "No. I can get there by myself. Besides, you need to look at the big boo-boo in the sand. I think God came during the storm and made a footprint."

Before Linc could ask her what she was talking about, she had turned and headed up the boardwalk.

Gracie raced farther up the beach, closer to his house, dodging large branches and brownish-green splotches of stranded seaweed. She stopped and pointed up toward the dunes surrounding his own boardwalk. "Come see, Linc. I think this is what she was talking about."

Linc followed her, then stopped in confusion. The landscape seemed to have changed. Instead of the fat rolls of sand dunes with sea oats and grasses clinging to the shifting sands, a large bowl had been carved out, then filled with sand and the ocean's debris.

Grace stood stock-still for a long moment, her head cocked as if listening to something only she could hear. Very slowly, she turned toward Linc with somber brown eyes, and he noticed how her eyelashes were sandy colored, a second before she started to scream.

CHAPTER 11

GRACE SLEPT FITFULLY IN HER MOTHER'S BED, PRESSING HERSELF against Jillian's side, her stuffed Bun-Bun clutched under an arm. Martha Weber had gone, and Linc now sat in the vacated rocking chair, his dark brows knitted in worry as he watched Grace sleep.

"I'm sorry, Jillian. I don't know what happened. She just started screaming. I picked her up and carried her home. I didn't know what else to do."

"I've never seen her like that before." Jillian blinked her eyes rapidly, trying to hide the sting of tears. "I've been sitting here, trying to understand why this is happening. I'm sure the divorce was tough on her, and then the move . . ." She rubbed her eyes roughly. "She's always had this imagination, but it's starting to scare me." She looked down at her hands, unable to look at Linc as she said the words. "You heard her talking about Lauren before you left. She talks to her all the time. I'm wondering . . . if I need to seek professional help for her."

She watched as he rested his elbows on his knees, bowing his head as his fingers ran through his hair. Finally, he looked up at her. "Or maybe she's gifted in a special way. Maybe she does see things we can't, or hear things we can't hear." He paused, as if unsure he wanted her to know his thoughts. "Maybe she really does speak with Lauren. Our Lauren."

"No." Jillian shook her head. "No. Because that would mean . . ." She glanced down at her sleeping daughter, feeling the full implication of what Linc was saying. She lifted her chin and looked at Linc directly. "Because that would mean Lauren was dead. And that my daughter was talking to a dead person."

His eyes looked as stricken as she felt. He stood suddenly, knocking the rocker into jerky motion. He kept his back to her, but she could all but see him building his barriers again. Their night together in the storm, she knew, had softened things between them, but he wouldn't let go so easily. That had never been Linc's way.

Without turning, he said, "She's dead. I think I've always known that. Even at the beginning. And your father seemed to believe it easily enough." He stuck his hand in his pocket and pulled something out of it, keeping it in his fist. "He was so sure she was dead that he tried to have me thrown in jail for her murder."

Jillian sat up straighter, trying not to disturb Grace. She tried to keep her voice quiet. "What are you saying?"

He turned to face her again, his hands now cupped around the object from his pocket. He looked at her, his eyes hard, and she barely recognized him. Gone was the boy she had known and the man who had offered her hope and sanctuary the night of the storm. The man in front of her was trying very hard not to allow her to see past his barriers. But it was too late.

"I don't know, Jillian. But I think Grace has a gift—a gift you and I don't understand and probably never will. If she can . . . communicate with Lauren, then maybe we can find out what really happened all those years ago." His hands squeezed tightly over the object they held. "Assuming you really want to know the truth."

The baby whimpered in his sleep, and Jillian looked down at him in the cradle Linc had made for him. Her breasts responded to the sound, filling with milk and beginning to ache. She looked back at Linc. "I won't use my daughter, Linc. I'm . . . scared of what it might do to her. Grace has already been through so much. . . ." Her voice faded as she looked again at her sleeping daughter, noticing for what seemed the first time the small smattering of freckles on the bridge of her nose and how long her eyelashes were. Her much-loved bunny was clasped in the crook of her arm, one eye and most of its fur missing, an ear hanging by just a few threads. *How did you learn to love so hard, Gracie? Who taught you?*

Linc had moved closer to the bed. "I didn't suggest doing anything that might hurt Grace. But I knew before I asked that you wouldn't want to dig very deeply into what happened. He is your father after all is said and done, isn't he?"

She pulled back from him, anger and hurt mixing in equal doses. Her voice came out like a hiss. *"What are you saying?"*

He leaned closer to her. "Grace told me that Lauren said that you had something of mine. What is it, Jillian? And why won't you show it to me?"

Jillian thought of the box and of the letter inside and was tempted to show him, to let him know. But then she remembered the man who had crossed the dunes in a storm and had shone the light into her darkness and put his arms around her. Somewhere deep down inside of her, where the darkness still held her, she saw a glimmer of light and Linc standing in the center of it. No, she wouldn't tell him. Couldn't. He would need to understand on his own.

"I'm tired, Linc. I need to sleep now." She burrowed down on the pillow next to Grace, feeling her child's warm breath on her cheek.

"We're not done with this conversation. I have not worked all these years and put myself in a position to return here, only to find that I'm no further ahead than I was when I first left. I'm a patient man, Jillian. I will find out the truth eventually."

He dropped something on the bedclothes between her and Grace, then crossed the room toward the door. He seemed to stop himself with a visible effort when he reached the doorway. Without looking at her, he asked, "What time will Martha be back?"

Jillian kept her voice even. "Any minute now. She just ran to the grocery store to pick up a few things."

He paused for a moment before responding. "I'll wait downstairs until she gets here."

"Thank you," she said to the empty doorway, listening to his feet clattering down the steps. She picked up the small object that Linc had tossed on the blankets, knowing what she would see before she opened her palm. Smoothing her fingers over the wooden star, she wondered briefly how it had come to be in Linc's possession. She held it up to the white painted ceiling, clasped between her forefinger and thumb, and imagined the sky beyond it, her wooden star the only constellation in the stark whiteness.

"It shines, Jilly-bean. It shines like a real star." Grace spoke with a voice still filled with sleep, her eyes mere slits.

"It's trying to, Gracie. And I'm trying to let it."

Her daughter's hand found her own and squeezed. Before Jillian could squeeze back, Grace had fallen back asleep. She nestled down into the covers and put her arm around the little girl, listening to the soft breathing of her children with an odd sense of contentment, until she, too, fell asleep.

Linc stood in the sand, staring at the yellow tape that surrounded the sunken portion of the dune. *God's footprint.* That's what Janie Mulligan had called it. He smirked as he spotted Officer Mason Weber approaching him from the boardwalk. *More like God's kick in the pants.*

"Hey there, Mr. Rising."

As he shook hands, Linc stared at his reflection in the officer's Ray-Bans. The grip was firm and strong, and Linc knew that the slow drawl and affable smile hid a keen eye and bright intellect.

"Officer." He jerked his chin to indicate the yellow tape. "Thanks for coming out so quickly and marking this off. I don't think there's a real danger, but I didn't want anyone getting hurt before I had a chance to take a closer look."

"What do you think happened?"

Linc shifted his feet in the sand, feeling the grit of it inside his shoes. "It looks like some sort of man-made cave or something. Your sister Lessie seems to think it's an old tunnel used to hide from pirates or Indians. I'd like to do a full-fledged excavation right here."

Mason offered a stick of gum to Linc before putting one in his mouth. "Good luck with that. These dunes are protected. You'll have every environmental group breathing down your neck—from the turtle people to the wackos who love plants more than people—if you so much as bring a measuring tape to these dunes."

"Yeah, that's what Mrs. Michaels said. She called right after Lessie did. News travels fast on the island."

Mason wedged a toe of his boot into the sand, being careful to avoid a thatch of seaside spurge. "Yup. Sure does." His sunglasses looked up at Linc again. "So, what do you think you'll do? I've got a list of all the environmental groups that will need to have their say, but I figure you've probably already covered that."

"Yep. I've already navigated my way through a lot of the red tape involved in renovating the two houses here and a few I've done in Charleston." He watched as Mason neatly folded up his gum wrapper and stuck it in his shirt pocket. "I've got some people from the South Carolina Department of Health and Environmental Control coming tomorrow. I'm not sure if they'll agree, but I'm thinking I'll have to fill in the hole with more sand, but not until I make sure that whatever is under there is completely collapsed first. I have a feeling that if I'm going to do any more exploring, it will have to come from inside the house—assuming there's a connection."

Mason moved to the side of the large pit, staring into it. "Lessie is convinced there is. There are three other houses that were built at about the same time as this one and Jillian's. All three have either a secret room or a small tunnel that runs from the inside of the house down to the beach, to give the residents an escape route. With all the erosion, though, the tunnels are mostly underwater now. Not that it stopped one of the owners during Prohibition." He grinned at Linc. "High tide flooded his tunnel, but it didn't hurt his moonshine bottles, so he'd just leave them in there until the boat arrived at low tide to take them away."

Linc tilted his head back and looked at the silhouettes of the two houses against the cerulean sky. He'd always felt that houses, particularly old ones, talked to him. He seemed to know instinctively where the wood rot was worse, where the roof leaked, and what floor joists were cracked. It was as if they released their secrets to him in dreams, knowing that a part of him was a part of them, that his builder's hands would be able to help them. He stared at the two silhouettes again. But not these two; they kept their secrets, held tightly against old plaster and faded wood.

He thought of Grace and of her screaming when she'd seen the pit. *God's footprint.* The skin on the back of his neck inexplicably tightened, and he rubbed his fingers over it. "I'll figure it out somehow. And don't worry—I'll work with the environmental people on this to make sure I don't harm a leaf on any plant."

Officer Weber removed his sunglasses and stuck them in his shirt pocket. "Just keep me informed about what's going on here." He reached toward Linc again and shook his hand. "You look real familiar to me. Have we met before?"

Linc faced him and noted that the officer's eyes were a soft, unthreatening gray. "I don't know. Anything's possible, I guess."

Mason dropped his hand. "You do look familiar. Just can't place the face, that's all. It'll come to me eventually. Always does." He smiled broadly, not fooling Linc for a second with its casual warmness. "Well, that's all for now. Just keep me posted, and I'll come check on the progress every once in a while. People are supposed to stay off the dunes, but I'm going to bring out some warning signs just in case."

"Thanks. I appreciate it." Linc slid his own sunglasses on and stared at the retreating back of Officer Weber before turning to gaze back into the pit again. *God's footprint.* He could almost hear Janie Mulligan's voice in his ear, standing behind him and mixing with the soft ocean breeze. He stared at the steep impression in the sand, at the uprooted sea oats and grasses, and at the small puddle of water that had been left from the tidal storm surge. Leaning over, he caught his blurred reflection and that of the sun behind him, and wondered what it was that had sent little Gracie Ryan into a screaming fit.

Jillian stepped out of her car, then adjusted the straps of the baby carrier on her shoulders, feeling the soft warmth of her son against her chest. She reached in for the plate of lemon bars as Grace climbed out from the backseat, closed the car door, and leaned against it.

"Come on, Gracie. Let's go see Miss Mulligan." Jillian held out her hand.

Grace continued to stare at the small pink-painted cottage—a four-room structure built on squat brick pillars. Slowly, she lifted her hand and allowed herself to be led up the broken-shell path to the house.

After Jillian knocked, it took a long time for the door to be opened, and she was about to turn away when she heard the latch turn. It only opened a crack at first, and Jillian spotted Janie's deep brown eyes gazing inquisitively at her.

"It's me, Miss Janie—Jillian Parrish, and Gracie. I brought the baby, too, since you didn't get to see him for very long when you came to visit." She held up the plate in her hands. "And I brought lemon bars. Martha Weber told me they were your favorite. It was the least I could do to thank you for the beautiful hat you gave Ford."

Janie stepped back slowly, opening the door enough to let them pass. She held her finger to her lips. "Shh. Baby's taking her nap, so try not to wake her."

Quietly, they followed Janie past a small portable crib where the rag doll lay facedown on a teddy bear quilt, then through the house to the back deck. Once they were outside again, Janie turned to them with a smile. In her breathless voice she said, "Come see my garden."

Jillian put down the lemon bars on a patio table before following Janie down the deck steps.

Janie's house backed up to the marsh, and the briny odor and soft breeze left Jillian feeling slightly bereft, a painful tug of returning home after a long absence. She mentally shook herself and turned to Janie with a smile.

She had been to Janie's house with her grandmother many times as a child, but she didn't remember anything about it. She thought that maybe she had been too terrified of the rag doll that Janie treated as a real baby to notice much of anything else.

Gracie giggled, and Jillian turned around to see, noticing in amazement the brightly colored flower beds that hugged the outline of the house and clustered around the deck steps and back brick pillars. There were begonias and gardenias, and even a small splash of sunflowers, all gazing garishly back at the still brown-and-olive marsh like ladies of the evening sitting in the back pews of a church.

Jillian moved toward a low bush of tea roses the color of the setting sun and stooped, holding Ford's head so it wouldn't fall backward, to sniff the sweet rose aroma. She sniffed hard, but smelled nothing but wet earth and marsh air.

Gracie giggled again, and Jillian turned around in confusion. "They're not real, Jilly-bean. They're all pretend." She put her hand over her mouth and giggled again, looking up shyly at Janie.

With her finger and thumb, Jillian touched a rose petal, amazed at how real it felt against her skin.

Janie came to stand next to her. She held her fingers together and swung shyly side to side. "They're silk. I buy the fabric when Miz Weber takes me into Charleston, and then I make them all by myself. It takes a long time."

"I imagine it does." She bent closer to examine the tiny seams and the intricate folds that so closely resembled a real flower. "But how do you keep them looking so lovely out here? Doesn't the weather and the sun damage the fabric?"

Janie's eyes widened as she nodded with self-importance. "Oh yes. I have to be very careful. I bring them inside when the weather gets nasty. And I cover them when the sun is too strong or when the wind blows too hard. They're my children. I have to keep them safe."

Ford stirred, and Jillian nuzzled his head with her chin and he settled again. She didn't know where she'd learned that and was still amazed how just her touch could settle him. Janie's soft brown eyes watched her closely. Turning from the intense gaze, Jillian noticed how the beds of flowers were actually carefully arranged pots, each overflowing with blooms.

"You mean you lug all of these pots in and out of the house, depending on the weather?"

Janie nodded solemnly, her voice breathless. "Of course. If I don't take care of them, who will?"

Jillian turned to stare into the face of a realistic sunflower, its brown stamens individually rolled cords of silk. Gracie moved up beside her and slid her hand into Janie's. "It's okay, Janie. She said it was okay."

Janie squatted so that she was face-to-face with Gracie. No more words passed between them, but there seemed to be some form of communicating, an understanding that needed no spoken words. It occurred to Jillian to think it unusual, this immediate connection between her daughter and Janie Mulligan, an odd but thoroughly harmless woman who seemed as lost in the world as Gracie. Her child had always kept to herself, never making friends easily, and to see this friendship blossom warmed her. Jillian had always blamed herself for Grace's inability to fit in, to be like other children, as if her own inability to remember what it was like to be a child had somehow been passed down unwillingly to her daughter.

Her gaze captured the bloodred blooms of a Confederate Rose, and Jillian stepped toward it, completely amazed at its authenticity. She reached for the stem, then drew back sharply as the prick in her skin started to bleed. "Ow!"

Janie appeared at her side, Grace's hand still held in hers. "That's a real one."

"I could tell." Jillian raised her finger to her mouth and began to suck, the coppery taste of blood in her mouth.

Janie handed her a clean tissue from her dress pocket. "Don't tell the others," she whispered, indicating the beds of potted artificial plants, "but these are my favorites. I love the others, but these are real." She looked down at where Jillian was wrapping the tissue around her finger. "Even though the real ones can make you bleed."

Jillian looked out at the brown marsh, teeming with insects, reeds and mud, then turned back to the roses. "How on earth are these growing here? And this early in April, too? You must truly have a green thumb."

Janie blushed at the compliment and awkwardly knelt in front of the bush. "I dug the hole myself and filled it with dirt I had Mrs. Weber order for me from New England. I fertilize and prune and talk to them every day." She looked up at Jillian, shielding her eyes with her hand. "Sometimes our children are put into places that are very hard to survive. I've had a lot wilt and die, and it makes me so sad. But some do very nicely. I think the fight makes them stronger. I think it makes them better roses."

Jillian stood as Ford squirmed again, finally opening his eyes with a loud yawn. Janie smoothed the back of a finger along his cheek. "He sure is cute—just like his big sister." She winked down at Gracie, who was squatting down in front of the rose bush. Her eyes smiled into Jillian's. "You just fertilize, prune and talk to them. And in all that taking care of them, you find that your own heart is just about full to bursting with love and pride. It's no big secret."

Jillian felt her eyes burn, and for one horrifying moment, she thought she might cry. She blinked and turned away from Janie's scrutinizing gaze. "Come on, Gracie. We need to get going. Thank Miss Janie for showing us her beautiful garden."

Gracie surprised her by throwing her arms around the older woman. "Thanks, Miss Janie. You have beautiful flowers. Can I come back some time and help you take care of them?"

Janie squeezed her back. "That would be fun. You just need to make sure it's all right with your mama."

"Jilly-bean, please? Please?"

They both regarded her with identical pleading expressions, and it made Jillian want to laugh. "Sure. We could both help. It looks like a big job."

Janie let out an exaggerated sigh. "Taking care of children always is."

They went around the house instead of cutting through the inside, because Janie said that Baby was still sleeping. As Jillian buckled Ford into his car seat, she looked back to where Janie stood at the rear of her house, a corner of her garden visible from the road. As they pulled out, Jillian waved, watching the woman amid her bright-hued children disappear in the rearview mirror.

CHAPTER 12

JILLIAN SAT NEXT TO LAUREN ON THE WINDOW SEAT IN LAUREN'S room, watching the April sun glint off the silver bracelet Mason had given her as a sixteenth-birthday present. She was painting her toenails with Lauren's fuchsia polish and trying to pretend that nothing had changed between them since the summer before. She looked up from her big toe and watched Lauren pacing the room.

"Look, why don't we go swimming? I've been here for two days already, and we haven't gone down to the beach once. I want to see all the damage from the hurricane last November. My dad wouldn't let me come up with him when he came to check on the house at Thanksgiving—he said he could barely recognize the shoreline because of the storm. Besides, spring break is only a week, so we just have until Sunday to hang out."

Lauren stopped her pacing and folded her arms across her chest. "I don't want to. Besides, none of my bathing suits fit me anymore." Almost reluctantly, she added, "I've gained some weight." She flattened her hands against her abdomen, outlining a roundness Jillian had never seen on Lauren before.

For the first time, Jillian scrutinized her friend, noticing the baggy T-shirt she wore. So different from the tank shirts and halter tops Lauren always liked. "So what if you've gained a little weight? I didn't notice anything. Besides, you could afford to gain a little. You hardly eat anything anymore—like you're starving yourself on purpose or something. Come on—let's go to the beach. You can keep your T-shirt on over your bathing suit, if that makes you feel any better. I promise not to pay any attention."

Lauren stared at her for a few moments, and the look on her face alarmed Jillian. It was a look of desperation and misery—the look of someone caught in a riptide who was slowly being dragged out to sea.

Jillian stood. "What is it? Tell me, Lauren—what's wrong?"

Lauren opened her mouth to answer, but stopped when the front doorbell rang. She walked quickly to her closed bedroom door and put her ear up close to it, motioning for Jillian to stay quiet. Jillian heard Linc's voice below, talking with Mrs. Mills.

After a moment, Jillian heard Mrs. Mills climb the stairs and knock on the bedroom door. "Lauren, it's Linc. Will you see him?"

Lauren pressed her forehead against the door and squeezed her eyes shut. "No, Mama. I don't want to see him. Tell him I'm not here."

There was a pause on the other side of the door. "This is the third time he's been here today, Lauren. You're going to have to see him sometime—it might as well be now."

Lauren's voice sounded frantic. "No! I don't ever want to see him again. Tell him that. And tell him not to come back."

There was no answer, just the sound of Mrs. Mills' footsteps retreating back down the stairs.

Lauren moved back to the window seat and peered out. Jillian joined her. They didn't wait long until the top of Linc's dark head appeared below them as he made his way down to the beach. When he reached the boardwalk, he stopped and turned. Jillian ducked back behind the curtain, spying at him through a crack in the fabric. But Lauren stared down at him from the window, leaving no doubt that she wanted Linc to see her.

He stared up at Lauren, but there was no malice in his expression. Only hurt and confusion. Shoving his hands into his pockets, he turned around and disappeared down the beach, not looking back again.

Something heavy and awful pressed at Jillian's heart. How could this be happening? She depended on the closeness she shared with Linc and Lauren as much as she needed air to breathe. The thought of not having them here on the island to return to each summer felt as if somebody had set her adrift on the ocean, in a boat without an oar. "What's wrong?" she heard herself ask in a voice she barely recognized.

Lauren avoided her eyes. "I broke up with Linc. I don't want to talk about it."

Jillian tugged at her arm, forcing Lauren to face her. "Are you sure? Maybe I can help you make up with him."

Lauren pulled away. "It's not that easy. Besides, I don't love him anymore. I told him that, but he doesn't want to believe it." She smiled at Jillian's wide look of shock. "Look, it doesn't mean that you can't be friends with him anymore. It just means that Linc and I won't be spending time together, that's all. But you can still be friends with both of us. That part won't change."

There was something else. Something Lauren wasn't telling her. Something that made Lauren avoid looking Jillian in the eye.

"Is there somebody else?" Jillian's voice came out in a whisper.

Lauren didn't say anything for a while, and Jillian had begun to think she wouldn't answer her when Lauren finally spoke. "Yes. There is."

"Who?"

Lauren sat back down on the window seat and stared out, not answering.

"Is it Mason?"

Lauren smiled a little and shook her head. "No. Mason and I are just friends. Besides, I think he's only got eyes for you."

Jillian blushed but didn't look away. "Then who?"

"Somebody who's different from any boy I've ever dated. For one thing, he's more mature and treats me as a woman and not a girl." She smiled softly. "A lot of people think he's cold and unfeeling, but with me he's warm and caring."

Jillian moved closer, a sick feeling in her stomach. "Who is it?"

Instead of answering, Lauren got up from the window seat and motioned Jillian to do the same. Then, kneeling before it, she lifted the lid, the brass hinges squeaking softly. "I want to show you something."

She leaned inside, and Jillian leaned with her to see over Lauren's shoulder. She watched as Lauren's fingers traced along the bottom of the storage compartment under the lid and then stopped on an almost invisible button.

Lauren moved her head to look at Jillian. "Do you see it? You have to pretty much feel for it, but when you find it, all you do is press." She pushed on it, and Jillian heard a faint clicking noise and watched as the side panel inside the window seat popped open.

"Wow. Has that always been there?"

Lauren shrugged, then reached in farther to take something out of the hidden compartment. "I don't know. It's been here since we moved in, is all I know. I'm pretty sure my parents don't know it's here."

She sat back on the floor, her hands cupped around whatever she'd taken from the compartment, and regarded Jillian evenly. "I need to give you something."

Jillian sat next to her, trying to push back the feelings of panic and excitement that spread through her. "Is it a present? Because my birthday isn't until July." She tried to make Lauren smile, but failed.

"Can you keep a secret?"

Deeply offended, Jillian said, "You know I can. I never told your parents about that pack of cigarettes my grandmother found in her kitchen."

"This is much more serious. You have to swear that you'll keep this safe and that you'll never open it after today." She paused for a moment, looking down at her hands. "I might have to go away for a while—Don't worry. I'll let you know where. But I won't be able to bring a lot of stuff with me, and I didn't want my parents to find this. So can you swear that you'll keep this safe for me?"

Jillian held up her right hand. "I pinky swear."

Lauren closed her eyes for a moment. "No, Jillian. Just promise me. This isn't kid stuff I'm talking about."

In that instant, Jillian realized that Lauren was already gone from her, that her friend had already crossed that invisible barrier into adulthood and had left Jillian behind to find her own way.

Jillian swallowed, then slowly lowered her hand. "I promise."

Lauren leaned over and put a small wooden box in Jillian's upturned hands. "Here."

The solid box of pine felt cold in her hand, and she felt even colder when she saw the two intertwining *L*s carved in the lid. When she lifted it, she could hear something small and solid rolling around inside. Lauren opened the lid, and Jillian saw a folded note and a wooden heart that had been pierced with a gold chain to wear around a neck.

Lauren stilled her hand when Jillian reached for the note. "I don't want you to read it." She picked up the necklace. "But I wanted this. Linc made the heart for me, remember? I'm going to put it on now, and I'll never take it off. It will always make me think of you and Linc after I'm gone." She fastened the chain around her neck, then put the lid back on the box.

Jillian wiped her eyes with her fingertips. "How long will you be gone?"

"I don't know. It might be a long time."

Jillian gripped Lauren's hand. "Don't do this, Lauren—you're only seventeen. Your parents love you. You've got friends and a happy family and only one more year before you graduate. Please. Don't do this."

Lauren pulled her hand away and stood. "You don't understand, and I can't explain it to you. Just trust me that I'm following my heart and that I know things will work out in the end."

Jillian dropped her pretense of trying to be mature and began to cry. "I don't want you to go. I know it's selfish, and I know you have a lot more to lose than I do, but I don't want you to go."

Jillian was surprised to see tears in Lauren's eyes, too. "I know it's hard. We both just got to get through this. It'll work out in the end. You'll see."

"Does Linc know about it?"

A stricken look passed through Lauren's eyes. "No. And he can't know—promise me you won't tell him. He'd kill me if he found out."

"He loves you, Lauren. He'd never hurt you. You know that. Maybe if you tell him, he'll help you out and you won't have to leave."

Lauren was sobbing now, her head on her folded arms on the window seat cushion. "No! Now promise me. Promise me you won't tell him."

She pressed her forehead against her friend's, as if to somehow keep their friendship within them, to maybe ignore the sure knowledge that it had already fled. "I promise, Lauren. I'll keep it safe. And I won't tell anyone." She squeezed Lauren tightly, and Lauren hugged her back as Jillian felt her friend's tears on her cheeks. They cried and rocked together, sitting on the hard floor of Lauren's bedroom, while Jillian clutched the small box with the entwined *L*s and sharp corners that bit into the skin of her palm.

Jillian leaned back against the sofa, stretching her legs out in front of her, feeling the sharp edges of the box with her fingers. She wasn't sure why she'd brought it from her bedroom. She'd had it in her hand when Gracie had called to her, forgetting that she'd been holding it as she made her way downstairs. But now, sitting opposite her daughter, she realized Gracie was the last person she wanted to see the box. There had never been a question worth asking, or that Jillian hadn't want to answer, that Gracie hadn't asked. Shoving the box under the sofa behind her, she watched Gracie stack the folded fliers advertising Jillian's new catering services into small piles against the wall.

Spot stood nearby, watching closely. Occasionally, his gaze would drift from Gracie, as if following the passage of an unseen person across the room. Jillian frowned at him, then flicked her bare foot in his direction, making him run from the room.

Gracie finished placing the last stack against the wall and straightened. "What if nobody reads these and nobody calls you to order food and stuff?"

Jillian tried to be flip and pretend that she hadn't asked herself the same question over and over already. "Well, first I'll have a tantrum and throw things and probably use bad language. Then I'll make prank calls to everybody on the island, telling them that their refrigerators are running. Then I'll rob a bank so I won't need their business, anyway."

Gracie regarded her solemnly. "Okay. But can I help you with the prank phone calls?"

Jillian nudged her with her bare toe, and they both started laughing. Jillian reached her hand out to tickle Grace. "Come on, Silly Pie. Help me up, and we'll think of something fun to do. We've been working all afternoon, and I think we deserve a break before you tackle your spelling homework."

Grace grabbed both of Jillian's hands and let out an exaggerated groan as she hoisted her mother to her knees.

Standing, Jillian asked, "So, what would you like to do?"

Gracie frowned. "Mrs. Michaels said I needed to practice my handwriting. She says she can't read it. She also wanted to know all about the night that Ford was born and why Linc was here, but I remember hearing Mrs. Weber tell you that even though Mrs. Michaels is a wonderful teacher, she's also the biggest gossip, so I didn't say anything."

Jillian looked at her daughter for a long time, trying to phrase a response that would adequately address all the topics in Grace's monologue. She finally gave up. "We can practice your handwriting after dinner. Let's do something fun now."

Gracie ran to the bookshelf and pulled out a CD case that had been sitting on the portable stereo. "Let's listen to music. Linc said I could borrow this, and I haven't listened to it yet."

"When did he give you that?" Jillian walked over and took the CD.

"A few days ago. He was checking the air in our tires because he said the tires looked low. He had his stereo outside and it was playing, and I liked the music. He said I could borrow it if I'd be careful."

"I see," she said, even though she really didn't. She looked down at the cover. *The Tams Greatest Hits.* Reluctantly, she smiled. "This is good stuff."

She walked over to the stereo and popped in the CD. "We can't play it too loudly because Ford is napping."

After pushing the PLAY button, she moved over to the sofa and sat next to Gracie. As soon as the music started playing, she noticed Grace's fingers and hands moving to the beat. Then she looked down at their feet, both pairs bare with matching toenail polish, and saw all four moving to the same rhythm. She nudged Grace with her elbow. "Wanna dance?"

Gracie grinned. "Sure!"

They got to their feet. "This is going to be scary, but bear with me. Do you want to be the boy or the girl?"

"I'll be the girl. You can be the boy."

"Thanks. OK. Give me your hands. Now you're a bit shorter than me, so we'll have to make allowances. Instead of putting your hand on my shoulder, put it on my elbow. That's right."

Jillian put her hand on Gracie's back between the shoulder blades. "Now, if you were taller, I'd put my hand on the small of your back, but we'll just have to make do. And this hand"—she reached down and grabbed Grace's—"goes in mine." She smiled in satisfaction that they had managed to get that far. "Are you ready?"

Gracie grinned up at her. "Yep!"

The opening bars of "Be Young, Be Foolish, Be Happy" began, and for a moment, Jillian could almost feel the sand beneath her feet and the light of a summer moon on her face. Slowly, she began to count out the dance steps from memory for Grace, smiling down at the earnest expression on her daughter's face.

"Just follow my feet. Everything I do, you do, but backward. Okay. One, two, now step. One, two, and rock back. Now rock forward." Jillian grinned, ignoring the way her daughter's feet trampled her own. "See? Isn't that easy?"

"Are my feet supposed to be on top of yours most of the time?"

Jillian snorted. "Not exactly. I'm afraid you got your dancing talent from me."

They both laughed and put their feet in the starting position again. Jillian cleared her throat. "Okay. Let's start again. One, two, now step." Their knees bumped as they both tried to lead at the same time. They stumbled together but managed to stay upright as they tried to fumble their way through the remaining steps, eventually giving up completely and just bouncing to the rhythm of the music, their hands clasped together, their voices shrieking to the words of the song.

"If Gracie wants to learn how to dance the shag, I think she'd learn faster watching somebody who actually knows what he's doing."

They both stopped in midbounce and turned toward the voice. Linc stood in the doorway, a measuring tape and clipboard in one hand and a heart-stopping grin on his face. For a moment, Jillian found it hard to catch her breath, and stood there staring at him.

His thumb indicated the open front door. "I saw you through the screen and knocked, but you couldn't hear me." He gave her a lopsided grin. "I thought I'd better intervene now, before Grace's dancing ability is ruined forever."

Feeling flustered and not really knowing why, Jillian attempted to smooth her ruffled hair and pull down her old shorts to cover at least a little bit of thigh. She hadn't seen Linc since they'd argued, and his presence now was doing strange things to her. Maybe it was the memory of Lauren's box, or maybe it was the fact that she was wearing shorts that were too short and her hair was a mess.

His eyes flickered for a moment over her chest before returning to her face, and she blushed, realizing she wore an old blouse that was stretched way too tight over her lactating breasts.

She crossed her arms over her chest. "We were working, and I wasn't expecting any company."

He smirked. "I can see that. You must be exhausted from all that work."

She smiled back at him. "Oh, not that exhausted. How are you?"

"Good. Busy." He paused for a moment, looking her up and down again. "You look smaller than when I last saw you."

"I think you mean 'less big.' Amazing what losing eight pounds, nine ounces can do for a girl's figure."

His lips twitched. "I was going to measure your kitchen and draw up some plans for your expansion we talked about a while back. I'm still waiting on permits from all the environmental groups for excavating the dune and had a bit of free time, so . . ."

He stopped, and nobody spoke as the Tams sang the first line of "What Kind of Fool Do You Think I Am?" Finally, Jillian said, "Thanks. That would be great. I'm not promising I'll actually have the work done, but if things go well, I'd like to have an estimate to put in my business plan."

"Nothing wrong with thinking ahead. You'll also have to discuss it with the National Trust. I had this house listed on the register before I renovated. It helped me financially, even though they're pretty tough about what they'll allow you to do."

Grace, bored with the conversation, moved between them and chirped, "I want to see Linc do the shag."

Linc raised his eyebrows. "I can't shag alone. I need a partner." He reached his hand out to Grace, but she shook her head.

"No. I want to see you dance the shag with Jilly-bean. Then I can learn how it's supposed to go."

Jillian forced a smile, wondering again where the awkwardness between them had come from. "It'll be just like old times. Except I'm a little heavier now and it might hurt your toes a bit more when I stomp on them."

Gracie plopped herself on the sofa and crossed her legs, her elbows on her knees as she smiled at them expectantly.

Linc put down his tape and clipboard, then shrugged his shoulders as if it didn't matter to him. But there was an intensity in his gaze as he approached Jillian with his arms outstretched. "You don't scare me." As they had done so many times before, they clasped hands, and then he placed his other hand on the small of her back, moving her closer to him. She stumbled into him and became aware of a slow heat that filled every pore on her skin until she thought she might be having a hot flash. She waved her free hand in front of her face. "Pregnancy hormones," she said before resting her hand on his shoulder.

This is Linc, she kept reminding herself as she felt his muscles move under her palm and felt his hand on her back through the thin cotton of her blouse.

"Relax," he said, looking down at her with a flash of amusement in those dark gray eyes. He started moving and she tried to follow his lead, crashing into him as he went forward and she forgot to go backward.

"Sorry," she said, completely flustered now and not even sure she could remember her own name, much less the steps to the shag. *What is wrong with me?* She glanced over at Gracie and saw the little girl roll her eyes.

Linc moved her into the starting position again. "Look, you need to relax. And forget about the steps. Just listen to the music and follow my lead."

The Tams were in the middle of "Untie Me," one of her favorites, and after a few false starts, she allowed the music to take over. She shifted her hips to the music, feeling Linc's hand slide across her back, touching bare skin as her blouse rode up. She tried to pretend that it didn't matter, that she barely noticed it, but she felt the sweat start between her breasts as her body reacted to the heat.

At first, she looked down at their feet, but as her confidence grew she was able to look up into his face, and immediately wished she hadn't. He was so close she could feel his breath on her cheek, smelling of mint and beer. He was watching her the way she remembered he watched Lauren as they danced together, and it made her want to throw back her head and laugh like Lauren had, the sound contagious enough to make others smile.

He shifted her closer and there was barely any space between them, and she realized then why she felt awkward. There was no pregnancy to hide behind, no physical barrier and no maternal image. She was a young girl again, dancing on the beach with bare feet and suntanned legs, and this time she did throw back her head and laugh.

The music ended and they stopped dancing, but he didn't release her. She didn't pull away, either. There was something holding them together, making it impossible for her to step back. His dark eyes seemed almost black to her, his expression indecipherable, and for a long moment she had the strangest thought that he was going to kiss her. And that she wouldn't mind if he did.

They seemed to remember Grace's presence at the same moment, because they both turned toward the little girl. And then Jillian heard Ford crying on the baby monitor and felt the letdown of her milk at the same time she saw the growing wet spots on her blouse.

Mortified, she stepped back, almost relieved to find the spell between them broken. She turned away, her back to him. "I've got to get the baby. Gracie, stay out of Linc's way while he measures the kitchen, okay?"

Without waiting for a response, she dashed up the stairs, still feeling the heat of his hand on her back and trying to shake off the overwhelming feeling that there had been a fourth person in the room watching them in the steps to a dance that neither of them had truly forgotten.

CHAPTER 13

L INC STOOD IN THE KITCHEN, FACING THE STAR CHART ON THE WALL, almost mesmerized by the tiny, neat handwriting labeling the constellation of Boötes the Herdesman. NEKKAR, SEGINUS, IZAR, ACTURUS. He said the familiar names in his head, picturing the glowing orange Acturus and remembering how Jillian had once told him it was her favorite star.

He traced his finger around the constellation, noticing the precise placement between the Big and Little Dippers, and imagining Jillian leaning over the chart with pencil and ruler to make sure everything was correct. It was so like her, trying to capture and make sense of something as vast and confusing as the universe. She charted it and studied it, and still found a place to hope for the sight of a new star.

He turned his back on the chart, trying to wipe his mind clean of thoughts of Jillian just as easily. He shouldn't have danced with her. He shouldn't have touched her. But once he had, he couldn't seem to stop. The warmth of her underneath his fingertips and the smell of her so close had made him almost forget who she was. And he'd almost kissed her. There was no doubt in his mind that if they hadn't been interrupted, he would have pulled her closer in his arms and kissed her. And he could tell by the look in her eyes that she would have let him.

Whatever secrets there might be between them, there was a strange force that seemed to propel them toward each other, like the magnetic north on a compass forcing the arrow to point in its direction. Not for the first time, he wondered if it had always been that way between him and Jillian, but that with Lauren in the middle the way to true north had been blurred. He shook his head. He couldn't allow himself to act on that attraction. There were secrets he needed to unbury, and there wasn't a doubt in his mind that she would do anything she could to distract him.

After a frustrating swipe of his hand through his hair, he picked up his measuring tape and began determining the dimensions of the kitchen layout, jotting down numbers and ideas on his clipboard. He was so completely immersed in what he was doing that at first he didn't notice that he had company. A movement to his left brought his head up, and he started at the sight of Grace's cat, Spot, sitting on the kitchen counter in a confident stance that dared anyone to ask him to leave.

Their gazes met for a moment, and Linc had the strangest feeling that he wasn't looking at a mere animal and that it would speak to him at any moment. He grinned to himself and bent back to his work, but stopped again when another movement from the cat made him look up.

The cat was still on the counter, but his head was turned slightly, eyeing something over Linc's shoulder. Linc turned around, expecting to see Jillian or Gracie, but only saw an empty room. *Dust motes.* The cat must be looking at dust in the light from the window.

Slightly unnerved, he faced the cat again and watched as the animal continued to follow the progress of the dust motes move behind Linc toward the door. With a loud meow, the cat leapt off the counter, landing on the floor with a soft thud, and trotted out the doorway and into the foyer.

Realizing his mouth had gone dry, Linc moved to the cabinet and pulled out a glass. As he began filling it with water from the sink, he felt a tap on his back. The glass slid from his hand, shattering against the faucet, and spraying him with shards of glass as he spun around.

"Sorry, Linc." Gracie smiled up at him, her hands clasped behind her back.

Linc felt his heart pound all the way up to his head. *I'm going to have a heart attack.* He tried to smile back while sucking on his finger where he'd been cut by the flying glass. "That's all right. You startled me, that's all." In truth, he'd never been so scared in his life, but he'd be damned if he'd admit that to a seven-year-old. "Did you need anything?"

She shook her head but didn't move away. Instead, she tilted her head as if listening to somebody standing beside her and speaking to her.

Swallowing thickly, he asked, "Are you talking to Lauren?"

Slowly, she nodded.

The hair on the back of his neck stood up, and he caught sight of Spot in the threshold again, his gaze staring at something against the wall behind Grace.

He grabbed Grace's arm, her hand still held behind her back, and pulled her out of the kitchen in a desperate need to exit the room. Once in the foyer, he squatted down and looked the little girl in the face. "What does Lauren look like, Gracie?"

She looked down at her feet, clad in red sparkly shoes that seemed too small for her, avoiding his eyes.

More gently, he asked, "How old is she, and what does she sound like?"

Keeping her head down, she shrugged again.

He felt vaguely relieved. He could deal with a child's vivid imagination. He doubted he could handle the alternative.

Gently squeezing her shoulders, he said, "She's just your imaginary friend, isn't she? You just heard your mother say her name once and that's where you got the name Lauren from, didn't you? You don't need to be embarrassed. It's a good thing to have such a great imagination."

He stood, gently patting her on her head. "I need to find a Band-Aid. Could you send me in the right direction?"

She looked up at him with those beautiful brown eyes. "She told me to give you this." She brought her hands around to her front, something bulky squeezed between her two flattened palms. Slowly, she lifted the hand on top.

Linc gripped the newel post, feeling foolishly like he was going to faint. In her hands lay the box he had made for Lauren so long ago, the *L*s of their first names intertwined just as their lives had once been. He somehow found words to speak. "Who gave you that?"

"It's Jilly-bean's. She keeps it hidden because that's what Lauren told her to do a long time ago. But Lauren thinks you should have it now. There's something inside she wants you to see."

For a long time he didn't say anything, just stared at the box in the little girl's hand, his breathing slow and deep. Finally, he reached for it and plucked it up with his uninjured hand. The wood was as smooth and warm as a young girl's skin, and he thought for a moment that he could smell Lauren's sun-warmed hair. His fingers traced the two *L*s on the lid, and he stared at the scar between the thumb and index finger of his right hand that he had gotten while carving the second letter. It had bled for a long time, almost as long as his heart had bled for the girl to whom he'd given the box.

He turned it over in his hand, listening for any sound to give him a clue as to what might be inside. He even put a hand over the lid, about to twist it off, but stopped. He looked back at Grace, who was staring at the closed box with anticipation. With a great deal of effort, he held it out to her. "I can't open this without your mother's permission. It wouldn't be right."

Grace's brows knitted. "Why not? It belongs to Lauren, and she gave you permission."

She tried to push the box back toward him, but he held firm. He felt the temptation grab at him like a wave at high tide. It would be so easy to open the lid and look inside without Jillian ever knowing anything about it.

Still, something held him back—and not just the wrongness of it. He admitted that part of him wanted Jillian to give it to him herself, to prove to him that she had nothing to hide. Another part of him was afraid to know. *Know what?* He held the box tightly for a long moment. *There are some who always believed your innocence.* Why was it so important to him that he believe this of her? *She* didn't matter; only the truth did. So why didn't he open the box?

Before he could argue himself out of it, he forced the box back into Grace's hand. "Take this back and hide it where you found it. If your mother wants me to see it, she'll show it to me."

Grace frowned, her lower lip trembling slightly, and Linc quickly sat down on the stairs to look her in the eye. "Why don't you tell me where to get a Band-Aid, and when I'm done, and if it's okay with your mother, I'll take you for ice cream."

A bright smile lit her face, and Linc wondered for a moment if he'd been had. "The Band-Aid box is in the medicine cabinet in the hall bath upstairs." Then she turned around, and with pigtails flopping, skipped into the front parlor.

He turned and headed up the stairs, trying to forget the smoothness of the wood against the bare skin of his hand.

When he reached the upstairs landing, he turned right, just the opposite of his own home, and began to cross the hall. He had almost made it to the bathroom when he made the mistake of looking into the open doorway of the third bedroom.

This bedroom was the smallest of the three, and the walls were still white, as he had left them. But someone had stenciled gold stars around the perimeter of the ceiling, and in the middle of the far wall, directly across from the door, was written a poem in glowing gold letters.

> *The Angels were all singing out of tune,*
> *And hoarse with having little else to do,*
> *Excepting to wind up the sun and moon*
> *Or curb a runaway young star or two.*

Linc felt a surge of warmth in his chest as he read the neatly stenciled words from Lord Byron's poem, and remembered. The summer before Lauren's disappearance, he'd kept up a steady employment of doing odd jobs on the island and a few in Charleston. He was known as being very handy with wood, and word of mouth had been free advertising.

That summer, he was hired to put wainscoting in a baby's nursery in one of Charleston's old mansions on Meeting Street. It was probably that house that had started his love affair with old architecture, and he'd never forgotten it—nor the beautiful room designed for a child, not even born yet, but loved and cherished sight unseen. He had loved the poem painted on the wall above the canopied crib and had shared it with Jillian one night as they lay on the beach, counting stars. She had told him it reminded her of the two of them, two tetherless stars adrift in the universe, waiting for whatever sun or moon to pull them close.

He smiled at the memory and was about to turn away when a movement in the corner of the room caught his gaze. Jillian sat in a rocking chair, one he recognized from the front porch, cradling the baby. Her head was down, looking at Ford, and Linc could only see the bottom portion of her face. Her mouth was curved in a half-smile as she bent forward to kiss the top of the baby's head and then leaned back against the rocking chair, her eyes closed.

It was then Linc realized the baby was nursing. Jillian's blouse was unbuttoned all the way and rippling slightly in the breeze from the open window, her bra exposing one full pale breast. Ford's head covered anything that Jillian might consider indecent, but the effect on Linc was the same as if she stood before him naked. He suddenly felt as if he'd stepped off a sandbar into water over his head.

He wanted to turn away or close his eyes, but found that he couldn't. He was even more embarrassed to realize that it had less to do with her near nakedness than it did with the maternal tableau she had unwittingly set herself in. He watched as the baby reached up a small hand and grasped hold of a fistful of Jillian's hair and tugged. She smiled, and it made her glow with maternal satisfaction, and made Linc choke on undisguised desire for this woman.

He must have made a sound, because Jillian's eyes snapped open, her gaze meeting his. The baby mewled, slapping his fist against her bare chest. They stared at each other in the silence, only the baby's nursing sounds filling the air between them.

Finally, Linc cleared his throat. "I'm taking Gracie for ice cream," he said, feeling completely lost.

Jillian nodded, not saying anything, and just kept her expressive brown eyes settled on him. He turned away, forgetting the Band-Aids and everything else except getting as far away from Jillian as he could, and away from all the feelings she seemed to evoke in him.

Jillian grasped Grace's hand and paused at the front entrance of the Low Country Day School as groups of recently dismissed children streamed by them. Hearing her name called, she turned and waved as she spotted Martha Weber coming toward her.

"Hello, Mrs. Weber. What are you doing at the school today?"

The older woman smiled down at Grace, patting her head and stealing a glance at Ford asleep in the front pouch Jillian wore. "Please, Jillian, call me Martha. Otherwise, you'll make me feel older than I am."

Jillian smiled. "Old habit. Sorry."

They turned together and began walking toward the parking lot. "I work at the library every Friday afternoon. Lessie's children go here, and they get such a kick out of seeing Grandma in the library." She smiled, deep creases forming at the corner of her eyes. "You aren't by any chance heading in my direction, are you? Lessie's taking Mary Ellen to the dentist right after school, and if you're heading right home, I'd love to hitch a ride with you instead. Besides, I have all those plates from the wonderful goodies you've been sending our way to give back to you. Joe and I have gained about five pounds apiece. But I say it's a small price to pay to be able to be your official tasters."

Jillian smiled. "I'd be happy to—but only if you're not in a hurry. I was planning on taking a long walk before heading home." She glanced down at the sleeping baby. "Ford only seems to like to nap in his little pouch. As soon as I take him out or lay him down, his eyes pop open for good and then he's cranky because he hasn't had enough sleep."

Martha held out her hand to Grace, placing the little girl between the two women as they walked. "Well, then. We'll walk slowly." She winked at Jillian. After a few moments of silence, Martha said, "Have you forgiven Mason yet? That boy is beside himself with guilt. When the storm hit, he headed right over to your house, but got called to a bad accident involving a fallen tree over on Ocean Highway. He tried to call you, but your phone was dead. He even got Mr. Rising's cell number from Lessie, but nobody answered." She shook her head slowly. "He had two more emergencies he had to see about before he made it to your house—and that was at about the same time the ambulance showed up. It's eating him alive knowing that it was his fault that you were alone during the storm and had that baby by yourself."

Jillian paused and placed her hand on Martha's arm. "I wasn't alone, remember? And everything worked out. I haven't blamed Mason for a minute—and I've told him that at least a hundred times. The change in the weather was a fluke of nature, something that not even the forecasters had predicted. No, I don't blame Mason. He's a dear friend, and I don't want to be on his conscience." She smiled secretively. "I'll bake him something real good to get his mind off of it."

Martha smiled back, relief evident on her face. "By the way, I've been meaning to ask you if your house sustained any damage during the storm. We had several roof tiles blown off. Nothing as serious as when Hugo blew through in 1989 and demolished all those houses on the south end of the island, but it was pretty scary for a while. Nobody saw the Gray Man, though, so I guess it wasn't too serious."

Jillian tried to get Martha's attention to switch the subject, but

Grace had heard every word. The little girl turned to Martha. "Who's the Gray Man?"

"Oh, you haven't heard of him, have you? Nobody's really sure who he was when he was alive—just that he was somebody who really loved Pawleys. His ghost appears before a hurricane or serious storm to warn people. Whoever sees him, if they're smart enough, will leave the island, and their property will be spared. And if they don't"—she leaned down toward Grace's face with an ominous look—"then all is lost."

Grace stared back matter-of-factly. "I haven't met him yet. I wonder if he knows Lauren."

Jillian had a litany of excuses prepared when Martha glanced over at her, but instead of seeing a confused expression on the older woman's face, Jillian saw only understanding. Gracie broke free of their hands and ran ahead to look at something in the grass. Martha turned to face Jillian.

"I've known Janie Mulligan too long to try and think that the human mind is all the same. Some of us are gifted in ways others will never understand." They both turned to look at Gracie before Martha continued. "Even Janie. There are some who say she's slow and dull-witted, but I think she's one of the smartest people I've ever met. She's not like you and me—or anybody else I know, for that matter—but she sees the truth in everything and won't be cowed into keeping it to herself."

Gracie ran back to them, a broken conch shell in her outstretched hand. "Look, Jilly-bean! I'm going to keep it for my collection." She dumped it inside Jillian's backpack, along with the bottle tops, rocks, sticks and shells that Gracie had added to her collection on a walk the previous morning, and Jillian hadn't had a chance to clean out yet.

Gracie ran on ahead of them again and the two women began walking, keeping a slow pace so Gracie could catch up to them. They passed under a huge old oak, its thick and ancient branches hovering low over the road, making them duck to be able to pass. Jillian squinted, wishing she had remembered to throw her sunglasses into the backpack. Eager to steer the conversation away from Grace, she said, "Who is Janie Mulligan? I mean, who's her family, and how did it happen that you and my grandmother have always taken care of her?"

Martha looked down, her mouth set in a firm line. "Well, Barbara—

that was Janie's mother—was a good friend of mine and your grand-mother's. We'd known each other since elementary school. Barbara and Annabelle were quite a few years older than me, but we lived close by and I walked to school with them every day from my first day at school. We were best friends since then on, even after we were married and had our own families." She looked up at the sky as a plane buzzed in the far dis-tance. "I guess that's what happens when you grow up in a small place and never leave."

A faraway smile lit her face. "It was so nice having children together—even though their ages were pretty spread out. Annabelle had your father first, so he was the oldest. I don't think I had my first until your daddy was twelve or so." She grinned, and she looked like a young girl again. "And then I had all of mine right in a row, and then I was drowning in diapers for a long time, so most of those years are a blur. But I do remember how we'd take all the kids to the beach and go oyster catching in the marsh, just like we'd done when we were chil-dren."

They stopped for a moment, watching as Gracie sat down to plop off a red sparkly shoe and empty it of gravel before Martha continued. "And then Janie was the last to be born. Her mother only had Bill, her eldest, and a bunch of babies born and buried too soon. . . ." She paused, her brows folding together in her sun-browned face. "Well, we knew Janie was different right from the start. The doctors said it was because Barbara had her so late in life—she was almost forty-four when Janie was born, after all. She was real slow-like; never crawled until she up and walked one day when she was three. Wasn't potty trained until she was in school full-time. But so beautiful, and what a sweetheart she was—still is."

They walked in silence for a few moments, watching Gracie zigzag in the grass, picking up more treasures and stuffing them in the already bulging pockets of her shorts. Jillian lowered her face to brush the soft fuzz of Ford's head, smelling his sweet baby scent. "So where's her fam-ily now? Is there anybody left on the island?"

"No—nobody left. Just me. Tragic, really. Bill drowned right after high school—he was trying to save a swimmer and they were both lost. Barbara and Tom were never the same after that. And then they were killed in a car accident a few years later. Janie was already a legal adult, living in her parents' house when it happened, and she just stayed there. The house was paid for and they'd left her enough money to get by, and that's where she's been ever since. She's lived there her whole life—except for one year she spent in Charleston when she was fifteen."

Jillian tried to picture a younger version of Janie on her own in a big city, but couldn't. "Did they send her to school there?"

"Sort of. It was a convent—but they boarded troubled teens and taught them practical things. I think that's where she learned so much about cultivating flowers." She sent Jillian a wry smile. "Not that there's a lot of cultivating involved with silk flowers."

Jillian thought of all the hard work it took to keep the silk flowers clean and dry, with the constant hauling in and out of the house, but kept her thoughts to herself.

"I don't know if it was such a good idea, though. She seemed so much more withdrawn, more fragile even, when she came back."

They had returned to the parking lot just as Ford had started to stir. Martha smiled brightly as Jillian unlocked the car and began strapping Ford into the infant seat. "But she seems happy now and mostly able to take care of herself, so we let her be. I see that she's become good friends with Gracie."

They both turned to see the little girl skipping toward them, her hands and clothes smeared with dirt and sand. She stopped near the car and smiled hesitantly up at Jillian. A large rock fell out of her overstuffed pocket and rolled at her feet. "I think I got a little bit of dirt on my fingers. Are you mad, Jilly-bean?"

Jillian bit back a laugh. "No, sweetie. I'm not mad." She made sure Grace was buckled in securely, then slid behind the steering wheel to drive the short distance to Martha's house. When they arrived, Jillian turned to her daughter. "You'll have to wait outside for a minute while I go in with Mrs. Weber to get my dishes. I know she doesn't want little dirty footprints all over her floors."

"Oh, don't be silly, Jillian." Martha turned to Grace. "There's a faucet right over there, by the side of the house, and a towel on a peg right next to it. Just rinse off your hands and face and come on in. I've got fresh-baked cookies waiting for somebody to enjoy them. They're probably not as good as your mama's, but I think they're pretty close."

She winked at Jillian as Gracie threw open her car door and skipped toward the side of the house. Jillian climbed out of the car and lifted Ford back into his pouch.

Martha held open the screen door but stopped Jillian with a hand on her arm, her eyes kind as she regarded Jillian. "You should let her call you Mama. She wants to, you know. She's just waiting for you to ask."

Jillian looked down at the baby, feeling his warm body cuddled up against her own. "Did she tell you that?"

Martha shook her head slowly. "No, dear. She didn't have to." She reached up a sun-spotted hand and smoothed down Ford's wispy hair. "Motherhood is a mixed bag. You make of it what you can. And nobody expects you to be perfect—most of the time all you have to do is just show up."

The baby started to fret, as if he knew he should be part of the conversation. Jillian met Martha's gaze. "It's . . . it's not easy for me."

Martha held the door open wider, placing her hand gently on Jillian's back to propel her forward. "I know, dear. The best things in life are always the hardest won."

Jillian rubbed Ford's back, soothing him, and felt a small surge of hope. She stepped forward into the house, hearing the snap of the screen door close behind her.

CHAPTER 14

JILLIAN SLID THE LAST SHEET OF CRAB CANAPÉS OUT OF THE OVEN, wiping her fingers on her apron before turning off the timer. She heard the creaking of Grace's rocker on the back porch, and walked over to the open window to call out to her.

"Why don't you go play in the yard, Gracie? It's too pretty for you to be sitting out here on the porch."

"I don't want to. I'm fine right here." She craned her head toward the side of the house, as if she were expecting to see somebody come around the corner.

"I'm almost done in here. Do you want to go down to the beach when I'm through?"

"No!" The answer was almost a shout, but Jillian let it go. Gracie hadn't been down to the beach since the day after the storm, when she and Linc had found the collapsed dune.

Jillian paused for a minute. "Okay. Then maybe we'll go visit Miss Janie and see if she needs any help with her flowers."

Grace's voice sounded distant. "Maybe." The creaking continued as Jillian went back to work.

A car door slammed, and as Jillian walked toward the front of the house, Gracie opened up the back door and called, "Tell him we've got plans, Jilly-bean." The screen door snapped shut before Jillian could question her.

She spotted the police Jeep through the sidelights by the door and had opened it before Mason had a chance to knock. "Hi, Mason. You're just in time. You're not allergic to seafood, are you?"

He came inside, taking off his hat. "No, ma'am. Definitely not. Couldn't call myself a native islander if I were, I don't think." He grinned his grin that had once made her want to kiss him. Now it just made her heart go soft at the memory of how impossibly young she had once been.

"Great. Donna Michaels wanted me to make a few things for a little faculty party she's throwing next week, so I've been doing some experimenting. I need a new taster—Gracie swears she's going to start growing a shell if I stuff another seafood canapé into her."

"And I'd hate to see that happen. I will gladly sacrifice myself so that she won't suffer." He smiled again and she warmed to him, much as she might warm to flannel sheets on a cold winter night. They had seemed to find their way back to the easy companionship they had shared before Ford's birth, even though she still found Mason looking at her every once in a while with remorse.

She led him into the kitchen. "I'm assuming this is a social call since I can't remember parking illegally or getting a speeding ticket."

He sat down at the table, and Jillian busied herself with fixing him a plate. "No, nothing official. I'm actually running an errand for Mama. She and Daddy are having an oyster boil on the fifteenth, and they wanted me to stop by and see if you could come. The invitation's coming in the mail, but she wanted to make sure that you put it on your calendar now."

She slid a plate and a glass of water in front of him, then sat down across from him. "I'd love to. Tell her I'll call her later and find out what I can bring."

He put a canapé in his mouth, and she eagerly watched his expression. He closed his eyes for a moment and then said with a half-full mouth, "Bring these."

Jillian laughed. "Good, huh? I think I finally got it right."

He looked behind her to the tray on top of the stove. "Are you saving those for anybody?"

"You really do know how to flatter a girl." Grinning, she jumped out of her chair and got a plate and plastic wrap. "Just for that, I'm fixing you a plate to take home. And don't feel the need to share it with anybody—I won't tell."

He watched her with a soft smile on his face as she busied herself preparing his plate. "If you like, I could stop by and pick you up before the party."

She fumbled with the wrap, not sure how to respond, but was spared a reply by a voice in the threshold. "Hello, Officer Weber. Aren't they missing you at the doughnut shop?"

Mason stood quickly. "Rising," he said in greeting, nodding his head in Linc's direction. "Shouldn't you be digging in the sand?"

"Believe me, I wish I were. I've got my lawyer arguing with the SCDHEC about allowing some heavy digging equipment on the dunes. They're afraid I might harm a sea oat and ruin life on the island as we know it. Can't do anything until they give me the go-ahead."

Mason silently regarded Linc for a moment before speaking. "Us native islanders are a little particular about those dunes. They're all that stand between us and erosion. That's something most people not raised near the ocean can't appreciate."

The two faced each other, sizing the other up, and Jillian thought for a moment that Linc might tell Mason a thing or two about being a native and knowing things like the schedules of the tides like the back of his hand. She watched his jaw tighten, and noticed absently that he wore jeans and a T-shirt, both of which fit very nicely over his various body parts. She felt confused for a moment, trying to remind herself that this was Linc. He'd been in Charleston for more than a week, and maybe her reaction was simply because she'd missed the security of having him next door.

Trying to release the tension that had built in the room, she walked forward with the plate for Mason. She saw that Linc carried a small pair of rubber boots and an equally small pair of gloves.

Her suspicions were answered when Grace bounded into the room. "Mr. Rising's taking us oyster catching!"

"He is?" She looked accusingly at Linc.

Linc slid his gaze to Jillian as a look of realization filtered through his eyes. "Something tells me that when a little girl calls me at the office to make plans, I should probably ask her to put her mother on the phone." He dropped the boots and gloves on the kitchen floor. "You didn't know anything about this, did you?"

Mason rolled the brim of his hat and looked like he'd rather be anywhere else than where he was.

Gracie interrupted. "She does now! Can we go, Jilly-bean? Please?"

Jillian felt the strong need to teach her daughter a lesson or two about subterfuge, and to refuse. But her gaze caught sight of the sand dollar necklace under Linc's shirt, and something shifted inside her chest. Whatever motivation might lie in Grace's mind, it had to be somehow connected to her daughter's large, generous heart. It was a precious thing, and Jillian knew from experience how easily it could be bruised.

She faced her daughter, leveling her with a steady gaze. "I'll say yes under two conditions: one, that you apologize to Mr. Rising, and two, that you will expect and accept whatever punishment I think necessary."

With just a glimmer of contrition, she tugged on Jillian's hand. "Okay, okay! Can we go now?"

Jillian raised her eyebrows. "No, not quite. I've got to find somebody who can watch Ford for me. I don't think he'd enjoy getting oysters as much as we might."

Mason slid his chair under the table. "I can see you're busy, so I'll just be going. But call Mama if you want her to watch the little one. She hasn't had a new grandbaby in a few years, and she's itching to get her hands on a baby again."

Jillian smiled up at him. "Thanks, Mason. I'll give her a call. And thanks for stopping by." She picked up his wrapped plate from the table and handed it to him again.

He slid his hat on. "I'll see myself out." Facing Linc, he said, "And remember, oyster season's over May first, so don't let me see you out after today. I'd hate to write you a ticket." His expression made a liar out of him, but Linc simply nodded. Mason said his good-byes and left.

Absently, Jillian wiped her hands on her shorts. "Well, then, I'll go get Ford up from his nap and nurse him before we leave. . . ." Her words trailed off as her gaze met Linc's, and she knew they were both thinking of the scene he'd witnessed up in the baby's room. Something had changed between them then—a specific moment in time that forever marked their before and after. Nothing between them would ever be the same again.

Without another word, Jillian turned and headed upstairs, wondering if it was a good thing or a bad thing before deciding not to wonder at all.

As Linc returned to the dock after parking his truck and trailer, he tried to keep his gaze off Jillian, but failed. She wore white shorts and a blue button-down blouse that was tied at the waist and had the sleeves rolled up. She had long legs, still pale from being out of the sun, but beautiful and slim. He noticed her hips and waist, more rounded than he remembered, but he knew without a doubt that she certainly didn't look like anybody's mother. His gaze slid lower and he saw that her feet were clad in bright yellow patent-leather flip-flops with huge daisies on top. He noted Gracie wore a matching pair.

He looked away, busying himself with untying the rope that anchored the boat to the dock. He had been in Charleston for a week. He told himself it was to catch up on all the work that he'd missed while working at the beach house. But some part of his mind kept calling him a liar, and said that the reason he'd gone away was to get this woman out of his system. Either way, he'd failed.

Jillian eyed the craft appreciatively. "Nice boat, Linc."

"Thanks," he said, stepping into it. Jillian handed Grace to him and he swung her into the boat.

Putting her foot on the running board, Jillian said, "I think you'll find I'm a better sailor than I am a dancer."

He reached up for her and kept his face straight. "That's a relief."

Gracie peered around Linc. "He's only teasing you because he likes you, Jilly-bean."

Jillian colored, but he pretended not to notice. Effortlessly, he lifted her by the waist and brought her into the boat, his hands lingering on her a little longer than they needed to. He turned away quickly and dragged out three life jackets from under the seat. Handing two of them to Jillian and Grace, he said, "Put these on."

Linc maneuvered the boat out into the marsh, heading toward Midway Creek. The motor rumbled at low speed as he turned his head over his shoulder to speak. "We're at midtide now, so the oyster rakes should be easy to spot between the tide lines. If you see one, just holler."

Gracie, on surprisingly sturdy sea legs, made her way closer to where he was and stuck her chin out into the wind as the boat gained speed. He looked back at Jillian, who had struck the same pose, and for the first time saw the resemblance between mother and daughter. It wasn't so much their physical looks, but more of how they saw the world: chin first, facing life and ignoring the strong wind hitting them head-on.

Jillian moved forward on the bench seat near Gracie, lifting the child to sit in her lap and holding back the long blond braids that snapped in the wind. They laughed together as he passed over the wake of another boat, making them bounce and their teeth chatter. The briny splash of the marsh, of seawater mixing with decaying plants and new life, settled on them like holy water, making him think of baptisms. Mother and daughter smiled into the rainbow-colored spray, holding out their fingers to touch the life-giving water.

Jillian spotted the oyster rake first, in the small bend of the creek in front of the old church that had long lost its steeple. "Over there!" she shouted, putting her face close to Grace's and pointing out the gravelly colony of knobby white shells. Gracie bounced in her seat as she spotted it, too.

Linc slowed the engine and circled back to where the colony clung to the creek bed, abandoned by the retreating tide and awaiting the life-renewing surge of seawater. As he anchored the boat, Jillian slipped on the boots he'd brought her and then helped Gracie put on the ones he'd borrowed from his partner's daughter. He slid on his own pair, and then handed out gloves, small mallets and pails. "Those shells are really sharp and can slice open your hand, so keep these gloves on at all times."

He jumped out first, then helped them, almost laughing at Gracie in her too-big boots and gloves, carrying a mallet and a pail and looking serious. Guiding Gracie over to the edge of the water, he bent down and showed her how to grab hold of the edge of a shell and use the mallet to set it free.

With grim determination, she squatted down, soaking her shorts, and began pounding. He smiled down at her. "And if you're really brave, I'll show you how to eat them raw."

"Eww," mother and daughter chimed in unison.

Jillian started banging with her mallet. "Damn!" She cradled her thumb on her left hand. "I hit it with the damned mallet." Wincing, she stretched out the thumb and bent it again.

Gracie put her fist on her hip. "Jilly-bean, you're not supposed to swear around me."

Looking chagrined, Jillian faced her daughter. "Sorry." As she bent back down, she mumbled, "Although it's not like you've never heard it before."

The stern look on Gracie's face almost made Linc laugh out loud, but he kept it to himself as he began pounding away again at the oyster rake.

They worked for nearly an hour, keeping in mind the legal limit of oysters allowed per household. Gracie kept up a nonending stream of chatter that didn't require any response from either him or Jillian, and he bent to his work, enjoying the cadences and lilts of her voice. Occasionally, he'd steal a glance over at Jillian and notice that she was smiling to herself, as if also enjoying the music of her daughter's voice. On the few occasions when Grace stopped to catch a breath, the marsh settled to the sounds of the mallets, the clink of shells against the metal pails and the water bumping into the sides of the boat.

Jillian took a break, straightening and dumping her mallet in the bucket. Looking around, she said, "You know this place well."

Linc straightened, stretching his back muscles. "I came here a lot as a kid. Not many people seemed to know about it, so I always had the oysters to myself." He looked up at the deserted church, with its missing roof and hollow windows that gaped at the brightness of the day. "A long time ago, they used to have baptisms here. They'd dip them into the water right here at ebb tide." His gaze met hers. "They say it's the best tide for washing away sins."

She didn't smile as he thought she would, but gazed somberly back at him. "Is it?"

He shrugged and looked away. "Don't know for sure. Can't say I've ever been baptized." He moved over to where Gracie was pounding on an oyster, trying to set it free. His back was to Jillian, but every pore on his skin felt her looking at him.

He looked at Grace's half-full bucket. "You've done real good for a first-timer, kid." He pulled on one of her braids, and she smiled up at him. "What do you say we call it a day and head back?"

Without complaint, she handed over her mallet and bucket, but frowned as she turned to her mother. "Jilly-bean said we might see a dolphin."

He glanced over at Jillian. Her face glowed with sweat and her shorts and shirt were splattered with water and hugging her body. He almost groaned, but remembered the child standing beside him.

Jillian tossed her mallet into her bucket and waded over to them.

"I said we might, Gracie. We'd have to go further out, and Linc's been kind enough to take us this far."

Linc watched their matching expressions of disappointment and knew he'd lose any argument he'd have with himself about why he should go back home. There was something so childlike inside the woman, a child prone to disappointment but who never gave up hope. He had recognized it in the girl she'd been, and was still amazed by it in the woman.

With a deep sigh, he looked from face to face. He did have an appointment with the construction supervisor, but the man could wait. Taking both buckets, he motioned for them to get inside the boat. "Come on. I know just the place—it's not too far. I can usually spot one or two."

Jillian restrained herself from jumping up and clapping as Linc loaded everyone onto the boat. Grace sat next to her again and laid her head on Jillian's lap, yawning loudly. Sleepily, she said, "I really want to see a dolphin."

Jillian placed a hand on her cheek. "We'll find one. You look really worn out. Why don't you go on to sleep now, and I'll wake you if we spot any dolphins."

Gracie nodded slowly, yawned again, and immediately fell asleep.

Linc kept the motor on low as he maneuvered his way out of the shallow water. Jillian watched as the muscles rippled under his shirt, his forearms tanned and strong as they rested on the steering wheel. This was more of the boy she remembered, the boy who knew every inch of the island, every nuance of the shifting tides. He was more a part of the island than she was, and she wondered if that was the bond she felt between them. This was the place that called her home, and she felt his presence pulling at her as much as an outgoing tide pulls at the shoreline.

She held her hand over her eyes to block the sun as she faced him. "Thanks for doing this. I know you've got things to do, and I really appreciate it." He nodded in acknowledgment but didn't face her. She stared at his broad back and saw him shift his shoulders, as if physically moving a barrier between them. She'd expected it. The warm afternoon spent together had affected her in ways she hadn't thought possible, and she didn't doubt that it had done the same to him. She stared out over the boat and waited for whatever words he thought would rebuild the old barriers.

Gently turning the boat toward open water, he asked, "Did you invite your ex-husband to come see his new son? Or did you just leave a message on his answering machine with all the pertinent details?"

She'd expected it, but his question caught her off guard. She didn't answer, but continued to stare into the briny water, willing a dolphin near the surface. Linc put the boat into high gear, drowning out all possibility of conversation as they moved along the surface of the water, watching the tide come in, blurring the edges of the marsh.

When they reached open water, he idled the engine. "You don't want him here, do you?"

After a moment, Jillian shook her head. "No. Not really." She met his eyes. "I know this is stupid, but I've always felt the island was my own special place. I think that's why I never suggested we come here when we were married." She shrugged. "When I called Rick last week, he said he wanted to come see Gracie and the baby and was going to make arrangements for a quick trip at the end of the month. He's supposed to be in Singapore until next Christmas, and I thought that then maybe I could handle seeing him—and his new wife." She stared out at the shoreline where a snowy egret stood silently waiting. "I'm just not sure about now."

"Do you have custody of both children?"

She nodded. "We share custody—for now, anyway. He said we'd talk about it again once the baby was born, after I figured out what it was like with two children." She smoothed her hand against her now-flat stomach. "During the divorce negotiations, he asked me if I wanted him to take them. I'd be lying if I said I didn't think about it for a minute." She looked at him, expecting to find condemnation, but found none, and it gave her the courage to go on. "But I knew in my heart that they are meant to be mine. I couldn't fail at this one thing." She sensed the boat rock beneath her, and she felt the truth of it settle on her. Looking up at him, she didn't bother to wonder why she was confessing something to Linc that she had only just admitted to herself. "I have no idea what I'm doing, and sometimes I feel like I'm floundering in the surf with my hands tied behind my back. But I can't fail. Because that would mean I'm just like my mother." Her last words were whispered and she looked away, toward the water.

"It's just that . . . I needed to be on my own. With Grace—and the new baby. I needed to know that I could do this on my own." She stuck her hands toward the water, the sun's bright signature marking the surface. "I never thought I could."

His gray eyes reflected the late afternoon sky. "And now?"

She smiled. "And now, well, I'm still not sure. But I try. Martha Weber told me that most of the time all I have to do is just show up, and I think she's right. For the rest, I just close my eyes and take the next step and hope for the best. So far I haven't fallen into any deep pits. Yet."

His eyes held a light she didn't recognize, and something flipped in her chest. His words were soft. "Don't sell yourself short. It takes a lot of courage to pick up and start over."

"Like you did?"

All softness faded from his face. "I didn't have a choice. Your father made sure of that."

She looked down at her sleeping daughter and brushed away the wisps of blond hair that stuck to the sweat on her cheek. Maybe it was being on her beloved island again, in the water that coursed around it, that suddenly made her see the truth so clearly. She met his gaze and stuck out her chin. "I am not responsible for his sins. I wasn't then, and I'm not now." She took a breath, finding strength in the water around her. "Sometimes you just have to let go of the past and live on hope. It's a thin meal, but it gets you by. And someday, bang, it's better. It's like wishing on dolphins: You know they're out there, and if you wait long enough, they'll come."

Just then, a splash of movement jerked her attention to behind Linc's shoulders. *Dolphins.* At least one—probably more. "Over there!" She pointed, and Linc started the engine, moving it closer to the spot before idling the engine once more. The distinctive smooth gray back of a dolphin appeared for a moment above the surface and then was gone.

She shook her daughter's shoulder. "Wake up, Gracie. We see a dolphin!"

Slowly, the little girl opened her eyes and blinked once before the words seemed to sink in. She bounded out of her mother's lap and leaned over the side of the boat. "Where?"

Jillian pointed to a spot about twenty feet from the boat. "We just saw the dorsal fin of one somewhere out there. Just keep looking and you might see him come up again."

Everything was silent except the slapping of the water against the side of the boat. Suddenly, not five feet away, Jillian spotted a churning of the water. She pressed her hand into Grace's shoulder, showing her where to look.

And then, as if riding the waves of a prayer, three dolphins leapt from the water, close enough that Jillian could see the wide dark eye of the one in front looking into hers for a brief moment before they disappeared beneath the surface again, its grin seeming to tell her *I heard. I listened.*

Jillian stood and moved to stand next to her daughter, staring out into the now quiet water, the disturbed surface the only clue as to what had just happened. Grace laid her hand on Jillian's and pressed. Quietly, she said, "Can you do it again?"

Jillian looked back at the rippling water teeming with forms of life too small to see but enough to change the color of light as it trickled from the surface, altering it so that it was almost unrecognizable by the time it reached the water's depths. For a moment, Jillian saw it all clearly, could see the three dolphins below the surface like some miracle waiting to break forth, if only one was strong enough to ask.

"Yes," she answered. "I can."

Before she had finished speaking, the dolphins leapt from the water again, closer this time and spraying them with water, and Jillian could taste the salt on her lips.

Gracie threw her arms around Jillian. "Thank you, Jilly-bean. Oh, thank you!"

Jillian sat down with a thud, the effort of her wanting making her weak. She felt the warm, soft body of her daughter next to her, and she knew deep down that somehow she had done something very right.

CHAPTER 15

Sixteen-year-old Jillian faced Grandma Parrish over the kitchen table, biting her lower lip hard enough to make it bleed. She watched as her grandmother dipped her fork into the fried peach pie and brought it up to her mouth. Jillian scratched her nose as she waited, belatedly remembering that her hands were covered in flour.

Her grandmother, chewing slowly, closed her eyes for a long moment. Finally, her eyes popped back open and she smiled broadly. "You have truly outdone yourself, dear. This is simply perfect."

Leaning forward and still frowning, Jillian said, "You mean the peaches aren't too tart?"

"No—they're sweet with just the right balance between too tender and too firm."

Still not convinced, Jillian pressed on. "The crust isn't too tough? I was wondering if it was too brown on the edges because I'd left it in the oven longer than I should have."

Taking another bite, her grandmother shook her head. "Oh, no—it's perfectly flaky. Cuts like a hot knife through butter."

"But what about . . . ?" Jillian was cut off by her grandmother's firm hold on her wrist. Warm brown eyes stared back at her. "It's perfect, Jilly, and you know it. Don't ever let me see you second-guess yourself." She put her fork down and slid the plate to the side before taking both of Jillian's hands in her own. "I know there're reasons why you lack confidence in yourself." She squeezed her hands tighter. "But that's all nonsense."

Grandma Parrish stood, seemingly agitated as she began straightening the kitchen counter, placing measuring spoons and cutting boards in the sink. She stuck a stick of butter in the refrigerator, then closed it slowly, her hand resting on the handle. "I can't make excuses for your parents—it's not my job and it's not what they want, anyway."

Jillian regarded her grandmother quietly for a moment, and then blurted out the words that had been boiling in her for more than a month. "I think my daddy has another girlfriend. He and Mama have been fighting a lot about it since Christmas. I think they might get a divorce."

Grandma Parrish squeezed her eyes shut for a moment. "Pay no mind, Jilly. Your daddy, well, he loves your mama. But he's got a big weakness where women are concerned. He was such a good-looking boy that he just kind of got used to women throwing themselves at him." She came and stood by Jillian's side and put her hand on her head. "They'll work it out—they always have, one way or another."

Jillian remained silent, wondering if divorcing might be the best thing for all of them.

Her grandmother turned back to the sink. "I do know that your father loves you in his own way. He doesn't know how to show you and he's too distracted with other things to figure it out. And your mother." Grandma Parrish sighed, straightened a towel on the oven handle that already hung perfectly straight. "Well, maybe one day they'll tell you the story." She turned around and looked Jillian in the eye. "She wasn't ready for motherhood and found herself with you before she could prepare herself. Always remember that—her indifference has nothing to do with you. It's all inside of her."

Jillian felt a prickle of uneasiness tiptoe across the back of her neck. She'd never seen her grandmother so troubled before, her movements jerky, her words angry and clipped. She stood and approached her grandmother.

"Grandma, what story? What are you talking about?"

Her grandmother faced her and shook her head. "It's not important, Jilly. But you are. And I want you to remember something. You are strong and beautiful and talented. You're bound to make mistakes, make the wrong choices and say the occasional stupid thing—you're only human. But never doubt the truth of those three things." Her grandmother leaned over to kiss Jillian on each cheek, then stared her in the eyes. "Most importantly, never forget that no matter how bad things look, it always gets better. All you need to do is have a little bit of hope."

Slowly, her grandmother straightened, then took her dirty dishes to the sink and began to wash them. Jillian felt giddy, almost lightheaded. She'd always known how her grandmother felt about her, although she'd never before expressed it in words. Jillian looked down at the perfect pie she had created, not seeing the hours, tears and sweat that she had put into it. Instead, all she saw was the way a pie was supposed to be.

Jillian stuck her finger into the flaky crust and brought it up to her mouth. Chewing thoughtfully, she said, "This is really good."

Her grandmother ran the water in the sink. "Of course it is. Now get over here and help me clean up this mess."

Taking another fingerful of pie, Jillian joined her grandmother by the sink. She grabbed a dish towel and began to dry the clean dishes in the strainer. "When we're done here, I'll bring some pie over to the Millses'. Lauren adores fried peach pie."

"They're not home. Mr. and Mrs. Mills left for Charleston this morning to spend the day antiquing, and I saw Lauren about an hour ago outside. She said she was heading to Janie Mulligan's with one of Mrs. Mills' casseroles to take for supper. Don't imagine she'd be back yet."

Jillian dried in silence for a moment, wondering why Lauren hadn't invited her to tag along. She folded the towel and put it on top of the dishes. "I'm done. I think I'll just go to Janie's and meet Lauren there. My parents are coming next week to take me back, and I don't think I've spent all that much time with her."

Her grandmother turned off the faucet and stood there without moving, her hand gripped tightly on the knob. She didn't say anything but turned to face Jillian, her eyes searching Jillian's with confusion.

Jillian met her gaze, feeling a soft swell of panic. "Are you all right, Grandma?"

Her grandmother continued to stare at her for a long moment without saying anything. She broke her gaze and looked around her, blinking rapidly as if seeing her surroundings for the first time. Slowly, her grip loosened on the knob and she took two deep breaths. Leaning against the sink she said, "I'm sorry. I was just having one of my . . . moments. I . . . I just sort of forgot where I was for a bit." She tried to smile but faltered. "I guess it's just part of getting old."

Worried at how pale and fragile her grandmother suddenly seemed to be, Jillian led her back to the table and made her sit down. Grasping each hand in her own, just like her grandmother had done for her earlier, Jillian faced her across the table. "Should I call the doctor?"

Grandma Parrish shook her head, her attention focused on the gold wedding band on her left hand. Jillian had never seen her grandmother's hand without the ring. It was as much a part of her as her white hair and purposeful stride.

Slowly, Grandma Parrish slid the ring off her finger, tugging on it as it snagged on her knuckle before sliding it all the way off. She held it for a moment between her thumb and forefinger, her short nails devoid of polish, sitting atop capable and loving hands. With a shaking smile, she handed it to Jillian. "I want you to have this."

Almost afraid to touch it, Jillian kept her hands down and shook her head. "No, Grandma. It's yours—you should be wearing it."

Her grandmother pressed it into her hand. "No. I want to make sure I give this to you now—when I'm still thinking clearly enough to remember. It's important to me."

Jillian swallowed, then nodded. "All right. Thank you." She slid the ring onto the fourth finger of her right hand. "It fits."

"I thought it would." She spread her fingers out in the air between them. "We have the same hands."

Jillian blinked hard, trying to hide the tears from her grandmother. She held her right hand out in front of her, fingers spread like a young bride. Grandma Parrish linked her fingers through Jillian's and smiled. "I want you to think of me whenever you see this ring, you hear? It's like those stars you stare at every night—they're to remind you that you're never alone."

Jillian gave up trying to hide her tears. "You're talking like you're going to die soon."

Grandma Parrish squeezed Jillian's fingers tightly before letting go. Handing Jillian a tissue from her apron pocket, she said, "No. I'm not planning to, anyway." She patted Jillian's cheek, then stood and wiped her hands on her apron. "You go on to Janie's and see if you can't catch up with Lauren."

Pushing back her own chair, she moved over to her grandmother and kissed her on the cheek, making Grandma Parrish smile with surprise. As Jillian turned to go, her grandmother grabbed her hand one more time. "Don't forget, Jilly."

"I won't. Promise." She turned and left, forgetting to pick up her shoes on the porch before she headed up the driveway. As she made her way to Janie Mulligan's house, she kept her head down, looking for the softest spots to place her bare feet, noticing not for the first time how in the midst of all the broken shells on the path, a few had managed to remain whole.

The sun chased light and shadow on the gold band on Jillian's hand as she rocked in and out of a slice of shade on her back porch. The lull of the salt air coupled with an evening spent with a fretting baby that had kept her up most of the night was quickly pushing her eyelids closed. Even the sounds of power saws next door couldn't seem to convince her to stay awake.

The back door swung open and then slammed shut as Gracie rushed through it, a Mason jar held aloft. "Jilly-bean! It's hatching!"

Fully awake now, Jillian's eyes popped open. Gripping the arms of the rocking chair, she said, "What's hatching?"

Gracie thrust the Mason jar at her. "My caterpillar from my school project. She's trying to come out of her cocoon, but I think she's stuck."

"Let me see." She took the jar in her hands and held it up. The once green chrysalis was now a smooth, clear shell with a split at the bottom. The folded orange-and-black stripes of an emerging monarch butterfly's wings could be seen clearly, offering glimpses of a miracle from the mundane world.

Jillian smiled at her daughter. "You're right. I guess it figured it was time to come out."

Gracie frowned. "Maybe I should call Mrs. Michaels and ask her what I'm supposed to do now. I think I need to help my caterpillar. How is she going to get rid of that cocoon all by herself?"

Jillian felt Linc's presence before she saw him turn the corner of her house, a large bundle slung over his shoulder. She and Gracie watched him approach until he stopped at the foot of the porch steps. He dropped the bundle and indicated the jar with his chin.

"Is that Constance Caterpillar?"

With a worried frown, Grace nodded vigorously. "I think she's stuck."

Jillian looked from Grace's face to Linc's. "Constance Caterpillar? And who came up with that?"

Grace took the jar from Jillian and handed it to Linc. "Linc did. He said that since my caterpillar was a girl, we needed to come up with a girl name for her."

Jillian tried not to smile. "It's a good thing Linc can tell if caterpillars are boys or girls. His talents never cease to amaze me."

Linc glanced at Jillian, his eyes alight with amusement. "What can I say? It's a gift."

She moved to stand next to him, and peered into the jar. "So, Mr. Expert, can you tell us what we need to do now? Gracie seems to think she needs to help Constance with the process."

Her gaze shifted to his long, beautiful fingers gripping the jar, before looking up to meet his eyes. She could see the stunning contrast of dark lashes against gray eyes, and the way he seemed able to see deep inside her to the person she was meant to be. It had always been that way between them, an understanding they had never shared with another person. *Even Lauren.*

He squatted, and she followed so that they were both eye level with Grace. Linc's face was serious when he spoke. "As hard as it is to believe, your butterfly is completely equipped to set herself free. If you broke the chrysalis yourself to let her out, you would damage her."

Grace sputtered in protest. "But, Linc, I'd be very careful. I wouldn't want to hurt her."

Linc smiled at her, and something in Jillian's chest seemed to flip over. "I know. What I meant is that the butterfly has to find its own way out. See, the whole process is designed to strengthen her wings and get her ready for flight. She knows that after she comes out, she needs to hang around a little longer to squeeze stored fluid into her wings and let them dry. If she doesn't struggle through the small hole she makes in the cocoon, she'll skip that whole step and never learn to fly. And what sort of life would that be?"

Jillian watched her daughter's face, seeing the understanding pass over her small features, and realized that she actually knew what Grace was thinking. It was a small connection, but more than she had once thought possible. She clasped her hands together, feeling the press of her grandmother's ring.

Slowly, Grace took the jar and set it on the floor of the porch by the door. With her elbows on her knees, she peered in at Constance. "They're kinda like people, huh?"

A stiff ocean breeze blew in over the dunes, twisting Grace's hair behind her back. "Smart kid," Linc said.

Jillian stared at Grace as if seeing the wonderful person she was growing into for the first time, and felt profoundly blessed to be allowed to witness it. It was as if the angels of her childhood had not deserted Jillian at all but had instead passed into her safekeeping this small token of love and hope.

"Yeah, she sure is," Jillian answered, sitting heavily in her rocking chair and wondering if Grace's presence in her life had not been an accidental whim but was rather meant to be all along.

Linc felt a tug on his pants leg. "My daddy's coming for a visit." Grace's face was serious, a small furrow in her brow.

"I bet you're excited." He stole a glance over at Jillian to catch her expression. She didn't look up at him, but fiddled with the gold ring on her right hand.

Somberly, Grace nodded. "I am. I don't think Jilly-bean is, though. She thinks it's okay since Daddy hasn't seen Ford yet, but she's glad he's not bringing that slut Joanie with him."

Linc held back a laugh as Jillian jerked to a stand and faced her daughter. "Gracie! Where do you come up with these things?"

Gracie considered her mother soberly for a moment. "From you. Those were the exact words you told Mrs. Weber on the phone last night. You thought I was in bed, but I got up to get a drink of water and I heard you." After a brief pause, she asked, "What's a slut?"

Jillian crossed her arms over her chest, her cheeks darkening. "You're not supposed to be broadcasting personal conversations to other people."

Grace focused her attention on the struggling chrysalis again, already bored with the conversation. "But it's only Linc!" Her expression made it clear that she assumed everybody would understand why Linc should be included in all personal matters.

Linc watched as Jillian fought for composure. "Grace, please go pour us all some iced tea. And don't forget to wash your hands first. And remember to refill the ice tray after you take out the ice."

With a heavy sigh, Grace stood and stomped her way toward the door, her displeasure at being dismissed evident in the slamming of the door.

"Don't slam the door—you'll wake the baby."

The only response was a loud groan.

Jillian shoved her hands into the pockets of her shorts and she smiled weakly at him. "Sorry about that. I don't mean to get you involved in all our dirty laundry."

He noticed the pink sunburn on her nose and cheeks, and how her hair was pulled back from her face in a ponytail, and he was silent for a moment, stunned at the effect she seemed to have on him.

He cleared his throat and grabbed hold of the bundle he'd dumped on the porch. "Grace told me that when Ford fusses at night you come out here to calm him down. I figured one of these would come in handy."

Jillian's face brightened. "A Pawleys Island hammock! Oh, Linc—it's wonderful!" She moved toward him and held out her hand to grasp the heavy white rope knots before surprising him with a hug.

The hammock slipped from his grasp onto the sandy ground as his arms reached around to hold her. She smelled of sun and baby and milk; so different from the old Jillian, but still very much the wonderful girl he'd known. He held her tightly for a moment, holding close to the good memories before letting go.

Her arms fell back to her sides, and he could tell she felt the same embarrassment he did. They were like two ships facing each other on the ocean without clear signals as to how to pass.

She blushed again. "Sorry. I can't tell you the last time somebody gave me a present. And it was real sweet of you."

He bent to pick up the fallen hammock, wondering yet again why he was there. He'd been in his car, heading for his Charleston office, when he'd passed a store selling hammocks. The next thing he knew, he was standing on Jillian's back porch, getting ready to hang one for her. He straightened. "Actually, I have an ulterior motive. I've been sleeping with my windows open and didn't want a baby's crying to keep me up at night."

She shifted her weight and grinned up at him. "Yeah. That's what I thought. But it was sweet of you, anyway."

Feeling oddly pleased, he reached for his tool belt that he'd brought with the hammock. "Just show me where you want it."

She folded her arms across her chest for a moment and walked slowly down the length of the porch. Finally stopping in the far corner, she said, "Right here. It'll get the late-afternoon sun, but be in the shade during the hottest part of the day. And at night, well, it'll be perfect."

Pulling out the screw eyes he needed, he dragged the hammock to where she wanted it, trying not to notice the long, bare legs she'd pulled up as she sat in a chair, or the way a hint of abdomen showed below her short top. He couldn't remember the last time a woman had pulled at all five senses like this woman did. He'd dated many, but none that had haunted his thoughts daily like Jillian did. *Not since Lauren.*

He turned his back on her and began working the screw into the wood, not wanting her face to soften the memories of her father's accusing glare, or the thin mattress of the cot he'd slept on during his two nights spent in jail.

He reached for the second screw eye he'd clamped between his teeth. "Do you remember that box I made for Lauren? The one with our initials on the top?" The screw fell from his mouth onto the floor of the porch, where it jammed itself between two boards. Cursing silently, he tried to yank it out, only scraping up his fingers for his efforts. He grabbed another from his tool belt, then straightened to face her.

Some of the color had bled from her face. Her brown eyes were wide, her mouth slightly opened. Slowly, she lowered her legs and leaned back in the chair. "Of course I remember it. I was the one who bought you the edging tool you needed to carve the initials." He watched her swallow. "I gave that to you for your seventeenth birthday."

He could almost feel the hard metal of the tool in his fingers as he stabbed the stubborn wood, and then the feel of it slicing into his hand and the warm blood dripping down his fingers as he refused to quit working. And then Lauren had been there, cleaning the wound and bandaging it. Linc looked down for a moment at the screw he held in his scarred hand, at the puckered ridge of pinkened skin, and squinted in confusion. No, it hadn't been Lauren. *It had been Jillian.*

He looked at her again, forcing himself to continue. No matter that he knew he was pressing on old bruises that had never healed. His youth had been stolen from him, and it was past time for somebody else to share the pain. "Do you know what happened to it?"

She shook her head as he watched her chest rise and fall as if she were struggling to stay calm. "She cherished it. I know she would have made sure she put it somewhere safe."

"How safe, Jillian?"

She met his gaze without flinching. "She had her reasons. Maybe one day you can ask her yourself."

He studied her for a long moment, waiting for her to say more. When she didn't, he turned his back to her again and finished hanging the hooks for the hammock, trying to push back his disappointment. *What was in the box?* For a brief moment, he wished he'd accepted it when Gracie had handed it to him. Then he'd know—what? He'd find out eventually. He had all the time in the world.

When he was done hanging the hammock, Jillian joined him standing next to it. "Thanks, Linc. I know I'll use it often."

He grunted his acknowledgment as he hoisted his tool belt again and slid his hammer back into its slot.

As he turned to leave, she put a warm hand on his arm, pulling him back. Her face was close to his, close enough for him to read the apology in her eyes. "Are you coming to the Webers' boil next Saturday? Gracie has been helping me practice my shag steps. You and I could really show them how it's done."

He hadn't planned to. Martha Weber had asked him, and he'd already made up an excuse just out of habit. He remembered as a boy sitting on an abandoned dock and looking across the creek to see cooking fires and clusters of island neighbors laughing and talking. He and his mother had never been invited. Instead, he had sat alone, an outsider looking into a place he could never call his own.

But now he looked at Jillian, at her bright eyes and wide smile and the promise of a dance. He remembered to shrug first. "I don't think I'm doing anything else. I might as well."

"Gee, Linc, you really know how to flatter a girl. But I'm glad you're coming."

"Do you need a ride?"

She shook her head. "Mason's picking us up."

He tried to ignore the feeling of disappointment as he slung his tool belt over his shoulder. "Now that I know you'll be expecting me to dance with you, I'll wear my steel-toed work boots to protect my feet."

Her retort was interrupted by Ford's crying on the baby monitor. Jillian opened the screen door and looked back at Linc. "Stay here for a few minutes—Gracie's bringing out the iced tea. She'll be disappointed if you leave after she's gone through all that trouble."

The door banged shut behind her, and he stole a glance at her retreating backside through the screen. A moment later, the door opened again as Gracie backed her way out of it, a dripping glass of iced tea in each hand. Moving forward, Linc took a glass.

Taking a sip, he nodded appreciatively. "Thank you, Grace. Hanging a hammock is hard work."

Grace smiled up at him as the ice banged her teeth. "Did you find Lauren's hiding place?"

The warm day seemed to turn suddenly cool, and he felt the hairs on his arms stiffen. "What hiding place, Gracie?"

"The one in her room. Jilly-bean knows it's there, but she couldn't get it open."

"No, I haven't. Where is it?"

But Grace had already shifted her attention back to the glass jar with the emerging butterfly. "How long do you think it'll take before Constance is ready to come out?"

Linc placed his empty glass on the side railing and moved closer. Squatting, he studied the oblong shape of the chrysalis, hanging by mere threads to the twig that held it. The small split in the side was larger now, the subtle movements shifting the chrysalis on its thread.

"I'm not sure. Maybe a day or two would be my guess."

Gracie put her head close to his and peered into the jar. "I think it should take years. It's a big thing to go from crawling to flying, don't you think?"

He stared at her profile for a long time, contemplating the wisdom of youth and how little of it adults seemed to retain as they moved away from childhood.

"Yep, it's an amazing thing to see, that's for sure." Linc stood and thanked Grace for the iced tea again before saying good-bye. As he turned to leave, Gracie said, "Are you really going to wear steel-toed boots?"

He smiled. "Is there anything you don't hear?" Shaking his head, he said, "No, I've already got plenty of protective calluses on my feet. They'll survive dancing with your mother."

Sticking her hand in her glass, Gracie pinched an ice cube between her fingers and brought it out. "Lauren says you're the best dancer."

Again, he felt as if a cold hand had touched the back of his neck, and his smile faded. "Who is Lauren, Gracie?"

Mischievous brown eyes stared up at him. "You know."

"No, I'm confused. Tell me."

They both turned at the sound of Jillian coming down the wooden stairs. Leaning up, Gracie stood on her tiptoes to whisper in his ear. "Look in the window seat."

Before he could question her, Jillian came out onto the porch, carrying Ford. He said good-bye again, then left, his thoughts churning between caterpillars and butterflies and of a girl he used to know—a girl whose face kept blending with the face of a woman he couldn't seem to stay away from.

CHAPTER 16

LINC STARED AT THE CARCASS OF THE BLUE CRAB, ITS WHITENED belly exposed to the warm late May sun, its claws supine in wordless supplication. He nudged it with the toe of his shoe, shuffling it until it fell into a dip in the sand. Then, slowly and methodically, as his profession had trained him to work, he kicked sand over the dead crab, not completely sure why he felt the need to do it, only that he felt a strong pull out on the dunes to bury the dead.

A dark-haired child chased the surf on the beach as his mother started to pack up coolers and sand pails, the father busy filming with a video camera. The mother raced after the little boy with a large towel, her shoulders pinkened from the sun.

Linc shifted his gaze down the stretch of sand, noticing a scattering of beach chairs and umbrellas, like flowers in a desert garden, their bright colors harsh against the paleness of the sand. The spring visitors had come, and soon the summer tourists would arrive. The island would be awash with people again.

Panning his gaze out over the ocean, he savored its vast emptiness, hearing the liquid music that had always brought him home to this place of tidal marshes and swollen dunes. His mother had moved him from apartment to apartment during his childhood, but here, out amid the pelicans and sea grasses, he knew he was home. The sun settled low and bloodred on the late-afternoon horizon, waiting to be swallowed by the ebbing tide. Linc felt the pull, as if he were a grain of sand or a discarded shell, much as he imagined his own ancestors had. They had been marauding pirates who had once haunted this part of the South Carolina barrier islands, men determined to take what they could not earn: ownership and respectability. He kicked more sand over the dead crab, and sometimes wondered if he wasn't all that different than his infamous ancestors.

He ducked under the yellow CAUTION tape that encircled the collapsed dune, being careful to test for firm footholds as he neared the sinkhole. He hadn't yet received permission to use heavy equipment to dig, so he'd ordered the long and arduous job of excavating the site by hand. Shovels and trowels were now stabbed into the sand like slender grave markers around the perimeter of the gaping hole.

Squatting, he reached down and picked up a red brick that had been pulled from the dune. It was an old brick, familiar to him because of the vast number he'd reused in his renovations of historic houses. Yes, there was something down there. Something man-made. Probably a tunnel of some sort, to be this far from the house. He stood again, staring up at his house. *What secrets are you hiding?*

After his little talk with Grace, he had gone to the window seat to look for a hidden compartment, feeling almost foolish, and had surprised himself by finding the small button in the corner near the bottom. But when he'd pressed it, nothing had happened. He'd wait until full light tomorrow to examine it more closely, and hopefully find a way to force it open without damaging anything. He respected old things; he wouldn't destroy the window seat and its compartment just because of something a seven-year-old had told him. It could wait until tomorrow. Or later. He couldn't explain, even to himself, why he was so reluctant to find out what was hidden in Lauren's window seat.

He looked back up at the house in the fading light, imagining he saw shadows move behind the windows. With workmen gone for the day, he never felt alone when he went inside. Even out here, on the dunes, he could almost sense a presence.

"Hello there."

He almost slipped into the hole at the sound of the voice behind him. Scrambling to regain both his composure and his foothold, he took a huge step backward, almost knocking over Janie Mulligan, who stood inside the yellow circle with him.

Linc gripped her upper arms, steadying them both. "Sorry, Miss Janie. You startled me."

She looked up at him with soft brown eyes, her hair blowing out of its braids and around her face like seaweed adrift in the open ocean. She held her arms protectively around the front baby carrier, the yellow yarn hair of the doll pulled into a thick ponytail at the back of her head. The doll's face was turned to the side, and he could see the wide, sightless eyes staring back at him with what Linc thought looked like commiseration. Janie's soft voice spoke into the ocean breeze. "It's lonely here."

Linc dropped his arms. "It won't be for long. I saw more tourists on the beach today. Summer's not that far off."

Janie didn't follow his gaze down the beach. Instead, she stared down into the hole. "I smell the ocean."

He picked up another brick and tossed it up on the dune. "The bottom of the hole fills with water at high tide—although I don't think it always did. Probably when it was first built—most likely as a hiding place—the beach was much farther away and the water not so much of a threat. But now"—he shrugged—"it's pretty much useless unless you bring diving gear with breathing equipment."

He smiled at his own joke, but stopped when he caught Janie staring at him with concentration. "What would happen if you didn't have any?"

"Well, you'd drown. Unless you could find an unlocked exit before the tunnel completely filled. There must have been one out on the dunes at one time. Maybe even one leading to the house—I'm not sure. I have to do some more investigating to figure that one out."

Janie bent to kiss the top of the doll's head, then rested her cheek against the yellow yarn hair. "I wonder what it's like to drown."

Linc looked sharply at her, remembering stories of how her brother tried to save a summer tourist who had suffered a heart attack not twenty yards from shore. They had both drowned. Gently, he said, "I'm sure it's quick. Maybe a little bit like falling into a deep sleep where you're not really aware of what's happening."

Her smile was sweet and grateful. "I think you're right. Yes, that's it exactly."

He gently took her elbow and led her under the yellow tape and away from the pit. He realized that he had been talking to her as he would a child. Maybe because her high-pitched, wispy voice and wide, innocent eyes reminded him so much of Gracie. With one last look up at his house, he smiled down at Janie. "Are you going to the Webers' party?"

She nodded enthusiastically, the sun throwing flecks of gold into her brown eyes.

"Good. Me, too. Would you like me to drive you?"

Her eyebrows puckered for a moment. "Yes, thank you. But do you have room for Baby's car seat? It's dangerous for a child not to have one."

He regarded her steadily for a moment, sensing not for the first time that there was much more to Janie Mulligan than an aging woman with a confused mind. He saw the small bones and the fair skin, the delicate nose and wide-set brown eyes. She was like a single grain of sand, easily dislodged and lost in a strong ocean breeze. Linc realized with a start that he was comparing her to Jillian. Except Jillian had never given up or let go in a storm. She clung fiercely, keeping the hope close to her heart that all would be well.

Janie placed her hand in his as if she were a little girl, and he walked her up the dunes toward the road. Her hand felt frail and cold in his, and her other hand stroked Baby's head. He watched as Janie retreated back into her own little world. He imagined it was an adequate self-defense for those whose hope lay lost and abandoned like a shipwreck deteriorating at the bottom of the ocean.

Jillian took one last look at Ford in the portable crib before stepping quietly out of Martha's bedroom and clipping the baby monitor on her belt. At six weeks of age, he was already a dependable sleeper, and she knew he was down for the count for at least six hours. Just in case, she had stored several bottles of formula in Martha's refrigerator if he decided to wake up sooner.

She hadn't had a beer in more than a year, and she felt like a giddy, underaged teenager thinking about the prospect of having one. Feeling a bit guilty, Jillian had even visited her doctor the week before to work out how many formula feedings she'd have to give Ford before she could nurse him again after drinking. She could tell Dr. Clemmens was trying to hide a smile as he told her it was a common question of new mothers. He'd then helpfully told her that she was completely healed and could start having sex again. She'd blushed, then rolled her eyes and stammered something about living like a nun. Smoothing her shirt down now, she blushed again just at the memory.

As she made her way down the stairs, she felt a small jolt of exuberance as if she were about to go out on a first date. *He's going to be here.* She felt heat rush to her face, and she paused at the bottom of the steps to look in the hall mirror. The tanned, slender woman in a tank top and denim miniskirt hardly resembled the pregnant woman who had driven from Atlanta nearly three months before. Thank God.

She was in time to catch Gracie and Mary Ellen barreling out the kitchen door. Gracie stuck her head back in. "Mary Ellen wants me to spend the night, and her mama says it's okay. Can I?"

Feeling magnanimous, Jillian waved her hand. "Sure—I'll pack up a bag of your stuff and bring it over after the party."

Gracie ran over to her mother, gave her a loud kiss, then ran out the door to follow her friend.

Martha faced her, a large bowl of coleslaw in her hands. "Could you take this on down for me? And if you can pull Mason away from the oyster pit, would you mind sending him back up here? I've got a whole pig's worth of pulled barbecue pork that needs to be brought down to the food table." She wiped her forehead with the back of her hand as she looked around the kitchen, as if assessing what needed to be done next. "I know it's the wrong time for an oyster boil, but I had put all those oysters you brought me in the freezer, and I thought that would be enough reason to have all the neighbors over. Can't really have a private party once the summer people come."

Jillian smiled and moved to leave.

"Are you and Mason dating?"

Jillian almost dropped the bowl. "No. He just gave us a ride here. Why? Has he said anything?"

Martha shook her head. "No, but he doesn't have to. I've always been able to read his mind—more so than any of my other children. And I know he's always had a thing for you, Jillian. Just don't break his heart, all right? I don't think I could stand to see that."

Jillian forced her eyes to meet Martha's. "I like Mason—I always have. But, well, it's just not like that between us."

Martha lifted a basket of hush puppies out of her deep fryer and put it aside. "I figured as much. Guess I got my hopes up when he told me he was bringing you here tonight. Should have realized that as long as Linc's around, Mason wouldn't stand a chance."

This time Jillian set the bowl down, no longer sure of her ability to hold on to it. "Martha . . ."

"Don't be embarrassed, Jillian. Joe and I knew who he was the first time we saw him."

"But you didn't say anything to him?"

Using a spatula, Martha began scooping out the hush puppies into a bread basket. "No, we figured he had his reasons. He'd left Pawleys under all that suspicion. Not that me and Joe ever thought he could have hurt Lauren Mills. But I figured Linc wasn't the kind of guy who'd believe it if I told him. He strikes me as the sort of person who'd want to figure it out on his own."

Jillian moved to take the basket from Martha and placed it next to the coleslaw. She turned her back on Martha before lifting them both, glad for the excuse not to have to face the older woman. "Linc and I are old friends, Martha. There's nothing between us but old memories. And when he looks at me, he only sees somebody he thinks once believed the worst of him."

She lifted the bowl and heard Martha do an unladylike snort. "Trust me, dear. That's not the only thing he sees when he looks at you."

Martha opened the kitchen door to let Jillian out, and Jillian focused her gaze on the coleslaw as she stepped through the doorway, then made her way down to the beach.

Several long picnic tables, covered with red-and-white-checked tablecloths, had been set up far away from the surf in anticipation of the oncoming tide. The scent of barbecue and roasting oysters curled through the warm evening air, accompanied by the familiar beach music. Jillian found herself humming along as she found spots on the food table to put down the two dishes she carried.

She straightened, looking around at the groups of people who had started to gather near the open pits, and spotted Mason. He raised a beer bottle in her direction, and when she nodded, he moved to a large cooler and pulled out one for her.

Kicking off her sandals and leaving them under the table, she approached Mason. Taking the opened bottle, she thanked him and took a deep swallow.

He looked different out of uniform, more boylike, almost. He was watching her closely, and she found she couldn't meet his eyes. "Your mother needs you up at the kitchen to help bring a few things down."

He nodded silently, then took a long drink from his bottle. "Would you hold my beer until I get back? Otherwise, Lessie will find it and put sand in it. You'd think as siblings got older, they'd also get more mature."

She smiled and finally looked at him. "I wouldn't know, but I'll keep your beer safe."

He smiled back at her and was about to say more when his attention was distracted by something behind her. She glanced around and saw Linc accepting a beer from Lessie, while Grace tugged on his jeans-clad leg for his attention.

When she looked back at Mason, his eyes were shadowed. "I'll be right back," he said before heading toward the house.

She took another swig of her beer and sang along with The Drifters for a moment with words from "Save the Last Dance for Me." The music and the smells of the ocean combined with that of roasting oysters, pit barbecue and beer made her smile to herself. She could almost believe she was young again, waiting for Mason to come ask her to dance while she watched Lauren and Linc moving together to the music, barefoot on the beach.

Feeling lightheaded, she tipped her beer bottle to her mouth again and finished it before heading down toward the water's edge. The first night stars had begun to punch holes in the dusk sky, and she sat down in the moist sand to watch them, only slightly aware of her empty bottle and Mason's full one tipping over in the sand next to her.

With a long sigh, she fell back into the sand, feeling the still-warm sand beneath her shirt, and stared up at the endless sky, searching for her star.

She felt Linc nearby before she saw him, but didn't speak until he was lying in the sand beside her, the top of his head touching hers.

He held the beer bottles by their necks above them. "Are both these yours?"

"Nope. One is Mason's. I definitely don't think I could handle a second. That's the first beer I've had in a year, and I think it's gone straight to my head."

"Oh, great. You never could hold your liquor. You're not going to start singing, are you?"

She threw sand at him, and he turned his head away for a moment.

His voice still held a smile when he spoke. "What were you looking at?"

"Ursa Major. It's hard to make out the stars right now because it's still light, but I was trying to remember how you used to help me find the North Star."

He was silent for a moment, then said, "Give me your hand."

She placed her hand in his, feeling his artist's fingers grasp hers and then maneuver her hand until he was pointing with her index finger. She tried to concentrate on what he was saying and ignore the heat that swelled down her arm and filled her body.

"Remember Merak and Dubhe?" He moved her hand in the direction of the two stars that made up the right side of the dipper.

She nodded, and he began to draw a line in the sky with her finger. "Let's draw an imaginary line from Merak through Dubhe, out of the cup of the dipper, and continue five times as far as the distance between them."

He swept her hand across the galaxies, painting a picture with stars that were older than the sand on which they lay, and guided her toward the polestar. It lay almost invisible in the dusk sky, its light no more than a fluttering pinprick, but even with her eyes closed she knew that the ancient star that had guided lost travelers for thousands of years hung in the sky, waiting for her. She felt as if she were on a journey through the night sky, led only by the light of the stars, and Linc's hand firm on hers, guiding her.

Slowly, she realized Linc had sat up and was staring down at her, even though he still held her hand. The music beat faintly behind them, the words clear enough to sing along with. He stood and pulled her up with him while the words of the Tams swept over the dunes toward them. What kind of fool do you think I am? Pulling her closer, he set her hands on his shoulders and then began to dance.

She stumbled at first, her legs feeling more like rubber than limbs, and then she moved in his arms as Lauren once had, feeling beautiful and graceful and wanted. He didn't smile at her as they danced, but looked at her with an expression on his face that made her feel as if he'd never really seen her before. She closed her eyes, seeing him again guiding her through the night sky, helping her find her way.

When the song ended, they stood where they were, close enough together that the wind blew her hair into his face. Brushing her hair back, he cupped her face and brought his lips to hers.

She tasted the salt air on his lips first, and then forgot everything else except for the heat that seemed to burn from the inside out as she opened her mouth and welcomed him in. He pulled her closer until the heat and hardness of his body lay against hers and she could feel his need for her. Her full breasts ached as they pressed against his chest, but she couldn't feel the pain—only the need to be absorbed by him and his kiss. *I'm drowning,* she thought, fighting for air and balance but not wanting him to stop.

Her hands found their way to his hair, and she smiled against his lips as she realized she'd always wanted to feel it like this, with her arms around his neck and her fingers plunging into the dark strands. His hands slipped their way under her shirt, and she pictured his long artist's fingers against her skin, warm and sure where they touched her, as if she were an unfinished block of wood waiting to be made into something beautiful. He said her name before pulling away abruptly and only then did she realize that somebody nearby had cleared a throat.

Mason stood about six feet away, looking everywhere except her face. "I was looking for my beer."

She looked around for the bottle in the sand and then spotted it lying on its side. "Sorry. We were dancing. . . ." She was unable to finish the sentence and found she couldn't look at Linc or Mason. Wiping imaginary sand from her skirt, she said to no one in particular, "I'm going to go check on Gracie."

It wasn't until she was halfway toward the picnic area that she realized the sky had gone completely dark while she had danced in Linc's arms, and she hadn't once remembered to be afraid.

CHAPTER 17

LINC SAT UP IN HIS BED, NOT SURE OF WHAT IT WAS THAT HAD AWAK-ened him. The full moon cast a blue-tinged glow around his bedroom, seeming to smother all outside sounds. But he had heard something somewhere inside the house.

Quietly, he slid from his bed and found a pair of jeans and a T-shirt to slip on. His flashlight lay on the floor by the empty milk crates he'd been using for a dresser, and he picked it up in case he might need a weapon.

He crept out onto the landing at the top of the stairs and listened. The house spoke to him, as it always did in its silence, the testament of years threaded through the faint sounds of the ocean. But beyond that, he heard something else. He was quite sure it wasn't a sound, exactly; it was more of a physical pull, as if someone were tugging on his hand and guiding him downstairs. He wondered why he wasn't afraid.

Without turning on any lights, he cautiously made his way down the steps, his bare feet silently padding on the freshly sanded wood risers. He moved surely through the dark, the moon shining through the door transom, showing the way with arms of blue light.

He stood in the foyer for a long moment, and then it was as if a voice had told him to turn around, although he was sure nothing had been spoken and that he was definitely alone. He turned slowly, then stopped, his heart stuttering in his chest as the feeling of standing in the path of an oncoming train came over him.

The door to the hall closet, the one that had been permanently shut due to warping wood, now lay wide open, its doorknob embedded in the wall behind it, the closet gaping black and open. He smelled the ocean then, the salt and wet sand, as if he were standing in the surf, close enough that he could feel the water between his toes.

The house is shifting, he thought, trying to explain the open door. He moved closer, his hand clutching the doorframe, and peered into the darkness, unwilling to shine the flashlight inside. The small room lay empty and open, with unanswered questions hovering somewhere in the darkness. Pressing his forehead against the wood, he clenched his eyes shut, almost hearing the voices, but resisted being pulled into the past.

"Hello," he called, feeling foolish. With a deep breath, he reached out and flipped on the hall light, throwing an arc of yellow light into the black interior. He peered inside, his eyes adjusting to the light, recalling briefly what it had once looked like. But now there were no coats or fishing boots or table centerpieces. Just old grocery bags filled with yellowed newspapers, and a single wire hanger on the chipped white painted rod.

Stepping back, he turned off the light, being careful not to close the door completely and get it stuck again. It must have been the shifting of the house or a dramatic change in the humidity that had forced the door open. It had to have been.

He searched the downstairs to assure himself that he was alone, checking the locks on the doors and flipping on the lights to be able to see better in the dark corners. The house was empty except for him, but he still couldn't shake the uneasy feeling of someone watching him.

Coming back to the hall, he returned to the closet, opening the door wider. He thought he heard the voices again and clenched his eyes shut, finally allowing himself to be pulled back into the past.

The three teenagers ran up onto the back porch of Lauren's house, pressing themselves against the cedar siding to avoid being seen by Mr. and Mrs. Parrish, who were now approaching the Millses' front door.

Lauren turned and opened the back door, peering in to make sure nobody could see them. "It's clear."

Linc's eyes met Lauren's. "I can't go in there—you know that. Your dad told me I'm not to have anything to do with you. That probably includes me not even being on your porch—much less inside your house."

Jillian was crying now. "I don't want to get y'all in trouble. I've got to go home with them, and hiding will just make it worse."

Lauren rolled her eyes, impatient with anybody who didn't see a situation the same way she did. "Don't be silly, you two. We just won't get caught. Besides, if they can't find us until suppertime, they'll probably stay, and you can spend another night with your grandmother." Lauren yanked the door open further and motioned for Linc and Jillian to go ahead.

Linc looked at Jillian, at her pale face and trembling hands. She was fourteen, only three years younger than he was, but at that moment she looked more like the six-year-old he'd met all those years ago on the beach with her grandmother. He felt a flash of anger, then anger at the two people who could make the strong-spirited girl he knew into the quivering picture of fear she was at that moment.

Defiantly, he held out his hand to her and she grabbed it, her skin cool and clammy. He smiled at her. "I will if you will."

He watched her swallow before she nodded, and then he led her into the Millses' kitchen. Lauren moved silently through the room toward the foyer, then paused, her finger to her mouth to remind them to be quiet. The sound of the TV came from the front parlor, and she made a move toward the steps leading upstairs when a knock came from the front door. All three pairs of eyes fell on the closet door.

"No!" Jillian's mouth formed the words, but no sound came out. She pulled back, but Linc kept her hand firmly held in his own.

Lauren quickly opened the closet door and motioned for them to follow before ducking inside. Jillian's look of terror was real, as if she believed boogeymen really lived in dark spaces. And when he thought of her parents and the things Jillian had told him and he had seen, he realized that to her, boogeymen probably did.

"Come on," he whispered in her ear. "You'll be with me, and I'll make sure nothing hurts you, okay? I won't let go of your hand—not once. Promise."

She looked past his shoulder toward where her parents waited behind the front door, then up at him with terrified brown eyes. Clutching his hand tightly, she nodded and allowed him to pull her into the closet behind Lauren.

The closet was dark and deep. They ducked under winter jackets and stepped over fishing boots and a tackle box to get to the back of the closet, where they could sit down along with Christmas decorations and a Thanksgiving centerpiece. He didn't once let go of her hand.

Lauren sat down across from them, her knees touching his as he sat next to Jillian. Jillian kept her knees up with an arm wrapped around them, as if for protection, and clung to his hand like a life preserver on a white-tipped ocean. They listened to faint voices in the foyer; the louder voices of Jillian's parents mingled with the soft, reassuring tones of Mrs. Mills. Linc couldn't distinguish most of the words, but could hear enough to know the Parrishes were angry and weren't content with the noncommittal answers from Lauren's mother. Finally, he heard their retreating footsteps and the front door being soundly shut.

Jillian's trembling subsided, and Linc knew she had heard her parents' departure. Still, she clung to him, burying her face in his shoulder and hiding from the darkness and the unseen things he knew lived in her fear. Closing his eyes, he smelled the ocean. He wondered for a moment if the smell came from the fishing boots, not understanding how the scents of salt and decaying sea life could be so pungent within the four walls of the closet.

"I'm hungry," Lauren whispered, shifting restlessly across from him.

"Not yet." Linc squeezed her knee. "Your mom's going to be looking for us. We should stay here for a while longer."

Lauren sighed heavily, and he heard her head thunk lightly against the closet wall. "I'm restless."

Linc felt a flash of irritation. "Then you can leave. Just don't tell anyone where Jillian is."

He heard her snort softly. "Like I would. You know, Jillian's dad is always nice to me—at least when Mrs. Parrish isn't around. It's like he's a different person when she's not with him. Maybe I could find him and talk to him. There's no reason why they can't stay a few days. I mean, it's silly for them to drive all that way just to pick Jillian up and turn right back around for the long drive back to Atlanta."

Jillian's voice was soft. "I don't think my grandmother and my mother get along. I've heard them arguing, and it always seems to be about something my grandmother forced my mother into doing—something she said once that she wakes up every day regretting." Linc felt her turn her face up to his. "I asked Grandma about it, but she just said it wasn't her place to tell me. And I'd never think about asking my mother."

Linc tightened his hold on Jillian's hand, knowing what she meant. He felt Lauren stand in the darkness. "Let me go see what I can do. My mom says I can charm anyone into saying yes." He heard the smile in her voice.

Lauren stuck her hand out and brushed his face, but her hand didn't stop until it was resting on Jillian's head. "You're safe in here. Linc will take care of you."

He felt Jillian stir next to him. "I can take care of myself. I just need somebody . . . here."

Lauren straightened. "I know." She paused for a moment. "I'll make sandwiches for everybody and bring them down on the beach. I'll see you there."

Linc closed his eyes at the bright light when she opened the door and just as quickly shut it. With his eyes still closed, he began to speak quietly to Jillian, telling stories of his pirate ancestors and their imagined exploits as kings of the sea isles. He didn't realize that he was almost asleep until he felt her warm breath on his cheek.

"Thank you," she said before laying her head on his shoulder. Her grip on his hand slowly lessened, as if her fear had been absorbed by him and dispelled, a conquering no less powerful than that of taking over a ship on the open sea. Her hand rested lightly in his, and they slept.

Even now, all these years later, he could picture the welts on Jillian's legs made by the buckle of her father's belt. He was sure she still carried the small, curved and purple scar on her upper thigh. Despite her punishment, her parents had relented and had stayed for three more days.

Linc stared into the gaping darkness of the closet, the voices finally diminished. Leaving the door open, he turned and slowly climbed the stairs.

He paused on the upstairs landing, his gaze focused on Lauren's old bedroom. *Look in the window seat.* He could almost hear Gracie's voice in the darkened hallway. He looked at his watch: three thirty. It was the middle of the night and he was wide awake. With a soft curse, he went to his bedroom to retrieve his toolbox, then made his way to the window seat.

The light from the overhead bulb shone dimly into the small space, but Linc could see enough to know that the button released the entire side panel inside the seat. He could force it with a screwdriver or break it with a hammer, destroying it either way. But he just couldn't wait any longer. It almost seemed as if there were an invisible pull forcing him to lift his screwdriver and jam it into the small crack in the edge of the panel. The splintering and heave of the wood didn't bother him at all.

He lifted the panel out and stared into the exposed secret compartment and blinked twice. Inside lay a stack of envelopes, their edges frayed and worn, held together by a rubber band. Sticking his hand inside, he pulled them out, the movement making the old rubber band break, then fall back inside the compartment.

The paper was warped and bowed, as if the envelopes had been at one time exposed to extreme dampness. Lifting the stack to his face, he sniffed, and for the second time that night smelled ocean waves full of sea life.

He sat down on the floor with his back against the seat and picked up the first envelope. It was blank, without even a name scribbled across the front, and the flap was intact, as if the envelope had never been sealed but just folded inside. Without pausing, he pulled out the letter and unfolded it. He stared at the bold black handwriting— definitely that of a male. Gooseflesh feathered the back of his neck, as if someone were standing behind him, reading over his shoulder.

Without reading the first letter, he flipped through the rest of the letters and examined the handwriting again. All of them had been signed with the single initial M. Small pricks of recognition floated somewhere in the back of his brain. With a deep breath, he opened the first letter again and began to read.

My dearest Lauren, it began, and Linc closed his eyes, not sure if he could go on. But he forced them open again and continued to read. At first, he didn't realize that he was holding his breath until he had to gasp for air. He read letter after letter, feeling more and more as if he were sinking into the deep water of the ocean, his head drifting farther and farther from the surface.

And then he felt as if somebody had punched him in the gut before he'd had a chance to prepare himself. He sat where he was, breathless, the feel of the paper against his skin his only connection to reality. *This must be what it's like to drown.* He stumbled to his feet when the first roll of thunder sounded, but he didn't move. All he could do was stand there and feel the anger, the hurt, the disbelief. When lightning flashed and the lights flickered, he moved toward the door.

"Oh, God," he said softly as he forced his feet to move in the direction of the stairs and then out of the house, as the first raindrops began to fall.

Jillian rocked back and forth, watching Ford's eyes drifting closed, his cheeks dimpling in brief smiles as sleep tugged him into the land of nod. He hummed to himself, a milk bubble forming on his lips, bursting only as his mouth opened in a huge yawn before settling in a wide, toothless grin. His eyes stayed closed this time, but his smile didn't fade.

She knew she was supposed to put him in the crib while he was still awake so he would learn to put himself to sleep, but there was something almost addictive about holding a drowsy baby. The sweet smell of him and his small, warm body against hers almost made her weep. She knew she must have felt the same with Gracie, but all of her memories of her first child seemed to be drowned in her own feelings of incompetence and self-doubt. But now, looking down at her son, she felt different. It was as if the salt-drenched air of the ocean and tidal creeks were breathing a newfound strength and courage into her. Or maybe they had been there all along, and she just hadn't known where to find them. She leaned forward and kissed Ford's cheek and sighed softly to herself. She still didn't think she'd ever be the perfect mother. But she was here, now, for both of her children, and maybe that was enough.

She rocked for a few minutes longer, reluctant to put him down, especially since Grace was spending the night with Mary Ellen again and Jillian would be on her own. Jillian lifted the baby from the crook of her arm and settled him on her shoulder, resting her cheek against his fuzzy head as she rocked. She spotted her bare thighs below her nightshirt, seeing the faint purple crescent scar that was so much a part of her now that it seemed it had always been there. It wasn't as noticeable as it had once been, and one part of her wanted it to fade completely. But another part of her wanted it to stay, to remind her of things she should never forget.

Standing suddenly, the chair rocked in her wake as she walked toward the crib. Ford murmured something in his sleep, reminding Jillian of how her grandmother used to say that children could talk to the angels. She kissed him again and whispered, "Put in a good word for me," then placed him down in his crib. He stretched and wiggled to find a comfortable spot before Jillian pulled the yellow blanket Martha had given him up over his shoulders.

The lights flickered briefly and she cast a worried look toward the window. It had rained several times since the stormy night of Ford's birth, but nothing so severe that the electricity had been knocked out. A flash of fear ran through her, and she forced it back. She now had a flashlight with working batteries in every room.

She bent to flip on Ford's night-light, but stepped back quickly as a blur of black fur streaked by at her feet. Spot stopped long enough to look back at Jillian, as if to make sure he'd frightened her enough before continuing on his way in a more sedate walk. The lights flickered again as Jillian straightened. With one last glance over at the sleeping baby in the crib, Jillian left the room, leaving the door cracked open behind her.

She flicked on every light she passed as she moved across the upstairs hallway and then down the stairs. She stopped on the bottom step when she saw Spot waiting at the front door, staring at it expectantly. Lightning flashed and the lights dimmed at the same time a knock sounded on the door.

Swallowing heavily, Jillian made her way to the door and looked through the sidelight, feeling visible relief when she recognized Linc on the other side. She turned the latch and the wind pushed the door in toward her, almost knocking her back, and then she was moving back, but it was Linc who was pushing his way inside.

She opened her mouth to say something but stopped when she caught sight of Linc's face up close. He was pale under his tan, his lips tight and white rimmed. His eyes stared at her as if seeing somebody else, and she stepped back farther to put distance between them. He slammed the door closed.

"Linc?" she managed. She was alarmed but not afraid. Not of Linc. He was soaking, his hair black and slicked back off his forehead. He stood dripping on her wood floor and was staring back at her. She hadn't seen him since their kiss earlier, and she wondered briefly if his agitated visit had anything to do with that. But when she stared back into his eyes, she couldn't imagine that anything as beautiful as their kiss could wound a man as much as Linc appeared to be.

It occurred to Jillian that it was probably somewhere near three in the morning. "The lights aren't out yet, if that's why you're here. . . ."

"What do you remember about your father when you were younger?"

She furrowed her brows, his words taking her off guard. "My father? You know what my father was like. Why are you asking me this now?"

Thunder shouted outside, rattling the windows, but Linc didn't shift his gaze. Instead, he took a step toward her and gripped her shoulders. She met his eyes and saw confusion, hurt and anger in the same moment she realized that none was directed at her but at some faraway person or thing that still had the power to cut him down. It seemed that all the strength and power Linc harbored were as impotent to him now as a ship's sail in a hurricane wind.

Linc moved his face close to hers. "We need to talk—now."

Instead of pushing him away, she moved her hands up and cupped his hands. It was a maternal gesture, meant to comfort, and she fleetingly wondered how she had known to do that. She spoke softly. "Come with me to the kitchen. I'll make some coffee, and you can dry off and then we'll talk."

He narrowed his eyes for a moment, then nodded. "All right."

She turned from him, and she felt him follow her to the kitchen, pausing behind her briefly as she stopped in the powder room to grab a couple of hand towels.

He sat at the large oak table while she began making the coffee and putting together a plate of brownies. She turned to put the plate in front of him and almost dropped it. He had stripped off his shirt, revealing a smooth, muscled chest and arms. He was watching her as a predator would watch its prey, and he no longer resembled the respected architect she had become used to. This was the raw man the young Linc she remembered had grown to be. He was unmasked now, and she felt something ripple through her, something that felt remarkably like desire.

His eyes met hers. "Why do you do that?"

"Do what?"

"Feed people. It's like you think you need to have a reason for people to be around you. You don't have to, you know."

Water dripped from his hair down the side of his face to his shoulder. She picked up the towel and moved to wipe it, but he grabbed her wrist. She frowned. "You're dripping."

He took the towel from her. "I'll do it."

She moved away and poured coffee into mugs with shaking hands, then returned to the table, placing a steaming mug in front of him, trying to avoid staring at his bare chest. She remembered touching his hair when he'd kissed her and how she had always wanted to do that. She felt the same about his skin, about how smooth and warm it would be beneath her palms.

She sat down across from him as her gaze met his, and for a passing moment she felt he could read her thoughts, and she blushed hotly. Taking a quick sip of her coffee, she burned her tongue and quickly set the mug back down on the table.

Drawing a deep breath, she looked back up at him, trying not to notice how dark his gray eyes had become. "What do you need to know?"

He leaned forward, his elbows on the table, his expression intense. "You told me once that your dad was having an affair with your neighbor in Atlanta. Do you know if that was the only time your dad ever cheated on your mother?"

Jillian sat back, stunned, her thoughts racing back to a long-ago Christmas when she'd been fifteen or sixteen. Her parents were having a horrible fight, with her mother throwing pieces of her treasured glass menagerie and accusing her father of unspeakable things. They didn't know she'd heard, but she had. Every ugly word.

Slowly, Jillian nodded. "Yes. At least one other time that I know of—but there were probably more. I don't know the details, but I know my mother had found out something. I thought they were going to get a divorce."

"What happened?"

Jillian shrugged. "My dad packed a suitcase and left. He came here—I know that because I heard my mother on the phone with him, begging him to come back. And then she'd try talking to my grandmother to get my dad to come back and would end up screaming at her." She looked down at her hands, small and sensible, and thought of her grandmother. "They never did get along. I knew my mother had to have been desperate to be asking my grandmother's help."

Linc's eyes narrowed as he regarded her, and he was silent for a moment, as if doing some internal calculation. Finally, he asked, "Then what happened?"

"He came home. They still fought, but I stopped listening." She met his eyes again. "I didn't care anymore. I was invisible to them. I figured if I pretended they were invisible, too, then it wouldn't hurt as much."

His eyes flickered before he turned away for a moment. "Did you ever find out who the woman was? Did you overhear your mother mention her name?"

"No. Or if I did, I don't remember now."

She made a move to stand up and get more coffee, but he reached over and grabbed her wrists. "Are you sure? You lived with the man. Maybe you saw something and thought it best to keep quiet."

A spot of anger flooded the space behind her eyes. "No, I don't. And why are you asking me these questions about my father? What has he got to do with anything?"

"Just a name, Jillian. Don't you remember a name?"

She pulled her hands away from his and stood, disappointment and anger flashing through her in equal measure. "Why won't you trust me?"

He stood, too, the shadows in the dimly lit room slipping over the muscles and skin of his bare chest. "Why should I?"

She stepped away from him. She couldn't seem to think clearly when he was standing so close. He'd been right about the food. There had always been a need in her to keep people close to her by making things for them. She had learned that from her parents. But with Linc, she'd wanted to earn his friendship on her own terms. Only that was no longer possible. They stood staring at each other for several long moments, listening to the wind and rain beat at the house, obliterating the sound of their breathing as tears stung her eyes. "Who do you think sent you the money to get away from here?"

His eyes opened wide and he took a step toward her, then stopped.

"It was my emergency fund my grandmother had given me—just in case I ever needed to leave my parents and get to Pawleys." She wiped her eyes with the back of her hand. "I figured you being in jail was an emergency, so I sent it anonymously to Chief Weber. I knew I could trust him to give it to you."

Linc raked his hands through his hair, then looked back at her. "I didn't know." He took a step toward her. "Please don't cry, Jillian. . . ."

She held up her hand to stop him from coming closer. "I have something else I need to tell you." She left the kitchen and went into the front parlor before kneeling in front of the sofa and reaching underneath, searching for the box.

Panicking, her fingers at first touched only old dust bunnies and discarded change. But she remembered sticking the box under this side of the sofa. She shifted to the right and stuck her fingers in again, this time touching something small and hard. Sitting up, she pulled out the box.

She turned, not surprised to see that Linc had followed her and was standing in the doorway. "Lauren's box," he said, his voice uneven.

Jillian nodded and walked toward him before placing the box in his hand. Lightning lit up the sky, creating daylight for a brief second, and the lights dimmed as if in awe. She watched until Linc's long, elegant fingers wrapped around the dark wood before she left the room, waiting for the next roll of thunder to come.

CHAPTER 18

L INC WAS SURPRISED HIS HANDS COULD REMAIN STEADY AS HE moved toward the sofa and sat down, staring at the box as if it were a jellyfish getting ready to strike. He was aware Jillian had left the room and was glad she'd gone. He wasn't sure why; just that whatever emotions were unleashed when he lifted the lid, he didn't want them to hurt her.

His gaze shifted to the empty doorway, his thoughts startling him. When had Jillian's feelings become so important to him?

Rain pelted the house, the wind pulsing against the eaves, urging him to continue. He lifted the lid slowly. Inside, he saw the wooden star first and took it out, the wood oddly warm against his palm. *Here's your star—right here on earth. You can make it shine, and don't ever let anybody tell you different.* Linc smiled as he remembered what he'd told Jillian when he'd given her the star, almost embarrassed at how idealistic he had once been. Returning his attention to the box, he felt the surety that whatever idealism he had left was about to be destroyed completely.

He placed the star on the table in front of him, then reached in for the worn piece of paper. Slowly, he unfolded it, the middle crease tearing slightly as he held the letter open. For the second time that night, he felt as if someone were holding his head underwater, the feeling of drowning so intense he felt the need to gasp for air.

Linc recognized his own handwriting first, and then the actual letter. He could almost see a younger version of his hand, holding tightly to the pen as it flew across the paper, the words of an angry young man bleeding across the page.

> *I have started this letter about a hundred times, and I guess there's really only one thing I'm trying to say. I love you, Lauren. I thought we had something permanent. But now you won't see me, and I don't know why. You don't even have the guts to meet with me and*

explain. You once told me that there's a thin line between love and hate—and I think I now understand what you meant.

I've given you everything, and I've got nothing left. I should have known from the start that it would never be enough for you and that your heart was always for sale to the highest bidder. You have killed a part of me, and I hope I have the chance to return the favor.

Maybe it's best we don't meet. I want to shake you so hard, to make you see. To remember what we had. But I honestly don't think I can promise not to hurt you. I hate you as much as I love you, and that's a very dangerous thing.

Linc looked up from the letter, surprised to find himself alone in the room. It was as if the words on the page had somehow conjured Lauren, with her bright, knowing smile and her sun-bronzed skin. He could almost swear he smelled suntan lotion.

He stood, his legs shaky. Before he could call for Jillian, she was there, standing with a tall glass of iced tea and a plate of lemon bars. He almost smiled at yet another food offering, but instead took the plate and glass and set them on the table.

Holding the paper out in front of him, he approached Jillian. "You've read this, then."

She nodded, her dark eyes unreadable.

"And you never showed it to anybody. Even when you knew this could be considered strong evidence that I had done something to Lauren."

Again she nodded, and he saw her pulse beating rapidly under the soft skin of her throat.

He let the letter float to the ground as he closed the distance between them. He laced his fingers through her hair, cupping her head and tilting her face toward him. "Why, Jillian? Why didn't you tell anyone?"

She surprised him by bringing her hands up to his face, cupping them as he'd seen her do to Gracie when explaining something important. Her words were quiet, hardly audible against the sound of the beating rain upon the house. "Because I know who you are, Linc. I always have."

He gripped her to him as her words sunk in, feeling the small, slender shoulders that suddenly seemed so strong. Why had he never recognized the silent strength behind her need and hopefulness? *Because I know who you are, Linc. I always have.*

Relief, anger and hope fired at him simultaneously, leaving him drained and empty. He realized he still clutched Jillian as he sank down on his knees, and she followed him. His eyes searched hers, looking for the girl he thought had abandoned him, and instead finding a woman who'd never given up hope. It embarrassed him and it humbled him, and the only thing he could think to do was to lean forward and kiss her.

Her mouth opened to his as if she'd expected his kiss, and said his name as lightning flashed again, making the electric lights flicker before going out completely. He touched her face with his fingers as he kissed her, feeling the soft skin of her cheeks, the dampness of her tears, the solidness of her bones, and her invisible strength in the way she held her head. The strength of her presence seemed to make the tips of his finger burn in the same way they did when he was creating something. Except this time, the energy flew both ways, molding and creating him in the same way he would carve a star out of wood.

He lifted his mouth and pressed his forehead against hers. "Why didn't you tell me? All these months, you could have told me, but you didn't. Why?"

He breathed heavily in the darkness, feeling her curves and angles against his body and listening to the storm outside. She kept her forehead pressed against his when she finally spoke.

"Because . . . I . . . I guess I don't really know." His fingers on the smooth skin of her neck felt her swallow as she struggled to find the right words. "I think, though, that maybe I wanted you to like me again—to trust me—on my own. It was . . . it was sort of like an experiment." He heard the smile in her voice. "I didn't need to bring you food."

He rubbed his face against hers, feeling his desire for her like a flood tide moving from his fingertips and up his arms and throughout his body, until he thought he might drown from it. He hardened and moved her closer. "I wanted to hate you—don't you know that? All of these years I taught myself to hate you, thinking you were just like your father. I . . . I don't know what to say."

Her fingers threaded through his hair, moving like the rivulets of rain on the windows, slipping with purpose toward unknown destinations. She brushed her lips against his again. "Don't say anything at all."

He stared at her in the dark, seeing nothing but seeking the light she seemed to be shining in the blackness around him, like a polestar in the night sky. He reached for her then, laying her on the floor and then moving on top of her. Thunder rattled their world, and he bent close to her ear. "Are you afraid?"

Lightning streaked across the sky, illuminating her face and eyes for a brief moment, electrifying the air between them, and he thought he could smell the burnt ions melding together with the scents of wet sand and ocean. He felt her shake her head. "No. Just don't let go." Then he touched her lips with his and closed his eyes with a sigh.

Jillian was aware of the storm and of the pressing darkness around them, but Linc's weight anchored her, keeping her safe from whatever it was that hid in dark spaces. She shifted beneath him, opening her mouth to his kiss, and wondered fleetingly how it could all feel so right.

Her nightshirt had already slid above her hips and his hands followed, long and sleek against her bare skin, moving in rhythm to the rain against the tin roof. She could feel his rain-soaked jeans along the length of her legs, and said the first thing that came to her. "We need to get you out of those pants."

He grinned against her cheek, his stubble brushing her jaw. "I was just thinking the same thing."

She grinned back, acknowledging the lack of awkwardness between them, as if the two of them together had been meant to happen and all the years in between had simply been a waiting time. "Let's go upstairs."

He stood and pulled her with him, keeping her hand in his. Kissing her neck, he whispered in her ear, "I won't let go."

"I know." She buried her face in the warm space between his neck and shoulder before allowing him to lead her slowly up the darkened stairs, his hand solid against hers.

The wind pushed at the house as they reached her bedroom, and Linc turned to her. "Do I need to turn on a flashlight?"

Her heart jerked in her chest at the knowledge that he would remember her fear of the dark, and she lifted her hands to his face. "No."

She wanted to tell him that he seemed to give the room light—not the light that she could see, but a light that seemed to fill her from the inside. But she didn't say it out loud. Linc was still the boy who had been embarrassed by shows of emotion, and had once given her a wooden star by first poking her in the arm with it. She smiled at the memory, and pulled him with her toward the bed.

The raging sky and stormy ocean faded from the periphery of her awareness, leaving her conscious of only Linc: of his touch, his scent, his weight on her as he moved on top of her on the bed. They moved together without words, seeming to sense what the other needed. She lifted her hips and he slid her nightgown over her head, and they both worked on removing his wet jeans and underwear, dropping them in a sodden heap on the floor.

His bare skin was warm and damp and solid on hers, his fingers and mouth starving for her flesh, feasting on the curves and hollows of her body. *This is Linc,* she reminded herself. Only it was and it wasn't. This beautiful man with the beautiful hands that seemed to know her body was the man he had become, not the boy who had once belonged to Lauren and to the things he created and nothing more. This man belonged to her at this moment, and she felt as if they became a part of each other, belonging to each other as much as the tides belonged to the ocean and the grains of sand to the shore.

His hands and lips moved lower, tasting her, sucking on her, feeding on her, and she cried out with impatience, needing to feel more of him. He had always been a part of her, and now she wanted to make it real.

She opened her legs to him and he surprised her by pausing for a moment, supporting himself on his elbows, his face in the shadows but poised above hers. "Are you sure you're ready for this?"

She nodded, pressing her hips upward to rub against him, and she heard him groan.

"No, I mean . . . you just had a baby. I don't want to hurt you."

Smiling, she reached up and touched his face, feeling the soft stubble under her fingertips. "The doctor said I'm fine." Pressing herself upward, she kissed him softly on his lips. "And I want this—very much."

"Thank God," he said, lowering himself on her again, and she smiled against his kiss.

He slid into her with a hard, deep thrust, but she was hot and slick and ready for him. She cried out with the joy of it as he began to move with sure and steady strokes. He threaded his fingers through hers, drawing her arms above her head, opening her to him even more. They moved together in timeless rhythm, and he was saying her name while loving her with his hands and body. She didn't think to feel self-conscious of the new fullness of her hips and breasts. He made her feel beautiful and perfect, and she opened herself to him, feeling the heat between them build until they both reached fulfillment together.

"Jillian," he said, his body slick with sweat as he collapsed on top of her, then moved to her side, cradling her head against his shoulder. She could feel the blood pump through her veins, her body like the creek at high tide, the life-giving waters moving from its source into the tiny estuaries, bringing sustenance to all the parched places she had kept hidden all her life.

Linc kissed the top of her head. "I'm sorry."

"For what?"

She could sense he was struggling for the right words. Maybe to express remorse for doubting her, or maybe to apologize for making love to her before all the ground rules between them had been presented.

Pressing her fingers against his lips, she whispered, "Shh. It's all right." He had always expressed himself eloquently through his hands rather than with words, and she would not have him feel inadequate when his touch alone had shifted her world onto an even keel.

She closed her eyes, pressing herself against his side, feeling sleep pulling her under. "Just . . . be. Be here with me now. We'll deal with the rest later."

The rain tapped against the tin roof as he pressed his lips gently against her temple, his long fingers stroking her hair. She let herself drift off to sleep then, and she dreamt of being on a raft in an ocean of stars, drawing nearer and nearer to the one that shone the brightest.

Something tugged on her hair and she stirred awake, staring into the sweet face of her baby son. Pulling herself up to a sitting position, she looked past Ford to see Linc in jeans and with a bare chest reclining on the bed, watching her. She was startled to see it was full morning, the sun bright and sparkling off the remaining raindrops on the window.

"I didn't hear him cry—was he fussing?" She lifted the baby, settling him in the crook of her arm, unbuttoning her nightgown and preparing to nurse him.

"No, just talking to himself. But I thought he might be hungry."

She smiled self-consciously, remembering their night together. They had made love two more times, leaving her sore and exhausted but completely sated. "He slept through the night, then. He hasn't done that before."

"I guess he figured you were otherwise occupied."

Linc's eyes glittered with amusement, and Jillian looked away again, feeling her cheeks heat. She settled Ford on her breast and waited until he was suckling contentedly before looking back at Linc.

His face was serious now as he focused on the nursing baby. His eyes met hers. "You have no idea how beautiful you look right now." Slowly, he reached out a finger and touched the baby's cheek, then gently stroked the top of her breast before lifting her chin to face him. "This whole motherhood thing—it suits you."

She dropped her gaze back to her son, not wanting Linc to see the moisture in her eyes. She still wasn't completely convinced, but even she was beginning to believe it.

The bed shifted as Linc stood. "You've been painting."

She looked up at the border she had just started working on, the gold-painted words shimmering in the bright morning sun.

Linc read the words out loud. "He turns not back who is bound to a star." He stuck his hands in his back pockets. "Da Vinci, right? I remember that. You cut it from a magazine once and gave it to me. I kept it for a long time."

"Did you?" Jillian rubbed her cheek against the top of Ford's head. "It still reminds me of you."

He turned then to face her. "Funny. It always reminded me of you."

Her smile froze at the knocking on the front door. "Oh, no—it's probably Lessie bringing Gracie back."

Linc began to pull on his shirt. "It's okay. It's almost eleven o'clock, so there's no reason why I can't be here measuring your kitchen. I'll go see who it is and then I'll leave, okay?"

She nodded once. "But will you be back?"

He walked over to the bed and kissed her hard on the lips as his answer.

She heard his steady tread on the steps and then the sound of the door opening. And then she heard the deep voices of men talking before Linc came up the stairs again, an odd expression on his face.

Placing Ford on her shoulder and patting him on the back, she looked up at Linc. "Who is it?"

Linc bent down to retrieve his socks and shoes. "Your husband. Or I guess I should say your ex-husband. He says he'll wait on the porch."

Jillian felt strangely calm as she gathered up the baby and slid off the bed. "But it's Saturday—he said he wouldn't be here until tomorrow. Did he bring . . . ?"

Linc's lip twitched. "The slut Joanie? No—he's alone. If you want me to, I'll go to Lessie's and pick up Grace."

She nodded. "Thanks. I guess I'll get dressed and bring the baby down."

Linc looked at her, his gray eyes unreadable. "I'll see you later, then."

She nodded again, and he left without kissing her but with a promise to return. She thought of Rick downstairs, waiting for her, but she felt no jitters, no self-consciousness and no personal repercussions. She remembered Linc's touch and felt stronger somehow, as if newly emerged from a long, dark tunnel into a day of blinding brightness. She could face Rick now without anger, without recrimination. And somewhere, the thought came to her that maybe she should thank him.

Calmly, she placed Ford in the small cradle by her bed, then padded across the wood floor toward her closet. Pausing at her dresser, she bent to peer into the caterpillar jar Grace had left there for Jillian's safekeeping.

Inside, a completely clear chrysalis still perched on a twig, but it now gaped open like a mouth waiting to be fed. And there, at the top of the jar near the lid, was a monarch butterfly, waving its wings at her from the underside of a glossy green milkweed leaf.

If she doesn't struggle through the small hole she makes in the cocoon, she'll skip that whole step and never learn to fly. And what sort of life would that be? Jillian rested her elbows on the dresser, remembering Linc's words and watching the new butterfly rest after its journey of metamorphosis. It had managed to squeeze through the shell of the chrysalis, the gossamer wings like solid air, straightening and strengthening them so that they would be able to take flight.

With one last look at the butterfly, Jillian moved toward her closet with a light step, almost believing for the first time in her life that maybe it was time to learn to fly.

CHAPTER 19

JILLIAN STARED INTO HER CLOSET FOR A LONG TIME, FLIPPING PAST the hangers that held all the shapeless sundresses that had once made up her complete summer wardrobe when she'd lived in Atlanta. But now it was like staring into the closet of a stranger, and she couldn't imagine slipping into a single one of them, any more than she could stand the thought of wearing another maternity dress.

Shutting the closet door with disgust, she went to her dresser and pulled out a pair of denim shorts and a cotton T-shirt, items she'd bought since Ford's birth. They were comfortable and fit her new curves well. Rick might frown at the casualness of it, but she simply didn't care. She wasn't his concern anymore.

After slipping on a pair of flat sandals, she changed and dressed Ford, then carried him downstairs. She found Rick on the back porch and she watched him through the screen door for a few moments before he realized she was there. He hadn't changed at all. She hadn't really expected him to, but thought that maybe in their time apart from each other he would at least appear different to her.

He was still tall, sandy-haired and clean-shaven. Even in pressed khakis and button-down shirt, he looked like the successful lawyer he was—if one didn't notice the Ray-Bans in his shirt pocket and the Barbie doll that hung loosely in one of his hands.

She pushed open the door and he looked up, a confused expression passing rapidly across his face. He stood slowly but waited for her to close the distance between them.

"Hello, Rick. It's been a while."

He tried a halfhearted smile, and she gave him a full point for attempted civility. "Yeah, it has been, hasn't it?" His gaze moved down to the bundle in her arms. "And this must be Ford."

Jillian moved closer and held up the baby, not yet handing him over. She was oddly reluctant to let her son pass from her grasp, even if into the arms of his father. It was as if the closeness she'd built with her son couldn't be shared with this man who was as much a stranger to her as he must be to Ford. "Ford, this is your daddy. Rick, this is Ford."

Rick slowly touched the baby's nose, cheeks and earlobes, finally allowing his finger to be grabbed by a tiny fist. He smiled fully this time. "He's great." His gaze settled back on Jillian. "I'm sorry I'm a day early. I found a few connecting flights that made it here sooner, so I booked them. I couldn't wait to see Gracie and Ford."

"I understand. Nice tan, by the way." *One point for civility for me, too,* she thought.

He rubbed his hand self-consciously across the nape of his neck. "Thanks. And you look, well, you look good. I didn't expect . . ."

She met his gaze, waiting for his words.

Finally, he shrugged. "I don't know. . . . You just look different. You seem . . . happy."

Jillian swayed with Ford in her arms. "You make it sound like a foreign word."

He studied her for a moment. "Well, for you, yeah, I'd say it was. To be honest, I was a little worried about what I'd be finding here. I had visions of you holed up on the sofa and both kids wondering what to do with you."

She frowned, remembering the woman he had known and realizing she couldn't picture her face. She felt a little sick. "Was I really that bad?"

He shrugged again, not answering. "This place seems to agree with you." He turned around, taking in the porch with the hanging flowers, swaying hammock and rocking chairs. "I can almost understand why you never brought me here." Rick moved toward the small brick wall that surrounded the porch and looked out at the ocean. "I can certainly see why you love it—it would have been great to vacation here in the summer."

He looked as if he would say more, but stopped. Turning back around, he moved toward her and the baby. "Can I at least hold him?"

Reluctantly, she handed Ford over, feeling bereft when the heat of the little body left her own. Rick's large hands cupped the baby's head, holding him at arm's length to get a better look at him. "He's a big guy."

"Yes, he is." She watched her ex-husband smile at their son, and she thawed a little toward him. With a small smile, she said, "Wait until you see Gracie—I think she's grown six inches since you last saw her." Jillian crossed her arms over her chest, studying the man she had once felt so grateful to. Grateful enough to give him two children. "She's missed you."

"I've missed her, too. Where is she?"

"She spent the night at a friend's. Linc went to pick her up—she'll be back any minute."

"Yeah, I met Linc. Is he a good friend of yours?"

Jillian blushed under Rick's probing gaze. "I've known him since I was a kid. He restored this house and sold it to me. He was going to use it as a rental—that's why it was all furnished—but when he knew I was looking at it, he went ahead and sold it." Jillian blushed again when she realized she was rambling to change the subject, and mentally kicked herself for giving so much away.

Rick looked down at Ford as the baby began to root on his shoulder. "You've changed, Jillian. You don't seem like the same woman who didn't like to go to the gas station by herself."

Jillian squinted up at him, shielding her eyes with her hand. "I'm not her anymore." She turned her back on him and looked out at the sea oats moving under the warm sun. "And I'm glad. She wasn't a person I particularly liked."

She faced him again and his brown eyes met hers over the head of their son. He didn't say anything, and she wondered if her rejection of her old self had seemed like an affront to him. After all, he had once loved that girl—the girl she had buried as soon as she had felt the warm Pawleys sand under her toes. A twinge of regret gripped her. Regardless of how things had ended up, she would always owe Rick a great deal.

She moved toward the door. "Come on in and I'll get you something to eat before Gracie gets back."

"I was wondering when you were going to do that."

"Do what?"

"Give me food. You're always feeding people."

Jillian held open the screen door and waited for Rick to go past her. "Linc says the same thing."

Rick stopped in front of her, his brown eyes gazing thoughtfully into hers. She tried to remember the years of being married to him, sleeping with him, making children with him. But it was as if she'd already packed those years away and forgotten them like an old pair of jeans, remembering how comfortable they were but not what they looked like.

Rick didn't say anything and walked past Jillian into the house.

Ford was swinging in the baby swing, and Rick and Jillian were sitting at the kitchen table, sharing a plate of pecan pralines when the front door banged open and Gracie came running into the room and threw herself at her father. Jillian felt an unfamiliar stab of gratitude as she watched Rick embracing their daughter—gratitude that Rick could find so much love in his heart for the child he shared with a woman who had never really loved him the way he had deserved.

"Daddy!" she squealed, throwing her arms around his neck. She jerked back and stared at the other people in the room, including Linc, who had followed her inside at a more sedate pace and now towered in the doorway. "Did you bring . . . ?"

"No!" Linc and Jillian shouted simultaneously. More calmly, Jillian said, "Daddy came alone."

Gracie turned back to Rick. "I've got *so* much to show you. There's the creek and dolphins and Mrs. Michaels—that's my teacher—and my school and Mrs. Weber. And you have to meet my best friend, Mary Ellen. Have you seen Spot yet?"

Jillian patted Grace's head. "I think you've worn him out already, Gracie. And don't forget the beach."

Grace looked up at her with somber brown eyes. "No, I don't wanna. It rained a lot last night. And remember what happened last time it rained a lot."

Jillian's eyes met Linc's for a brief moment before she turned her gaze back on Rick and Grace. "There was a little cave-in on the beach during the last storm. It scared Gracie, and she hasn't wanted to go down there. But maybe you can take her further up the beach by the Webers'. She'll show you."

Grace crawled off Rick's lap and walked over to Linc. She tugged on his hand, and he squatted so he could look her in the face. "She can see the sky now. But she can't breathe. She just wants to breathe."

Jillian felt the rush of cold all over her body, as if she'd just plunged into a pool of icy water.

Rick sent a questioning look to Jillian, who responded by shoving the pralines closer to him. She mouthed the words "imaginary friend," and that seemed to satisfy him. He put another praline in his mouth as Grace skipped back to sit on his lap.

"Are you gonna stay here with us?" She smiled up at her father, and Jillian realized perhaps for the first time how she didn't resemble him at all. It was as if her features had shunned her father's genes and clung to the ones of her mother's ancestors.

Rick choked a little and said, "Ah, no. I'm staying at the Pelican Inn. It's close by, though."

"But why not stay here? Jilly-bean's bed is big enough for both of you."

Jillian could feel Linc's stare on her, and she refused to look at him. She plucked Grace off of Rick's lap. "I'm sure Daddy is more comfortable at the inn, sweetie. Why don't you run upstairs and put on your swimsuit with some shorts, okay?"

Gracie shot her a look complete with furrowed brows, but ran upstairs to do as she was told.

Rick had stood and moved away from the table, leaving the dirty dishes. "She still calls you Jilly-bean."

Jillian wiped her palms across the front of her shorts. It hadn't sounded like an accusation, but she still bristled. "Yes, well . . ." Stealing a glance at Linc, she looked at Rick again and took a deep breath. "I'd like to talk about custody arrangements while you're here."

Rick acted as if he hadn't heard her and instead looked toward the doorway where Gracie had disappeared. "She's . . . wonderful. I've never seen her so energetic. Or happy." He turned to face Jillian again and studied her for a long moment. "I came prepared to take them both back with me, you know. Without opposition."

Jillian stabbed her fingernails into the sides of her legs, afraid to move. "And now?"

"We'll work it out before I leave," he said, running his fingers through his hair, and doing nothing to ease the tenseness Jillian felt. "I'm going to go back to the inn and change into shorts. Tell Grace I'll be right back."

She hadn't realized how much she needed an answer from him. But she would wait. And somehow, she wasn't afraid. She took a deep breath, smelling the ocean, and felt strengthened.

"Thank you," she said, looking into his eyes again and wondering what it was she had always been looking for there and had never found.

He nodded to her and Linc, then left. She felt Linc move up behind her, enfolding his arms around her. She leaned back into his embrace, thinking that maybe here, with him, she might finally find what she had sought all her life.

Jillian sat in the hammock on the porch, watching the sun sink lower in the sky and holding a very tired and sunburned Grace. Her daughter had spent a fun-filled day with her father, which unfortunately hadn't included sunscreen for either one of them. Gracie was tired and cranky and complaining about her reddened skin, despite the soothing lotion Jillian had applied.

"I don't know why Daddy couldn't spend the night."

"I know, sweetie. It takes a bit of getting used to, doesn't it? I know Daddy wanted to spend more time with you, but we're not married anymore, so he needs to stay in his own place. That doesn't mean that we both don't still love you very much. Okay?" She leaned down and kissed Grace's forehead, the skin hot under her lips. "And Daddy said he'd be back for breakfast tomorrow morning, so you won't even have time to miss him."

Gracie stuck out her lower lip. "Yes, I will. I'll miss him all night until the morning time."

Jillian didn't bother to raise the point that Gracie would undoubtedly be sleeping the entire time. They swung for a little longer before Jillian remembered the butterfly. "Constance hatched today."

Gracie sat up quickly. "Today? Really? Where is she?"

"She's upstairs in the jar on my dresser."

Gracie scrambled out of her mother's lap and onto the porch floor. "I've got to go see her."

The little girl ran inside, her sandals clattering on the wooden stairs. Jillian stood, the hammock swinging in her wake, and moved to rewind Ford's baby swing. Straightening, she stared out across the way to Linc's house. All was quiet there and on the beach, with the workers taking the weekend off. The roof was completed now on all sides, and the stark new wood made the house resemble a phoenix rising from the sand. *So much like Linc.*

Linc had gone to Charleston for the long weekend, and she found herself aching for him. Jillian smiled to herself, remembering their night together and feeling her hunger for him. It wasn't the need she'd had for Rick all those years ago; that had merely been the need to escape. No, the need she felt for Linc went much deeper, rooted with her need of air and food.

The screen door slammed shut, making Ford start as Gracie raced back out on the porch, the glass jar held out in her hands. She stopped in front of Jillian and held up the jar, her lower lip trembling. "She can't open her wings all the way because the jar's too small."

Jillian squatted down and took the jar. "What do you think we should do?"

Grace squinted up at her mother in the fading light. "We need to let her go."

Softly, Jillian said, "I think you're right."

They decided they would set Constance free at the creek, and while Jillian bent to unhook Ford from the baby swing, she sent Grace back into the house to get the front carrier Jillian would wear to hold the baby.

As she waited with Ford in her arms, swaying lightly with the breeze, she looked down at the beach, past the thick stand of white-tipped Spanish bayonets and brushy patches of saltwort, and spotted Janie Mulligan standing still and alone at the mouth of the collapsed dune.

Baby was in her front carrier as always, the straggly yellow hair tossed about in the wind. It was hard to see at that distance, but Jillian was quite sure Janie's lips were moving and her head was nodding, as if she were talking to some unknown companion. Jillian watched in silence as Janie turned around toward the surf, then walked slowly away, her head and shoulders bowed, her feet kicking sand behind her.

There was something so familiar about the way she moved, about the way her back arched and her feet splayed as she struggled through the dunes to the packed sand of the surf. It struck Jillian as odd when she couldn't think of what was so familiar about it, and she wondered why she'd never noticed it before.

Gracie raced out again, followed by the expected slam of the screen door, and handed her mother the carrier. "What if Constance doesn't know what to do when we let her out of the jar?"

Jillian sat down with the baby lying across her lap and began tying the carrier around her neck and waist. She paused for a moment, thinking about what she should say. "I think all of God's creatures are born with a certain knowing. For animals and insects like Constance, it's a knowing of how to find things to eat or seek shelter or even fly. It's passed down to them generation to generation, from mommies and daddies to their babies. It's a way of taking care of their children, really, that's inborn in every single creature."

Grace looked at her baby brother with a frown. "But what about people? Ford doesn't know how to do anything except pee in his diaper and drink milk."

Jillian smiled. "Well, yes, but there's more, too." She tried not to think of her own dark childhood, of unmet wants and needs and black closets. But always, always there had been hope. Maybe God had made sure that she had been given an abundance of hope and a grandmother who would make it grow. And now, when she looked into the faces of her two children, she thought she could finally understand why.

"I think all babies are born trusting in their parents to take care of them—to pick them up when they cry or feed them when they're hungry. They somehow know that things will work out—even though sometimes it's not quite clear right away. Sometimes it takes time to figure it out." And then Jillian thought of something her grandmother had once told her. *Sometimes mothers can only do their best. It's all God ever asks of us. And all he can expect with what we're given.*

She looked away and spotted the distant shape of Janie Mulligan, remembering the beautiful flowers and faded rag doll that the older woman mothered blindly but with so much love.

Lifting Ford into the carrier, she turned to Gracie. "Come on— grab the jar and let's get this done before it gets too much darker." The purpling sky loomed above them, the first stars of the evening shining faintly, and she felt a part of her fear diminish, as if a light from another source shone around her.

They crossed the street and walked down the boardwalk to the creek at low tide, the muddy earth seeming to melt into dark water. A mass of moving fiddler crabs scurried away from the dock, disturbed by the approach of footsteps.

Jillian and Grace squatted at the edge of the boardwalk, their eyes meeting over the lid of the jar.

Jillian smiled at her daughter. "Are you ready?"

Gracie nodded, her expression serious. Slowly, she unscrewed the lid and moved it away, then stared with expectation at the lip of the jar. At first, Constance did nothing but flutter her wings a couple of times. *Yes,* thought Jillian. *It's hard flying off the first time. But you'll be fine.*

Leaning over, Gracie spoke to the insect. "Fly, Constance. Fly away."

The butterfly fluttered her wings a few more times, seemingly to sample the fresh air above her, then lifted off her branch into the space between Jillian and Grace before disappearing in the dusk over the marsh.

Gracie stood, watching her butterfly vanish, her face turned toward the sky. She clasped her hands together in front of her, a broad smile on her face. "Did you see that, Mommy? She remembered how to fly!"

Jillian stood and brushed the hair out of her eyes. "Yes, she sure did."

She helped Gracie gather up the jar and lid and begin the journey back home. It wasn't until much later that she realized what Gracie had called her, and how long Jillian had known it to be true.

CHAPTER 20

JILLIAN SAT ACROSS FROM MARTHA WEBER AT THE WEBERS' KITCHEN table, poring over several ancient low country cookbooks and old recipe cards, jotting down notes and ideas for a prospective menu. Her plans had already progressed from catering out of her own kitchen to a full-fledged bakery with a small lunchtime restaurant. She'd even found a place in the Litchfield Beach area that seemed the perfect spot.

She took a sip of her coffee and looked over at Martha, who was holding Ford and making a big deal out of his cooing. He was perfectly content where he was, lying supine in the lap of luxury and being doted on by the women in his life. Martha tickled his chin, making him laugh, so she did it again.

Jillian smiled. "Guess you didn't find that recipe, huh?"

Martha shook her head with a grin, her eyes not leaving Ford's face. "No, sorry. I was busy."

Leaning back in her chair, Jillian watched the laughing baby and doting woman. "All I need to do is give that boy a TV remote, and he'll be ready for manhood. Just like his daddy."

Martha raised her eyebrows. "Speaking of which, where is Rick today?"

"He spent all morning with Gracie, but he said he had to work for the rest of the day. Personally, I think he's over at the Pelican Inn trying to soothe his sunburned skin. He got himself and Gracie real burned yesterday at the beach." She held up her hand. "Not that I'm complaining. Gracie had a wonderful time. I think she enjoys having a man around."

Martha nodded. "Well, there's certainly things a child could only learn from a man. Mason could surely teach them a thing or two about the remote." She looked up at Jillian and said, "Or Linc."

Jillian felt her cheeks flush, but didn't say anything.

Softly, Martha said, "So it's that way between the two of you, is it? Poor Mason."

"Martha, it's not that Mason's lacking in any way. . . ."

Martha shook her head. "You don't need to explain a thing, dear. We all have to follow where our hearts lead and not the other way around. Your grandmother told me that once, you know."

"Smart lady."

"Yep, that she was, God rest her soul. And don't worry about Mason. He'll get over it, because that's what he's supposed to do. But I don't doubt I'll live the heartache with him." She studied Jillian carefully for a moment. "You'll find with your son that you share a special bond. Not that the one you share with your daughter is any less special—it's just different and completely unexpected."

Jillian looked down at her hands, pressed flat against the table in a spot between cookbooks. They were the same hands she remembered, the same ones that had looked so much like her grandmother's. She liked them, she decided then. She liked them not only because they were a link to her grandma Parrish, but also because they were flat and square and capable of doing all the things Jillian had never thought she could.

She smiled up at Martha. "I'm finding bonds with both children that are completely unexpected. I didn't have . . ." She couldn't finish and looked down at her hands again.

Martha stood and moved Ford to the baby swing that had been used for Lessie's children. "I know, dear. And you're not to blame for any of that. Do you have any contact at all with your parents now?"

"Not really. I send them a Christmas card each year with a picture of Grace, and my dad calls on my birthday, but that's pretty much it."

Martha switched on the swing and gave it a gentle push before returning to the table. "I'm wondering if you should invite them down here. To see the children, to see you. To see you as you are now."

Dread, fear and nausea seemed to ball up inside at once, and Jillian found her hands clenched without any recollection of doing it. "No. Never. I've found a haven for me and my children. I can't let them destroy it for us."

Martha turned warm eyes on her. "But I think the haven you've found has been there all along—on the inside. You choose who you let in or out. It's harder when you're a child because a child lets everyone in. But you're an adult now. Maybe it's time for you to face them as an adult and realize that you don't need to be afraid anymore."

Her fingernails bit into her palms. "No." She shook her head vigorously. "I can't. I won't."

With a pat on Jillian's arm, Martha stood and started stacking books. "I understand, dear. I won't bring it up again." She moved to the large kitchen window that looked out toward the ocean. "Would you like some more coffee?"

"I'll get it." Jillian stood, too, and moved next to Martha at the window, and they both looked out. She spotted Gracie and Mary Ellen crouched over something in the sand and was surprised to see Janie Mulligan with them, standing above them and pointing. She wore a wide-brimmed straw hat that obscured her face, but Jillian could tell she was talking because the two young girls were nodding as if in agreement with something Janie was saying. She noticed with amusement that Baby was being worn on Gracie's back. The doll's head fell forward as Gracie leaned down so that it looked like Baby was peering over her shoulder at whatever had captured the girls' attention.

Jillian glanced over at Martha. "How long has Janie had Baby?"

Martha pursed her lips for a moment as if in deep thought. "Well, I know she didn't have it when she was a little girl. I would have remembered that because I used to see Janie just about every single day when her mama was alive. We were real close."

She unscrewed the lid of the coffee thermos and filled up Jillian's mug before filling her own. "I'm thinking it must have been while she was at the convent school in Charleston. She was fifteen years old, but maybe her mother gave it to her when she left home as a sort of security blanket. I guess now Baby reminds Janie of her mother. It's all she's got left, you know. Except for her house, of course."

"And her flowers," Jillian murmured absently, remembering the beautiful and garish colors in Janie's backyard. Her gaze flicked toward the sky, at the heavy clouds that seemed to be hugging the horizon. "I think it's going to rain again."

Jillian watched as Janie pulled out Baby's blanket from the carrier, then knelt in the sand. She wrapped something inside the blanket before standing again, carrying the bundle with as much care as a mother holds her newborn for the first time.

Janie and the two girls turned and started making their way toward the house. Mary Ellen and Gracie broke into a run and ran the rest of the way, but Janie kept her pace slow, the bundle secure in the crook of her arm. Once again, Jillian was struck by something familiar about the way Janie moved. She frowned, trying to think of what it was.

The screen door swung open as the girls spilled into the kitchen, talking excitedly at the same time. Martha put an arm around both of them to try and calm them down. "Now that you've found your breath, how about one of you telling me what you're both so excited about?"

Mary Ellen began to jump up and down, and Grace frowned furiously at her. "I found it, so I get to tell."

"But she's *my* grandmother."

They paused in their arguing when Janie reached the screen door and stood behind it, looking through to the kitchen. "Knock, knock," she said, her smile wide and innocent and reminding Jillian of Gracie.

Jillian called out a greeting, then opened the door and let her in. Everyone watched as Janie shyly glanced around her before approaching the table and gently putting down the blanket in the middle of it. Sand cascaded onto the table as she slowly unfolded the blanket. When she was done, Jillian spotted the small, Ping-Pong–sized white egg sitting in the middle of the blanket.

Martha turned to Mary Ellen and Gracie with a look of reproach. "Oh, girls. Did you take this from a nest?"

Gracie shook her head vigorously. "Oh, no, Mrs. Weber. We know not to do that. We were playing on the beach and saw it. We looked everywhere for the nest but couldn't find it. Miss Janie thinks it was stolen from its nest and then accidentally dropped."

Jillian moved closer to get a better look. "It doesn't seem to be cracked or anything. I'm wondering if we rebury it if it will have a chance."

As if in answer to her question, a small roll of thunder came from outside, followed closely by the tapping of rain against the tin roof. Martha began wrapping the blanket around the egg again. "Well, it will have to wait until after the rain's stopped. For now, we'll just have to keep it warm."

Janie laid her hands on Martha's, stopping her. Her voice was light and breathless. "I'll do that."

Martha nodded and stepped back, and they all watched as Janie carefully brought the ends of the baby blanket up and across in intricate folds, like a baby's swaddling. "I'll find where the baby goes. I know sometimes babies are taken from nests and that's a very sad thing. Her mommy is probably missing her a lot right now."

Martha and Jillian exchanged glances but didn't say anything.

Janie continued. "I need to find the right nest, because if I don't the other mommy won't take care of this one and might hurt it."

Martha put her arm around Janie's shoulders. "Sweetie, loggerheads lay their eggs and bury them, then swim out to sea. They never know their babies."

Janie frowned and shook her head. "No. All mommies know their children. I'd never forget if my baby was stolen from my nest. I'd find her and I'd take care of her."

The two young girls were looking from Martha to Janie, as if waiting for someone to say it was all a joke and that they could have the egg back. But no one spoke. Jillian watched as Mary Ellen took Gracie's hand and led her silently from the room.

A car door shut outside and then Mason appeared at the back door, rain running off his uniform hat. His smile faded slightly when he caught sight of Jillian. She remembered the last time she'd seen him, when he'd come upon her and Linc in the sand, and she felt herself color. "Hi, Mason," she said as she began to gather the remaining cookbooks and recipe cards and shove them into her tote.

He greeted his mother and Janie, then turned to Jillian. "Hi, Jillian. Good to see you again."

"You, too. You should stop by soon. I've been experimenting with Brunswick stew and I've got tons of it in my freezer. I'd be happy to give you some."

"I will. Thanks." A roll of thunder rattled the sky outside.

"Well, I've got to be off. It's getting dark, and the children will want to be fed."

Mason turned to peer out the screen door. "I didn't notice your car. Do you need a ride home in the rain?"

Having to force a conversation with Mason was the last thing she wanted to do, but when she followed his gaze, she saw that the rain was now coming down in sheets. She could walk through the rain, but not with her children. Without looking up at him, she said, "Actually, that would be nice. But you just got here. I don't mind waiting if you want to visit with your mother."

He rolled the brim of his hat in his hands briefly before speaking. "Actually, I wasn't making a social call. I was looking for William Rising. I've been everywhere else and I can't seem to find him, so I thought I'd try here. Mama always seems to know where everybody is."

Jillian waited for Mason to explain why he was looking for Linc, but he didn't elaborate. Martha reached up and gave him a kiss on the cheek. "Sorry to disappoint you, dear, but I haven't seen him."

Jillian lifted the tote to her shoulder. "Actually, he's gone to Charleston for the long weekend. He's behind with his paperwork and needed the time to catch up while the workmen here were taking a three-day break."

Both Martha and Mason looked at her with the same expression— each looking as if they wanted to ask her how she would know so much about William Rising's whereabouts.

"He'll be back Tuesday," she added weakly. She smiled and her gaze met Janie's, who'd been standing silently behind her, as if to escape being noticed. Jillian touched the older woman on the elbow and turned back to Mason. "Would you mind driving Janie, too?"

His face seemed to soften as he looked at her, making Jillian feel guilty and awful all over again. "Not a problem. Let me go find Mary Ellen's old car seat and stick it in my car for Ford. Mama doesn't throw anything away, so I'm sure it's here somewhere."

"Thanks, Mason. You're a good friend." She wasn't sure why she'd added that last part but wish she hadn't as soon as she said it. She saw Mason clamp his lips together before turning and leaving the room.

Jillian fetched a reluctant Gracie and then they all ran out into the rain to Mason's patrol car. It was a tight squeeze, but they all managed to fit in, with Jillian in the front seat and Janie and the children in the back.

Mason leaned forward, straining to see past the torrential rain that covered the windshield and tapped on the car's roof like persistent fingers on a shoulder. Jillian saw his uniform shirt was stained dark, soaked through when he'd put Ford's car seat into the patrol car.

He didn't look at her, and Jillian kept her gaze focused out the windshield, but she was unable to see the road past the car's hood. She heard Janie and Grace whispering unintelligibly in the backseat and was relieved to know at least Grace wasn't afraid of the storm or the approaching dark.

Finally, Mason spoke. "How much do you know about this William Rising, Jillian?"

She squirmed uncomfortably in her seat, her wet legs sticking to the vinyl. "Enough, I suppose, to call him a friend." He looked at her then, but she glanced away. "Why do you want to know?"

He was silent for a moment before he said, "Because I've been doing a little investigating. Seems there's no record of a William Rising before six years ago. It's like he just appeared out of nowhere and started up the business of Rising and Morrow. And his partner's not talking, either."

Jillian gripped the car handle and tried to keep her voice calm. "Why are you doing all this? Has he done something wrong that would warrant your investigation of him?"

Mason shrugged. "It's my business to know who's living on the island, that's all. And I just think it's a little interesting to find out that your new neighbor has no past." He slid a glance at her, his eyes probing. "Thought you might find it interesting, too."

She turned away from him and took a deep breath to cool her anger. "I don't. He's been a good friend to the children and me. That's all I need to know."

They rode in silence, listening to the patter of the rain against the metal roof of the car. Even Janie and Grace had fallen quiet, and Jillian resigned herself to the fact that Grace would hear every word of her conversation with Mason.

"Why were you looking for William?"

He didn't answer right away, and Jillian felt rather than saw Grace lean forward so she wouldn't miss anything.

"Nothing important. Just that there's been practically swarms of gulls over by that pit, and I'm thinking his workmen must be dumping garbage in there. I need him to clean it up."

Jillian relaxed against the seat, not sure why she felt so relieved. "Oh. Well, if I see him before you do, I'll be sure to let him know."

They pulled up in front of Janie's house, and Mason shifted in his seat to face the back. "Stay there, Miss Janie, and I'll come around and get you with my umbrella."

Jillian felt the spray of rain as Mason opened the door, then sat and waited while Mason escorted Janie, Baby, and the turtle egg to her front door in the growing darkness. She'd almost forgotten Grace's presence until she felt an icy cold hand on her arm. Jillian jerked and turned to find Grace's face very close to her own.

Grace leaned closer to Jillian's ear and whispered, "She can see the sky now."

A chill that had nothing to do with the dampness on her skin rushed through her. Grace had said that the other day to Linc. And they had both brushed it off as being one of her conversations with an imaginary friend. *But why would she repeat it?*

"Who, Gracie? Who can see the sky?"

Grace lowered her eyes and stared at the back side of Jillian's seat. She didn't answer.

"Who, Gracie? Tell me. I promise I won't tell anyone. And I won't be mad."

It was hard to hear her daughter's voice above the sound of the rain, but Jillian somehow knew what she was going to say before the words were even formed on the child's lips.

"Lauren," she whispered.

Gracie slid back into her seat as Mason opened the door, letting in droplets of rain that did nothing to cool off Jillian's suddenly feverish skin. *She's dead.* The thought hit her so surely and so completely that she didn't even try to revoke it. And then the second thought came, and it made her feel as if she might faint. *Grace is talking with a dead person.*

Mason started the engine, and they rode the rest of the way in silence. Jillian's teeth chattered, but she wasn't cold. She kept turning around to look at Grace, and was met each time with solemn brown eyes that seemed much too old to be set in a child's face.

Jillian allowed Mason to escort them to her front door, holding the large golf umbrella to keep them dry. Gracie ran on inside, calling for her cat, while Mason lingered, as if waiting for an invitation to come inside. Jillian noticed he'd shut off his car engine, and she thought of the Brunswick stew, but she said nothing.

Mason took a step back, glancing at the front windows. "Looks like you're expecting company."

For the first time, Jillian noticed that a light shone from every window visible from her vantage point on the porch. She knew without looking that the same would be true about the windows she couldn't see, too. "I . . . I didn't turn them on." She paused, dread filling her. "Gracie's in there."

Mason dropped the umbrella and motioned her aside. "I'll go get Gracie and send her out. Then I'll check out the rest of the house, okay? I'm sure you just forgot about turning on the lights."

She nodded, pressing her hand against Ford's sleeping head, knowing that she hadn't forgotten. Nor did she completely believe they had an intruder. Not the kind that Mason would expect to find, anyway.

Jillian let out a breath she hadn't realized she'd been holding when Gracie came through the front door holding Spot.

"Why'd I have to come out? Spot's hungry, and I was fixing his bowl."

Jillian set her hand on the beautiful blond hair, feeling the precious curve of her daughter's head. "Just to be safe, okay? Officer Weber and I both noticed all the lights were on, and I didn't remember turning any on. He's just checking to be sure."

Gracie looked up at her with calm eyes and didn't look away.

You're an old soul, Gracie. Jillian didn't put her thoughts into words any more than Grace had. The communication was mutual yet silent, and Jillian wondered briefly if that was a gift borne of the closeness they had shared since coming to the island. Or maybe it had always been there and Jillian simply hadn't recognized it.

Mason came out several long minutes later, verifying that the house was empty. "I could stay for a while—if that would make you feel any better."

Coming from any other man, except maybe for Linc, his words would have sounded suggestive. "No, but thank you. I must have forgotten I'd left the lights on. We'll be fine."

"Are you sure?"

She nodded vigorously to add solidity to her words. She wasn't at all sure she wanted to be alone without adult companionship.

"Lock your doors."

"Really, Mason—I don't think that's necessary."

"Sorry, Jillian. It's just that I don't like that Rising fellow hanging around here when we have no idea who he is. Would you at least promise me that you'll think twice before opening your door to him?"

Jillian forced back a smile as she remembered the night she'd let

Linc inside her house—and a whole lot more, too. "Really, Mason. There's no need to worry on my account, all right? And I promise to call you if there's a problem."

He hesitated for a moment before leaning down and picking up his discarded umbrella and placing his soggy hat on his head. "All right. But please be careful. And do call me. I don't mind sleeping over, if that would make you feel better. Downstairs, of course," he hastily added.

She couldn't see his blush in the dim light but knew that it was there. "Thanks, Mason. I'll remember that."

She held Ford close to her as she watched Mason drive away, then went inside the house, making sure she locked the door behind her.

It didn't take Jillian long to get the children ready and put them to bed. She kept all the lights on, except those in the children's rooms, and went down to the kitchen, where she poured herself a glass of wine. Her nerves were raw, and she desperately needed to talk to someone— someone who wouldn't think she and her daughter were crazy. *She can see the sky now.* Jillian took a long gulp of her wine, trying to block out the words. But the more she tried, the more she felt the goose bumps rise on the back of her neck.

Twice she picked up the phone, ready to call Linc, but both times she'd placed it back in the cradle before the first ring. He had called her two times during the day—each time with an excuse about checking his doors to make sure they were locked or asking her to close his patio umbrella in case of strong wind. But they had remained on the line both times for almost an hour, talking of nothing and everything. Even now, in the dim light of her deserted kitchen, her skin ached, missing his touch. She moved away from the phone with a determined step— she'd call him first thing in the morning. Now she needed to convince herself that she was good enough company even when she was quite alone.

After refilling her glass, Jillian left the kitchen and moved toward the family room, where she would try to settle down in front of the television to calm herself before bed. As she crossed the foyer, a slight movement caught her eye through the sidelights next to the front door.

She froze, trying to decipher what it was she had seen. Slowly, she moved closer to the door, cautiously peering out of the small side windows and grabbing the doorknob to check that it was locked.

Jillian spotted something on the porch floor in front of the window—something that looked remarkably like Baby's blanket.

Jillian set down her wineglass on the foyer table and slowly unlocked the door. She pulled it open carefully, prepared to shut it quickly if she needed to. The rain had slowed to a steady drizzle, the tapping of it against the wet sand and grass and wooden porch like that of a bored child waiting for attention.

She recognized the blanket immediately as the one Janie had wrapped the egg in. Jillian stepped out onto the deserted porch, then squatted and gingerly lifted the blanket, feeling the egg inside. "Janie?" she called out, not expecting an answer.

Stepping back inside the house, she shut and locked the door again. She wasn't afraid, she realized. Just curious. She opened the sodden blanket and took the egg out, examining its flawless white smoothness. She looked out the side windows again to make sure the porch was empty, and she frowned. Why had Janie given her the egg? To return it to Gracie to bury instead of Mary Ellen? It didn't make much sense—although it probably made as much sense as Janie's silk flowers. Slowly, she took the egg to the kitchen to wrap it in a warm, dry towel to wait until tomorrow.

It wasn't until later, when she was hanging up the blanket to dry, that she got a good, long look at it. Yes, she'd seen it before—always wrapped around Baby. But she'd never really taken a good look at it. She held the bottom right corner with the J. M. initials, and stared at it for a long time. She recalled another blanket, one she had found in a cedar chest she'd taken from her parents' attic. It was identical to this one—the colors, the weave, the pattern and fringe. She had used it for Gracie and had put it away somewhere, she wasn't sure where. She fingered the initials again, remembering the pulled threads on Grace's blanket in the same spot where there had once maybe been a monogram.

She finished hanging up the blanket in the laundry room, securing the clothespins to the line she'd strung from one end of the room to the other.

She picked up her glass of wine again and made her way to the family room. But instead of turning on the television, she sat on the sofa, drinking her wine, playing with all the small pieces that didn't yet quite know they were a part of a puzzle. She swirled her glass, watching the red liquid toss itself against the sides, and wished Linc were there.

After draining her glass, she finally let her head fall back on the edge of the sofa and closed her eyes, and dreamt of silk flowers the color of crimson, and turtle eggs that hatched human babies with yellow yarn hair.

CHAPTER 21

Lauren sat next to Jillian on the blanket, so close that their knees touched, Jillian's unshaven legs prickly against Lauren's skin. Lauren swore to herself, vowing to buy a damned razor for Jillian's thirteenth birthday, regardless of what Jillian's mother would say. It wasn't right that any twelve-year-old could be so clueless just because her own parents never bothered to remember her existence.

Lauren took a sip from her can of Tab, which Jillian's grandmother had put in the cooler for them, then put her arm around her friend and squeezed. "It's all going to be all right, you know."

Jillian stared out into the night sky over the ocean, and Lauren followed her gaze. The reflections of the bright stars on the water made them appear as if they were at the bottom of the ocean, staring up in wonder at themselves. "I know. Grandma Parrish tells me the same thing. I figure the two of you can't be wrong. I just wish I knew when everything's supposed to be all right."

Lauren pulled her knees up and rested her chin against them, smelling of coconut lotion and Charlie perfume. "I don't have a crystal ball, but I know things sometimes. And I know that you'll be okay—that you'll grow up to be successful at whatever you choose to do. And you'll have a great husband and a wonderful family, and all of what's happened before just won't matter anymore."

They listened for a moment to the sounds of night crawlers and the slap of waves in the dark. "I don't want kids."

"I know, you say that all the time. But I think you'd make a great mother."

Jillian turned her head and laid her cheek against her upraised knees. "Really?"

"Yeah—really. You remind me of Mama sometimes. You're both truly kind people. Even with all the crap you have to put up with, you've never even talked back to your parents. God—instead you go bake them a cake or something when they're mad at you. And you never take no for an answer—and not just from other people. But from yourself, too." She grinned at her friend. "It sometimes makes you hard to live with, but it's still a great quality. Speaking from a kid's perspective, it makes me want to try harder."

Jillian's teeth glowed white under her smile, and Lauren watched silently as it faded and her face became serious again. "Will I always be afraid of the dark?"

Lauren studied her friend in the moonlight, at the way the yellow light bathed her face and made her eyes appear full of hope and faith. This was the way she always imagined Jillian when she thought about her during their long winter separations. She smiled. "Yeah—I'm positive." She began brushing sand off her pink-painted toenails, wiggling them in the warm air, and feeling wise. "See, it's not really the dark you're afraid of. I think you're afraid of all the unknown stuff in your future; it's like the inside of a big black bag where you can't see what's in it. You think it's full of all the things you don't get now from your parents, and you're afraid that that's all there's ever going to be. You hope it's going to be different; I truly think you even believe it. But you're afraid to stick your hand in that black bag and find out for yourself."

Lauren sat back, propping herself on the heels of her hands, and smiled smugly to herself, feeling for once as if she knew all the answers. She sensed Jillian looking at her and turned to face her, waiting expectantly for gratitude at explaining the meaning of life.

"You're full of shit, and you know it."

Lauren looked at her in stunned silence for a moment, then threw back her head and started to laugh. Jillian joined her, and soon they were both lying back in the sand, struggling to breathe through their laughter. Slowly, they regained their composure but remained in the sand, staring up at the black canvas of painted stars, each one placed and named with a purpose by their creator.

Lauren heard the hint of desperation in Jillian's voice. "Grandma Parrish told me they're coming Thursday to take me back to Atlanta. I don't think I'll be able to stand it."

"Yes, you can. You always have." She got up on her elbow and looked down at Jillian. "Your dad's not such a bad guy, you know. He's been over several times to our house to apologize for things your mom has done or said to my parents and to me." She blew out a puff of air. "No offense, but your mom has issues. Big issues. I kinda feel sorry for your dad—he has to put up with it. He must love her a lot."

Jillian shrugged in the sand. "They're always either fighting or making up—I don't think they ever just sit and have a normal conversation. I don't really pay attention anymore."

"Well, I think if you appeal to just your dad when your mom's not around, you might make things easier for yourself."

Jillian didn't answer, and Lauren continued. "And remember that no matter what, whether we're together or not, I'll always watch out for you. You don't ever have to feel you're all alone."

Jillian wiped her hands over her eyes, then looked up at Lauren. "Do you pinky swear?" She held up her hand, her little finger rounded into a hook.

"I pinky swear," Lauren said, and hooked her little finger with Jillian's and squeezed. Then she fell back on the sand and looked up at the stars. "And to make it more binding, I'm going to tell you a secret I've never told anyone—not ever."

Jillian lifted her head. "Really?"

Lauren nodded and took a deep breath. "I'm afraid of water. Always have been. Mama says as a baby I used to scream when it was time to take a bath."

Jillian sat up completely. "But you're a great water skier and swimmer. You can't still be afraid of water if you can do that!"

"That's only because of something my mama told me. You have to face your fears. It's the only way to overcome them."

Jillian sighed into the salty air. "Are you still afraid?"

"Yeah—a little bit. I'm afraid of drowning. But each time I dive into the ocean or strap on my water skis, I'm that much closer to getting over it. Some things take time, you know? I guess you and Mama have rubbed off on me a little bit. I simply couldn't accept that I would never enjoy the water. So I just jumped in. You do it every day of your life, Jilly, whether you realize it or not."

They stayed on their backs, and Lauren pointed up at the sky. "What are we supposed to be looking at?"

Jillian grabbed her hand and moved it to the right. "You can't really see it well without binoculars, but that's Sagittarius." She swept their hands in a circular motion, and Lauren squinted to see better. "He's the archer, and Linc says it's supposed to look like Sagittarius is shooting at the giant scorpion, Scorpius." Jillian snorted and let their hands drop. "I told him I thought it looked more like a teapot. I think he got mad at me."

"Sounds like Linc."

"Yeah, well. He said that the center of the galaxy was tucked inside Sagittarius—but twenty-seven thousand light-years farther away. He said it was a lot more dignified to find the center of the galaxy inside a warrior than at the tip of a teapot's spout."

They laughed again, then Lauren reached into her pocket. Holding it up over Jillian, she said, "Look what Linc made for me."

Jillian took the small object from her and held the tiny wooden heart close to her face. "Wow, it's beautiful."

"Yeah. He said he was going to carve something for you from the same piece of wood—but it wouldn't be a heart. It'll be something that reminds him of you. I bet it'll be a star."

Jillian cupped the heart in her hands as if memorizing it, then handed it back to Lauren. "Will you always keep it with you?"

"Definitely. It means a lot to me. I think I'm going to varnish it, then have a necklace made out of it with a gold chain my parents gave me last Christmas."

They fell into silence, listening to the surge and retreat of the waves. After a while, Jillian jumped up, spraying Lauren with sand. "Let's go inside. I'm in the mood to bake something."

Lauren laughed. "You always do that."

Jillian snatched up the blanket and snapped it in the air to free it of sand. "Do what?"

"Make food for people. It's like your way of giving them a gift for no reason at all."

"I don't hear anybody complaining."

Lauren looked a few feet ahead of them and saw the water creeping up the shoreline. "The tide's coming in."

Jillian finished folding the blanket and tucked it under an arm. Something seemed to catch her attention and she pointed to the water. "Look—glowing fish!"

Lauren moved closer to watch a cluster of tiny phosphorescent fish glowing like they had swallowed moonlight from the surface of the water. They moved back and forth, as if dancing to the ancient rhythm of the tides, performing for no one but themselves and the moon.

Jillian stood next to her, staring in awe at the beautiful fish. "It's a little bit of magic, isn't it?" She found Lauren's hand and squeezed it. "I'm going to remember this night. Always."

"Me, too." Lauren squeezed back. "You'll always be my very best friend, you know."

"Really?"

"Yeah, really."

"Promise?"

"Promise."

They gathered up the blanket and cooler, then struggled up the thick sand of the dunes toward the house with the light in the kitchen window, leaving behind glowing fish and a ribbon of stars that led far out into the galaxy, taking with them youthful wishes and memories that would last a lifetime, and maybe even beyond.

Linc pulled his car up behind the house and turned off the engine. He sat for a while, willing himself not to move while he berated himself for returning to Pawleys before he had made much more than a dent in the work waiting for him at his Charleston office. He rubbed his hands over his eyes. *Jillian.* He'd missed her. He wanted her. He could almost believe that he needed her.

He opened the door and climbed out, and found himself heading next door before he'd so much as checked to make sure his own house was still standing. After knocking on Jillian's door and receiving no answer, he found Jillian and the children on the beach, farther down from where they usually were, far beyond the pit in the dunes behind his house.

Jillian turned toward him before he had called out to them, almost as if she had sensed him. She wore a pale pink sundress, the skirt long and flowing around her calves. Her hair was swept back in a ponytail, one that matched Grace's, with loose strands that danced around her face. Her hands were coated with wet sand, and as he watched she scratched her nose, leaving a streak of sand on her sun-browned skin. He'd never seen anything so beautiful.

He shoved his hands into his pockets, clenching them in a vain effort to staunch the rush of desire that seemed to propel him forward. He stopped in front of them, patting Grace's head first before directing his attention toward her mother. He'd needed to do that first so he could find his voice.

She smiled at him, her eyes glowing in the sunlight. "You're a bit overdressed for the beach, aren't you?"

He realized for the first time that he still wore his suit and tie and that his Italian loafers were caked with sand. He blew out a breath of air and smiled ruefully as he loosened his tie and unbuttoned the top button of his shirt. "I'm sure somewhere in the world this is appropriate beachwear."

She gave him a knowing smile as he squatted down to pat Ford in his infant carrier and greet Gracie. "What are you girls up to?"

Grace regarded him with wide brown eyes for a moment. There was something in the way her eyes widened and the color of sun reflected in them that reminded him of someone else. Not her mother; someone else he couldn't recall.

She put a sandy hand on his pants leg. "We just brought back a turtle egg and put it back in its nest. Her name is Tammy. Mommy brought Ford so he could help, but he's pretty useless. Mommy and I did all the work, as usual." She finished this with a heavy sigh.

Mommy? He looked over at Jillian with raised eyebrows, and she smiled back at him. His thoughts were interrupted by the feel of sandy hands on his neck. "You wore your sand dollar necklace I made you."

He tried not to wince at the feel of sand grains dropping from the neck of his shirt onto his chest. "I wanted to bring a piece of the beach with me to the city—to remind me of the ocean until I could get back. Otherwise, I'd miss it too much. And you, too, of course."

Gracie giggled, then wiped the remaining sand on her hands off on his pants legs as she helped herself up. "I'm gonna go look for shells." She spread out the skirt of her sundress, showing them the large front pockets. "I'll put them in here, okay, Mommy?"

Jillian nodded, and they watched as she raced off and began searching for treasures. He reached for her then, cupping her face in his hands and kissing her. Her lips tasted of salt and sand and warm sun, and he kissed her again, lingering longer.

"She's calling you Mommy."

Jillian nodded, her eyes shining. "She didn't ask or anything—she just started doing it."

"Is it a good thing?"

She didn't pause. "Yes. Definitely. It's almost like waiting your whole life to open a present—and when you finally get to, you're not disappointed."

Jillian bent to pick up Ford, lifting him to her shoulder and adjusting the baby's hat to protect him from the sun. The sun skipped under a thick cloud, creating intermittent patterns of darkness and light on the water and dunes. "Let's walk," she said, and started in the direction Gracie had gone.

"I missed you." She didn't look at him.

"I bought you some pans." It was so inadequately stupid he wanted to pull the words out of the air and swallow them.

Her cheek creased in a smile. "Really? For me?"

"Yeah, for your new kitchen. They're the blue porcelain-coated ones you were admiring last week. I thought you'd like to have them."

She turned to him. "Thank you. You didn't have to do that, you know, but thank you." Then, keeping her eyes focused ahead of her, she said, "Rick is spending the afternoon with Gracie again, if you want to come over later."

He looked at her and saw the telltale pink of a blush creeping across her cheeks. "I'd like that." He realized that they had been walking in the direction of his house and toward the dune with the yellow safety tape still stretched around it. Grace had halted suddenly, making them stop short so they wouldn't run into her. She was staring over the dunes, and he followed her gaze. "What the . . . ?"

A swarm of seabirds had settled around the yellow tape, a few of them flapping their wings and cawing to each other.

Jillian put her hand on his arm. "Mason was looking for you yesterday. He thinks your workmen have been dumping garbage in the pit, and wanted you to take care of it before the birds became a nuisance."

"Damn," he said before he remembered Grace's presence. He bent his head to apologize to her, but stopped when he saw her face. Her eyes were wide with terror, her face the color of a sand dollar bleached by the sun.

Jillian was looking at her with worry. "Are you all right, Gracie? Are you sick?"

Gracie shook her head slowly. "No. I want to go home now." Her small voice sounded strangled.

Jillian knelt in front of her, feeling her forehead. "She's a little warm. She got a little too much sun yesterday, and it must be catching up with her. I'm going to take her home and let her get some rest before her father comes."

Gracie continued to stare at the damaged dune, her eyes wide and unblinking. It almost looked as if she were listening to somebody speaking to her.

Jillian tugged on her arm. "Come on, sweetheart. Can you walk? We'll go home now."

Slowly, Gracie's eyes drifted to her mother's face. "She can't breathe. There's water over her nose and mouth, and she can't breathe."

Jillian's face paled to the same shade as her daughter's. "Who, Gracie? Who can't breathe? Is somebody in trouble?" She looked into her daughter's face. Quietly, she asked, "Is it Lauren?"

Linc felt a chill pass through him as Grace nodded, before her head dropped so that she was staring at her bare feet, the pink nail polish chipped and faded. Linc reached down and picked the little girl up in his arms, noticing how light yet how solid she felt. "I'll carry her up to the house." Gracie looped her arms around his neck and laid her head down on his shoulders. There was something so right about the way she felt in his arms—something so right in the way that he was able to help make her hurt go away. He realized with some surprise that he still thought of Gracie as a young Jillian. He had always wanted to take away Jillian's hurts, and now maybe with her daughter he had been given a second chance.

They moved across the sand and boardwalk and then up to the house, where Jillian held open the door for them to pass. Grace had fallen asleep, so he followed Jillian upstairs to Grace's room. He held still while Jillian did the best she could to wipe the sand off the child's feet before pulling back the sheets and gesturing for Linc to lay her down.

They stood for a few moments, their shoulders touching, and watched the sleeping girl. Spot leapt on the bed and crouched next to the child in a protective gesture, a movement so doglike it almost made Linc smile. Jillian had turned to say something to him when Gracie sat up suddenly, her eyes closed as if still asleep. Her voice was soft and languid and not her own. "I'm sorry, Linc. I'm so, so sorry."

Grace fell back on the pillows, her chest rising and falling in the soft rhythms of sleep. She turned on her side, grabbed Bun-Bun and snuggled it under her arm. With a faint voice, she said, "I love you, Linc. I never stopped."

Her brow softened and she burrowed further into the pillow, as Linc felt an icy blast blow down his spine. He glanced at Jillian and saw that she was crying silently, the tears wetting her cheeks. She held the baby closer to her as he touched her elbow and took her from the room.

They descended the stairs without speaking, and he led her into the kitchen. For once, she sat down at the table and he put the kettle on to boil. Neither of them said anything until he'd put a steaming cup of tea in front of her. Her eyes were red and swollen when she looked up at him. "Is this really happening? Could she really be talking to Lauren?"

He put his hand on her arm and noticed how cold she was. "I think . . . yes. I think she could be. I believe that Grace might . . ." He stopped, unsure of how to go on. He pushed his fingers through his hair. "I think she might have heightened awareness—a sort of sixth sense. She might be able to see things you and I can't. I've read about things like this before. There's nothing at all wrong with her—that's the most important thing you have to realize. You might want to take her to a child psychologist just to help you both understand it better." He squeezed her arm. "You have to believe me—there's nothing wrong with Gracie. She's a wonderful little girl with a very special gift. And I know that you'll handle this."

Jillian put her cup down slowly. "I think you're right. I think I've known it for a while now. I just didn't want to accept it—I still don't. Because not only does it mean my daughter communicates with ghosts, but it also means that Lauren . . ." She couldn't finish.

He nodded, then touched his forehead to hers. "Yes. I think she is."

She clenched her eyes for a long moment, then stood and adjusted the baby on her shoulder. "I can't deal with this right now. I just can't.

I'm going to get the baby changed and down for a nap, and then take a long, cold shower. Then I'll think about it. But I know one thing— Gracie will not be singled out or ridiculed. If Lauren somehow talks with her and tells her something we need to know, I will not allow anyone to know that it came from Gracie. She is my *child*. I will *not* let her suffer for this."

Linc had the oddest urge to stand up and shout, "Bravo!" It was the first time he'd ever witnessed the true Jillian he knew stand up and let the world see it, too. Instead, he kissed her gently and patted Ford on the head. "We won't let that happen, all right?" She looked at him, and her eyes were warm. He touched her cheek. "I'll come back later, okay?" Gently, he added, "You and I have to decide what we need to know about Lauren from Grace."

She nodded, and he left. An odd prickling sensation in the back of his neck prodded at him as he crossed the sand between the houses. He had reached his car and was about to lift his overnight bag out of the trunk when he heard the combined cry of birds, a raucous sound that seemed to rise on the salt-drenched air and burst over his head like confetti. It chilled him to the bone.

He dropped the bag and ran to the back of his house and moved down to the boardwalk to see the birds. The collapsed dune was peppered with gulls, their dirty white-and-brown feathers like shadows on a palette of sand. He began to walk closer, and as he approached he got a better look at the ground around the yellow tape and saw it move, each grain seemingly covered with crabs and other seaside scavengers. The skin tightened over his shoulders, the fear plucking the air from his lungs. *She can see the sky now. But she can't breathe. She just wants to breathe.*

"Oh, God," he whispered, stumbling forward, not wanting to go but compelled to do so, anyway. He ducked under the yellow tape and stood at the edge of the pit for a full minute before moving closer and peering in, knowing what he would find before he'd even looked.

Half covered by water and sand lay the smooth, curved bone of the top of a skull, the lower jaw missing, the water and sand like a gloved hand pressing tight against what had been a nose and mouth, smothering out air and life. The sightless sockets stared up past him at the blue South Carolina sky, where the moon and stars could not be found.

CHAPTER 22

J ILLIAN SAT AT HER KITCHEN TABLE IN SILENCE, THE ONLY SOUND THE
swish of the ceiling fan. She twisted her grandmother's ring on her
finger, the gold warm beneath her touch. Holding her hand out in
front of her, she thought for a moment it was her grandmother's hand,
warm and knowing and capable. It was with a small jolt that she realized that the hand she was staring at was her own.

She had just decided to make crab cakes for Mason, as a sort of
peace offering, and had her head buried in the cabinet where she kept
her pans when she heard the short bursts of a siren. At first she thought
she'd left the television on, because the sound was so completely unexpected in her little world out on the dunes of Pawleys Island. But when
she pulled her head out of the cabinet and listened, she could tell that
the sirens were outside and very close by.

After quickly checking to see that Gracie and Ford still napped, she
headed outside, not bothering first to find her shoes. She felt an inex-
plicable urgency pressing her forward, and she didn't want to waste any
time.

She recognized Mason's vehicle first. The sirens had been turned off
but the lights were still on, the bright flashes nearly surreal in the sun-
lit front yard of Linc's house. Behind the patrol car was a dark brown
sedan and an ambulance, and Jillian's heart raced when she spotted it.
Ignoring the pinching of broken shells on her bare feet, she raced to
Linc's door and began hammering on it with her fist.

When no one responded, she tried the knob but found it locked.
Trying to keep her panic in check, she raced to the rear door. As she
rounded the corner of the house she caught sight of movement on the
dunes and walked down toward the boardwalk. She stopped there, trying to find her breath and almost crying with relief when she spotted
Linc near the collapsed dune, his hands thrust into his pockets.

He still wore the clothes she'd seen him in last, his loafers completely covered in sand now. He was staring inside the pit, his face calm and serene as if he were asleep. But she could see the tenseness in the fall of his shoulders and the line of his jaw. He looked so much like the vulnerable and lost young boy she had known, and her heart lurched in her chest. He needed her now. She felt it as strongly as if he had just said the words out loud.

As if she had called to him, he lifted his head and his deep gray gaze met hers, moving her forward. He met her halfway and he held her while she kept her eyes closed, knowing that when she opened them, she would have to face whatever nightmare lay beneath the sand in the open, dark pit. But here, in his arms, she felt safe and cherished. *I love him.*

Then Linc held her away from him, his hands on her shoulders, and she saw the stretcher and the bright orange body bag behind him, and she knew.

"Why didn't you call me?" Her voice choked, the words coming out in a whisper.

He shook his head. "I don't know. Maybe because I wanted to spare you this." He indicated the scene behind him with his chin.

"Lauren?" she managed.

"It's too early to tell. All they know for sure right now is that the body's been there for some time. They'll take the . . . remains for an autopsy. Weber said they'll see if there's enough of the upper and lower mandible to try and compare with Lauren's dental records. Old Dr. Nordone still practices here, so that shouldn't take very long."

His voice trailed away as he looked past her toward the ocean, the horizon reflected in his clear eyes much as she supposed the South Carolina shoreline had once reflected in the eyes of his pirate ancestors.

They both looked up as Mason approached them. His eyes were cold as he directed his gaze on Linc, like a gull circling over its prey. "I'm going to need to ask you some questions, Rising. I'd like for you to come down to the station right now, if you would."

For a moment, Jillian thought Linc would refuse. Instead, he nodded his head. "I need to get changed first. I'll meet you back here in about ten minutes." He gave one last glance toward Jillian, then made to move up toward the house.

"Wait!" she called, and kissed him quickly. "Call me when you're done. I don't care what time."

He nodded again, the skin around his mouth pale, and moved toward the boardwalk.

"Jillian."

She turned toward Mason, her back stiff. "Do you need to question me, too?"

"Not now. I'll let you know."

"Fine," she said, hearing her clipped voice. Her gaze strayed toward the pit, where two men wearing surgical gloves were squatting over something in the sand, while a third took pictures. She didn't want to see, and looked back at Mason.

His eyes had softened. "You go on home now, Jillian. It's not safe here."

She could tell that he wasn't just talking about the pit. But she had no energy to argue. She turned and began walking toward her house.

"And keep Gracie away from here, too. I don't want to see her getting hurt."

She half turned and sent him a cooling glance. "Don't worry, Mason. Neither one of us will be likely to step foot on this beach for quite some time."

Each step felt labored and tedious, as if she had just begun the longest journey of her life. It was only when she had reached her own back porch that she realized why the beach had descended into silence. Every last bird had disappeared.

Jillian sat cross-legged on the end of the boardwalk, clutching her binoculars, her flashlight and baby monitor nearby. She kept the binoculars pressed against her face, checking off the stars one by one and trying not to think of the dark pit just a short walk away across the dunes.

"Looking for your star?"

Jillian startled at the sound of Linc's voice, but didn't turn around. "It's keeping my thoughts busy."

He sat down next to her, bringing one knee up to rest an arm, but didn't touch her. "Mason knows who I am. Did you tell him?"

She brought down the binoculars. "No, I didn't, although I knew he was getting pretty close to figuring it out. He'd already done some checking on you and found out that William Rising had no past. Joe and Martha Weber have known all along."

He sent her a sharp glance. "And they never mentioned it?"

Jillian shrugged, feeling the tenseness in her shoulders. At least that was something. She'd spent the afternoon completely numb, unable to penetrate the stabbing grief that had haunted her for sixteen years and had finally jumped out of the dark closet to confront her. She felt like a glass shattered into so many pieces she wasn't sure she could find them again.

"There was no need. They understood your desire to blend in and leave the past behind. You're not a criminal."

He let out a deep breath. "Not everybody believes that. And when they find out that the body's Lauren's, there'll be a lynching party."

"But it might not be her." Even to her own ears, her words sounded hollow.

He stroked her cheek and wiped away a tear she hadn't been aware had fallen. "It is."

Something in his voice made her stiffen, but she still couldn't abandon her hope. "How can you know? It's too early to tell."

He studied her in the dark for a long moment, and Jillian held her breath, a sick feeling in the pit of her stomach. With deliberate movements, he reached into his pants pocket and pulled something out. Taking her hand, he placed the object on her palm.

In the yellow light of the moon, she could see it was cracked and splintered, the varnished wood brittle against her skin, as if it had been submerged in salt water for a very long time. The small heart had a split in the middle, nearly severing it into two pieces, like a broken heart. Still clinging to a hole in the middle of it was a gold chain, the yellow dully reflecting the moonlight.

She felt the darkness descend on her like a great tidal wave trying to pull her under. But Linc was there, his arms around her, his shoulder under her cheek, and his hands, with the long, beautiful fingers that had once carved a heart and a star out of wood, stroked her hair while she cried.

Her grief gave way to hard need. She reached for Linc, like a drowning victim reaching for an offered limb, their need for each other mixing with their need to prove their own survival. As Linc pressed her into the sand, she thought irrelevantly of soldiers after a battle.

Their loving was frantic and rough, neither one wanting to take the time to remove all their clothing. He moved over her, touching and ripping and devouring her, and she felt his heat and the retained heat of the sun on the bare skin of her back and arms as she settled more deeply into the sand.

The grains stuck to his sweat-soaked chest and rubbed her breasts as he slid into her in one hard thrust. She lifted her hips, bucking against him, and cried out with pain and pleasure as he continued to push into her, fast and quick until she thought she would go mindless with her need for this primal comfort, for this man and how he made her feel. He stilled for a moment, reaching his own release, and her cry drifted off across the dunes toward the ocean, where the dark water waited.

They lay on their backs for a long time, watching the stars without speaking. The breeze blew on Jillian's skin, chilling her, and she rose to get dressed. She could feel Linc's eyes on her as she searched for her bra and shirt. Buttoning up her blouse, she faced him.

"What happens next?"

He stood, zipping up his pants and keeping his head down. He moved closer to her and took her in his arms. "We wait. People are going to be asking a lot of questions, and I don't doubt that I'll be made a scapegoat again. I guess I'll find out who my real friends are."

She moved away from him, feeling chilled from the inside. "Do you mean me?"

He raised his hands to his head, and she pictured him running his fingers through his hair. "I don't know. I don't know anything anymore. How did she get to be there? It looks like an underground tunnel, but I've looked and looked through the blueprints and all through the house and I can't find anything." His eyes caught the reflection of the moon for a moment as he watched her in silence. "And who else knows she's there?"

She saw him bend down and his hands sweep over the boards on the boardwalk, searching for something. He straightened, and she knew he held the wooden heart necklace. Walking toward the water, he pulled his arm back and threw it as far as he could.

Jillian ran to him and grabbed his shoulders, trying to shake him. "Why did you do that? It was evidence."

He looked coolly down at her and said softly, "I know. One less piece of incriminating evidence against me. That's one mark in my favor. That makes it a million against one—not really good odds, is it?"

She moved away from him, stumbling in the sand until she reached the boardwalk. "I'm going to bed. Call me when you're finished with your self-pity and you're ready to do something about this mess we're in."

"What do you mean—the mess *we're* in? This doesn't have anything to do with you."

If she'd been closer, she would have hit him. "Damn you, Linc Rising—or whoever in the hell you really are. Forgive me for thinking that maybe we were having a relationship and that we'd work our problems out together. My mistake."

She yanked up the flashlight and the baby monitor and began walking toward the house, trying very hard to hold back tears.

"Your father's name is Mark, isn't it, Jillian?"

She faced him, furious, hurt and thoroughly confused. "What has any of this got to do with my father?"

"Just remind me, would you? I always knew him as Mr. Parrish. I'm pretty sure it started with an *M*."

"His name is Mark. Why? Why do you need to know?"

But all he said was "Good night, Jillian." He bent and picked up his shoes, not bothering to look back at her.

"You can be a real shit—you know that?"

He paused and called over his shoulder, "You always had a foul mouth, Jillian. It was one of the funniest things about you."

She was amazed that she could feel embarrassment over all the other emotions that were running through her head. She jammed her balled fists into her sides. "Well, shit, Linc. I'm sorry as shit that I've offended you. I promise to try and stop saying 'shit' so much."

She heard him laugh quietly. "No, don't. There's not a whole hell of a lot to laugh at anymore." He continued walking away from her, up toward his house, and she stayed where she was and watched him until she heard his back door shut.

Linc stared up at the ceiling of his bedroom, too wired to sleep. He hadn't meant to argue with Jillian. But he remembered the flicker in her eyes when he'd picked up the little wooden heart necklace. He'd thought it was doubt, and it had angered him enough to toss the heart out into the ocean. He wasn't even sure why he'd done it; only that it had everything to do with Jillian and his need to pull at the bonds that seemed to inextricably link them together. He had learned how from a pro, after all. His mother had been the queen of emotional bondage, testing and pulling on him until he had simply given up and disappeared from her life. He was good at that—the leaving. And some foolish part of him had believed that he had finally come home for good.

Until they'd found Lauren.

He threw the sheets off of his naked body and pulled on a pair of jeans. Barefoot, he padded downstairs to the kitchen and pulled a beer from the refrigerator. Maybe if he got drunk enough, he could pass out in mindless oblivion.

And then he smelled it again—the briny smell of salt water, strong enough that it seemed as if the ocean had moved outside his doorway. He paused with the beer halfway to his mouth. *The closet.*

Slamming the bottle down on the kitchen counter, he half ran to the closet and stopped outside the open door. He hadn't shut it since that night he'd found it open, and as he stood there, he could almost swear he heard the lapping of water nearby.

Turning on the light, he got down on his hands and knees, examining each crack and crevice of the wooden plank floor. It had bothered him since the beginning when the dune had collapsed and revealed what had once been a tunnel of some sort. But a tunnel from where? As his fingers searched the floor, he thought he might have an answer.

When he reached the left back corner, he noticed how the last length of board nearest the paneled wall wasn't flush with the other boards. It reminded him of the hidden switch upstairs in the window seat. Wiping sweat out of his eyes, he slowly moved his hand toward the place where the board met the wall and pushed.

With his breath held, he heard a slight clicking sound. Two wide boards on the wall had separated from the rest. He inched forward and pushed on them, and a small door formed before it stopped on squeaky hinges. He could hear the water louder now, hear it slapping against something solid. Moving closer, he put his shoulder to the hidden door. *Shit.* It wasn't going anywhere.

He retreated to the kitchen and found his flashlight, a can of WD-40 and a hammer. He grinned ruefully at the hammer. This simply wasn't a time for finesse.

Returning to the closet, he sprayed the seams of the hidden door-way with half of the WD-40 can, then gave the door another shove and was rewarded when it swung open enough for him to squeeze through it. With one last look behind him, he stepped inside, allowing the dark to swallow him.

He felt gritty sand and brick beneath his feet. Flipping on his flash-light, he found himself at the top of a narrow flight of circular brick steps. He pictured the outside of the house in his mind, trying to fig-ure out where he was standing. *I'm inside one of the brick posts.*

The light illuminated brick-and-mortar walls. Definitely old brick. Shining the flashlight at his feet, he saw the steps moving down in a spi-ral pattern until a path sloped away from the circle of light.

He descended the stairs and found himself in a narrow tunnel, big enough for a man to crawl. His knees and hands scraped against moist brick as he followed the old tunnel, noting the timber supports that bolstered the ceiling. He paused for a moment, glancing behind him, and saw only blackness. He thought briefly of stopping and going back, but continued on.

The sound of water was louder here, echoing off the brick. He felt the moistness of the ground and realized the water had climbed almost to his elbows. He stopped and looked ahead, realizing that his explor-ing had come to an end. A few feet ahead lay a steel door, the kind he'd seen at the old debtor's prison in Charleston. The bottom foot of it was covered in water, almost to the large dead bolt that was clamped down in the locked position.

He leaned against the brick wall for support, feeling the clammy, cold brick against his bare arm. He sucked in air, barely getting enough to fill his lungs, and wondered how long the oxygen would last once the secret doorway was shut. His gaze shifted back to the door. *How did you get on the other side of this door, Lauren? And who locked you out?* He looked at the lock again, at the firmly latched bolt, and felt the cer-tainty that this had been no accident.

Gripping the flashlight like a weapon, he turned around and made his way back into the closet, the sounds and smells of an unforgiving ocean at high tide lapping at his back.

CHAPTER 23

W HEN JILLIAN RETURNED FROM THE GROCERY STORE THREE DAYS later, it was to find an answering machine with a red light flashing insistently. Holding Ford in one hand and a bag of diapers in her other, she leaned over to stare at the display. Forty-eight messages. With one foot, she wrapped the cord around her ankle and yanked the plug from the wall.

She had made it as far as the kitchen when somebody knocked on the front door. Before she could check to see who it was, Grace rushed past her, shouting, "I'll get it!"

Jillian turned on her heels. "Wait to make sure we know who it is. . . ."

But Grace was already welcoming whoever it was. Dropping the diapers, she shifted Ford in her arms and went to the front door.

Lessie Beaumont, in typical floral capris and yellow patent-leather sandals, sent her a sympathetic frown. She stuck a vase full of daisies at Jillian and walked inside, followed closely by Miss Janie and Baby. "You poor, poor thing! Mama and me have been just sick with worry about you. Your answering machine must be broken or something because we keep calling and calling and leaving messages, but you haven't been calling back."

Lessie made her way to the kitchen, and everybody followed. Weariness won over annoyance, so Jillian tagged along, too, noticing that Janie had her arm around Grace's shoulders.

Lessie barely paused for breath as she filled the vase with water from the sink. "You here all by yourself now that William—or I guess it's Linc, isn't it?—has gone back to Charleston while the police tear his house apart, looking for clues. I don't know why you don't come live with Mama or with me and Ken. We've got plenty of room, and you know Mary Ellen would just *die* to have Gracie come stay with us. Plus, I need to get all the details about that tunnel. I'm almost done with my paper, and all this will be the perfect way to end it, don't you think?"

Jillian didn't say anything, but just put Ford in the baby swing and started passing around a tray of homemade pralines. Gracie pulled a pitcher of sweet tea from the refrigerator and began filling glasses. Lessie sat down at the kitchen table and patted the seat next to her. "Come on, sweetie, and get off your feet. You look exhausted."

Too tired to argue, she sat down next to Lessie and took a long sip of her tea, watching as Grace scooted her own chair close to Janie Mulligan's. Jillian leaned over the table to speak to her daughter. "Don't eat too much. Your daddy will be here within an hour to take you up to Myrtle Beach for some lunch and miniature golfing."

Gracie bounced up and down in her chair. "Yippee! Can I wear my new dress with the little cats all over it? You know—the one Linc bought for me in Charleston?"

Jillian felt Lessie's gaze on her. Stiffly taking a sip of tea she said, "Sure, honey. That would be fine."

Gracie shoved an entire praline into her mouth and then, being careful not to spit too many crumbs, asked, "May I please be excused?"

Jillian nodded, and Gracie leapt up, but first whispered something to Janie, who took Baby out of her pouch and handed her to Gracie.

"I want to show Baby my room."

All three ladies at the table watched Gracie run from the room. Lessie turned, knowing eyes on Jillian. "She's a sweet child. I hope none of this business with the body in the tunnel has upset her."

"Actually, her father—my ex-husband—has volunteered to stay for a week to get Gracie away from all this. I took her out of school, too. Even in first grade, I'm sure the children will have heard something, and I don't want Gracie to be upset. She's . . . sensitive." She took another drink of iced tea, grimacing as a large ice cube hit her front teeth. "I just wish I knew how the news traveled so fast. I've had reporters calling me from the *Savannah Times-Courier* and even the *Atlanta Journal-Constitution*."

"Well, actually"—Lessie sent her an apologetic smile—"my room-mate from Agnes-Scott is a staff writer for the *AJC* and, um, I might have mentioned the story to her when we spoke last."

Jillian stood to go get Ford out of the swing. It was nearing his nap time and he was starting to fuss. "Well, thanks, Lessie. Then I'll let you return all the phone calls, okay? Only forty-eight today, but there were fifty-six yesterday. Have fun."

Janie approached her, her arms outstretched. "Can I hold Ford? I'm really good with babies."

Jillian stared into the soft brown eyes turned up at her with expectance, and nodded. Carefully, she handed the baby to Janie and watched her sit down with him, her small, girlish hand patting him on the back.

Janie rubbed her cheek against the top of Ford's head, a small smile playing at her lips. "He smells so good. I remember that smell. It's like cotton candy and angels, and it makes you never want to let go." She closed her eyes and sighed. "I did, you know. But only because they made me and said I wasn't smart enough. Sometimes you really do know what's best for your baby, and you have to fight for them." Opening her eyes, she drew a deep breath. "I think when that happens is when you become a real mama. It's like earning a badge." She giggled and then slapped her hand over her mouth when Ford stirred, his eyes opening drunkenly for a brief moment before closing again.

Lessie leaned forward and patted Janie on the hand. "I think you're right, Miss Janie. And my mama, with all eight of us kids, would have a suit of patches covering her from head to toe. She'd look funny in it, but I guarantee she'd want to wear it every day."

Jillian and Lessie laughed, easily picturing Martha Weber in her suit of motherhood patches, but Jillian noticed how Janie's eyes seemed to glaze over and get teary. Jillian pushed the pralines over to her and put her arms out for the baby.

"I'm going to go put him up in his crib. I'll be right back." She took Ford, then watched as Janie picked up a praline and began nibbling it all around the edges, just like Gracie did, the crumbs going everywhere. With a bewildered glance at Lessie, she excused herself and left the room.

She had just finished closing Ford's door when she heard another knock on the front door. Jogging down the stairs, she peered through the side windows, then hid her disappointment behind her smile. For one brief moment, she'd hoped it was Linc. They hadn't spoken since their argument out on the beach. Her emotions seemed to be swinging along a clock, stopping at regular intervals on anger, remorse, reconciliation and disbelief. Several times, while stuck in the hour of reconciliation, she'd picked up the phone to call him, but had stopped before she'd dialed the last number. She had a Key lime pie in the refrigerator she'd made for him at two o'clock in the morning. She had carried it halfway to his house at the break of dawn, before coming to her senses and turning back.

Opening the door to Mason, she smiled and greeted him warmly. "I'm glad you stopped by. I made you some crab cakes. They're in the refrigerator, and all you have to do is reheat them. . . ."

She let her voice trail away when she noticed the grim expression he wore. "I'm afraid this isn't a social call, Jillian. I have some news for you, and I don't know how you're going to take it."

"Come in," she said, motioning him past her and watching as Janie entered the hallway and then began making her way up the steps. "Lessie is in the kitchen and Janie and Gracie are upstairs, so if you don't want them to hear, you'd best tell me now."

"You might want to sit down."

"I'm fine," she said, wishing everybody would stop treating her as if she were a lone sea oat on a windy dune. She'd learned over the years that bending in the wind kept you from breaking in half. "Tell me."

He pursed his lips. "Dental records taken from Dr. Nordone's office were a match. We can now positively identify the body in the tunnel as that of Lauren Mills."

Jillian clenched her jaw, softening the blow. She'd known the truth already, but hearing the verification of it was like going to the same funeral twice. It still hurt.

"Have you located her parents yet?"

"Not yet. We're still trying." He looked somberly into her eyes. "There's more, but I really think you should be sitting down before I tell you."

She knew he was only being kind, but she wanted to push him away, to make him leave. "No, just tell me."

He paused for a moment, his head nodding slightly to an unheard beat. "We also found the remains of an infant. Looks to be almost full-term—as far as the medical examiner can determine with what was left."

She sat down hard on the bottom step and put her head in her hands, hearing Lauren's voice again from that long-ago summer. *None of my bathing suits fit me anymore. I've gained some weight.* "I wasn't expecting that. Oh, God. No, I wasn't." She took several deep breaths before looking back up at Mason. "The baby—how did it die?"

"So much of the physical evidence is gone that it will be almost impossible to come to a definite conclusion. There's a chance that it could have been expelled postmortem from Lauren's body."

She didn't ask him to elaborate. Resting her elbows on her thighs, she dug the heels of her hands into her eyes. "Poor Lauren. Poor, poor Lauren." The tears were warm and wet in her palm.

Mason squatted in front of her. "Look, Jillian, this casts a strong light of guilt on Linc. They were seeing each other before her death. I know she broke it off with him, and he was upset. Considering she had no other enemies, that's a pretty strong motive. Especially if she was pregnant." He paused, as if to let his words resonate in her brain. "You might be in danger. Do you understand that?"

She shook her head several times, not even able to put her objections into words. "No," was all she managed.

He stood, brushing imaginary lint from his uniform pants. "Without a confession, we don't have enough to hold him—for now. But I wanted you to know that he's our number one suspect, and you need to be careful."

Jillian clenched her eyes, seeing in her mind's eye Linc and Lauren dancing in the sand. "No," she said again, her voice sure.

She felt Mason's hand on her shoulder. "I want you to think about moving you and the children over to my mama's. She's extended the invitation to you, if you think you'd feel safer. But it's up to you—you just let her know. And I strongly encourage you to take her up on her offer."

He let his hand fall from her shoulder and stepped away toward the door and avoided looking at her. "One more thing. Your father called my office. He was looking for my daddy and got me instead. He said he's been trying to reach you for several days but keeps getting your answering machine. He saw the story about Lauren in the Atlanta paper. Said he thinks Linc's guilty and is also concerned about your safety. He and your mama are on their way to Pawleys. Should be here by tomorrow."

Jillian rested her hands on her drawn-up knees and stared at the familiar blunt fingers and her grandmother's ring, finding the strength there to continue to breathe in and then breathe out.

She stood. "They won't be staying here. If they find you first, direct them to the Pelican Inn."

He nodded, and she knew he understood.

"And I have a lot more to fear from them than I ever would from Linc." She leaned against the banister, the solid oak newel post digging into her back and keeping her grounded.

Anger flashed across Mason's face. "How can you be so sure of him? All of the evidence is against him, but you don't seem to have any doubts. Why, Jillian? After all this time, why?"

She moved away from the newel post and fingered her grandmother's ring, feeling it warm beneath her touch. "I'm not sure. I just think that long ago I figured the best way to get through life was to find something to believe in. It's like the new star I look for every night. It keeps me believing in possibilities."

Mason regarded her silently for a moment. "That's either the smartest thing I've ever heard or the dumbest. Either way, I hope you're right—for your sake. Otherwise, I wouldn't give a damn if Linc Rising rotted away in jail for the rest of his God-given life."

He pushed open the door, but she grabbed his arm. "Mason, wait. I'm sorry. I'm sorry that things couldn't work out with us. But see, even when we were younger, you never had enough faith in me. You thought you could be my salvation—just like my ex-husband did. But neither one of you believed that I was strong enough to survive on my own." She shrugged, not really knowing what else to say. Finally, she said, "Linc always did. He still does."

She put her hands on either side of his face and stood on her toes to kiss his cheek. "You're a good friend, Mason. I hope you always will be."

He looked away from her, then nodded before passing through the door and leaving. He didn't look back once as he walked toward his truck and drove off.

Jillian closed the screen door gently and walked toward the kitchen. Something caught her attention from the corner of her eye, and she looked up the stairway and saw Janie and Gracie sitting next to each other and holding hands. Janie was crying, and Gracie was patting her on the knee with her free hand.

Jillian walked up the stairs toward them and sat down on a lower step. She touched her daughter's cheek lightly before turning her attention to the older woman. "What's wrong, Janie? Were you listening to what Officer Weber was telling me?"

Janie nodded as she wiped away strands of hair that had stuck to her wet cheeks.

"Was it about the baby?"

She didn't respond, but sniffled loudly and closed her eyes. Jillian had to lean forward to hear her when she spoke.

"I'm afraid."

"What are you afraid of, Janie? Tell me. Maybe I can help."

Janie's brown eyes darkened as she scooted forward on the step. "They're coming. They're coming to take the baby."

"Who, Janie? Who's coming to take the baby?"

"They are. They're coming, and I've got to keep the baby safe. Poor Lauren's baby. Nobody's going to take that one. Poor Lauren. She used to visit me, you know. She was my friend."

A cold breeze ran up Jillian's spine as she patted Janie's hand. "Yes, she was. She was my friend, too. I know you miss her as much as I do." She heard Lessie join them in the downstairs hall but didn't acknowledge her. "But who's coming, Janie?"

Janie leaned forward to whisper in her ear, "You know." Janie began to look around frantically. "Where's Baby? Where is she?"

Lessie called from below. "Gracie must have left her in her bedroom. I'll go get her." She came up the steps, squeezing by them.

Jillian grabbed Janie's shoulders to calm her down. "See? Baby's safe. Everything's going to be okay."

Lessie retrieved the doll and ran down the stairs to put it in Janie's waiting arms. "I'm going to take Janie home now. I think there's been too much excitement this afternoon."

Gracie crawled onto Jillian's lap as they watched Lessie help Janie down the stairs. Jillian closed her eyes for a moment, breathing deeply of her daughter's scent of baby shampoo and sweat. *Who's coming, Janie?* She squeezed her daughter harder. *You know.*

She took a deep breath. "I know who Lauren is, Gracie. And I do believe you've been talking to her. I'm sorry I didn't believe you at first."

Gracie put her finger in her mouth and sucked on it, just like she'd done as an infant. Jillian felt a stab of remorse that she'd forgotten that, and so much more about Grace's babyhood. She shoved the regrets behind her, mentally locking them in a box, and tried to think of the future. It would be different, and if she believed that, then it would happen.

She rested her cheek against her daughter's head. "Has Lauren said anything else, Gracie? Anything that might help us know how she got hurt?"

Gracie shook her head, pressing against the sand dollar necklace Jillian wore. "She's gone now. She said she'd be back, but that you didn't need her anymore."

Jillian's eyes stung with tears. "She said I didn't need her? Is that all?"

Gracie's words were muffled as she spoke around the finger in her mouth. "And she said that you didn't need to be afraid of the dark anymore."

Jillian bit down hard on her lip, stifling the tears that threatened to spill. Nothing was making any sense, and she still felt chilled by Janie's words. Who had she been talking about?

She remembered what Linc had said the last time she'd seen him, and felt her heart skip a beat. *Your father's name is Mark, isn't it, Jillian?*

Gently moving Gracie from her lap and forcing her voice to stay calm, she said, "I've got to go find Linc. First, I'm going to call your daddy and tell him I'll drop you off at the inn. And then I'm going to see if Mrs. Weber can watch Ford for me for a few hours." She stood and pulled Gracie up with her.

The little girl looked up at Jillian. "And then what?"

"And then we're going to finally find the star that I've been looking for all these years."

CHAPTER 24

LINC RAN HIS HANDS OVER THE SMOOTH PLANES OF THE OLD DOOR that was laid flat over his worktable. Layers of paint had finally given way to its hidden treasure of solid mahogany after nearly a week of meticulous stripping. As Linc had already discovered, the best things life had to offer were the hardest won.

He stepped back, wiping away the sweat and paint chips from his cheeks, letting his gaze roam around the beautiful high-ceilinged room with the water-damaged hand-painted wallpaper. When he'd seen the house on Tradd Street, in Charleston's historic district, it had called to him in a way he couldn't explain to anyone—even his business partner. There was something about taking something old, damaged and un-wanted and breathing new life into it. He'd done it with his own life, and found it to be his calling to do the same to this house.

He heard the sound of the large brass lion knocker against the front door, and threw his T-shirt over his head as he went to answer it. He pulled open the door and stared at Jillian in surprise.

"Hi, Linc." She gave him a tentative smile. "I called your office and they told me you'd be here. I hope you don't mind."

He shook his head, then stepped back, allowing her to come inside. She stopped on the black-and-white marble-tiled floor and looked up at the floating stairway, a hallmark that had clinched the sale of the house for him. Silently, she moved to touch the newly stripped mahogany ban-ister and the termite-eaten rosettes that crowned each spindle.

He studied the tilt of her head, the curve of her cheek and the openmouthed wonder as she looked about her. She had always under-stood his elemental need to create beauty where most only saw dirt and neglect and raw ugliness. The two of them had always seen the core of things that existed under all the surface flaws. He imagined they both regarded people in the same way.

"It's . . . beautiful." Her voice vanished in the empty foyer. "It's like the inside of an oyster shell, isn't it? Not many would bother to pick up the ugly shell to see what's on the inside." She swept her hand over the smooth swell of the curved plaster of the stairwell, her fingers brushing at the heart of him.

"Thank you," he said, moving closer. He waited for her to speak.

She turned around and pressed her back against the wall, creating more space between them. "Mason came to see me today. He said that Lauren was pregnant when she died."

For a terrifying moment, he thought he might throw up. He raked both hands through his hair, searching for something to grab hold of. He reached for Jillian and grabbed her arms, pulling her to him. She felt stiff under his fingers. "You think I killed her? Because she was pregnant?"

She pressed her forehead against his chest, and he didn't move away. "No, Linc. I don't. And that's not why I came here." Pulling her head back, she gazed directly into his eyes. "I wanted to know why you asked me about my father."

He pushed away, and returned to the supine door and picked up a square of sandpaper before putting it down again. "You don't want to know. Trust me, you don't want to know."

Jillian crossed the room in three angry strides. "Yes—I do. I will not allow you to dismiss me again. I love you, Linc. And I'm sorry if that makes you uncomfortable. But being in this position makes me care a great deal about what happens to you, and I don't want to see you sent to jail for a crime we both know you had nothing to do with. So I'm asking you why you had to know my father's name. And I need you to trust me that I can handle it."

He looked at her with narrow eyes, feeling torn between the desire to shout at her or to kiss her senseless. He felt her impenetrable strength and knew there was no going back. He said nothing and moved to the far side of the foyer to a tall door and went inside. From his back pocket, he pulled out a key and unlocked the bottom drawer of the desk that had been pushed in front of wide French doors. He stared at the familiar letters for a full minute before deciding to take them out and show them to Jillian.

Not bothering to shut the door behind him, he walked over to Jillian and handed her the letters. Slowly, she sat on the bottom step and placed the stack on her lap.

"Where did these come from?"

"I found them in a hidden compartment in Lauren's bedroom." He cleared his throat. "Gracie told me. She said Lauren wanted me to look there."

He stood quietly and watched her open each envelope and unfold and read each letter. When she was done, she calmly laid her hands over the scattered letters in her lap and looked up at him, her eyes bright.

"How long have you had these?"

"A few weeks, maybe longer."

"And you didn't show them to me or anyone else."

His eyes met hers. "I might have if it came down to me facing prison. But I would have left that up to you."

"Why, Linc?"

"Because he's your father. Because I was trying to protect you in the same way you tried to do for me by keeping Lauren's box a secret. I didn't want him to hurt you any more than he's already done." He took a deep breath and stared up at the plaster medallion under which a chandelier had once cast a brilliant light over the now ruined foyer. It was in the shape of a star, each tip pointing toward unknown destinations. "And because I think I love you."

She stood, the letters sliding to the dusty floor. "So you're admitting that we have a relationship?"

His arms slid around her waist. "Yeah, I guess I am."

She closed her eyes, and he watched her chest rise and fall. When she opened them again, she said, "Great. Then you're coming with me to give Mason these letters. But we will definitely finish this conversation later."

She moved away from him, but he tugged her back. "Aren't you even going to ask?"

"About what?"

"About the baby."

"No, I wasn't. It doesn't matter to me."

He let her go and watched as she put the letters in a single pile, then picked them up. "My hands are shaking too badly. You're going to have to drive."

After locking up the house, he opened the car door for her, then slid behind the wheel. They were silent as he made his way through road construction and narrow alleys that defined Charleston's historic district and headed toward the highway. He didn't speak until they were headed north on Highway 17. "I never slept with Lauren. It's not that we both didn't want to. It's just that I could never risk doing to my own kid what my mother had done to me." He gripped the wheel tighter. "I never even knew she was pregnant."

He heard her expel a deep breath. He turned to look at her, and saw her head resting on the seat back and her eyes closed. "What was that for?"

"It'll be a lot easier to make Mason look at other suspects if you're not the father of the baby. *I* didn't need convincing."

His heart skidded in his chest, and he couldn't find any words. Instead, he reached out a hand to touch her cheek, and she smiled into his hand.

It was nearly six o'clock by the time they returned to Pawleys, and Jillian's breasts were full of milk and aching. She held the seat belt strap away from her chest to prevent any undue pressure or unfortunate wet spots on her blouse.

"We need to stop at Martha's first to get Ford. I left a few bottles with her so he won't be starving, but I need to feed him as soon as possible."

Linc glanced her way and saw her adjusting her bra and just nodded.

She closed her eyes to escape the turmoil of her thoughts, but found her mind straying to a summer night on the beach long ago when she'd been fifteen. She could hear Lauren's voice as if she were speaking from the backseat. *I thought your dad and I could have a reasonable conversation over a little drink. He's agreed that you can stay another week.*

Jillian covered her face with her hands, then turned to stare out the window, unable to meet Linc's eyes. *Oh, Lauren—what did you do?* She let herself doze, imagining she could still smell the suntan oil and stale beer.

When they arrived at the Webers', Jillian was relieved to see

Mason's Jeep and the chief's car parked in front. They walked around the porch to the kitchen door and rapped on the screen door. Joe, Martha and Mason were sitting at the kitchen table, and all three stood and motioned for them to come in.

Joe offered his hand to Linc to shake. "Good to see you again, son. Didn't get a chance to say good-bye last time I saw you."

"No," he answered, shaking Chief Weber's hand, "I didn't. All those people breathing down my neck wasn't conducive for good manners. I left in a hurry."

Mason stepped forward. "I'm surprised to see you back. Thought you'd be hiding out in Charleston a while longer."

Before Linc could respond, Jillian stepped in between them and handed Mason the stack of letters from her father to Lauren. She was surprised at how easy it was. "I think you and your father need to see these."

He glanced at them and opened one, quickly scanning the *to* and *from* lines. "Who's M?"

"My father—Mark Parrish. I recognize his handwriting."

"Are you saying that Lauren and your father had a relationship?"

She felt Linc's hand on her shoulder. "Yes. I have reason to believe it was an intimate one." *I thought your dad and I could have a reasonable conversation over a little drink.*

Mason's eyes narrowed slightly as he took in both Linc and Jillian. "I see," he said, glancing down at the letters. "I'll look into this. And while your father's in town, I'll have a talk with him."

"He's here—now?"

"Yes. They arrived around noon. They came to the station first thing, and I told them what you said about getting a room at the Pelican. They said they'd wait for you at the house."

Jillian looked at her watch. "That's wonderful—just what I need right now. I suppose Rick is back there already with Gracie. I'm going to go up and feed Ford, and let Rick stew there for a while with my parents. It's the least he could do."

"Ford's not here, Jillian." Martha frowned. "Rick and Grace came by around four o'clock. I'd just fed the baby and he was in a good mood, so Rick asked if he could take him back to the house. I didn't think you'd mind."

"No, I don't mind—I'm just a bit surprised. But that's fine. And I thank you for taking him this afternoon. I hope he behaved."

Martha smiled. "He's a lovely little boy. No trouble at all. I only hope you call me more often to babysit."

Martha began packing up the diaper bag Rick had left behind, but Jillian felt an urgency to leave the house, to see her children. To make sure they were safe. "Don't worry about the bag—I'll come back to get it. I need to go."

Without waiting to hear anybody's farewells, she left through the door they'd come in, letting it slam shut behind her. She heard Linc shout, but she didn't slow down.

He caught up to her. "What's the rush, Jilly? I'm sure Rick is taking good care of the children. He might have been an awful husband, but he seems a capable father."

She shook her head, taking long strides down to the beach where the sand was packed flat and she could walk faster. She thought of her son and felt the letdown of her milk, feeling it soak through her nursing bra, but she didn't stop. "It's not that. I just . . . have a feeling. I need to get home. Go ahead and take the car. It's just as quick for me to walk."

He didn't answer but took her hand and continued to walk with her, and she was glad. They reached the part of the beach that lay directly below their two houses, beneath the scarred dune and the two shrugging houses. Jillian breathed in deep gulps, sustained by the salty taste of the ocean on her lips. Her gaze traveled to the part below the dunes near her own house, and spotted Rick and Gracie.

She moved forward and started to wave but stopped suddenly, watching Gracie walk purposefully toward her father. It was there in the way her back arched and her feet splayed as she struggled through the deep sand. All that was missing was Baby in her carrier. *Janie.*

Linc touched her arm. "What is it, Jilly?"

She shook her head, her vision blurred. "I don't know yet. I'm trying to figure something out." She met his dark gray gaze. "Stay with me, okay? I need you with me."

She broke into a run until she reached Gracie, and the little girl threw herself into her mother's arms. "Mommy! I beat Daddy at golfing, and he said I could have an ice cream. I spilled some."

She stretched out her yellow T-shirt, which was now covered in varying shades of chocolate ice cream. Jillian tugged on Grace's sun hat, one she didn't recognize with the words DADDY'S LITTLE GIRL on the brim. "Nice hat, sweetie. Guess Daddy doesn't want you getting sunburned again, huh?" Rick walked up to them, clutching a red Frisbee. His forehead and shins were peeling, and he wore white sunblock on his nose.

Jillian cupped her hand over her forehead and looked up at him. "Where's Ford?"

Rick's smile dimmed. "Up at the house. He was getting a little cranky, so I changed him and put him in his crib. He fell asleep right away."

"Is he alone?"

"No, your parents are up there waiting for you. They said they didn't mind listening for Ford while I took Gracie down here to the beach."

Linc was already ahead of her, walking quickly toward the house. "Come on. We'll do this together." He grabbed her hand, and his skin was warm against hers. It calmed her and gave her the strength she needed to open the door and walk inside.

They found them on the front porch, sitting straight-backed on two rockers. They were both drinking martinis in the fading light, her mother's immaculate manicure displayed against the near-empty glass. She drained it as Jillian approached and set it down on a side table, but didn't stand.

Her father stood and gave her a tentative smile. He dropped it when it met with no response from Jillian. His gaze slid to Linc, and Jillian saw the recognition flit over his face.

Jillian crossed her arms, trying to hide the wet spots on her blouse. "What are you doing here?"

He stuck out his hands, palms up. "I know this is unexpected—I'm sorry. I've been trying to reach you for days. I kept leaving messages on the answering machine, but you never called me back."

"And it never occurred to you that maybe I didn't want to talk to you?" Jillian thought she was more amazed than anybody else at her response. Just a mere month before, she would have apologized. And then she would have gone into the kitchen to make something for him. Now, feeling Linc behind her, she felt no compunction to do either.

His eyes held remorse as he regarded her. Jillian found herself looking at him as an outsider would and realized that he was still a very handsome man. But she knew there had never been any real strength in his broad shoulders. She almost felt sorry for him.

"I'm sorry, Jillian. When I read about . . . Lauren in the Atlanta paper, I knew I needed to talk to you." He looked beyond her shoulder at Linc for a moment. "Alone. But when I couldn't reach you on the phone, your mother and I decided we needed to make the trip to speak with you in person."

Jillian hugged herself, drawing strength from Linc's presence behind her. "There's nothing you need to say to me that I don't already know. I know about you and Lauren. I just gave a bunch of letters you sent to her to Chief Weber. He'll be wanting to ask you some questions."

Her father's lips whitened. "I had nothing to do with her death." He pointed to Linc. "He's the one who should be questioned. He was the one who kept stalking Lauren when she dumped him." He dropped his hand. "She loved me. And Linc couldn't stand knowing that she loved somebody else."

She felt Linc tense behind her and she grabbed his hand, willing him to be silent. "She was only seventeen, Dad. And you were a married man. Did you ever stop to think about that? About the people you'd be hurting?"

He shrugged, his eyes skittering away from her face. "She loved me."

Jillian stared at him for a long moment. "Did you know she was pregnant?"

He lifted his gaze to meet hers. Slowly, he nodded. "I knew. Nobody else did, though. I was supposed to take her away to a home in Charleston where they would take care of her until the birth and adopt her baby. I was going to have her call her parents to let them know she was okay so that they would think she'd just run away." He turned back to look at his wife, whose fingers had turned white around the stem of her glass. "Lauren thought we were running away together. I never told her the truth because I knew she'd tell her parents. But then she didn't show up where we were supposed to meet." He stared hard at Linc. "And I always knew she would have been there if she could have been. Was she already dead then? Or did you make her suffer first?"

Linc moved forward. "You bastard. Is that why you've driven all the way down here? To make sure that all fingers are pointing at me instead of you? You did that before, remember? But it's not going to work this time. Too many people know the truth about you. There's nowhere to hide."

Jillian put a restraining hand on his arm as he moved closer to her father, his hands tightened in fists. Her mother stood, wobbling on high heels. She stuck her hands out to support herself, knocking the martini glass onto the ground and shattering it. Glass sprayed in all directions, a final, irreversible act. Jillian smelled the alcohol and turned her head as her mother stumbled forward.

"And you knew about his affair with Lauren—and you didn't stop it. And you never said anything when she disappeared. Why? How could you be so blind for him?"

Her mother's lips quivered. "You could never understand. I love your father, and he loves me. We've learned to overlook each other's faults. Maybe if you had a heart, you'd understand that."

Anger erupted inside of her, and Jillian took a step toward her mother. "If *I* had a heart? Isn't that a little odd coming from a woman who never once showed an ounce of affection for her own daughter?"

Her mother's face paled, and bright spots of color sprang onto her cheeks. "You ungrateful wretch. I fed you and clothed you and took you to the doctor when you were sick. I never got a word of thanks from you."

Jillian's voice was barely louder than a whisper. "You were my mother. You were supposed to do those things out of love, not out of obligation. Don't you know the difference?"

Joan Parrish's eyes were bright with unshed tears. Her voice was low but clear when she finally spoke. "You weren't the child of my body, no matter how hard I wanted it to be. So you could never be the child of my heart."

Jillian's mouth opened, trying to suck in air, and finally knowing what it must feel like to drown. Linc stepped forward and wrapped his arm around her shoulders. Jillian could see his jawbone clenching. "This isn't the time for family confessions—Jillian needs to feed the baby. You can save it for your chat with the chief. Right now, we want you to leave. You've already done enough damage."

Jillian felt the clawing hurt and the need for a thousand questions. But her mind shut and all she was left with was the fullness of her breasts and the urgency to get to her son. She turned her back on the woman she had called Mother all her life, and saw the baby monitor Rick had evidently set up on the porch. She noticed it was turned off. "Wasn't anybody listening for the baby?"

As she brushed by her father, she had the satisfaction of seeing a chagrined look on his face. "I'm going to go feed Ford."

Linc came inside with her. "I'll go get something to clean up the glass."

Jillian took the stairs two at a time and threw open the baby's door so hard that it bounced off the wall behind it. She cringed, preparing herself for the wailing of a baby suddenly awakened by a loud noise. But no sound came.

She rushed to the side of the crib and stared inside, her gaze roaming from one end of the baby's bed to the other, then back again, her brain not really registering what she was seeing.

The crib was empty except for a balled-up blanket at the foot of the bed—the yellow one that had once covered a turtle egg and now only carried the powdered scent of an absent child.

CHAPTER 25

Linc heard Jillian scream. He ran up the stairs and found her next to the crib, clutching a baby blanket. He didn't need to ask her what was wrong.

"He's gone." Her eyes lacked the light he'd grown used to seeing in the past few months.

"Come on," he said, grabbing her hand and pulling her out the door. She followed him mutely, her hand limp like a child's. When they got downstairs, he grabbed the cordless phone from the cradle and pushed it into her hand. "Call Mason. Tell him to get here now." Her breath was coming in short gasps as she took the phone. "We'll find Ford. I promise."

She nodded and began dialing the number. Linc left her and went to the front porch and spotted her parents climbing into a dark blue Lincoln at the end of the driveway. He started running.

He caught up with them before Mark Parrish had a chance to turn the car around. Linc grabbed the door handle of the driver's-side door and yanked it open, then stuck his hand in and tore the key from the ignition. Jillian's mother struck at him, her long fingernails raking his cheek.

Linc grabbed Jillian's father by the neck of his shirt, making them almost nose to nose, and feeling for the first time in his life that he was perfectly capable of murdering another human being with his bare hands. "Where is he? Where is the baby?"

Genuine confusion passed over Mark's face. "Rick said he was upstairs in his crib, napping. I didn't go up and check."

Linc loosened the grip on the shirt and Mark pulled back, closing the door and rubbing his neck. "He's not there. Was anybody else in the house?"

Mark looked annoyed. "No—I swear it. But we were on the front porch. Anybody could have come in the back, I guess, and gone upstairs without our seeing it."

Linc straightened, glaring at the older man. "Or heard anything, either, since you had the monitor off." He pocketed the car keys. "I'm hanging on to these for now. Officer Weber is on his way over, and I don't think he wants you going too far. Just don't come in the house. Jillian doesn't want to see you, and I might kill you."

Mark tried to push open the door and step out, but Linc held it firm. "You can't hold me here! I've done nothing wrong. Give me the damned keys now, you son of a bitch."

Linc pressed against the door, and glanced past Mark to where Jillian's mother was pressed against the side of the car, looking as if she might be sick at any moment. "I don't think so. I guess you can't be arrested for an inability to watch a sleeping child, but there is the matter of your relationship with a minor."

Mark's face paled. "She was past the age of consent in this state. There's nothing there to charge me."

Linc grabbed the man's collar again. "Except for her murder—and that of her unborn baby."

Jillian's father pushed on the car door again, his eyes narrow and his lips white. "Was it your baby? You probably killed her when you found out she'd found a real man instead of a street punk whose mother was a whore. Lauren decided it was time to come up in the world."

Linc felt the rage consume him but was amazed at his control over it. Maybe because the rage wasn't in defense of himself. He marveled at how calm he was as he pulled the door open and yanked the man out of the car. He pulled his fist back and felt a finger break as he plowed it into the older man's jaw. "This is for Lauren, you son of a bitch." Then he pulled his fist back and pummeled the man's nose, feeling bone snap beneath his hand and barely feeling the pain from his own broken finger. "And that was for Jillian. You never stood up for her. You never cared enough to just show up for her."

Linc stood back, panting, as he watched the man collapse against the side of the car and slide down into the grass, blood streaming from his nose and lip. He glared at Linc but didn't move.

Linc turned away toward the house, knowing he couldn't stay in the man's presence for a minute longer without finishing the job he'd started. He found Jillian where he'd left her, the phone still clutched in her hand, the baby blanket in the other.

"Did you reach Mason?"

She hung up the phone. "He's coming right away with the chief." Her voice was faint, as if from far away.

"Do you think Rick had anything to do with Ford's disappearance?"

"No. He wouldn't do anything like that. I know he wouldn't."

She started fraying the fringe around the edges of the blanket, her hands shaking. "This isn't Ford's blanket. It was on the porch with the turtle egg, and I'd left it in the laundry room." She looked up at Linc with wet eyes. "Why was it in his bed?"

He gently touched her shoulders. "I don't know. We'll tell Mason when he gets here."

"Janie said that someone was coming to take the baby. She said, 'They're coming to take the baby.' Who was she talking about?"

A cooling breeze blew through the screen door, chilling his spine, and he noticed the setting sun. It would be dark soon. He pulled Jillian closer. "I don't know. I don't think your parents had anything to do with it, though. I really don't think they'd go to that much trouble and risk getting involved in your life."

"She's not my real mother," she whispered.

He smoothed his hand over her head. "I'll help you find your real mother. When this is all over, we'll do it together. But first we need to find Ford. And we will find him—I promise."

Jillian rested her forehead against his chest, and he felt her nod her head. She was silent for several minutes, and he could hear Grace's laughter outside through the screen, a welcome reprieve from the thickness of the air inside. He could feel Jillian still pulling at the blanket.

She lifted her head. "This is identical to a baby blanket that was in a chest in my parents' attic. I always thought it had been mine. But why would Janie have the same one?"

Bright pockets of air seemed to burst inside his head and he felt the breeze again, almost as if it were a hand pushing at his back, urging him toward the door. Jillian must have felt it, too, because she pulled away from him and moved to the door, throwing it open and then stepping out onto the back porch. She walked toward the boardwalk, where she could see Gracie and Rick throwing the red Frisbee in the growing dusk.

He watched as Gracie missed a toss, then trudged up the dune to retrieve it. There was something so familiar in that walk, and he remembered again how he had once thought that her expression had reminded him of someone, too—someone whose identity still hovered on the edges of his consciousness.

Jillian touched his arm. "Do you see it, too?"

"She reminds me of someone—someone I can't quite place." He furrowed his brow and stared back at the beach where Rick and Grace had stopped playing and were now gazing back at them.

Gracie pushed the hair off her face with both hands as they watched. He felt Jillian's hand fold itself into his. Her voice was thick with tears. "Where's Mason? What's taking him so lo—"

Her voice stopped in midsentence, and Linc followed her gaze toward Gracie. Jillian's fingernails dug into his palms. "Janie," she said quietly. "How old do you think Janie is?"

"I don't know—definitely not more than fifty. Why?" He felt that same breeze against his spine again, like a storm breeze that blows right before lightning strikes.

"Oh, God," she whispered. She squeezed his hand, tighter now, and he knew she'd broken skin on his palm, but he didn't feel any pain. "Oh, God," she said again, and sank down into the sand, finally letting go of him and burying her face in her hands.

Her voice was mumbly beneath trembling fingers. "It's something Janie said to me—when she found that turtle egg and then left it on my doorstep with the blanket. She said something like how all mothers know their children. And that if her baby were stolen from its nest, she'd find it and take care of it." She stared up at him, and he knew all of her secrets at the same moment he realized that they were both learning them for the first time.

He squatted down on his haunches and cupped her head in his hands. "We need to go to Janie's. I'll tell Rick to let Mason know where we are, and also about your parents." He patted his pants pocket. "They're not going far. They'll be very helpful in figuring out all the missing pieces."

He kissed her forehead soundly and then pulled her up. He expected her to lean heavily on him, to clutch at his arm. Instead, she pulled away and started moving quickly toward Rick and Grace. "Hurry, Linc. I can't wait another minute." She put her hands on her hips while she waited for him to catch up. Her gaze swept behind him, up the dunes toward the two identical houses. "I'm going to find out the truth, Linc—I'm not afraid. But I need you with me."

He watched her face closely, at the way her chin jutted forward and her arms were at her sides, not bothering to hide the large, round wet spots that were beginning to dry around the edges. The ocean wind whipped at her hair, and he thought with a brief smile that she looked like Mother Earth, an elemental role she played with grace and beauty. If he hadn't known it before, he knew now that he loved her, and probably always had. It was hot and lovely and humbling as the emotions shot through him, making him sway on the dunes like the sea oats around him.

Nodding, Linc took her hand and they went to talk to Rick together before heading off in his car to Janie's house on the other side of the island; the house with the silk flowers that bloomed all year long under a mother's loving care.

Janie answered the door with a tentative smile that broadened when she realized there was nobody else behind them on the front steps. "I'm so glad you're here. Ford's hungry and needs to eat, but he wouldn't take a bottle from me."

Jillian nearly swooned with relief. The whole ride over she'd kept fighting the thought that she had been wrong, and that Ford was somewhere else with a stranger. But when she saw Janie's brown eyes that were so much like her own, she knew her first instincts had been right.

Linc followed her inside as she moved through the front room to a corner where Baby's crib was set up. Ford cried out a loud, impatient cry, and Jillian reached for him, her own tears spilling over as she held her baby next to her heart, a part of her whose capacity to love she was only beginning to realize.

She sat down in an armchair and began unbuttoning her blouse, oblivious to the other occupants of the room. As soon as the baby began to nurse, she sat back in the chair and felt the relief flood her. She bent her head to the baby's as she cried into the soft down, remembering how she hadn't wanted him when she was pregnant, and how now she couldn't imagine life without him.

Something cold touched her shoulder, and she looked up to see Linc holding a glass of ice water. "I thought you could use this."

She took it and drank a grateful sip, carefully leaning forward to place it on the coffee table in front of her.

Janie picked up Baby from a chair and sat down on the sofa next to Jillian, not raising her eyes from the yellow yarn of the doll's head. "I didn't want them to take Ford. So I rescued him. I wanted to ask your permission, but you weren't there. It was so important that they didn't take Ford, so I didn't wait for you. I'm sorry."

Jillian looked at the older woman and felt no anger, just gratefulness and a lifetime's worth of sorrow. She reached over and patted Janie on the hand. "I know. Thank you for that." She met Linc's gaze for a moment, then turned back to Janie, looking into eyes that mirrored her own. "Why did you think my parents would take Ford?"

Janie bent her head back to Baby's. "Because they did it before. I had a little baby girl once, and they came and took her." She looked up briefly at Jillian. "Your grandmother said it would be best if she had a mommy and daddy instead of just me. But they said it was because I couldn't take care of her, but I knew I could. That's why I have Baby—to show them that I know how to take care of my own child. So that maybe one day they would give me my little girl back."

Jillian felt the sob deep in the back of her throat, but she managed to find her voice. "What happened to your little girl, Janie?"

She saw that Janie was crying, too, with fat tears sliding down the rounded cheeks. "They took her away to live in Atlanta. But they always brought her back in the summertime, and that's when I got to see her."

Jillian wanted to ask the question, to bring her life to this point of change. She felt Linc at her side, touching her knee as he squatted in front of them.

"Janie, what did they call your baby—the one they took to Atlanta?"

Her voice was hardly audible. "Jillian. They named her Jillian."

Jillian had known that, of course, but to hear it was like stepping into a tall wave and feeling as if the world had no top and no bottom for a moment.

Linc placed his hand over Jillian's where it lay on the baby's leg as she nursed, and his gentleness made Jillian want to weep. She noticed for the first time the scrapes on Linc's face and the way his second finger hung at an odd angle. Glancing down, Jillian saw that Ford had fallen asleep. Carefully laying him on her lap, she fixed her bra and rebuttoned her blouse before putting the baby up on her shoulder.

Linc spoke gently again. "Janie, do you know how babies are made?"

She buried her face in Baby's belly and slowly nodded her head.

"So you know that every baby has a mama and a daddy?"

She nodded again, peeking up at Linc with one eye.

"Who was your baby's daddy?"

Janie clenched her eyes and buried her face against her doll. Her voice was muffled but her words were clear. "It was him—it was Mark."

Jillian turned her face away, settling her cheek against Ford's in an attempt to ground her world and keep it from shaking.

And then Linc's voice drifted over to her again. "And did Mark ever do to another girl what he had done to you?"

"She was my friend. I didn't want him to take her baby, too."

"Who was your friend, Janie? What was her name?"

There was a short pause, and Jillian lifted her head to watch Janie answer. "It was Lauren."

Linc sank back on his heels and held his head in his hands. Slowly, he stood and moved toward Jillian. He had almost reached her when Janie spoke again. "She told me that she and Mark were going to run away together."

Fear and panic rose in Jillian at Janie's words. She wanted to tell Janie to stop, but she sat silently with the sleeping baby in her arms and listened to the rest of Janie's story.

Janie tapped herself on the forehead. "But I'm a lot smarter than he knew. I knew that he only wanted to take her baby like he took mine."

The silence in the house was like a deafening roar, and Jillian realized it was now full dark outside, the sky surrendering its last light with a pale pink banner. Her eyes met Linc's for a moment, half wanting to tell him to stop, but knowing there was no going back. She kept her gaze on him as Linc walked back to Janie and sat on the coffee table in front of her.

"What did you do, Janie? To stop them?"

She smiled up at Linc. "I told Lauren that Mark had changed their meeting place and wanted to meet her in the tunnel instead."

"You knew about the tunnel?"

"Oh, yes. My brother told me about it. He had a girlfriend that lived there before the Millses did. But then he died, and I was the only one who knew. I know how to keep a secret." Her smile halted halfway.

"Why did you tell her to go there?"

Janie didn't answer at first. Instead, she moved to the crib and put Baby inside it, humming a little lullaby as she did. Slowly, she moved back to the sofa. "So I could lock her in there until Mark went away by himself, and then Lauren and her baby would be safe." She paused, and Jillian watched as Janie's face crumpled. "She was my friend."

Linc's voice was patient. "We know that, Janie. We know you wouldn't hurt Lauren on purpose." He squeezed her hands. "But what happened when you went to unlock the tunnel?"

Janie started sobbing, her words unintelligible, and Linc's arms went around her in the same way Jillian had seen him comfort Grace. "It was all water. It was deep and I called her name, but she never answered. She didn't want to come out again."

Jillian stood on shaky legs and carefully laid Ford in Baby's crib, moving the rag doll to the corner, where it sat like a guardian angel. Jillian went into the kitchen and got another glass of water and returned to the sofa where Janie and Linc now sat, and handed it to the older woman. Janie stared at it for a long moment, as if wondering what to do with it, but then took it and drank with long gulping sounds.

Jillian sat down on the other side of Janie. "But you never told anybody where Lauren had gone?"

Janie shook her head, her braids flying. "I told you. I'm good at keeping secrets." She paused, looking first at Linc and then at Jillian. "And Lauren told me that it would get me in trouble. She said she wasn't afraid of the water anymore and she would wait."

Jillian's eyes met Linc's and neither one spoke, but Jillian was sure they were thinking the same thing. *Gracie.* If the genetic bond had not already been established, there would be no doubt now.

Janie looked down at her hands, and Jillian noticed the green stains from Janie's beloved garden. These were nurturing hands, caring hands that knew everything about coaxing life from brown earth, silk flowers and a child's heart.

With a sigh, Janie laid her head on Jillian's shoulder. "Am I going to get in trouble?"

Linc patted her shoulder. "We're going to take good care of you so you don't have to worry, okay? I have a lawyer friend in Charleston I'm going to call tonight. He'll know what to do."

Jillian met his eyes again and mouthed the words "thank you."

Janie sat up straight and looked toward the front window as if noticing for the first time that night had fallen. "I've got to go turn on the lights in my garden. My children are afraid of the dark."

Jillian stood. "I'll go with you and help."

Linc grabbed her hand. "Are you sure you wouldn't rather stay here with the lights on and wait for Mason?"

She kissed him lightly and smiled. "I'll be fine."

She gave a quick glance at Ford in the crib as she walked by, then followed Janie out the back door to the sleeping garden. She descended the stairs and stood behind Janie amid the unscented begonias, gardenias and roses, but smelling the air of the marsh at night and feeling the beauty and serenity of this place. Darkness surrounded her, but it held none of its former terror. She reached for Janie's hand, thinking that maybe the dark wasn't full of things she couldn't see, but rather filled with all the colors of light that remained hidden until you opened your eyes wide enough to see.

CHAPTER 26

JILLIAN FINISHED ZIPPING UP THE BACK OF HER BLACK DRESS AND shook her head at her reflection in the mirror, making her bright pink shell earrings dance. They were similar to a favorite pair of Lauren's: pink, shimmery and fun, and Jillian wore them to honor her friend in a way that wearing black to her funeral never could. Spot sat on the bed watching her, and Jillian could almost swear that she read approval in his eyes.

As she was walking down the stairs, she heard a knock on the front door. A loud thump—most likely Grace jumping off her bed—sounded from upstairs, followed in quick succession by racing feet. Jillian called up the stairs, "Don't you dare come out of your room until you're dressed. I'll get the door."

A gratifying silence answered her as she moved toward the door and peered through the sidelights, surprised to see Rick there, holding a small flower arrangement.

She held the door wide and took the flowers from him. He smiled softly. "I came to say good-bye to Gracie and Ford. But I"—he shuffled his feet before speaking again—"I wanted to send these to the funeral. I didn't know her, but I knew she was a good friend to you. I hope you don't mind bringing them for me."

"Of course I don't mind. It was very thoughtful of you and I appreciate it, and I know her parents will, too." He stepped past her, inside the door, and she closed it with her hip.

His eyebrows raised. "They found her parents?"

Jillian nodded, leading the way into the kitchen. "Yes—Mason did. They've been in California all this time. I guess they felt they needed to move as far away from here as they could. I don't blame them—losing a child must be a horrible thing."

"Yes, it would be."

Jillian placed the flowers on the counter and turned to face Rick. "I suspect you didn't come here just to say good-bye to the children."

"You're right—I didn't." He stuck his hands in his pockets and walked across the kitchen to stare out the large picture window.

"Would you like some homemade fudge? I made it last night."

He faced her, a small grin on his face. "No, you don't need to feed me—but thank you." He patted his stomach. "I'm trying to lose a few. Joanie's tracking my cholesterol. . . ." He trailed off, as if realizing he'd used a dirty word in the presence of children.

No large hammer slammed into her chest, and Jillian smiled. "I'm glad she's taking care of you. It's about time somebody did, huh?"

He didn't answer, but turned to look out the window again. "I'd like to say you've changed, Jillian, but you haven't."

Her heart sank a little, but she continued to watch him, being careful not to let her emotions show.

Rick continued. "I think you've always been this wonderful strong person. You just needed to be out from under the wings of your parents—and me—to find your own strength." He faced her and smiled. "It's amazing, really, how much my leaving has done for you. I'd almost say you owed me a thank-you."

"Not quite," she said, finding a smile. She moved closer to him, wondering where all his newfound wisdom had come from. Maybe it had been there all along and she had only now started to listen. She looked into the eyes that had once held such love for her, a love that had made her ashamed of her inability to return it. A feeling of gratitude washed over her—gratitude for this man who had once loved her and taken care of her and made it better—for a while. She stood on her tiptoes and kissed him on the cheek. "But thanks for saying all that other stuff."

"You're welcome." His face was serious again. "I've been thinking about our custody arrangement."

She tried to remember to breathe evenly as she waited for him to speak again.

"I'm going to contact my lawyer and see if we can't make some adjustments. I want liberal visitation rights, and for them to spend alternating holidays with us. But I think they should live here with you. If that's all right with you, that is."

She threw her arms around him and hugged him tightly. "Of course that's what I want—more than you could ever know."

They heard the sound of a door upstairs being flung open, and then the sound of Grace's feet, clad in patent-leather Mary Janes, clopping down the stairs. And then she was in the kitchen, throwing herself at her father. "Daddy! I'm going to Lauren's funeral. Are you coming, too?"

Their eyes met over Grace's head. "Grace knows about Lauren, and she wanted to go. She knows she'll have to be quiet and behave. Ford is too little, so Lessie is watching him and will bring him by after the service. I'm sure she won't mind if you stop by to say good-bye."

Grace looked solemnly up at her father. "Mommy bought me a new dress and new shoes to wear to the funeral."

Rick nodded as he straightened, lifting Gracie in his arms. "I can see that, Pumpkin, and you look very pretty." He kissed her on the cheek. "Now, you and I need to say good-bye. I've had a lot of fun with you this week, and I'm going to work it out with your mommy so that we can see each other again real soon, if that's all right with you."

"Will I get to meet Joanie the sl—"

"Yes, Gracie, you'll get to meet Daddy's new wife, Joanie," Jillian interrupted, her smile apologetic. "Now give Daddy a kiss and a hug good-bye. The chief and Mrs. Weber will be here any minute to take us to the funeral."

They said their good-byes, then Jillian sat out on the front porch with a sniffling Gracie while they waited for the Webers' car.

Jillian sat in the backseat with Rick's flowers and Gracie on the short drive to the old cemetery and chapel at All Saints. Martha met her reflection in the rearview mirror. "I'm assuming your parents won't be at the funeral."

"No, they won't. They're on their way back to Atlanta right now."

Martha raised an eyebrow in question.

"They stopped by this morning, hoping to come to some sort of truce."

"What did you tell them?"

Grace reached for her hand and held it. "I asked them to leave. That maybe one day I'd contact them again, but for now they have no place in my life." She smiled at Martha. "I've learned a lot these past few months. I'd always thought there was something wrong with me because my parents couldn't find anything to love. I can almost under-stand now how my mother must have resented me, but that's really no excuse." She looked out the window, seeing the tall palmetto trees rush by. "I think motherhood has very little to do with biology—except for maybe the color of your eyes or the shape of your hands. All it takes to be a mother is a little effort and a lot of love."

"And to show up," Martha added, her eyes bright.

"Yeah, that, too."

Gracie held up their hands, Jillian's grandmother's gold ring reflecting the sun. "Look, Mommy, we have the same hands."

Jillian leaned over and kissed her on the forehead. "We sure do. Just like my grandmother's."

When they arrived at the church, Martha and Joe were pulled away for a few moments by an older couple Jillian didn't recognize. Grace tugged at her skirt, demanding Jillian's undivided attention.

"Are we going to say good-bye to Lauren now, Mommy?"

"Yes, sweetie, we are."

"But I've already said good-bye to her."

Jillian stopped, still holding Grace's hand. "You have?"

Gracie stared up at her mother with sad brown eyes. "She said she was going away and that she wouldn't be able to talk to me anymore."

Jillian put her arm around the small shoulders and squeezed. "Did she say why she had to go away?"

Gracie nodded. "She said you didn't need her anymore—that you had me and Ford." She grinned mischievously. "And Linc."

Jillian felt herself blush. "I see. Did she say anything else?"

"She said she would always be your very best friend, no matter what. And you don't ever have to feel you're all alone, that she'll watch out for you." Then Gracie held out her hand to her mother, the pinky crooked. "Pinky swear."

Jillian felt the tears on her face as she knelt in front of her daughter and hooked her pinky with Grace's. "Pinky swear," she said.

Grace reached out a hand and brushed her mother's tears away and smiled brightly. Then Jillian stood and led her daughter toward the chapel to say a long good-bye to a best friend who had once promised to watch over her always.

Jillian stumbled off the boardwalk in the dark, almost dropping the telescope and stubbing her toe. "Damn!" Guiltily, she glanced around for Gracie, then remembered that she was spending the night at Mary Ellen's.

She looked back at the two houses, at their identical shrugs outlined by the moonlight, and smiled. They had weathered another storm yet still sat on their perches behind the lovely dunes, standing sentinel over shifting tides and troubled lives. They persevered, their weathered facades growing more beautiful with each passing storm, with each passing year. Jillian drew a breath, feeling almost as resilient as the houses.

Only the moon and stars lit her way down to the packed sand below, where the ocean waited at low tide. She set up her telescope, then scanned her corner of the sky with her binoculars, checking off each memorized star. *Nekkar, Seginus, Izar, Acturus.* She made a second pass with the binoculars, moving from one section to the next, staring at the black spaces between the stars and looking for a spark of light that hadn't been there before. She never felt disappointment while doing this, only the hope that the possibility still existed. But tonight, with a free heart and a clear sky, she had expected something more.

She made a third pass of the final section and was about to give up for the night when she spotted something, a small pinprick of light hovering far out in the galaxy, a bright spot in an ocean of darkness. Memorizing its position, she slowly lowered her binoculars and moved to her telescope. It took her a minute to find it, and for a brief second she thought she'd made a mistake. But when she locked in on it, she knew she'd been right. After all these years, she had finally found her new star.

Feeling weak-kneed, she dropped to the sand and wrapped her arms around her legs. She wanted to laugh and cry at the same time, but found she could do neither. All she could feel was a longing to share her discovery with someone who would understand how much it meant to her.

She felt him before she turned her head to see Linc walking down the beach toward her. His pants were rolled up at the ankles, and he carried his shoes in his hand. He dropped them, then sat next to her, their knees touching.

"I thought you were in Charleston." She felt suddenly shy with him, bursting with contained emotions but unsure how to share them.

"I was. I wanted to be as far away from Lauren's funeral as possible."

Jillian rested her head on his shoulder. "You would have been welcomed there. Mrs. Mills said she wanted to offer you an apology in person."

"Yeah, well. I didn't want my presence to detract from everybody saying their good-byes to Lauren."

"She's gone now, you know. I think she's finally resting in peace."

He looked at her in the moonlight, his eyes soft. "I haven't felt her since the day we found Ford." He flexed his fingers, and she noticed he wore a splint on the middle one. "I'm glad. She deserves peace after all this time."

They stared out at the ocean, listening to the suck and pull of the surf, feeling the power of the moon sliding the huge ocean across the earth. Linc lay back in the sand and Jillian followed, their heads touching like they'd done a thousand times before in a time that seemed a thousand years ago.

Linc reached for her hand and held it. "What's going to happen to Miss Janie?"

"Her lawyer is confident she won't be facing any jail time. Right now she's receiving a psychiatric evaluation to see if she's competent. Either way, when all this is over, I'm going to have her move in with me."

"Won't it be a little crowded?"

"Oh, I don't know. I figured I'd put the children in the same room and give Gracie's to Janie. And I'll be starting a garden for her. Her flowers will flourish wherever they're planted."

He was silent for a long moment. "As much as I'm sure Janie would like being near you and the children, I have a feeling she enjoys her own space. Maybe it would be best to move her into the house next door."

Jillian got up on one elbow. "I could never afford it at market price, and you know it. Besides, where would you live?"

He looked up at her with a lopsided grin. "With you."

She felt her cheeks heat. "Linc, I couldn't—not with the children. It wouldn't . . . it wouldn't be a good example."

He laughed and reached up to her, pulling her down on top of him. "I was suggesting we do it legally."

She put her hands in the sand on either side of his face and looked down at him, forcing the thoughts in her head to override the stirrings in her heart. "Is this really where you want to be? I never thought you saw yourself living here on any permanent basis."

"I didn't. Until now. I bought these houses as a sort of revenge—a way to show people that I wasn't an outsider anymore. But I think I was the only one who ever felt that way. I put up barriers where none had really existed." He reached up to pull the hair out of her face and tucked it behind her ears. "And now I'm getting all sorts of interesting offers from the most unlikely people. Mason Weber's on the historical preservation committee, and he said they're looking for a new president. They thought somebody with my architectural background would be an asset to the community. I thought it might be nice to be considered an asset."

She smiled. "Yeah, I guess it would." Her smile faded as she felt his heat underneath her, and she moved her face closer to his. "I love you, Linc, and if you want to stay here and make our relationship legal, then I'm all for it. But only if you're sure that's what you really want."

He kissed her slowly, drawing her lower lip into his mouth and tasting her fully. When he pulled away, his eyes were serious. "I'm more sure of this than anything in my life. It's like everything I've ever worked for has led me right here, with you. Like my life has just been one big circle. Maybe that's the way it was supposed to be, and all I ever really needed to do was follow the stars home."

She moved off of him, and they both sat up. She leaned toward him. "I found my star today."

He smiled, and her heart flipped. "Congratulations. What are you going to call it?"

She shrugged. "Oh, I don't know. I was thinking of Mercury—so then I'd have a Ford, Lincoln and Mercury in my life."

He elbowed her in the arm. "Very funny. You wouldn't dare."

She laughed and rested her head on his shoulder. "Actually, I was thinking of naming it Annabelle Janie Grace—after the three most important women in my life."

He kissed her on her temple and spoke softly in her ear. "That sounds like a really good idea. But won't Ford feel left out?"

She touched his face, feeling the stubble on his jaw. "I'm saving his name for the next star I find. I can't imagine not searching for one. I guess it's become a habit to always be looking for light in my life."

She lifted her head, and he looked in her eyes. "So are you going to marry me or not?"

She smiled into his eyes. "Yes, Linc, I'll marry you."

He kissed her soundly on the lips, then helped her stand. They stood with their arms around each other, looking out at the moon marking its signature across the dark waves and hearing the quiet slap of water against sand. Linc took a deep breath. "Come on—we can watch the stars from inside, too."

Linc helped her pack up the telescope, and then they began to move up the dunes toward the two old houses that had always linked their lives together. They paused on the boardwalk and stared up at the endless expanse of the night sky, at the river of stars that flowed over the earth's ceiling, bringing light to the ocean and the marsh, and into lives that harbored hope through the darkest night.

She reached for Linc, and he took her hand as they turned together to walk over the sandy grass before stepping into the circle of light that flooded the porch of the old house. They went inside, closing the door on the night, and the dunes were once again left to the guiding light of the moon and stars.

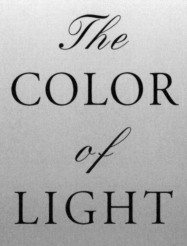

The
COLOR
of
LIGHT

KAREN WHITE

This Conversation Guide is intended to enrich the
individual reading experience, as well as encourage us
to explore these topics together—because books,
and life, are meant for sharing.

A CONVERSATION WITH KAREN WHITE

Q. What inspired you to write The Color of Light? *Is Lauren's disappearance based on true events?*

A. *The Color of Light* is not inspired by any factual events (which is probably a good thing). I'm a huge fan of plot twists, and the idea of Lauren's disappearance stemmed from that. I also love stories where the villain isn't always a villain—that there's something redeemable or understandable about the villain's actions. It's so much closer to real life, and more identifiable to readers.

Q. Are you a full-time mom, or do you work outside of the home? How do you balance these responsibilities with your writing life?

A. I am a full-time mom to two children. I'm very blessed to be able to pursue my career as a writer while staying at home to raise my children. This doesn't make it easy, however! I have to be very, very organized. Unfortunately, there's always a deficit of time and I find that my sleep is the first thing to be sacrificed when I'm working on a novel. It's a constant juggling act and when it gets too rough, I take a nap. I'm a huge believer in naps.

Q. Your characters evoke a great empathy, even though they are flawed. Jillian, Gracie, Linc and Janie are all very human. Who or what inspires these characters? Do you identify with any of them?

A. I enjoy reading books about believable characters. Believable characters, to me, are simply those who are not perfect—like real people. I like to see people grow and change, which means that at the beginning of the book, my characters have to have an impossibly high mountain in front of them. But I also give them something in their character to find the tools necessary to climb that mountain and move on. With Jillian, it's her boundless hope. With Linc, it's his need for justice. It's what made me love both characters and root for them.

These characters are strictly from my imagination—or maybe they're a collage of people in my life. I'm not sure because I never know where my characters come from. I imagine it's inevitable that an author will draw on his or her own experiences to create characters. As for identifying with any of my characters from *The Color of Light*, I'd probably say Jillian. She uses self-deprecating humor to smooth over the rough spots in her life, which is something I know that I do as well. That's where the resemblance ends, however, since I have a well-known aversion to cooking.

Q. Jillian and Linc share a very painful past, which, at times, seems insurmountable. Did you know how the book was going to end when you began it?

A. I vaguely had an idea of how the book would end when I started writing the book. I don't like to have everything mapped out in my mind before I write because that would be a bit like reading the end of a book first. The idea for the ending didn't come to me until I was halfway through writing the book. I knew what would happen to Lauren, but I didn't know who or why until that point. I also wasn't sure how Jillian's issues with her parents would be resolved until the final rewrite of the manuscript.

Q. What do you consider important themes or motifs in The Color of Light?

A. I always come up with the book title before I start writing a book because once I have it, I know what the book is about. In *The Color of Light*, I wanted to show how two very damaged people could learn to overcome their pasts by finding whatever it is that lies inside of them that will give them the strength to go on. I've defined this internal fire as light. It can be a combination of things—the love of family, faith in God, the gift of creating things, a low country marsh. It's what stirs the soul. In the same way a stained glass window can create a kaleidoscope of colors, so too do the small combinations of things bring light to a person's life.

Q. You describe the South Carolina low country beautifully, and in such vivid detail. Is this a place close to your heart? Did you spend part of your childhood there, like Jillian?

A. I had never been to the low country until about eight years ago. I had always been fascinated by stories and pictures and movies and recognized a pull toward the area for many, many years. On my first visit I can honestly say that I felt as if I had come home. There is something about the Spanish moss and the smell of the marsh that steals your heart. Each summer now, I pick a different South Carolina island and rent a house for a week with my family and I look forward all year to those visits. It was inevitable that I would use the low country for a setting for a book and I plan to do it again.

Q. In The Color of Light, *the main characters end up forming a less-than-traditional family by the end of the book. What components of family are most important to you? Are there any problems inherent in writing about family?*

A. Unconditional love is the most important component of family to me. Regardless of how many mistakes a parent can make, everything will be okay as long as the children understand that they are loved no matter what. Jillian was such an ambivalent mother at first—but she never let Gracie know. I loved watching Jillian learn how to love both of her children. It was never a question about if—it was always about how much.

I come from a very traditional family and that is what I usually tend to write about because it's what I know. This book was a bit of a departure for me and I'll admit to a little bit of trepidation as I pictured my parents reading over my shoulder as I typed. But in the end, I realize there's very little difference between my own family and my fictional family. Where there is unconditional love, there is family.

Q. Who are your favorite authors? Is there anyone who is particularly influential?

A. My two favorite authors are Margaret Mitchell and Diana Gabaldon. Their storytelling and characters are unmatched. Their books came alive for me, allowing me as a reader to be completely immersed. I strive to do the same for my readers with each book I write.

For wonderful Southern voices, I turn to Harper Lee, Olive Ann Burns and Pat Conroy. Their writing can make me taste sun-warmed watermelon and feel the cracked summer asphalt under bare feet.

Q. When did you realize that you wanted to be a writer, and when did you begin writing?

A. My sixth grade teacher, Mrs. Anderson, told me I should be a writer and I wanted to believe her. I'd been a huge reader ever since I learned how to read and I thought it would be fun to be a writer. But all through school, I'd always received bad marks on writing assignments due to a nearly illegible handwriting. I hated to write because of it; each word was torture and I usually ended up writing really large so I could fill a page quickly. I would either write the shortest story possible or just abruptly end it when the page ran out. It wasn't until I learned to type in tenth grade that a whole new world opened for me. I began to enjoy writing assignments for the first time and was encouraged by many of my teachers to write. But life got in the way. I was a business major in college, got married, then worked in the business world until I had my first child.

I didn't actually sit down to write my first book until I'd been out of college for eight years. I simply sat down one day and started writing. I found out that writing a book is a lot like having children—there's never a perfect time for either. You just do it.

Q. What is the most difficult aspect of writing for you? What is the most rewarding? Do you have any quirky habits that you indulge when you write?

A. Writing the first three chapters of a book is a bit like licking glass. It's very painful. It's like going to a family reunion where you don't know anybody but you're expected to converse with a familiar knowledge. I usually have to rewrite the first three chapters once I hit chapter ten or so because at that point I'm more familiar with my characters and I know how they should be acting/speaking and what sort of baggage they're carrying.

My favorite part about the writing process (and I do have many) is hearing from fans. Hands down—there's nothing better.

My most embarrassing quirky indulgence that helps me when I'm writing is usurping my son's GameCube and playing Pikmin. He's more embarrassed about this than I am. But there's something about attacking Bulborgs that really gets my creative juices flowing. Go figure.

Q. What are you working on now?

A. I just finished a book entitled *Stone Heart,* which is set in the North Georgia mountains. As with Jillian in *The Color of Light,* Caroline Collier is damaged and flawed but makes the most unbelievable journey to find her life again and to find forgiveness for a single event in her life that irrevocably changed it thirteen years before. There are a few quirky characters and a mother-daughter relationship that will make any woman with a mother nod her head and say, "Oh, yes. That's how it is."

Q. Do you have a recipe for those mouthwatering lemon bars that Jillian makes?

A. Yes, here it is:

1 C real butter (2 sticks)
¼ t salt
½ C powdered sugar
2 C flour

Grease 10" x 13" pan well. Blend above ingredients and press into pan. Bake at 350° F for 30 minutes (until lightly browned).

4 eggs
2 C sugar
5 T lemon juice
4 T flour
Grated lemon rind (optional)

Mix above ingredients and pour over first mixture. Bake 20–30 minutes at 350° F or until solid. Cool and then dust with powdered sugar and cut into squares.

QUESTIONS FOR DISCUSSION

1. In what ways are the constellations important to Jillian? Why do they hold such a fascination for her?

2. What role does forgiveness play in the novel? For whom is it important and in what different ways is it asked for and given?

3. Discuss the different ways motherhood is represented in the novel. Are they positive or negative? Why?

4. Why does Linc disguise his identity from the community? Is this effective?

5. How is Jillian's failed marriage related to her difficult childhood?

6. How is Jillian's relationship with Linc different from her relationship with Rick? How is it similar?

7. On page 241, Linc thinks to himself that he and Jillian "had always seen the core of things that existed under all the surface flaws." Why does he think this, and how do he and Jillian demonstrate this in their lives?

8. How do the townspeople feel about Linc returning to Pawleys Island?

9. Why is Janie's silk flower garden important to her?

10. How does the epigraph by Alfred, Lord Tennyson, relate to the story to come?

11. Why is Jillian afraid of the dark? How does she finally overcome that fear?

12. When does Jillian realize that it was she who drove Rick away? What brings her to this realization and how does it change her?